THE AETHER AWAKENS

The Aether Awakens

C.G. WYNN

C.G. Wynn

N
N
E
S
Tanvik
The Burnished Highlands
Quargonia
The Cliffs of Eidolon
The Sloughmire
Feyralis
Kav
The Jungles of Ruin
Pellucid Falls
Isyath
The Severed Wood
Aluka
Cantheas
The Lucid Strait
The Shole

~ One ~

CONSCRIPTION

Ophiera had forgotten how much she despised the sight of Feyralis. Other travelers would have rejoiced at the first glimpse of the magnificent city. But all she saw was a blight of civilization against a sparse, green countryside. Its towering stone walls loomed on the horizon, souring her mood.

The rhythmic clang of armor fell to silence along with her heavy steps. She needed to stop for a moment to catch her breath. And by catching her breath, she meant gathering her nerve before continuing toward the capital. Thankfully, no one else was in sight along the main road. No one could judge her actions but herself.

While chewing her lip, Ophiera studied the endless steeples of sharp crimsons and shimmering golds peeking shyly over the distant bulwark. Even from afar, the towers within the walls shone vividly in the midday sun. The varied chromatic spires created a picturesque skyline...or at least that's how others would have described it. But Ophiera found the city imparted a very different vision: one of bloodied fangs set within a stern stone jaw, open wide as if prepared to consume the sky. That was the Feyralis she remembered, the city she swore she'd never set foot in again.

Years had passed since Ophiera last viewed the centerpiece of the Tanvik nation. To this day, the capital city of beauty and beast caused her gut to churn with confliction. Or perhaps it was merely her belly aching after traveling on foot for half a day without breakfast. Regardless, now that the city was within sight, she would soon be relieved of the strenuous journey. Then her real task would begin.

Unlike the last time she'd stood in this very spot, years ago, the road before her now lay fully paved. Flattened and grey cobbled stones reached out from the city, all the way to the edge of the Severed Wood that she just left behind her. She guessed that before the next spring, the road would be paved in full, through the southern woods to the port city of Cantheas. Civilization had a few perks, she supposed. Her aching legs welcomed the smooth road ahead.

She had come from the south through thick forests, on gravel roads still muddied by spring rains. While luck had accorded her escape from the Severed Wood unscathed, prosperity would now ease the last leg of her journey. But no amount of good fortune could negate what was to come once she reached Feyralis.

With her lamentable destination in sight, she felt the sting of regret for what she left behind. Ophiera had departed Iluka with no notice to anyone except the village shaman. Like salt on a wound, knowing the small coastal village stood unprotected behind her hurt more than the sight of the city before her.

She tried to shake away her guilt with ratiocination while still catching her breath. Iluka had stood for millennia, she reminded herself. The quaint village existed and thrived long before she ever set foot on its sandy dunes. Most villages of the Southern Coastlands were long-lived and fiercely self-sufficient. Also fiercely traditional.

The coastlands were the last realm of Tanvik to still recognize the ways of the Phratries. A Phratries-trained shaman resided in every village, and every shaman appointed a Warden. The Wardens protected village interests along the sparsely populated coast. This meant that "protection" mostly involved keeping beasts away from the storehouses and helping prepare for the storms that ravaged the area year-round.

Though all coastland villages had Wardens, no other village had a Warden with Ophiera's skills. No other village had a Warden who had abandoned their post.

She wasn't very good at making herself feel better.

The only thing that could improve her mood was to return home. She missed her small cottage on the outskirts of Iluka. It had been the only place of peace she ever knew, the only place she'd chosen to be her own. But she had no choice anymore. She had been summoned by the Magistrate and thus, must continue this bitter march toward Feyralis.

Ophiera should have known better than to think herself free of the Magistrate's chains these last few years. Retirement was the proper term, despite its connotation of age. Though Ophiera couldn't recall exactly how old she was anymore, the shaman in Iluka guessed somewhere in her third decade. But her age never really mattered to her. It never did to someone who felt they had lived long enough.

She couldn't afford any more hesitation; it was time to move along.

Ophiera dragged her feet back to pace, resuming the rhythmic clanging of armor. She adjusted the straps on her pack, resetting the weight against her back.

The notice of summons felt heavy in her pack, although it was a simple piece of parchment. The writ had the Magistrate's sigil pressed upon it, a damningly weighty signet on its own. But the addition of the Cloister's seal beside it had crushed any remaining hope completely. She didn't need to read the notice to know she had been conscripted. Again.

Even knowing couldn't stop her from reading and re-reading the letter countless times. But it declared nothing outright as to the reason for the sudden summons. No task or intention was listed. The only clear message was the demand for her to uphold her Oath and return to Feyralis immediately. They even gave her a deadline, which fell on the morrow.

That's why she needed to keep moving. She'd hesitated for too long already and if she arrived late, the punishment would be severe. It was just hard rushing to a dismal destination with an unknown purpose.

While the writ omitted the exact purpose of her subpoena, she was unsurprised by the ploy. The Magistrate preferred to deal in impression over substance. Their doctrines were written with far too much flexibility, ensuring murky interpretations. Obscure technicalities provided maneuverability within their doctrine, enough to shift their will on a whim; guaranteed to fall in the Magistrate's favor. Ophiera had remained naive to their manipulations until it was far too late.

At least she'd managed a brief savor of freedom these last few years. More than any of her predecessors. She had thought herself so clever when she was released from her original contract with the Magistrate. All without returning to the Cloister, a feat no other had achieved. She had been relieved of all her duties and free to do as she pleased, under condition, of course. If she performed her duty ever again—upheld her Oath in any way—the retirement contract would be void. How stupid she had been to think she could outwit the Magistrate's doctrine. Still, it was less stupid than thinking she could escape her Oath.

Ambiguities woven into the very ink allowed the Magistrate to interpret her protection services for Iluka as a formal duty. The bastards had set her up to fail. A life claimed by the Cloister meant she possessed a very narrow range of skill sets. All of which required her Oath and the beaten claymore strapped against her back. The Magistrate had known when they signed her release that she was doomed to enact her Oath, sooner or later.

Ophiera wiped the perspiration from her brow, a by-product of exertion and irritation. The sun hung high in the cloudless sky, warming the air, far exceeding the shaded temperatures of the

Severed Wood. The trees along the road grew sporadically at the edge of the wood, widely dispersed in small bunches amongst the natural meadows. Quite unlike the dark and dense forest, this open landscape was peaceful, or so she had heard others describe it. Perhaps farmers or merchants found the rolling hills of farmland and thin thickets charming, but that was not how she viewed the veld surrounding Feyralis. She'd traded paved roads for exposure and vulnerability—which her lifetime of conflict left Ophiera painfully aware of.

Her stomach churned again, refusing to be neglected any longer. Perhaps she could spare time for a proper break. Procrastination was one of her several skills.

A suitable respite lay a short distance off the road, where an old, solitary tree with sprawling branches promised shade. After trudging through a small meadow, she arrived at the gnarled trunk. Ophiera first removed the massive claymore from her back, leaning it against the tree gingerly. The wide blade lacked a sheath—quite pointless given its size and condition. She studied the sword carefully for a moment, positioned against the trunk as if being laid to rest.

But wishful thoughts served no one.

With less care, she threw her leather pack into a rooted corner of the tree. Long ago, she had mastered the art of sitting in full plate mail, and yet the attempts always felt clumsy. Heavily, she sank down against the trunk with minimal grinding of her armor.

The bright foliage of spring's apex offered a welcome shade. For a moment, Ophiera sat like this, stiff and unmoving as she watched the breeze dance through the meadow. The motion of the reeds and whisper of the grass reminded her vaguely of the ocean. Of Iluka.

Before her thoughts grew too bitter, she pulled from her pack a skin of water and the last gemfruit she carried. The dark purple stone fruit would be all she'd eat today until she arrived in Feyralis.

The ancient tree was gnarled and knotted, but the protruding bark was of no discomfort. Ophiera's armor always served as protection, against foe and nature alike. Old and beaten, the ancient armor still functioned despite its scuffs and dents. And even beneath the shade of the tree, the golden hue of the plate mail gleamed, grandiose in style and unmatched in function.

The armor represented yet another duality of her existence: her most precious possession and a symbol of her chains. Most of her life had been spent in this beaten armor, nostalgic in the most painful sense. As she chewed the sweet and tart fruit, the flavor turned bitter against her tongue.

A faint rustle pulled Ophiera away from her darkening thoughts. To the untrained ear, the sound could be easily mistaken for heavy wind or a small animal crossing the meadow. But she recognized the sound of someone's feathered steps approaching from behind the tree. Whoever was here walked with intentional stealth, and sneaking was never a sign of innocent intentions.

Ophiera steeled herself to take the necessary precautions and touched her hand to the ground. Her open-palmed gauntlets allowed the scarred skin of her Oath hand to touch the cool dirt. In a whisper, she murmured words that none but those trained by the Cloister recited. An incantation in a dialect long dead, one she did not understand herself, yet the words had been burned into her long ago. As she chanted the guttural syllables, the ground glowed in fiery runes, encircling her in symbols of golden light. Like the skyline and her armor, the glowing glyphs brought her both comfort and regret.

The footsteps continued toward her. Three sets, to be exact. She had a feeling this wouldn't end well.

"Leave," she called, unmoving, from her spot against the tree.

The footsteps stopped. For a moment, the air held nothing but the gentle rustle of the meadow. Hoping they would heed her advice and flee, she stole another bite of her stone fruit. But as the steps resumed, she chastised herself for such foolishness.

"Sorry, dear," a voice growled, "can't leave without you."

The three sets of footsteps came round the broad trunk of the tree, two from the right and one around the left. Each step sounded sloppy, unburdened by conscience or packs.

Ophiera reasoned they must belong to a faction of outlaws. The main road was usually a popular hunting ground for new prey. She guessed they traveled light to ensure easy transport of their spoils. While theft itself was a crime by Magistrate law, that alone would not force her to enact her Oath. Only if murder was their intent would she be forced to enact her duty.

"I have nothing of value to you," she said. "So, I will repeat myself; leave."

The three footsteps became three men as they came into sight. They stopped, facing Ophiera and giving her a wide berth. She wondered if they recognized the emblazoned runes encircling her or were merely cautious. The golden armor was usually a dead give-away in the past, but so few recognized her kind anymore. They wouldn't dare proceed if they knew what the armor and the runes meant for their fate.

Calmly, she observed the three men, searching for their intentions. They were utterly filthy, dressed in deep brown leathers and worn linens. But the goldenrod bandanas they all wore about their biceps distracted her.

"That armor is worth something to someone, I'm sure," said the middle bandit. "And what's underneath's worth even more."

Bile rose in Ophiera's throat. Clearly, he had no idea what her golden armor meant if he dared speak so disgustingly. The Cloister only bestowed the gilded plate to those who received an Oath of Retribution: the Oath burned into her hand upon her kindling. So few underwent the rites these days, and even fewer survived them. It was no surprise he did not recognize what she was, though she wished he had. Perhaps then they would have fled.

"And what if I refuse?" she asked in a steady voice. It was a blunt question, one she had already guessed the answer to, but she needed an admission before she would act.

One of the other men, younger than the presumed leader, chuffed at her question. "Well, it'll be easier to take the armor if she's dead. Then we won't have to drag her back to camp."

Her stomach churned as he sealed his fate. Upon his confession, her Oath demanded Retribution. He was willing to commit the greatest sin in Erum, the greatest slight against the Aether: to murder another soul in cold blood. They were anathemas then; their souls were cursed with their sins.

Retribution must be sought. The scars she harbored demanded her obedience. Why must they make her do this?

Enraged, she flung the gemfruit pit at the young man with all her might. A sickening thud preceded the yowl of pain. The bandit leader smiled at his comrade's suffering, a loathsome expression. Based on the amount of blood, she'd likely broken the young man's nose.

Good.

"Take her alive, if ya can...Ya know the Reverend prefers to do the deed himself." The leader waved the other two forward, and they advanced upon her.

Ophiera didn't have the capacity to worry about this Reverend; she was too busy preparing to uphold her necessary but brutal Oath. If these men, these anathemas, intended to kill her, then they'd likely claimed the lives of others before. Those unfortunate souls taken in sin were lost, unable to return to the Aether for rebirth. It was her duty to seek Retribution for the lost, to cleanse these corrupted souls and claim them for the Aether as a meager recompense.

The golden runes surrounding her pulsed with anticipation. As the first bandit stepped a toe over the runic circle, the runes ignited. Thick flames of pure white energy erupted from the ground, engulfing the man's leg as his screams engulfed his comrades. The odor of charred flesh wafted in the air. Yet, with quicker reflexes than Ophiera expected, the bandit pulled himself from the pale, consuming fire, revealing the ashen stump left behind.

"The Reverend didn't say she was a paladin!" the second crony cried, attempting to support his comrade's collapsing weight. So now they recognized what she was, but it was far too late.

The agonized screams made it difficult to hear what the bandits yelled now, but their words meant nothing. Ophiera had begun to claim them for the Aether.

Ophiera remained seated with her back against the tree as the chant hissed under her breath. She dug her fingers into the dirt, commanding the runes with the foreign mantra. The golden symbols pulsated as she chanted, triggering the churning circle to widen. With a cry of fear, the leader turned tail and fled. The second man dropped his injured comrade with abandon.

They valued their lives enough to flee, yet had threatened to claim hers moments ago. The hypocrisy of these anathemas enraged her. Her chant became a shriek, a venomous voice coaxing the ring outward in chase. As the emblazoned circle crossed the injured man, white fire erupted from the ground again, burning him to ash before he could scream. Ophiera watched the two others stumble when it overtook them. Their anguished cries rang out before they became silent ash. The runes faded from the ground, leaving behind a bright green meadow marred by three tendrils of dissipating smoke.

Ophiera lifted her trembling hand from the ground, shaking the dirt from her palm. She placed her hand over her gilded breastplate. In the same ancient tongue as her rite, she prayed under her breath. Unlike the circle of flames, her words evoked no rite—this act was merely a convention. She'd found the prayer in a book, one of few passages translated from the symbolic language of the rites. Ever since, she recited the words for the corrupted souls she claimed for the Aether. And sometimes, like today, she added a plea for her own.

Three vespers rose from the ash. The small glowing orbs shone brightly despite the high sun. Her eyes burned against their light as she searched the vespers for the signs. Every soul she'd ever witnessed was different, as were these three. The leader's shade glowed in a monotone, burnt orange, like a miniature sun hovering in the grass. Another shined despite its muddied brown coloration, and the last was nearly camouflaged as bright, acid green.

Only one commonality existed between the vespers before her, and all the vespers she'd ever seen. Within the varied hues of their souls, darkness swirled. Ripples of black corruption danced within the orbs, silhouetted against the brightness of their natural shades. The leader's vesper held the darkest distortions, like a scrawled epitaph of his sins for the Aether to claim.

The first time Ophiera saw a vesper was the same day she began her service to the Magistrate. Trained by the Cloister and chosen by the Aether, paladins served the Magistrate by cleansing Tanvik of anathemas. Despite the dwindling numbers of the Cloister's clerics and paladins, and those who followed their teachings, the Magistrate still relied on those with an Oath of Retribution to maintain justice. To keep Tanvik free of the corrupted souls.

The Cloister taught that all souls were born of the Aether. Upon a natural death, their vespers would return to be cleansed and cycle anew on Erum. Murder was an unnatural death—the ultimate sin. Yet it was the murdered, the victims that suffered, even in death. When a soul was stolen from the cycle by the sin of another, there was little chance of reclamation for the innocent; their souls became lost to the Aether and the cycle. Thus, without a chance for reclamation, the Aether demanded Retribution instead.

Retribution of a sort only Ophiera could claim. She watched solemnly as the vespers disintegrated, scattering their dimming light over the ground. Like a spring shower, their essence adsorbed quickly into the soil, making their way back to the Aether below.

Regardless of the taboo, she could never tear her gaze away from the vespers as they returned to Erum. So few in Tanvik had seen a vesper in these times. As it should be.

One had to witness the moment of death to see the manifestation of the dying soul, short-lived and ethereal. In times of peace, like in recent decades, only the Cloister's clerics or the village shamans bore witness to the death of the sick and elderly. Whether driven by fear or taboo or convenience, the people of Tanvik didn't want to see vespers.

Ophiera didn't either, but, as a consequence of her Oath, she had lost count of how many vespers she had witnessed. All of them laced with the dark corruption of their sins. All of them returned to the Aether by her scarred hand.

She couldn't stay under the shaded tree with charred remains for company any longer. No matter how justified, she always despised taking life. The three piles of ash were a fitting and fateful preamble for what was to come when she reached Feyralis. How many more corrupted souls would the Magistrate demand of her?

Maybe the three vile men were the reason she had been conscripted. Maybe she'd already completed her task, and would arrive to Feyralis just to be sent back to Iluka.

Again, wishful thoughts served no one.

With a healthy pace, Ophiera reasoned she'd reach Feyralis well before nightfall. She could spend the evening in the first tavern she crossed and continue her killing streak on several pints before reporting to the Magistrate in the morning.

Humor was not her strong suite.

From beside the tree, Ophiera retrieved her pack and hoisted her oversized claymore onto her back. She carefully pulled her thick braid of snowy hair forward, avoiding the blade of her sword. The color of the waist-length plat wasn't reflective of her age, merely another consequence of her Oath. The shaman in Iluka often poked fun at her colorless hair, saying it matched the age of her soul.

Ophiera trudged her way back to the road, continuing toward Feyralis at a doubled pace. Her exhaustion went beyond physical and mental fatigue now. The rune rite had depleted most of her mana. Since her kindling at the Cloister, she held the holy flames within, and like true fire, it was short-lived unless fueled. Time and rest would restore her, just like every other person. But few others had powers and duties such as hers.

She still had her claymore for defense, but with little mana left, she could no longer call upon the holy flames without cost to her life. Just another reason to get to Feyralis as soon as possible. She hated herself for wishing that.

Bitterly, she wondered why fate had deemed it necessary to throw those three men before her. She had gone so long without any need of the holy flames, without seeing a vesper. The shock of how quickly she fell back in line disturbed her more than the sight of death itself. Had she even hesitated? Was her soul just as dark as theirs for so easily claiming lives? But she mustn't spiral down this path of what-ifs and whys.

In need of distraction, she started to hum a melancholy tune. Music always siphoned the woes from her mind, even if the Cloister had forbidden singing altogether. It remained to this day her sacred rebellion.

It would be hours before she reached the city walls, longer still to the South gate. Plenty of time to sing away her self-loathing, to forget the souls burned in the name of Retribution.

~ Two ~

FATE

Ophiera reached the edge of the enormous wall on shaking legs. Perhaps she'd pushed herself a bit too much during the last few hours of travel. But it would be pointless to slow now. The South gate of Feyralis was just a bit farther along the wall.

Stacked pale stones curved around the glorious city in a perfect circle of impossible height. The bulwark held only two passages into the city, the North and South gates. The limited access points only meant frustration for traders and travelers in peaceful times, herself included.

Feyralis proper lay behind an arm's depth of stone, yet the gate remained an hour's walk away. With a grunt, Ophiera adjusted her rucksack and continued upon the circumscribed path toward the South gate.

This portion of the lofty wall ran parallel to the Slumbrous River, which flowed between the circling outer road and the city. Swollen with spring snowmelt, the river frothed wildly with its short-lived excess. The lowlands surrounding the capital were in the warming season, but the last frost still clung to the distant mountains. These few days a year, the Slumbrous River no longer babbled sleepily but flowed with violent, icy energy from those peaks.

The sun soon dipped below the horizon, streaking the bright azure sky with warm shades of fire. Ophiera's constitution faded with the extinguishing light, drained of more than mere mana. The roaring waters drowned out the protesting aches of her legs and back.

A thud caught her attention, loud over the rush of water. She slowed, inspecting the riverbank beneath the wall. Large, irregular stones edged the water, mostly fallen pieces from the wall above. None looked recently felled though. Most were heavily weathered and covered in moss or by the high waters. But she knew she had heard something.

Barely noticeable on the opposite shore, a dark blue bundle of cloth lay half-floating in the water. She recognized the silhouette of a man, crumpled and unmoving. The water slowed against the nearby rocks, enough to keep him from being swept away, but only just. Gazing upward, Ophiera suspected he'd plummeted from the wall. An unfortunate accident or purposeful end?

She hesitated for a moment. Surely no one could survive a fall from that height, yet there was no vesper in sight. The man was either long dead before he fell, or still alive. She stood, studying the heap of cloth and flesh, watching for signs of life or death. His chest rose and fell with the slightest of movements, erratic and weak.

A dilemma began raging through her mind.

Neither Oath nor Magistrate required her to help him in the way he needed most. In fact, the Cloister would likely punish her intervention. She had been branded with an Oath of Retribution, not Mercy. A paladin of the Cloister, not a cleric. Only if his death had a murderous origin could she become *involved*. And even then, not in the way he needed.

But still, no vesper had appeared.

Even if she could help, she had no mana left and no potions in her pack. The bloated river prohibited any crossing. There were no bridges nearby. She would have to swim in the frigid waters, risking her own life, for what? His vesper was likely to rise from his crumpled body any minute now. No. He was beyond her Oath and beyond her help. With one last look at the unfortunate man, she took a heavy step forward on the road.

On her third step, Ophiera swore under her breath and turned on her heel. She reached the river's edge with a clenched jaw, preparing for a frigid swim. After swiftly removing every last piece of golden plate, Ophiera stowed the armor near a banked boulder, along with her claymore and pack. It was hidden well enough from the road, but she could keep her eyes on it from the opposite bank. She felt exposed without her armor, even if her dark brown underleathers covered nearly as much skin.

The tumultuous flow of the water forced her to hesitate for a moment. Freshly born from ice atop the distant peaks, she didn't need to touch the water to know it was cold enough to kill. Yet the unconscious man who lay half-submerged had still not succumbed to frigid death. The thought impelled her to dive headfirst into the rushing river.

Needles of pain pierced her skin as her breath froze solid in her chest. No measure of toughness or training could stand against the shock of plunging into frigid water. As she propelled herself forward against the current, every kick and stroke drained her of warmth and strength. By the time she reached the opposite bank, she was near collapse and downstream a way. Her limbs convulsed as she dragged herself up the bank, wet leather smothering her despite her gasping breaths. She held only a whisper of warmth within her core, like her mana.

Ophiera stumbled her way to the crumpled man, who lay facedown. With trembling hands, she rolled him onto his back and inhaled a scant breath.

For a moment, she mistook the man for a youth. His features were boyish, but the laugh lines and strong brow aged him as a grown man. Even slackened in unconsciousness, his jawline looked sharp and his high cheekbones painted a strong, but soft face that, somehow, remained unscathed despite his ordeal. Unscathed and absolutely beautiful.

Absentmindedly, Ophiera caressed the wet blonde hair away from his face, studying his features with unusual curiosity. To her surprise, his cheeks held warmth, nearly uncomfortable against her frigid hands. The temperature shock snapped her out of whatever the hell had come over her—hypothermia, most likely.

Aside from his warmth, however, the man was in poor shape. Even under the water, Ophiera could tell his legs were bent at unnatural angles. If they had taken the brunt of the fall, his spine was likely injured as well. He suffered damage that could never be healed with time and potions alone.

While the Cloister reserved the healing rites for the clerics, Ophiera had rebelled against her Oath of Retribution for a brief time after being kindled. Night after night, she snuck into the archives at the Cloister, studying the rites for those bound by an Oath of Mercy. She still wished the holy flames had demanded Mercy instead of Retribution from her soul. Only when the punishments became too severe did she stop learning and practicing the rites of Mercy. But she never regretted it. She had healed worse injuries than his before, a far more satisfying end than seeing a vesper return to the Aether.

But the problem now was her mana. No longer did the holy flames burn bright within her, and to cast such a rite would cost more than just her last bit of mana.

Once, while training at the Cloister, she let her competitiveness overtake her judgment and completely drained herself of holy flames. For a moment, she felt her rite take energy from elsewhere, feeding off her life force instead of mana alone. The Chaplain at the time had swiftly ended her rite, and the ensuing punishment had been harsh enough to ensure Ophiera never depleted herself again.

Though her stomach twisted with the guilt of rebellion, as it always did, she knew in her heart the Cloister could do nothing to stop her now. The little mana she had left, topped with a bit of her life force, would be a worthy sacrifice for saving the beautiful man's life.

Ophiera rubbed her hands together, attempting to regain circulation while she recalled the words of the healing rite. The cold fogged her memory, which was worsened by her apprehension of what this would cost her. All rites required the same foreign tongue, but the words were quite distinct. She couldn't recall if the last chant was *arrunmai* or *arruntai*.

Suddenly, a bright light peeked out from the man's chest. Whatever warmth she held in her heart froze in an instant. The curved crown of his vesper began to emerge, a glowing beacon of her failure.

How useless. She swam too slowly, hesitated too often, and now, the Aether had begun to draw his soul back to it. The pain gripping her chest went beyond exhaustion. His beautiful face shined in the eerie light cast by his vesper. But she realized that both man and vesper held still as stone. The vesper's departure had...stalled. The dome of brilliant blue remained embedded in his chest, vibrating as if straining against the call of the Aether. A shimmer of vitality within the vesper whirled violently as it clung to its vessel. The man's brow furrowed, reflecting the struggle of his very soul.

Of all the death she had witnessed, she had never seen anything like this vesper. Not only was its behavior strange, but the unadulterated elegance of an untainted vesper moved something within her. Cerulean swirls, utterly untarnished, pure, and magnificent without a trace of darkness. Tears fell down her cheeks, hot against her frigid skin. She couldn't recall the last time she cried.

A life of claiming Retribution had clouded her expectations; she had forgotten that vespers were never meant to contain the blackened corruption. The lack of darkness within this vesper, the exquisite purity displayed, was precisely as the Aether intended. And yet, an innocent soul was a sight none should ever see.

She could walk away; she *should* walk away and let the man pass in peace. That was what fate had clearly intended. Then why did the idea cause her such pain? Could she ever forgive herself for allowing something so beautiful and immaculate to perish?

Trembling in defiance, Ophiera placed her hands upon the man's chest. Careful to avoid the vesper, she watched it flicker like a flame against a draft. It was aware of her in some way.

She began to chant the healing rite. The rhythm of the mantra fell clumsily from her lips, but it was effective nonetheless. Her fingertips burned with the Aether, no longer taking the form of the white holy flames, but instead a pale light flowed from her scarred hand. The vesper only flickered more, and she feared her efforts were in vain. But slowly, the glowing orb began its descent back into the man's chest.

Just when hope flickered in her heart, she felt a disconcerting shift in the rite. Her mana fully extinguished now, she instead poured forth the very essence of her life from her hands. Every instinct screamed for her to end her rite, to take her hands away from the man. But until the vesper returned fully to its vessel, she could not stop.

The strain was immense. The pain was overwhelming. Her chest rattled as her voice dropped to a whimper, struggling to maintain the chant. The light from his vesper dimmed as it sank back into his chest. Darkness hovered at the edges of her vision.

The man's eyes fluttered open, revealing a brilliant, pale blue gaze. His infrangible stare matched the shade of his vesper, sky-blue and fading as the darkness encroached. She couldn't fight the fatigue that dragged her into the nullity.

At least she wasn't cold anymore.

~ Three ~

OVERDUE

Every muscle ached as Ophiera stirred, adrift on a sea of excruciating pain. She had never felt agony like this before. Everything hurt, but with no distinct cause or source. The pain only deepened when she tried to recall what happened, as if the memories themselves whipped against her skull.

Through the agony lashing over her, she managed to discern fragments of incoherent images. A single point of bright blue light overtook her thoughts and the dam holding her memory broke. His vesper. The healing rite. Was he alive? Was she?

Ophiera couldn't hear the rush of the river, nor feel the cold of the water. Where had the river gone? Stupid, she chided herself—pain fogged her mind. Where was *she* now?

After a moment of struggling, she eventually forced her eyes to open. Straining to focus through bleary shadows, she saw a dim light source cast from somewhere unseen. Through her spinning vision, she made out a dark, vaulted ceiling of aged wood and cobwebs. She only recognized the feel of linen and straw against her backside.

Ophiera failed to sit up several times. Eventually, she made it onto her elbows, the farthest upright the pain allowed her to move. At least now she was perched up enough to examine her surroundings. She clung to the bed linen, fearing she might spin away in constant vertigo. Her insides churned, threatening to rebel.

"I wouldn't move just yet," said a deep, warm voice.

Ophiera reeled, surprise overriding the pain for a moment. On the far side of the room stood a man she vaguely recognized. He looked livelier now, with a smirk she would never forget playing across his face. Long golden hair flowed over his shoulders, lustrous even in the dim light. Against the dark blue of his robes, his eyes held the spring sky, pale, bright, and unwavering. She only had a moment to rejoice in his vitality before she remembered her duty.

"My armor," she said, her voice graveled by disuse. "I need to go back—"

"That would be ill-advised," he said with a snort. "But don't fret—I brought your belongings here, armor included."

Ophiera closed her eyes in another futile attempt to halt the spinning room. "And where is here?"

"Feyralis," he said with another hint of a laugh. "My home, if that's what concerns you."

His smiling face multiplied and fanned out across her view. The room continued to waver, as did her strength.

"What's wrong with me?"

He released a heavy sigh. "Manasickness. Frankly, I've never seen someone so depleted. I did my best to keep you comfortable, but it's been a rough few nights."

"Nights?" Ophiera breathed.

No, no, no. She was overdue to report to the Magistrate.

Without thinking, she swung her legs over the side of the bed to abruptly stand. At full height, the room twirled at a dizzying velocity. The pain nearly forced her to collapse, to succumb to unconscious peace. But fear kept her mind alert. Would they charge her with abandonment? With treason?

A chill crawled over her skin, transforming to a burn of shame as she looked down at herself.

"Where are my leathers?" she spat. "What perversion is this?"

The floor beneath her swayed like a rolling ship.

"You were hypothermic," the man said, raising his hands in a gesture of innocence. "Removal of wet clothing is basic first aid, not perversion."

Her stomach churned at the thought of his hands on her unconscious body. She needed to leave.

"I need to get to the Magistrate," she said through gritted teeth.

His brows knit together. "I don't think that's a good idea."

She made to argue, but no words came forth. In a violent convulsion, she purged the few contents of her stomach onto the rough wood floor. Whatever strength she had was taken in the act, and she collapsed clumsily back onto the bed.

"I warned you."

Warm hands folded her cold limbs back onto the bed. Too weak to fight, she could only grunt her disapproval as he rolled her onto her stomach.

"Stay like this," he whispered. "It would be a shame if you suffocated on your own vomit after everything."

The mattress smelled pleasant compared to vomit. She might get sick again just from the horrid taste still lingering on her palate. Her bare back welcomed the blanket now being draped over her. As comforting as it felt, she couldn't allow herself to fall back asleep.

"The Magistrate...I–" She stopped, stunned to silence as he began to wipe her face and mouth with a damp cloth.

"Rest first," he said. His pale gaze bored into hers with a foreign tenderness. It made her feel uncomfortable, though far from threatened.

When he finished mopping sick from her face, sleep began to creep over her. She tried again to speak of her need, but all that escaped her was a pained moan.

"Please, just rest," he hushed.

And as if the strange man commanded it of her, Ophiera fell restlessly unconscious.

* * *

At her second waking, Ophiera felt less pain, though her body remained stiff and sluggish. Her vision and stomach remained steady this time as she sat up in bed. Aware of her lack of clothing now, she pulled the bed sheet over her chest as an unwanted flush crept under her cheeks.

Bright daylight illuminated the small circular bedroom. A worn dressing table and a rickety chair were the only other furniture in the room, both constructed from weathered driftwood. Oversized and ovular, a multipaned glass window sat above the bed, swung open wide. A gentle breeze flowed in, carrying with it the murmurs of a bustling city. The red and gold spires of Feyralis provided her little comfort.

"Feeling better?" said a familiar, warm voice.

Again, he hovered near the threshold. At least this time he did not multiply and instead smiled gently as their eyes met.

"A bit," she croaked.

"Better than nothing. Looks like the worst is behind you."

Her mind dragged, taking far too long to understand his meaning. How ill had she fallen?

"You have my gratitude," she eventually said.

"Ah, it's *I* who should thank you." He grinned. Something about the way he watched her made her wish he would look away.

"What happened after I...?" She struggled to complete the thought. What *exactly* had she done?

He crossed the room in a few strides and sat upon the bed, inches from her. She shifted uncomfortably. And somehow, he remained aloof.

"You collapsed on me just as I regained consciousness. I recognized the Oath inscribed upon your arm and assumed your armor was nearby. I've never heard of a paladin without armor," he laughed.

Ophiera stared at him with eyebrows raised. So few in Tanvik recognized the paladins these days, let alone knew of the Oaths branded upon their arms. The welted scars ran from her elbow to her fingertips, runic and savage, shared between all of the kindled, yet distinct to each. His eyes lingered on her bare, disfigured arm, and in habit, she withdrew it beneath the covers.

"Hypothermia and manasickness left you in a rather fragile condition. So, I brought you to my home to care for you," he said.

"I am grateful, truly," Ophiera began, her voice beginning to waver. "But I must go to the Magistrate immediately. They were expecting me to report for duty by the eve of...of..." She faltered as he glanced away from her. "How long have I been here?"

He smiled sheepishly, running a hand through his hair in silence.

"How long?" she demanded.

"Today will be the fifth day since the riverbank."

Any regained strength drained instantly from her limbs, leaving her numb. Five days late? The Magistrate's guards were likely already searching for her. And if the Cloister interpreted her tardiness as an abandonment of her Oath, the punishment would be severe.

"Come now," he said, "five days isn't so bad, considering the state you were in."

"The Magistrate does not tolerate abandonment...the Cloister even less so."

He chuckled. A very inappropriate response given the gravity of her predicament. The people of Tanvik may have forgotten the Cloister's teachings, but everyone knew the consequence of the abandonment of an Oath. What was a mere bedtime story to everyone else was a grim reality for her.

"I already informed the Magistrate," he said, reading her confusion with a smile. "I found the summons in your bag and sent a detailed explanation of your condition to the Justicar of Feyralis. They won't expect you to arrive until you've recovered."

Ophiera stared in disbelief at the man's smug expression. She admitted that was rather clever of him, and at the moment she was too grateful for his forethought to be angry at his nerve to rummage in her bag.

"Speaking of recovery, I bet you're famished!"

Without another word, he marched from the room, disappearing beyond the threshold.

What an odd man.

He seemed utterly unperturbed by her or his own near-death experience. Not everyone would act so flippant around an incapacitated, Magistrate-conscripted paladin. Paladins were rare, but the reputation of the Cloister transcended time. Those associated with it were often met with fear or apprehension, and yet he expressed neither.

Never before had a stranger recognized the ornate scars of her Oath. The brands were unique to all her brethren, who were few and far between nowadays. The holy flames burned Oaths and echelons into the flesh of paladins and clerics alike. The scars left behind spoke of their power and subjugation.

The man returned with a large tray laden with enough food to feed a small family: bread, cheeses, pastries, fruits, and cured meats stacked neatly on a worn wooden platter. Ophiera's eyes widened as he placed the tray on the bed. The sheer weight of it pulled at the sheets, still clinging tightly to her chest.

"My entire home holds less food than this tray," she murmured.

Head thrown back, he laughed. This man only ever laughed.

"I conjured everything, so eat until your heart's content...or stomach, I should say? I suppose both work. Food feeds the body and the soul, doesn't it?"

He rambled more to himself, musing. The word *conjure* was indeed strange.

Ophiera now found herself in a dilemma of where to prioritize her hands; holding up the sheet in her diffidence or seeking the sustenance she craved. As if reading her mind, the man strode over to the dressing table and removed from it a large cream-colored tunic. He tossed the garment to her, and the billowing material landed over her head in what would have been a comical manner had she been someone capable of humor. She tore it from her head, gripping the bed sheet tighter to her chest.

"You can wear that if you'd like," he said, watching her closely. "Or just hold it, your choice."

"Could you please turn away?" She tried to sound polite, but failed. Her annoyance broke through in every syllable.

Though his eyes rolled, he faced the other direction obediently. "I told you I'm not a pervert."

"I don't even know your name, let alone your intentions," she said matter-of-factly. With his gaze averted, she slipped the tunic over her head. It felt soft and clean, but she missed the weight of her armor. "Though I do appreciate your hospitality."

Before turning back around, he grabbed the shaky chair from the corner and dragged it over to the bed's edge.

"It's the least I could do after you saved my life," he said with a grin. Her heart fluttered at the sight. Manasickness afflicted more than just her body, it seemed. "And my name is Myronor."

He watched her expectantly.

"Ophiera," she mumbled. She might know his name now, but other than that, she knew nothing about him other than the brilliant shade of his vesper. How could the soul she saved belong to the flippant man before her?

"It's not poisoned," Myronor said, interpreting her grimace as distrust. He picked up several chokecherries and popped them into his mouth. She interpreted this as his way of telling her to eat, but the sarcasm was unnecessary.

Her stomach churned in need, and she heeded its call. With her scarred hand, she reached for the crusted bread. Myronor watched her with a jovial expression as she took a nibble off the end. She didn't like how he watched her. Golden armor tended to elicit prying eyes, so she was used to ignoring people's stares. But something about the softness of his expression made her feel self-conscious and awkward. She tried to focus on a large knot in one of the aged floorboards, avoiding his gaze while she chewed a few mouthfuls of sourdough.

"How did you come to find me on the riverbank?" Myronor asked.

A more pertinent question was how he ended up on the riverbank, she thought. But it seemed only fair she share her side of the story. At least some of it.

"I heard you fall and tried to heal you," she said, averting her gaze to the tray of food now. "The rite I attempted simply cost me more than I expected."

She refused to admit more, making no mention of the vesper. To witness someone's soul was to witness the most intimate part of a person. She had seen his bare soul on the brink of death. If she thought him a pervert for removing her wet clothes, seeing his vesper made her something far worse.

Myronor remained silent for a moment. She caught him again watching her with his pale stare. Was he trying to catch her lie, or was he simply strange?

"You could have stopped the rite when you felt it drain your life. So why risk yourself for a stranger?"

She hesitated. The truth was too revealing, too private. In deflection, she blamed the ultimate source of her strife.

"I was simply fulfilling my Oath."

Myronor raised his eyebrows. "I didn't realize your Oath would demand your intervention in my scenario."

"My Oath is Retribution, but..." Curiosity overrode her caution. "How do you know so much regarding the Oaths of the Cloister?"

He chuckled. "I read."

Avoidant again, she selected a pastry stuffed with chokecherries to occupy herself. As she chewed the tart and flaky pastry, it had a profound effect on her mood and energy. She felt restored—revitalized even. As she opened her mouth to inquire about the food, a stray crumb lodged itself into her windpipe. She cleared her throat, which only served to worsen the situation. Face reddening, she cascaded into a coughing fit.

"I always forget the damn water," Myronor said, thrusting his empty hand before her. A bright light glowed in his palm, a hue that matched the shade of his vesper. She watched the light transform into an ornate glass of water. Without hesitation, she reached and drained it in one movement.

"You're a mage?" she asked in a hoarse voice.

"That I am." He grinned boyishly, drinking his own pride from a cup.

"Enchanted food?"

"Best treatment for manasickness—if you're conscious." He grinned, standing up from the rickety chair. "And rest, of course, which you should get back to once you're done. I'll be downstairs if you need anything else."

His dark blue robes swished as he made his way to the door. And while she looked forward to the solitude of his departure, something compelled her to speak.

"You're surprised by what I did for a stranger," she began, and he turned to meet her eyes. Her words faltered a moment. "Y-yet you have done more without any Oath binding you to act. I'm indebted to your hospitality, so please, tell me how I can repay you."

"You owe me nothing, Ophiera. Besides, we're no longer strangers."

He looked more handsome with a smirk. She was glad he closed the door behind him before the heat flushed her cheeks.

Alone at last, she savored the silence before eyeing the breakfast tray again. She ate more than her fill, taking advantage of a rare excess.

Myronor had suggested she rest, but she found herself too on edge to even think about sleep. Too many questions remained. Who was he? How did he have knowledge of paladins? And had he really carried her all the way to Feyralis? Where he had fallen was still a long walk from the South gate, especially on two newly-healed broken legs. Ophiera had the weight and build of a warrior, muscular and tall. She doubted he could manage the strength to lift her armor, let alone herself along with it.

So she must assume he'd used magic. But she knew very little about mages. The Cloister kept the unkindled isolated from the world, their entire being dedicated to the holy flames. Once kindled, a paladin certainly held no need for knowledge beyond their Oath. Magic included.

Perhaps it was her naivety of magic that fed her growing curiosity about this man. A curiosity the Cloister oppressed with violence, but they weren't here, were they?

But then...if Myronor was a mage, how did he end up falling to his near death? The most plausible explanation was an accident: he must have tripped and fallen from atop the bulwark. Or had he thrown himself off? Or maybe someone pushed him. Her mood darkened at the thought.

Ophiera's obligation to Myronor would go beyond repayment for his hospitality if an anathema tried to kill him. Even if the mage still lived, the intention remained the same. And murder was a sin of intention. A sin that she was doomed to rectify.

With disdain, Ophiera examined the scarred runes carved upon her arm. Her doom. She couldn't recall what her arm looked like without the scars. The Cloister had claimed her life from a young age, so young she barely remembered the circumstances.

She had been an orphan, like every unkindled these days. But she had always despised the life the Cloister forced upon her. After receiving her Oath, the bitterness consumed her until it became unclear whom she hated more: herself or the Cloister. Perpetually stuck in a cycle of resentment and guilt, she charted a path no paladin had taken before. Retirement. Even if it only lasted a few years, it was more freedom than any of her brethren had attained. Too bad it was over.

She hadn't kept track of how much time passed while she was lost in thought. Myronor had advised rest, but the burn of resentment always prevented peace of mind. She couldn't truly rest anywhere besides her cottage in Iluka. The sooner she completed the Magistrate's task, the sooner she could return, assuming they didn't try her for abandonment. And with that, she decided it was time to face the consequences of her choices.

Gingerly, she set both feet on the rough wooden floor and stood. Unlike last time, the dizziness subsided rather quickly as she glanced down to examine herself. The tunic Myronor lent her was long enough to cover her modesty, yet she still yearned for the bittersweet cover of her armor.

Quietly, she searched the room for her lost items. The dressing table was filled with assorted linens and a few other tunics, but no armor or rucksack. Under the bed were some scattered books and empty ink bottles, but nothing that belonged to her. Perhaps she was asking too much of him to store her items near her. He had already done quite enough.

Given the size of the bedroom, she imagined his home was quite small. It was likely Myronor could hear the creaking floorboards downstairs. At least it would be no surprise to him then when she came down to find her belongings.

However, when she opened the door and peered beyond, she saw no other rooms. Only a small landing with a spiral staircase. It twirled downward in a dizzying fashion, the steps widening from the wall as they descended.

The pointed steeples of Feyralis outside the window ought to have been clue enough that she resided in one of the many towers throughout the city. The newer districts had taken to this architectural style, and she chastised herself for losing track of her surroundings. Myronor must be important if he lived in one of the fangs in the jaw of Feyralis. She wondered exactly what kind of mage he was, or what he did for a living. But she knew it best to leave her curiosities behind. The only thing that mattered now was getting to the Magistrate.

The tower descent tested the modest strength Ophiera had recovered. She clung to the stone wall, avoiding looking down the hollow tower. Eventually, she reached a level where the stairs became enclosed by two stone walls flanking either side. Surely this meant she was reaching the bottom.

The stairs ended quickly at a small landing with a large archway leading toward the center of the tower. It was the only path to take, and so she stepped over the threshold. She hadn't realized just how wide the tower had become the farther she descended. The room she now entered was massive in comparison to the bedroom above. She stepped onto a balcony that spanned the circumference of the tower wall. With a timid step, she grasped the railing and looked down in awe.

The balcony encircled an enormous, two-story library nestled below.

The bookcases were tall enough that she could almost reach a hand over the edge and touch them. If she did, it would only be to wipe the thick dust from the tops. It seemed Myronor didn't come up here very often, or perhaps he didn't care about the mess. More interesting than the dirt was the curious pattern of the shelves. Rather than straight rows, the shelves spiraled outward from an open central area. It looked quite like a flower of sorts from high above.

Within the spiraled shelves, Myronor had managed to cram an overwhelming number of books and manuscripts. Some had flowed over into small piles on the floor. The shelves that lined the outer wall were reserved for *other* items. Between the occasional book were instruments and sculptures and bottles and quills. It looked like utter chaos, but intentional somehow. The scent of parchment and musky leather hung in the air.

He hadn't lied; Myronor *really* liked to read.

~ Four ~

PALADINS

*T*hunk.

Myronor missed the first step down the spiraling, tower staircase, jolting him from his musings. He frequently ran into things or misstepped when lost in thought. Inside his mind was where his best work happened, after all. Still, he couldn't recall a time when a *person* had obscured his vision in such absolution.

Ophiera. A unique name, that was certain. One Myronor was glad to finally know. He *needed* a name for the vision that had haunted him for days on end. The image of a chanting woman with a tear-streaked face had been burned vividly in his mind. It was shocking enough for him to wake at all after his fall, but to find *her* above him, of all people...

Ophiera had fogged his mind for days with visions of stark white hair and intense violet eyes. They reminded him of amethysts and not just in color. They were bright and hard, warm and cold, beautiful and powerful. A perpetual contradiction. A bit like her, he was learning.

By the river, he had barely caught a glance of those eyes before she collapsed atop him. But from the moment he had awakened, he remained, for lack of a better word, mesmerized. He assumed his fascination with her was merely a side effect of a near-death experience. It was not every day someone saved your life. Especially not a beautiful woman. Especially not a paladin of the Cloister.

He'd suspected she was a paladin by the chants, but the scars had truly proved it. He couldn't believe she of all people had found him.

Ophiera was the first paladin he had ever encountered outside of a book. And speaking with her today only proved she held more interest than as his savior alone.

As he descended the spiral stairs, his thoughts wrapped themselves in reflection again. Myronor had spent a momentous effort recounting the events of the river whilst she recovered.

It was difficult piecing together coincidence and fate, notably when he lacked her side of the story. But now that she was awake, he found her to be quite surreptitious. Why would she only admit to healing him and nothing else? Manasickness was usually an ailment that afflicted mages, as far as he knew. Induced by casting magic far beyond their mana, an act forbidden by the Magistrate. How a paladin from the Cloister came to suffer so much from a simple healing rite was beyond him. Though he admitted he knew less than he'd like to about paladins, he couldn't understand how the rite had nearly killed her. Something else had happened, and a paladin refusing to confess only fed his curiosity.

At the end of the tower descent, Myronor stepped onto the balcony circumventing his library below. He followed the path around to the opposite side, running his hand along the wooden banister out of habit. From here, he could appreciate the cobwebs coating the variegated chandeliers and grimy windows. As he looked down, he ignored the thick layer of dust coating the tops of the spiraling bookcases. Below, in the library, he forgot the dust existed and preferred it that way. Sure, he could employ a few choice spells and magic away the grime to spotlessness. But that wasn't the point. Cleaning up here was a waste of time and mana when the exciting work happened below.

From this vantage, he could see the open center of his study. The spiral of inward-curving shelves always led him home. In his study, he couldn't see the neglected tops of shelves. There, he could greedily drink from the fountain of knowledge surrounding him in peace. His sacred, lonely place amongst the endless books.

Myronor reached the other spiral staircase, opposite the tower stairs, that twirled down into the library. The smell of musty tomes welcomed him home. Tall as they were, it was impossible to become lost amongst the shelves, as all paths led to the center. Often, he paced the outer path surrounding the spiral, circling the multitude of radial rows until an avenue appealed to him. Each day, his path was distinct, and each day, he browsed along the way to find unique tomes he had not yet perused. Like any good mage's library, it was so large that he would rejoin the Aether before reading every book contained within his tower.

Today, however, Myronor took the first path between the bookcases with an uncharacteristic sense of urgency. Ophiera's awakening had ignited his curiosity again.

When he reached the center study, the sight of his chaotic wooden desk invigorated him. Empty ink bottles and haphazard stacks of scrolls gave it the look of an unorganized mess, but it was exactly as he wanted it. Organized piles of books sat atop layers of worn and mismatched rugs. A single plum armchair remained free of clutter, permanently reserved for the only other being who frequented his tower.

"Mallow?" he called.

His familiar was not in the chair. A rare occurrence indeed, but she was never far. The perfect circular indentation of where she had lain still remained. More curious than worried, he searched the study for his small companion. It was more of a gesture than anything; if Mallow didn't want to be found, no amount of searching would yield results.

In his periphery, Myronor caught two enormous eyes peeking around a stack of books. A playful, half-hearted attempt to remain hidden. Her pale azure stare matched his own, contrasting starkly with the coloration of her fluffy fur. Her triangular face and pointed ears were a deep, blackened blue, the same shade of fur on her four limbs and tail. The dark blue faded to creamy white fleece on her torso, stark and beautiful. His Mallow was absolute perfection embodied in a catlike form.

"Spying on our guest?" he asked. She ruffled her fur indignantly before slipping out from hiding and back into the armchair. As Mallow curled into a ball, he found himself ignored. Yet again.

Returning to his desk, Myronor hoped to continue where he'd left off before tending to their injured guest. Information regarding the Cloister and their Oath-bound disciples was challenging to find, an exceptional frustration given the sheer quantity of books within his library. Never before had these tomes failed him so spectacularly as in recent days.

The Cloister's holy writ, the *Book of the Aether*, was as worthless to him as it was to everyone else in Tanvik. It only held nugatory rules and coercive prose while remaining devoid of any facts or theories. Some of their scripture was likely based in truth, but bloated by self-righteous musings on the purity of souls and the white flames of the Aether.

Did the people of Tanvik truly need their morality spoon-fed to them under threat to their souls? Of course, murder was a sin...who needed a book to tell them so? And more importantly, why was the victim of such a heinous act the one that suffered the consequences? According to the Cloister's teachings, a soul stolen by murder could never to return to the Aether. Yet the murderer, claimed by Retribution, would be cleansed and reborn. Even as a child, their doctrine made no sense to him. No one could adequately answer his questions, other than to point to the damned book. And "because I said so" was never a *real* answer to a question.

At least it seemed the rest of Tanvik was slowly waking to that realization that the Cloister could be questioned.

While the Cloister had an integral connection to the Magistrate of Tanvik, their role in government was now their greatest influence. Very few followed the teachings of the Cloister these days, and yet Tanvik remained relatively peaceful. Myronor could count on one hand the number of murders that had occurred in Feyralis since he moved here nearly two decades ago. That wasn't to say Feyralis was a utopia of peace and prosperity, but it was clear the people of Tanvik no longer required the Cloister to solve their problems.

Magic, on the other hand, could solve everything.

Needless to say, he never cared for the Cloister's teachings, nor their clerics or paladins. Not until recently.

Tossing the *Book of the Aether* aside, Myronor opened a different tome, one of far more use: *The Paladins of the Cloister*. More journal than manuscript, the old, tattered book had no author listed. He suspected his library housed the only copy. Over the last few days, this book had provided him *some* insight at least into the Cloister.

Myronor had a feeling the book was written by an outsider, someone dissociated from the Cloister. It held far too much useful information to be written by one of their priests. Because of this, he was able to glean a bit more perspective regarding its practices. If the tome was written by someone of the Cloister, they would have hidden more in vague details and avoidance. He was even able to decipher a few of the runes, cross-referencing them to those burned into Ophiera's arm. But the book was far from comprehensive. For instance, it nowhere mentioned the language she had chanted nor the various rites of the different Oaths.

The book served as a frustrating appetizer; a tease of knowledge, serving only theory when he desired a seven-course meal of details. What did the runes mean? What language did she chant? Were the holy flames a form of magic? Or the Aether itself, as so many speculated? How binding were these Oaths?

The most frustrating part of all was knowing that someone who could answer his questions lay incapacitated in his bedroom. But perhaps now that Ophiera had awakened, she could shed some light on the curiosities that plagued him.

Seated at his desk, Myronor gathered his ink and quill, ready to begin his study. Before he dove too deeply into *The Paladins of the Cloister*, he jotted down some notes on his interaction with Ophiera and the information she revealed, deliberately and not. As he scrawled down the important bits of their conversation and sketched what runes he remembered, he added the questions he hoped to answer.

He recalled how fearfully she had spoken of her Oath and duty to the Magistrate. But he had a hard time understanding the fear of tardiness. Quite regularly, he arrived late to the Magistrate's summons, sometimes outright ignoring them if the request was inconvenient enough. The worst rebuke he had received was a written notice. Then again, perhaps he was the exception and not the rule. Whatever favor he had curried with the Magistrate before was long gone by now.

When he finished purging his thoughts, he began to read again in a fervor. With hunched shoulders, Myronor traced the words in the book with one hand while his other stood poised to annotate his findings. His fair hair draped around him, providing a curtain of concentration. When he obsessed over a topic like this, his whole being drew to the task, the book like a vortex and he a ship without a sail. However, the draw of the whirlpool was a welcome escape.

* * *

Mew.

Mallow's call drew Myronor from his concentration. He looked at her expectantly, but she closed her eyes sleepily. Mixed messages were her forte. Only then did he notice the soft footsteps from above and sighed.

Brushing aside a stray scroll, he found the desk clock he seldom used. Only an hour had passed since he left Ophiera to rest, yet she was already up and about. Quill still in hand, he made a note of the impatience of paladins.

Her steps halted on the balcony above. Obscured by shelves and stacks of books, he assumed she could not see him amongst the clutter. Part of him desired to remain hidden, to observe her actions for his own knowledge and amusement. But a glance from Mallow convinced him of the rudeness in his ploy.

"Ophiera, shouldn't you be resting?" he said.

She remained silent and he wondered if she hadn't heard him.

"Where is my armor?" she said with a timid, yet stern tone. Another contradiction.

Myronor had every intention to answer her. He planned to invite her down to his study—maybe offer her tea and ask her more questions before showing her to her lost belongings. But he found himself silently distracted by a flip of the page.

A rough, charcoal sketch darkened the otherwise pale parchment. It looked to be a person engulfed in flames, both intriguing and disturbing. Below the black drags of flames, a small footnote referenced another page. He thumbed gently through the aging parchment, but the pages referenced were in an unrecognized language of foreign characters. Similar to some of the runes on previous pages, he wondered if these were perhaps the characters associated with the language of her chants.

Driven by a nearly manic curiosity, he searched the pages before and after. These remained written in his native tongue, but none referenced the burning image. He returned to the sketch, studying the pain and triumph captured in the eyes of the burning figure. The rest of their face, however, had been completely obscured by the drawn flames. Myronor *needed* to know who, or rather what, this was.

In his periphery, Myronor saw a movement that pulled his attention from the book. Ophiera entered the inner circle of his study with a wary posture; she had entered without invitation. Not that he cared or minded, but she seemingly did.

She wore nothing but a sour expression and the tunic he had lent her. Draped over her shoulder, her long braid fell past the hem of the shirt, dangling in front of her knee. He was fixated on the braid, of course, not her long, muscular legs running perpendicular to the floor. His stuttering heart gave him away, but he kept his thoughts to himself. She had already called him a pervert and he did not wish for his appreciation to be misconstrued.

Ophiera's stance became defensive without warning and for a moment, Myronor feared she had read his thoughts. He followed her gaze to the floor, where Mallow now landed after leaping from her chair. The familiar strode directly toward Ophiera with an inquisitive expression. But the paladin remained alarmed as if danger approached. He realized in pitying amusement that she had likely not seen a cat, let alone a familiar, before.

Unyielding as usual, Mallow rubbed her face along the woman's calves with a pitched mewl. Myronor relaxed as Ophiera's expression softened, her full lips teetering on the edge of a smile.

"That's Mallow," Myronor said as he vacated the comfort of his desk and stared adoringly at his minuscule familiar. "She's the sweetest familiar you'll ever lay eyes on."

"I see," Ophiera breathed. She was so damn near a smile. But her eyes hardened and the hint of amusement faded. "I do not wish to inconvenience you further. If I can gather my armor, I'll be on my way to the Magistrate."

Myronor observed the paladin for a moment, trying to decide if there was a way to convince her otherwise. She clearly hadn't grasped how close she was to death just five days ago. He couldn't believe she was awake, let alone able to stand before him now, stern and stoic. At full height, her presence now was far more formidable than when she had laid in his bed. She filled out his tunic in an alluring way, the material tight around her chest and hips.

It was probably best he didn't delay her any further.

With a wave of his hand, he beckoned to Mallow. As she trotted over, he pulled from his robes a clear crystal wrapped in a leather tassel. He held it out, expectant in the routine. The cat graciously leaped into the air, only to never land. She instead adsorbed into the crystal as it glowed and dimmed again in her absence.

Ophiera's expression shifted to something Myronor couldn't quite recognize. It wasn't a smile, but all the hardness left her eyes. Maybe it was a poor attempt at curiosity.

"It's easier for her to travel like this," he said, tucking the crystal back into his robes. He patted it affectionately for good measure. "Let's be off, shall we?"

Ophiera stared at him, face falling to expressionless stone again. "We?"

"Yes." He smiled, trying to reassure her. "I'll escort you to the Magistrate."

"Thank you, but I do not require an escort," she said with a stab of arrogance.

Her indignation was rather cliché. Obviously, he knew she could fend for herself, but that was beyond the point.

"Under normal circumstances, I would agree. But I doubt you're fully recovered from your ordeal."

"I feel fine," she said, crossing her arms.

He could have guessed she would be *difficult*; he remembered her glorious purge on the floor the last time she refused to listen.

"When was the last time you were in Feyralis?" he asked, changing tactics.

She glared at him and a shiver of fear ran down his spine. "Far from a year, closer to a decade."

Myronor smirked. He needed to add *sassy* to his notes as well.

"Feyralis may not be as you remember," he said gently. "It's grown quite dangerous."

She continued to glare. "Feyralis has always been a dangerous place."

Stubborn too, he thought with a sigh.

"But now it is dangerous for *you*. Opinions of the Cloister have changed rapidly of late." Though Ophiera continued to glare, he saw that hint of concern dance across her brow. Still, she looked as if to argue. She left him no choice. "I have business at the Magistrate anyway—so I either walk with you or follow you; it's your choice."

He watched her jaw twitch in annoyance, another peculiarly endearing expression. It appeared the only way to reason with a paladin was a challenge.

"Fine. As long as we depart promptly."

"Of course."

Myronor led her back through the bookshelf maze to the metal spiral staircase. They descended to the ground level, into the living space of his tower. Like the circular room above, this level held distinct areas segregated by the layout of furniture. Nearest to the stairway was a small reading area speckled with more mismatched armchairs of leather and velvet. He used this area to read for entertainment rather than study, a physical separation of work and leisure. Unfortunately, it had fallen into disuse in recent times.

In the center of the room, a slab of speckled granite sat atop petrified tree trunks, forming an archaic table surrounded by six stools of the same petrified wood. The style did not particularly appeal to him, but the table, like most of the furniture, had passed to him with the tower. And he had far too many priorities over the outdated decor.

On the far wall sat a small, unused pantry and kitchen area directly across from a massive hearth. Flames crackled in the stone fireplace and, with a mild embarrassment, he saw his blanket and pillow strewn over the leather couch. He often slept in front of the hearth rather than the bedroom upstairs, accidentally before, but by choice of late.

Next to the fireplace, Myronor kept a large wooden chest for cloaks and other outing items. He turned to Ophiera with a smile and opened the container, revealing her armor and gear.

"Thank you," she breathed. The pained sincerity in her voice gripped his heart. She ran her fingers over the golden breastplate as if reunited with a lover. The moment was too intimate, and his presence felt intrusive.

"I'll make some tea while you ready," he said before fleeing to the kitchen. He was still in her line of sight, though he kept his back turned for her privacy. Again, he wanted no more reasons for her to accuse him of perversion.

Tea was the only consumable Myronor made without magic. No matter his mastery of conjura, nothing could replace the routine of a steaming pot of tea. Since his hearth remained occupied by the dressing paladin, he compromised and conjured boiling water into an old teapot. He felt a slight twang in his chest as he cast, an early sign his mana reserves ran low. Perhaps he shouldn't have conjured as large of a feast as he had this morning.

From a clay urn, he tipped in an exotic blend of dried tea leaves, a parting gift from a special friend. The aroma filled him with nostalgia.

Quicker than expected, he heard the gentle clang of armor as Ophiera marched to the kitchen. As he turned to see if perhaps she needed something else, he found her completely dressed. The result was quite intimidating. Boots and all, Ophiera sat only a few fingers shorter than himself, yet still was much taller than the average Tanvik woman. More muscular too. More everything, in fact.

The addition of the bulky golden armor to her already impressive physique and the enormous claymore now strapped to her back added layer upon layer of threat. Armor segments covered her from neck to ankle, including massive pauldrons atop a flattering, fitted breastplate. Combined with her stark white hair and somber demeanor, she looked positively deadly.

"I assumed that would take longer," he said with a smile. But his light-hearted comment fell on deaf ears. She only responded with a blank stare, the armor seemingly encouraging her stiff personality.

Myronor busied himself setting out his old chipped teapot and two mugs on the small wooden table in the kitchen. "We have time for a cup, right?"

Again, she stared blankly. When her lips parted, he was sure she was about to protest, but the softness of her words surprised him. "One cup shouldn't hurt."

The armor was no encumbrance to her as she moved to the table, but he knew the golden plate carried much weight. He brought it here, after all. As he poured her cup first, he studied the worn, ancient plate armor. Despite its golden gleam, the armor lacked the luster associated with the precious metal. Drab with age, the armor itself was not nearly as impressive as the woman within it.

"I can see why you were so desperate for your armor now," he said. "What's the saying...'if looks could kill'?"

Ophiera snorted into her teacup. "Thanks?"

He laughed, wondering if she intended to be humorous. But her expression remained solemn.

"I do have a question before we depart," she began hesitantly. Myronor nodded with encouragement. He loved questions. "How did you fall from the wall?"

Over the rim of his cup, Myronor watched her carefully. Maybe he didn't love all questions.

"You won't like the answer."

She grimaced. "My Oath requires one."

He should have guessed this would come up eventually. She had said her Oath was one of Retribution, hadn't she?

"I fell," he said, feigning embarrassment.

She stared at him, unwavering and unnerving. The armor definitely didn't help.

"*How* did you fall?"

He too very much desired to know the answer to that question. The events leading up to his plummet were hazy still. He had once read about the ability of the mind to purposefully forget a traumatic event in an attempt to protect one's sanity. The last thing he remembered was climbing the stairs up to the wall with the intention to try a newer spell. But he knew what Ophiera was really asking him. Did someone try to kill him?

According to the *Book of the Aether*, there was no greater sin than murder, yet the paladins themselves killed in recompense. He had always found this hypocrisy curious. Still, all that mattered now was he was alive, thanks to the intervention of the taciturn woman before him.

"No one pushed me," he said, taking a sip of tea. "So, no Retribution is required."

"I see..." she said, relief loosening her jaw. "But then, why were you up on the wall in the first place?"

Myronor rubbed his temples. The truth was guaranteed to anger her, but no one in their right mind would lie to a paladin. She had saved his life, after all; she at least deserved to know why.

"The details are still fuzzy...but I was up on the wall to test a new spell," he said, not meeting her eyes. "It was intended to slow my fall from great heights. A float charm of sorts, but more powerful. Again, I can't remember, but I must assume it didn't work. The next thing I remember is you, chanting atop me by the riverbank."

Ophiera's face turned to stone as he spoke. One might easily interpret his actions as negligence rather than misfortune. As he watched her face redden in anger, he wondered if she was now regretting her decision to save the life of someone so careless. But she remained silent and still.

"Stupid, I know," he said with an uncomfortable chuckle. "In my defense, it had worked beautifully before on shorter falls." He had practiced that spell many times, yet upon the wall...Shaking himself from his thoughts, he addressed her again with a grin. "Thankfully, you wandered by at the right time."

Ophiera's armor rattled slightly as she glared at him, stone-faced and tense.

Though Myronor viewed the entire situation with mild amusement, he was not without sympathy for her. She had nearly given her life to rescue an idiot.

If she did not despise him now, he was confident she would after reaching the Magistrate. The thought saddened him, but there was no fighting what fate had so clearly planned.

"Speaking of time—shall we be on our way to the Magistrate?"

~ Five ~

TASKED

No matter the time or day or season, the main streets of Feyralis overflowed with people.

Ophiera's lackluster tolerance of crowds was hardly new. But recent years spent by the ocean in a tiny village had ruined any ability to cope with the throngs. Whether by personality or training, isolation or illness, her senses were overwhelmed by the slightest bump, smell, or sound. Her nerves yanked with every shouting trader or laughing child. Only five minutes after leaving the tower, her jaw ached, locked and tense.

The constant murmur and movement seemed riotous, yet her escort remained unperturbed. Myronor navigated through the throngs of people with grace, smiling like a fool as he led her to the Magistrate. A few people waved to Myronor as they passed, but the moment they saw who he led, they rethought stopping to chat with him. He said Feyralis may not be as she remembered, but at least that response was the same.

The people were still dressed in bright solid colors of flowing garbs. The clothes of the capital city were layered by custom, allowing for both individual expression and flexibility in wear throughout the shifting seasons. Most adults wore thinly layered wrapped dresses or loose, linen pants with tunics and vests of various lengths. Only the traveling merchants and laborers wore leather. On hot days, the laborers only covered their privates. Thankfully, today still held the brisk chill of spring so Ophiera did not have to witness *that* particular spectacle of Feyralis.

No single person stood apart from the crowd, as *everyone* stood out, homogenous in heterogeneity. Ophiera's white hair and violet eyes often went unnoticed. Occasionally, someone recognized the disparity between her physique and the aged coloration of hair, but the golden armor kept their gaze brief.

Few in Feyralis wore plate armor and none in a set cast in shining gold. When Ophiera was first conscripted by the Magistrate, the gawking and whispering from the crowds slowly broke her spirit. The voices became easier to ignore as time passed, and by the time she negotiated her retirement, she barely noticed the points and glares anymore.

She had learned most of the gawking occurred out of curiosity. Paladins had become a cultural myth well before she retired. They were part of a history that every child learned but rarely encountered. Even at times when most of Tanvik followed the Cloister's teachings, the paladins themselves were scarce. As far as she knew, she was the last paladin conscripted by the Magistrate; no one had replaced her. No one could. She was the last of the kindled to receive an Oath of Retribution.

In the distance, Ophiera's eye caught the massive ivory wonder that was her destination. The ancient architecture appeared out of place in the city's heart, a tall obelisk of white gleaming stone. A gold-dipped peak held a large finial at the top, pointing toward the sky. Against the blue, cloudless day, the inlaid golden flames shone like a beacon. The structure loomed powerful and foreboding, the intended message of the Magistrate.

Only within the last twenty years had Tanvik opened its borders to trade, culminating in excessive prosperity. Over time, the trade of magical commodities transformed Feyralis into an epicenter of commerce and knowledge. Mages had always existed in Tanvik, but of late, the Magistrate had become an oligarchy that favored magic. Even since her last visit years ago, the city had made substantial progress. The entire infrastructure shifted to accommodate the growing importance of mages and alchemicians. But such change came at a price.

Hidden in the narrow alleyways between the sod buildings and high towers, vagrants eked out a meager existence. Many more than she remembered from years past. Malnourished people lay crumpled against the walls while children huddled in small groups. Ophiera remembered planning food heists in similar gangs as a child and assumed they were making their own plans to avoid starvation.

Prosperity rarely fell to all citizens of Feyralis, but the divide had clearly widened since she'd retired. Perhaps this was what Myronor had meant when he said Feyralis had changed. Her stomach turned to iron at the juxtaposition of the market's excess and the vagrancy in the alleys. The breakfast she left behind this morning could have fed these poor souls. If Myronor could conjure that amount of food on a whim, why was anyone starving in a city with mages? This was exactly why she hated coming to Feyralis. Nothing made sense.

"Filth!"

Ophiera didn't turn her attention to the source of the shrill cry. She never did. It was likely a simple squabble amongst traders. None of her concern.

Only when she felt something smack hard against the back of her head did she realize the intention behind the cry. She closed her eyes and inhaled deeply before pressing ahead. Several paces beyond her, the mage remained oblivious.

"Anathema!"

Ophiera's heart froze. Were they referring to her?

She had grown accustomed to the stares and the whispers, but no one had ever used that vile word against her before. Any hope of discretion disappeared as the crowd peeled away from her. Myronor turned around and met her with an inquisitive gaze.

Another spiteful shriek pierced her ear. "No one needs your Retribution!"

"Please, keep moving," she whispered as she caught up to Myronor.

"I told you Feyralis wasn't as you remembered," he murmured with a hollow chuckle and turned on his heel. They continued only a few steps before three burly men stepped forward, blocking their path.

Stunned, Ophiera couldn't even imagine their intentions. Surely she had been shunned, even shamed on occasion, but never challenged by the people of Feyralis. She was about to step forward and demand they move, but Myronor's chuckling kept her silent.

"Good afternoon, gentlemen," Myronor said with a smile. "Something I can help with?"

"That anathema," snarled a man with dark eyes and a thick, tangled beard. He pointed at her with a trembling hand. "She's not welcome here. Not in Feyralis. Not in Tanvik."

Ophiera wished to tell this man that if not for the Magistrate, she would have gladly never set foot in Feyralis again. But duty and dignity held her tongue.

"Feyralis is welcoming to all sorts," Myronor said, gazing toward the crowd in mock question. "Or am I mistaken?" He gestured to a silver medallion hanging from his neck. Until now, the trinket had gone unnoticed by Ophiera; she wondered if he had kept it tucked beneath his robes.

The crowd murmured, recognizing some meaning behind the medallion that Ophiera couldn't understand.

"We meant no disrespect, sir," muttered the bearded man, his dark eyes widening. "But even mages ought not to keep the company of a vile anathe—"

"If you insult my companion," Myronor interrupted, "you insult me. So I would rethink your intentions."

For the first time since she'd met the mage, he sounded cold. She had viewed him as a silly man, but now he felt nearly dangerous. No blue light of magic emanated from his hands, yet a staggering power charged the atmosphere.

Nevertheless, the crowd backed slowly away, avoiding his invisible influence. The bearded man blanched as a few murmurs escaped the crowd. Ophiera heard her own racing pulse rise above the chatter of the distant market. But the bearded man moved aside, the crowd following his lead.

"Ready, Ophiera?" Myronor looked at her with a roguish grin.

With a nod, she followed Myronor.

It took far too long before the murmurs began again. The crescendo of the market's bustle could not silence the hateful words now ribboning through the crowd.

"I thought the Magistrate no longer conscripted paladins."

"How could they let that murdering filth in this city? *They're* the anathemas!"

"Did you hear how the Cloister trains them? Barbaric."

"Why would he defend her? You think *he* believes in the Cloister's teachings?"

As she trailed behind Myronor, the malicious cries rang in her ears, striking past her armor. Could they not see she existed only to serve their very souls? To seek Retribution against the anathemas? Could they not understand the Cloister had sacrificed *her* soul for *their* benefit?

She hated herself enough without their venom.

The sight of the Magistrate provided only a slight respite from her depressive mindset. As her greaves clunked familiarly on the white marble steps, she sobered. Neither Cloister nor Magistrate cared for her feelings, so why should she? All that mattered was duty now.

Myronor halted before her, and in her distraction, she nearly knocked him to the ground. He stood before the Magistrate's doors, solid wood and riveted with iron brackets. As always, he wore a smile, yet it felt disingenuous against the sadness in his eyes.

"Are you still mad about your escort?"

The question caught her off guard. She would not thank him for intervening because the crowd spoke the truth. By every definition, she was a murderer. An anathema. She simply had never heard someone *else* refer to her as such.

"I would have endured what justice they felt I deserved," she said.

"Cruelty is never just," he whispered. The sincerity of his voice was soothing but foolishly naive.

Without waiting for her response, Myronor pushed against the hefty doors.

She followed the mage into the Magistrate, still irked by his presence. Silence fell as the door swung closed behind them, sealing away the bustle of the city outside.

The quiet eased Ophiera's spirit, and she allowed herself a moment to center herself in peace.

The hall of the Magistrate was just as she remembered.

The Tanvik sigil dominated the view from the entrance parlor, a massive banner of silk and flame. Hung high from the vaulted ceiling, the crimson flag was embroidered with the white holy flames, outlined in gold thread.

Alongside the Tanvik banner hung other standards, those which represented the Five Realms of Tanvik. Ophiera had always favored the emblem of the Southern Coastlands, where Iluka lay. The standard was a simple, solid cloth of dark blue, sewn in the shape of an inverted wave. She paid the other four standards little mind as she passed beneath them.

Her greaves echoed on the marbled green agate floors. The golden geometric designs, inlaid into the stone, conveyed a semblance of structure to the chaos of the swirls and textures. She had always felt guilty walking on these beautiful floors with worn, dirty boots, but the stone clearly stood the test of time. Myronor's shoes barely made a noise as he followed close behind her.

"I'll join you in the Magistrate's chambers," Myronor said, his voice echoing in the empty hall. She nearly cricked her neck turning to him so quickly, startling Myronor into further explanation. "To ensure you're excused from the tardiness and whatnot."

She'd hoped this was where they would say goodbye. But the encounter outside had left her without the energy to argue. Ophiera turned, continuing through the lavish hall as Myronor trailed behind.

Feyralis may have changed, but the Magistrate seemingly hadn't. Everything looked the same, including the complete lack of guards. The Magistrate never had a need for guards; some nonsense of power balance that she never cared to recall. But that didn't mean the seat of power stood unprotected.

At the end of the hall, two lines of carved statues stood before an elaborate marble staircase. Each stone figure represented some pillar of Tanvik's history and culture. People of fame and importance from all Five Realms were represented, including a caricature sculpture of a paladin. She had never bothered to read the iron plaques beneath the statues because she never cared what they represented or what they accomplished. She only knew the statues were a gift from Krysas, the mage city-state overseas, soon after their trade agreements began.

The moment her foot touched the marble staircase, all thoughts of the statues disappeared. Instead, her nerves rose concomitantly with each ascending step. She hadn't climbed this staircase in years, yet the tension in her shoulders built just the same. She had never wanted to come back here. The only motivation for her continued steps toward the Magistrate's door was learning her task to come. Soon, she would understand the purpose of her summons.

Ophiera nearly forgot Myronor still trailed behind her until she pushed open the double doors. She led him into the vast but relatively vacant chamber of the Magistrate. A massive wooden table sat at the far end, where five ornately carved chairs faced the door.

From dawn until dusk, at least one of the five Justicars of the Magistrate held vigil here, constantly available to the people of Tanvik.

Only two of the Justicar's seats were occupied now. Ophiera recognized the Justicar of Feyralis and, to her dismay, the Justicar of the Cloister. They conversed quietly while sifting through rolls of parchment. Aleksander, the Justicar of the Cloister, happened to look up first. He was a cleric bound to an Oath of Mercy and thus wore the traditional white robes with black adornments, including a veil to cover his face. The sight never failed to increase Ophiera's anxiety. The Justicar of the Cloister was the only other of her brethren she knew outside of the Cloister, and even then, she hardly *knew* Aleksander. His role had always been the same: to ensure her obedience.

Ophiera's attention shifted to the Justicar of Feyralis, the unspoken ruler of Tanvik. Though the Magistrate claimed equal rule across the Five Realms, all denizens knew the Justicar of Feyralis held the reins of the council.

Eliana Diamont looked the same as she had the day she signed Ophiera's contract of retirement. In an ideal world, she would have *never* seen the Justicar again. But today, Ophiera was once again forced to bear witness to the terrifying beauty of the woman who had called her back to duty. As always, Eliana's pale green eyes shone cold and distant as she watched Ophiera approach. Sleek curtains of black hair framed her flawless, delicate face. Yet when Eliana smiled, she looked like a wolf baring its teeth.

"Welcome, Aspect of Retribution," Eliana boomed haughtily, her voice echoing in the empty hall. "Pleased to see you're still alive after failing to heed our summons."

Ophiera only acknowledged the Justicars with a silent nod when she arrived before the table. She refused to say more than necessary to those who had trapped her. Fulfillment of her duty was her only intention here.

However, Myronor stepped forward.

"*Failed* is rather harsh, Eliana," he said. "The Magistrate is well aware of the circumstances behind her delay."

Ophiera cocked her head, glaring at the mage. No one referred to the Justicars by their names, at least not without a title. Despite his disrespect, Ophiera appreciated his defense of her.

The Justicar's eyes fell to Myronor and somehow grew even colder. "Ambassador Ebontide, I'm surprised to see you unscathed after sharing a house with a disciple of the Cloister." She clicked her tongue in disapproval. "You'll be glad to know the Magistrate *did* receive your notice and will not seek punishment for the paladin's *failure* to present herself on time."

At least Eliana hadn't changed since Ophiera's retirement. The Justicar of Feyralis never allowed anyone to dictate the conversation, and the mage would fare no differently. From the corner of her eye, she saw Myronor's spine straighten, but he held his tongue. Maybe he wasn't a fool after all.

"We've wasted enough time," drawled a bored voice from beside Eliana. Aleksander's veil barely moved as he spoke, but his voice had the same effect on Ophiera as the sound of a whip. "Task the Aspect of Retribution so we may continue with our business."

The Justicar's words should have cued Myronor to leave, yet the mage stood still. Too still. Ophiera watched him from her periphery, but he only continued to stare at Eliana.

"Myronor must stay for this," said Eliana, perhaps reading Ophiera's darting eyes. A wintry smile played upon her lips. "It is by *his* request we've summoned you from your...retirement, did you call it? From whatever you've been doing all these years."

Ophiera tried to keep her expression stoic as the floor shattered beneath her. Myronor was responsible? Myronor, a fool mage she had come upon by chance, half-drowned and near death—*he* was responsible for her conscription? She couldn't understand why he would require Retribution.

"Once again, the Magistrate commands you to fulfill your Oath," Eliana said. "We demand your Retribution."

Though Ophiera had heard these words countless times before, they stung worse today.

"For twenty years, we have allied ourselves with the city-state of Krysas. And for those two decades, Tanvik has appointed an Ambassador to the foreign capital, as per Krysas's custom. Recently, we received word our dear emissary has returned to Aether. Details have come to light that have led us to suspect she may have died by...unnatural means. A suspected assassination."

Ophiera chewed on the conscription details for a moment. She hated when they used the word *assassination*; why did they need another word for the murder of a politician? She hadn't even known the position of Ambassador existed. She supposed it made sense to have a mediator of sorts between nations, but even during her conscription, she had never really paid attention to politics. Couldn't the accusation alone challenge Tanvik's alliance with Krysas? This could become complicated very quickly. And her Retribution wasn't enacted on suspicion alone, especially not for such a politically delicate task.

"Why does Krysas not enact its own justice?" Ophiera asked.

She caught Aleksander's veil shifting to her, presumably with his jaw dropped, but she couldn't tell. Every time she had stood before the Magistrate to receive her task, she had simply nodded and left. Never had she challenged a command, even with a simple question.

"The Consortia in Krysas declared her death one of self-destruction, and thus closed their investigation," Eliana said, flicking her hair as if a fly had passed nearby.

Summoned from retirement for a closed case? Ridiculous. Something else was going on.

"And what evidence exists to say she did not sacrifice herself to the Aether?" Ophiera asked. She tried to hide the frustration in her voice, but she was losing composure.

"It's more that the *lack* of evidence provided has left us suspicious," Myronor said, not looking at her. "And I know for a fact my mother would not have killed herself."

Her stomach clenched. His mother?

"Pyra Ebontide was a highly respected Ambassador and a gifted mage," Eliana said, her eyebrow raised at Myronor. "She single-handedly solidified our alliance with Krysas, sacrificing much of her personal life for the greater good of Tanvik. A claim of self-destruction goes against her character, and everything she has done for Tanvik. Therefore, we need to investigate these allegations ourselves, and thus, we task you, Aspect of Retribution."

The Magistrate had torn Ophiera away from Iluka only to demand she serve as some detective and yet withheld details from her. In the past, when the Magistrate set her tasks, they provided details closer to proof that a sin was committed. Judgment had always been a part of her duty, for there was no guaranteed way to deem someone innocent or corrupt without sight of their vesper. But now, they gave her nothing but questions to investigate before deciding for herself if her Retribution was even needed. Why did Aleksander allow this blasphemy to unfold without intervention?

"Investigation of a politician's death seems an inappropriate task for my Oath, especially when you have such little evidence to claim—"

Aleksander held up a scarred hand in silence. Unable to break the years of conditioning, she cut her voice with a flinch. An uncomfortable silence lingered in the room before Aleksander spoke.

"The Cloister has given this task their blessing, Aspect of Retribution. By your Oath, you will travel to Krysas and investigate the death of Pyra Ebontide. If you suspect her soul was claimed by an anathema, then you will enact Retribution on the Aether's behalf. Failure to comply will be interpreted as abandonment of your Oath and a breach of contract with the Magistrate, resulting in punishment for your transgression."

The cleric lowered his hand, resuming his statuesque disposition. His scars might have bound him to an Oath of Mercy, but he was far from merciful. Ophiera felt her chin tremble a moment and wished her face was veiled like Aleksander's. If the Cloister gave its blessing, the scars upon her arm would hold her to the task. There was nothing to be done but obey.

Myronor shifted next to her, his eyes staring at the floor with despondence. She imagined this had not gone as he expected either. While he may have read about paladins, no book could properly convey the bane of compliance.

"I will take my leave then," Ophiera said, ready to be done with this humiliation.

"We're not done," Eliana said, halting Ophiera's retreat. "There is one more task at hand. Myronor Ebontide is to be the next Ambassador to Krysas. Since you are Oath-bound to travel to Krysas anyway, the Magistrate also asks you to escort the Ambassador to his new home in Krysas. You must protect him at all costs."

So, Myronor was also a task himself. She wished she had left him on the riverbank more every minute. Was this her punishment for rebelling against her Oath? That now she must serve a purpose far beyond it? A Hand of Mercy from the Cloister would be suited for the task, not an Aspect of Retribution. Cleaning up political fallout and babysitting a foolish mage wasted both her time and skills.

"I will investigate Ambassador Pyra Ebontide's death, as required by my Oath, but taking on a charge is hardly—"

Eliana's cold voice cut in. "The Magistrate will hold you accountable should you fail to protect your charge. So, while you may not be Oath-bound to protect him, you will be held liable for any harm to him."

"And a breach of contract with the Magistrate will be investigated as an abandonment of your Oath by the Cloister," Aleksander chimed in.

The Justicars watched her expectantly, but Ophiera could not speak. Her face contorted with her held, angry breath. The wills of the Magistrate and the Cloister converged upon her, and she shook under their weight. Both Eliana and Aleksander were careful not to claim her Oath-bound to Myronor himself, but the situation was as good as such. She had found the man nearly dead already by chance. She doubted he was capable of surviving a day outside the city walls, let alone on a long journey to Krysas. He'd probably never traveled a day in his life, and if he had, it was not alone.

With ash on her tongue, Ophiera nodded her acceptance.

"Good," Eliana said with a simper. "*Now* you may take your leave, Aspect of Retribution."

Ophiera jumped at the opportunity to vacate.

She turned on her heel and, without another glance at the Justicars, marched toward the chamber's exit. Her greaves thundered in the now silent room, and she barely registered the tailing presence of a certain mage. Her vision tunneled as the holy flames themselves burned away her insides in existential self-destruction.

As she entered the hallway, one of the ornate guard statues caught her eye. It was a reflection of herself; a stone man carved with armor that would have been gold had he not been made of stone. Unlike her though, he stood proud and gallant, dramatically pointing a massive sword toward the sky.

What a pathetic sight. She reached for her own claymore and charged.

With a whine of metal, the sword effortlessly cleaved the head from the granite paladin's body. It clattered deafeningly to the floor. Unsatisfied, she struck again, dismembering his sword arm with another crash. The blade shattered to pieces upon impact with the swirled agate ground.

The injustice of her life powered each strike upon the stone reflection. Just when she'd finally become comfortable with her escape from duty, she had been reeled back into the Magistrate's chains. And for a task unlike any she'd had before. She never wanted this duty, this burden, this life. Why was she doomed to obey?

As always, what she wanted was insignificant. All that mattered was her Oath.

She ran out of stone to strike well before her anger had subsided. Still furious, she turned, seeking a new target amongst the statues, and found Myronor instead. He watched her with an inquisitive grin, and a fresh wave of fury descended upon her. *Him* and that stupid smile.

"I didn't realize," Myronor said casually, pausing to examine the crumbled stone, "that the Magistrate exempted paladins from vandalism."

His words broke her tantrum. She stared at the pile of rubble before her and cringed. Within minutes, she had reduced one of the precious gifts from Krysas to a heap of stone. What would be the punishment for destroying government property?

Myronor's laugh echoed in the hall as he strode toward her. Without a word, his hand hovered above the stones, glowing a subtle blue. The granite pieces appeared to rewind in time, re-assembling before her eyes in flashes of stone and light. Soon, two smug men stood before her: one of stone and one bearing brilliant blue eyes reflecting a whisper of guilt.

"Have another go if you'd like. Or maybe a different target this round—I think this one is a mage?" He pointed toward a statue of a woman whose palms had been carved to hold tendrils of ethereal stone.

She felt a burning need to punch or thank him, yet neither seemed appropriate. Myronor sighed and clapped a hand on her shoulder. She stiffened against his touch, a discomfort even through her golden pauldrons.

"You look like you really need a drink," he said as he began guiding her toward the door.

Every ounce of Ophiera's self-control was spent on not throttling this fool-turned-charge. But his safety was now supposed to be her top concern. She could not very well break his hands under a vow of protection.

"And maybe put your sword away before we leave," Myronor muttered with a chuckle. He let her go to swing open the massive doors, revealing the city again. "Unless, of course, *you're* willing to stop an angry mob this time."

~ Six ~

WILL

The nameless tavern had no patrons other than Ophiera and the mage. She watched the crowds in the street just beyond the dust-filmed windows. Myronor had led them here by back alleys and side streets in order to go unnoticed. But from her view inside the pub, the main drag of the market was in a full bustle. It seemed like a prime location for a nearly empty bar.

Nestled along a strip of several ancient sod structures, the small rickety tavern appeared to be ignored by people outside. She supposed it was easy to pass over a place like this for the convenience of food and drink stalls available in the marketplace. Like so many in Feyralis, this tavern now sat out of place, forgotten amongst the progress.

Ophiera slouched in the corner of a heavily worn booth, feeling slightly out of place as well. Her golden armor looked odd in the dank, musty establishment. Centuries-old wood covered the interior of the tavern, including the elaborate front counter. An entire tree had apparently fallen neatly into place within the tavern, and rather than move it, the proprietors had simply employed it exactly as it had landed. The top of the bar had been crudely whittled flat, while the remaining branches extended to the opposite wall of the room, decorated with clean, ceramic steins. It was not unpleasant, but her mood prevented her from truly appreciating the charm of the place.

Myronor was still gesticulating flamboyantly to the barkeep as he recounted some elaborate tale. She noticed the old bartender casting sidelong glances toward her as Myronor continued his monologue unabated. Though she had endured such looks most of her life, the events of the day still weighed on her heart. Like this tavern, she was often acknowledged but ignored—at least until today.

Ages ago, the disciples of the Cloister had stood great in number. The people of Tanvik named them by their Oaths; paladins with Retribution, clerics with Mercy, and priests with Sacrifice. Each disciple was branded with their Oath and the scars were unquestioningly revered across all realms of Tanvik. Most families had sacrificed at least one child to the trainings—a great honor to contribute an unkindled soul to serve the Aether. As the ancient wars waned, the Cloister came to serve as unofficial peacekeepers instead. The clerics served the people with their Oath of Mercy, while the priests served the Cloister itself. The paladins simply served the Aether's demand for Retribution.

But after peace had reigned in Tanvik for generations, fewer families were willing to sacrifice their children for a dying, pointless cause. Reverence became tolerance, sacrifice became reservation, and faith became a myth. With a dwindling place among the people, the Cloister allied itself with the Magistrate. They offered their own disciples to the Magistrate for conscription. The gesture earned the Cloister its own seat for a Justicar in the Magistrate, despite its dwindling numbers.

Ophiera had been the most recent paladin kindled from the holy flames; the most recent conscript with an Oath of Retribution. And as far as she knew, she was the last. Aleksander was the only other member of the Cloister she knew in Feyralis, and even he was bound by Mercy; though a cleric in name, he also served as Justicar. She wondered if he ever faced the same backlash she had faced today. Unlikely, given his Oath and authority.

Outside the grimy window of the tavern, she watched the people of Feyralis with a newfound wariness. Since her conscription, the people had always held an apprehension of paladins that she found quite understandable. But the outright hostility in the market today had never occurred before. What exactly had changed in Feyralis? She was well aware more and more citizens had stopped practicing the faith of the Cloister. Despite her Oath, she never viewed this as abandonment: as long as people were good, did it matter if or how they worshipped? She simply felt bitter that *they* were allowed to disregard the Cloister, while she could not.

The sound of a throat clearing nearby dragged Ophiera from her brooding. She hadn't realized how lost she had become in her thoughts until she saw Myronor before her brandishing two massive pottery steins. He looked excited as he set down the two drinks. Frothy golden liquid overflowed onto the dank, scarred table as he clumsily set a mug before her.

"Ubel has the best braggot in the city," he said with a covetous smile at his own mug. He slid into the seat opposite her, cradling the drink.

"Then why are we his only customers?" she said back, unable to contain her sour tone.

Myronor merely chuckled, ignoring her snark. He cocked his head to one side, then held up his mug in salutation. "To new partnerships!"

Ophiera's fist clenched around her mug. This was *not* a partnership. This was servitude enforced by the damned Magistrate and her damned Oath. Against her will, she had been bound to this idiotic mage. She refused to raise a drink to entrapment.

Judging by the falter in his smile, Myronor had received her message loud and clear. Yet he reached his mug across the table to meet hers and knocked them together sharply, spilling a bit of the braggot in the process. This final, absurd gesture broke her composure.

"Do you always act a fool?" she hissed.

"Depends on who you ask...but since you asked me, my humble opinion is...no. I might act *foolish* on occasion, but I'm actually quite brilliant." He took a few gulps of drink, looking self-satisfied.

She had never met a more frustrating individual. As an acquaintance, she could ignore his lack of seriousness, excusing it as an eccentric quirk. Yet knowing they must now travel together, and she must keep him safe, only ignited her fear for their very survival.

The bottom of the stein seemed a good place to drown her woes, and Ophiera brought the mug to her lips. Throwing back her head, she drank deeply, refusing to stop until the beverage had disappeared. As she set the hollow stein back upon the table, she refused to look at the mage, instead glaring steadfastly at the rafters.

"Another round, Ubel!" Myronor called over his shoulder. Not long after, the barkeep shuffled over with two overflowing steins. He left without a glance toward her.

"Ophiera—" Myronor said quietly, staring at the stein in his hands. "I truly am sorry for my role in this scenario. When I requested a wrongful death investigation for Pyra, I didn't imagine the Magistrate would summon a paladin for the matter. I would take it back if I could, but...we are both bound by the will of others—wills that are not so easily broken."

His sincerity caught her off guard. But he didn't *know* the meaning of binds.

"What are you bound by?" she asked, flexing her scarred Oath hand as if daring him to challenge her.

With a saddened smile, he pulled from his robes the medallion he flashed earlier. It dangled lackadaisically over his thumb. The inlaid design reflected brilliantly in the yellow glow cast by a nearby oil lamp. Three coppery stars aligned against the curve of a silver crescent moon. Both adornments were overlaid atop a full circle of fine silver. The two moons of Erum, she recognized, but the three stars of the insignia remained unknown to her. Still, the symbol must have meant something to the people in the marketplace.

"Almost everyone recognizes the insignia of Krysas now; you saw the fools in the marketplace. And while an Ambassador's oath of office is not nearly as damning as the Oath of a paladin, promises to family can still be quite burdensome."

Promises to family? A part of her thought to ask, but she ultimately chose not to. Her mood was slowly shifting with the strength of the libation, and a personal discussion of Oaths and bonds could only ruin such a hard-fought victory.

Instead, the pair sat in silence, sipping their drinks. She had thought the mage never stopped talking, but now he appeared content to merely sit in silence across from her. It was a peace she needed, but sharing it with someone else discomforted her. For once, she looked for words, a question or topic to break the quiet. And the question that still plagued her mind bubbled to the surface.

"Did you use magic to get us to Feyralis from the riverbank?" she asked.

Myronor held her gaze with eyes that always seemed too curious. He tilted his head slightly, comically reminding her of the strange familiar now residing within the crystal beneath his robes.

"Yes and no," he said.

"That's not an answer."

"It is," he said with a smirk. "Just not the simplistic answer you wanted."

She cast a silent glare upon him. "Explain then."

"I *spanned* both of us back to my home."

Ophiera blinked. "You what?"

"Spanned." He chuckled. "It's like instantaneous travel. I can disappear from one place and appear in another."

"I didn't realize mages could do such magic."

"Most can't."

The libations had slowed her mind, but a realization hit her like a falling fruit. "Wait—can you *span* us to Krysas then?"

Myronor shook his head. "I've never been to Krysas and, seemingly, I can only travel to places I know. Like from the riverbank to my home."

Though her heart sank, she was not about to give up. "Do you know another mage who has visited Krysas before? One who would agree to *span* us?

Again, he shook his head. "Like I said, spanning is a rare skill. Frankly, I don't know any other mages, besides my late mother, with the talent," he said. His voice was steady, but Ophiera sensed a hint of sorrow.

How cruelly she had behaved. Thus far, she had given him little acknowledgment or sympathy for his deceased mother.

"I'm sorry for your loss," she mumbled. "I should have offered condolences sooner."

Myronor simply smiled at her again. "Thank you, but there is no need. Just as Eliana said, Pyra sacrificed everything for her position, family included. The last time I saw my mother was when she left for Krysas twenty years ago."

This struck Ophiera as odd. If Pyra had also possessed the ability to span, what would have stopped her from visiting her son? It seemed a rude question to ask, and thus Ophiera remained quiet. Myronor had no qualms filling the silence.

"My father raised me in a small village near the coast. I was a fisher's son until my magic awakened." He smiled as he reminisced. It was a beautiful expression, though Ophiera hated to admit it. "He sent me off to Feyralis for my apprenticeships shortly after my mother left. I've only been back to Iluka a handful of times since."

Ophiera choked, a spray of drink exploding from her mouth across the table. Eyes wide, Myronor stared back at her as she wiped her mouth with her cold gauntlet.

"The oyster village?"

"Yes!" Myronor beamed at her. "You know it?"

She held silent as Ubel dutifully brought a rag to wipe up her mess. As the barkeep left, Myronor cleared his throat with expectation.

"Iluka has been my home during my retirement," she said flatly.

His eyes widened even farther. "Don't tell me...*you're* the Sea Warden?"

Ophiera closed her eyes. The day was filled with too much co-incidence.

"That title is ridiculous," she said through gritted teeth, "but yes."

The title of tradition had never sat well with her, but to hear it spoken outside the village stung her heart in a different manner.

Myronor whistled, low and dramatic. "Wow...I thought the river-bank was a strange coincidence, but this proves it. Fate clearly intended our meeting, Ophiera!"

Fate? The Cloister and the Magistrate already controlled nearly every aspect of her life, leaving little room for fate. Yet the events of late were difficult to reconcile as chance alone without invoking its cruelty. Again, self-pity threatened to sour her mood, so she pressed on in a different direction.

"Who is your father?"

"Berwyn Ebontide. He runs the—"

"Rubyfin boat," Ophiera interjected, watching the grin spread over Myronor's face. She searched the mage's face for resemblance, skeptical of the relation. Berwyn was a reserved man, a hard-working pillar of the community. The smile was the only similarity between the two.

"He's written to me with tales of the Sea Warden," Myronor said. "In fact, one of my favorites spoke of a time the Warden single-handedly fended off over a hundred raiding pirates from Iluka."

Ophiera said nothing. She knew her deeds for Iluka had reached the Magistrate's ears, enough for them to conscript her again. But for Myronor to know of the things she had done, and to speak of them with enthusiasm rather than distaste, only confused her.

"Is it true you never let them reach land?" he pried again.

"You heard a fisher's tale," she said. The second round of braggot now sat well with her, loosening her tongue along with the tension in her shoulders. "I only counted twenty-three. And they most definitely made it on land...though I suppose technically not *dry* land."

"Oh I need to hear this," Myronor barked with a laugh before turning toward the bar again. "Ubel! We're going to need another round!"

As much as she desired more drink, the looming thoughts of duty never left her mind for long. How could she forget when the man responsible for her return to service sat across from her now, grinning like an idiot? An idiot who did not shy away from her or fear her but instead conversed with enthusiasm. Damn, the braggot was strong.

"Shouldn't we begin our preparations for the journey?" she asked, trying to avoid his eyes.

Ubel sidled over and dropped the requested drinks. Myronor took up his fresh, frothy mug, peering at her over the top. His smile was no longer charming, but...challenging.

"We are preparing. Learning about your traveling companion is necessary for a smooth journey."

She stared at him, considering. If not for her Oath, it would have been a benign suggestion. But now, she was duty-bound to begin her investigation of Pyra's death and did not wish to waste any more time. The sooner she got this over with, the sooner she could return to Iluka. The mage seemed to sense her doubt.

"You're required to escort me to Krysas and *then* begin your investigation, correct?" he asked. She nodded in confirmation, Eliana's words ringing in her ears. His grin grew more devilish by the second. "Well, unfortunately for you, I'm a very *uncooperative* charge. I refuse to leave his pub until you, at the very least, tell me this tale."

She grimaced. "You're like a child; is this how you plan to act as an Ambassador?"

Myronor laughed, shrugging his shoulders. "Have you ever met a politician? I'll fit in wonderfully."

Despite herself, her lips twitched into a smile. He was rather good at manipulating rhetoric to his favor. Still, she couldn't understand why he'd want to hear a story of death with such enthusiasm. Like the vespers, talk of anathemas or murder was regarded as taboo. And yet Myronor avoided all social precepts thus far. It must be nice, to be free of convention.

But the braggot reminded Ophiera that she wasn't completely devoid of choice. Inaction was a choice. If her charge refused to co-operate, then she must oblige, mustn't she? The Magistrate ruled with principles of loose interpretation and self-serving rhetoric, so why couldn't she?

A rare smile parted her lips, and she raised her own fresh stein in salutation.

"T'was was a dark and stormy night..."

~ Seven ~

WARDEN

Rumors of the Grey Marauders' interest in Iluka had reached Ophiera weeks before their attack. The shaman's sight had proven useful in establishing a timeline, and the loose gums of inebriated pirates in nearby taverns gave away their tactics.

The Marauders were not the first, nor the last, group of outlaws that hoped to capitalize on Iluka's famous blushed pearls. At least, Ophiera assumed that was their motivation. Every other threat to Iluka, rare as they were, simply coveted the crop. Cultivation of the rare and valuable resource had been practiced and refined by the villagers over the centuries. Despite the clear target on their back, Iluka had existed in peace more often than not. Most villagers owned no real weapons, only tools that could be used in a pinch: machetes, fishing knives, and harpoons. They weren't prepared to defend themselves against an incursion of pirates. That was the responsibility of the Sea Warden. An old tradition amongst the Southern Coastlands established by the Phratries, the title served more as a station than anything. But becoming Warden of Iluka had been the first duty she had ever chosen. And despite her aversion to superfluous titles, she took her duty to heart.

Only the villages of the Southern Coastlands kept to the old traditions, maintaining a shaman and a Warden in each village. The shamans appointed the Wardens and tasked them. But only Iluka stood protected by a former paladin. The villagers not only knew her past, but protected it; they kept the rumors to a minimum outside the village. Few beyond Iluka knew a paladin resided within the village, let alone served as its protector. And from what Ophiera had learned, the Grey Marauders were included in that ignorance. They wouldn't have ever targeted Iluka had they known what they'd face.

Two villages near Cantheas had already succumbed to the Marauders. Pillaging and destroying, the pirates left nothing behind but death and ash. Precious few survivors had surfaced after their attacks, resulting in the delay of the murderous news. Despite Ophiera's retirement, her Oath remained burned into her flesh. She could ignore the acts of anathemas all she wanted, but now that they came to her doorstep, it left her little choice. Their souls must be claimed for the Aether, and she must breach her retirement contract.

When she had agreed to be Iluka's Warden, she expected a few thieves or petty bandits here or there. Crimes she could resolve without the need of her Oath or drawing the Magistrate's attention. Justice without Retribution was a strange, yet enticing concept. However, the Marauders would require her Retribution, no matter how much she wished otherwise. It had been years since she'd seen a vesper.

For several nights, Ophiera camped on the beach, readying for the Marauders' arrival. The shaman's sight had its limitations and thus could not predict the exact night of their attack. But the rumor mill filled in some gaps in knowledge.

The pirates' tactics relied on the sea and the darkness of night. Small boats and soft steps were impossible for most to distinguish from waves. This was how the Marauders surrounded a village without notice and ambushed without resistance. Ophiera reasoned if she could stop them on the beach, she would stop them in full.

And so she waited.

On the fourth night of Ophiera's lonely watch, a storm brewed off the coast. Storms weren't rare, but they were inconvenient. Senses dulled in the rain, and tonight she needed all of them.

She hadn't donned her golden plate armor since becoming Warden, and tonight was no different. While a part of her missed the heft and protection of a paladin's armor, the added weight in sand proved too much to bear. Besides, she wasn't returning to duty; she wasn't on this beach tonight for the Magistrate. She was here to protect Iluka. And that she could do without armor.

Instead, she wore a set of blackened leathers; a gift from the shaman when she agreed to become Warden. Similar to those she wore beneath her armor, they fit her snugly while providing modest protection. Dark and wet, she remained invisible against the dark beach. She did keep her claymore handy, resting it against her shoulder as she sat in the sand. Her arms lay lazily over her bent knees as she stared at the beach beneath her. Her alabaster braid had fallen over her shoulder and coiled upon the damp sand.

Ophiera remained quiet and still as it rained, listening for signs of others. Hours passed as she held a vigil in the storm. The onslaught of rain soaked through her leathers, chilling her bones, but she did not shiver. She maintained the stillness she learned from the Cloister until something disrupted it.

Only Ophiera could distinguish the faint skid and gentle splash of a small boat from the storm waters. The sound of boots in shallow water marked the beginning of the end.

As she stood, water flowed from every curve and crook of her body. Stiff with the cold, she stretched a moment before stabbing her claymore in the sand. The sound of grit against metal remained hidden by the waves and thunder and rain. She freed her hands and pulled a small bundle from a pouch on her belt. Silently she took a few steps toward the first stage of her resistance.

She had placed a line of oil-soaked rags and driftwood along the sand dunes every night she held vigil. As she struck the pieces of flint, she worried the rain might hinder her plan. But the true flames rose, bright orange and reaching high into the night with a few sizzles and pops in the rain. A wall of true firelight stretched down the beach, illuminating the dark waters as a barrier before the village. Its purpose was not for light nor warmth, but merely a dramatic scare tactic. Hopefully.

She turned to face the sea again.

Atop the choppy waves bobbed five wooden boats. Each vessel carried a handful of soaked figures, their shocked expressions visible in the firelight. Several had dropped into the water already, standing in knee-high waves with tow ropes in hand. Everyone remained frozen before her.

This was their preview, their warning for what was to come. Ophiera shouldered her sword, the hilt slick and cold, and stepped toward the boats. She stood feet away from where the waves reached the sand, distant but not far. And still, the Marauders waited.

"Take a single step upon this beach and the Aether will claim you!" she cried, her voice as harsh and cold as the night itself.

A man stepped forward, splashing in the shallow water. Lightning arced across the sky at his approach, illuminating his furious expression more than her wall of true fire had managed.

"You think some fire is goin' stop the Grey Marauders?" shouted the man.

"In a sense," Ophiera claimed, pointing her battered claymore at the man in a challenge.

The man laughed a toothless smile. "Come on...one stupid little girl doesn't stand a chance against us. But if you're willing to kill...why not kill for us instead?

"I'm not willing, simply compelled by your choices. You're an anathema and you have no place here."

"So, you still follow the teachings of the Cloister, eh? Shame." He turned to the boats. "Take the village!"

Caught in the chaos of a raging storm, the whipping winds and flashes of lightning distorted the events to come. The Marauders disembarked and splashed forward through knee-deep water, one by one.

This was *their choice.* Meanwhile, Ophiera had no choice when faced with such vile intent.

She sank low to the beach and dug her scarred hand into the wet sand. The familiar yet foreign words of her chant fell from her tongue as if she had never stopped calling upon them. Years had passed since she beckoned the holy flames, and yet they heeded her call, as if eager to reunite.

The glowing runes of her chant formed a line along the beach, mirroring the wall of flames behind her. She had warned them not to come ashore. But this was *their choice.*

The first man to cross her boundary burst into spectacular, white flames. The holy fire looked wrong against the orange glow of true firelight. Along with smoke and ash, the first soul reclaimed left behind a cloud of steam. It lingered in the rain, clouding the line of symbols extending along the shore.

In their haste, the Marauders spared no thought for their fallen comrade and instead charged blindly forward. Obscured by steam and storm and light, the holy flames claimed them, one by one in rapid succession. She was unable to hear her chants over their screams.

When the night fell to quiet again, Ophiera peered through the thick veil of fog. Only six figures remained; one lone person in a boat, and five in the water. The toothless leader still stood in the surf, though she hated calling him that; he hadn't led, only cowered.

The six remained still.

Slowly, she removed herself from the ground. As her fingers left the sand, so did the light of white flames, extinguished in her absence.

Ophiera drew her claymore to stance as she approached the water. With what little mana she had left, she ignited the blade in burning white with a few choice words. The leader yelled in horror as she charged.

Although she never considered pirates to be overly loyal, three of the brigands threw themselves upon her in an effort to shield their leader. Brave as they were, nothing could forgive their sins. With three powerful swings, Ophiera cut them down to ash with a blaze.

Only three remained.

Ophiera took a step into the water. The cold surf pressed uncomfortably against her boots as she closed in on the trembling leader, still paralyzed before his boat. The woman next to the leader turned cowardly and ran. She stumbled as she fled up the beach. Ophiera now had a choice. Did she think the fleeing woman an anathema, running from consequence? Or an innocent, fearful of death? Judgments like this were never easy.

In her soaked boot, Ophiera felt for the balanced knife stowed within. She felt the cold metal ignite as it flew from her hands. Lit by a strike of lightning, she watched the woman's ashes fall into a wave, a melted silver knife plunging into the surf.

The leader, now within reach, trembled as Ophiera approached. She held no sympathy for the fear in his eyes.

"D-don't—"

"Kill you?" Ophiera asked, interrupting his plea. Steady as ever, she placed her sword at his neck. "And how many have begged the same from you, anathema?"

He said nothing in return, but she read the tally of victims in his eyes. No words could change the sins committed, but Ophiera hoped to see a trace of remorse. Just once. Her moment of hesitation was all it took for the scoundrel to reach for his knife. His attempted action sealed his fate, though she wouldn't allow him to follow through with it.

Blood flowed from his throat as Ophiera flicked her wrist away. Like flint to steel, her sword sparked an eruption of white flames, and a receding wave carried his ashes from her presence.

One final Marauder sat still within a boat, unmoved since the others had shored. He did not look fearful or angry as he stared at the beach, now illuminated by the vespers of his comrades. Ophiera sought Retribution, but his reaction caused her hesitation.

"Why?" she called into the wind.

Whiskey-colored eyes, bloodshot and wet with remorse, stared at her through the darkness. His face was young, but drawn like someone who had suffered too much too quickly. She guessed him likely in his mid-teens, but the pain of his eyes spoke of terrors beyond his youth.

"I couldn't get out of the boat..." he said in a tormented voice, cracking slightly with his age. "I...I was born in Iluka."

Of all the souls she'd purged from Erum, he was the first to look upon her with eyes of regret. Was tonight his first raid? Was he an innocent after all? Perhaps forced here by the threat of family or just bad luck. But boy or man, in the end, he made a choice. Didn't he?

"Flee," she said. He blinked at her, dumbstruck. "Go. Don't ever return to Iluka."

With one last glance at the sorrowful boy, she returned to the beach. The vespers hovered in the storm, creating an eerie glow against the fog and waves. She counted twenty-three vespers in total, each a unique shade across the spectrum of colors, yet all were webbed by the same taint of corruption. Trembling with cold and cost, Ophiera recited her prayer as she watched the souls become like rain, falling in the sand.

The cold storm had numbed her to the pain of remorse. At least for the night.

***

Myronor watched Ophiera with rapt attention as she ended her tale. Throughout the story, his eyes had never left hers. He interrupted her very seldom and only to clarify details. She couldn't remember the last time she had spoken at length on any subject, let alone regarding such an act. It felt strange speaking of death, only to be met with blue eyes full of wonder. She reached for the last few dregs of braggot, uncomfortable with his silent stare.

"Fisher's tale or not, your story put my father's version to shame," he said. "So, what became of the Grey Marauders?"

"Disbanded," said Ophiera. "I claimed over half their legion and most of their leadership that night. They couldn't recover, or so I heard."

"Amazing!" Myronor exclaimed. "I feel much better about this journey now. Couldn't ask for better protection, eh?"

She twitched at his words, looking away. A guardian bound to an Oath of Protection would be better, she thought bitterly. But they were more myth than the paladins, even to the Cloister. Myth or not, any other Oath would be better suited for protection than hers.

She killed twenty-three people that night on the beach. And countless others before. What if she had claimed an innocent in her Retribution? Had she truly judged the Marauders? Well, she *knew* by their vespers she'd only dispatched anathemas...but the boy...She hadn't thought about him in a long time. Those whiskey-colored eyes held so much fear in them. Her actions were reprehensible and yet Myronor watched her with admiration instead.

"So, vespers are real, huh?" Myronor asked.

Ophiera averted her eyes from him, sudden guilt gnawing at her chest. All she could manage was to nod.

"As morbid as it sounds, I'd really like to see one someday," he said, rubbing his chin in thought. "On one hand, I understand why no one has studied them... witnessing a person right at the moment of death is rare indeed. Taboo even. But given their significance, you'd think we'd 'un-taboo' them and learn more."

Again, Ophiera merely nodded. They were coming dangerously close to a subject she wished to avoid. She had seen his vesper with her own eyes, had prevented it from returning to Aether to boot. It was taboo enough to have seen as many vespers as she had, but to have seen one that still belonged to a living person? That was unheard of.

"Can you describe them to me in more detail?" Myronor asked.

She could. But she wouldn't.

"Some other time, perhaps," she said, gazing out the dingy windows at the thinning crowds. It was dusk already, a perfect excuse. "I'm ready to retire for the night. Does this tavern have a room?"

Myronor tilted his head again. She found the expression quite endearing after several drinks. "Why would you stay here? There's a perfectly good bed back at my tower."

She couldn't tell if it was him or her making this more awkward.

She thought of his blankets on the couch, where he had slept as she recovered in his bed. Tonight could very well be the last night he ever spent in his tower in Feyralis. She wondered if he had thought of that as much as she had.

"I just thought...well, I cannot, in good conscience, take your bed away another night," she murmured.

He was laughing yet again. "Oh, I prefer to sleep on the ground level anyway...No windows, no damn sun. It's perfect."

The libations left her in a silly state of mind. That was the only explanation for the words that blurted from her mouth. "Sounds like one of those children's tales—some troll keeping prisoners locked up in a tower whilst he sleeps in the dark."

He laughed at her again. "Come, then!" he said, standing with a grin. "I'll gladly play the role and keep you captive for one more night."

She flushed but guessed that was his intention. "Troll or not, *captive* is a bold choice of words, considering I hold a sword."

He laughed yet again. "Fair point. But am I not your charge now? You wouldn't hurt me, would you?"

The braggot made his silliness nearly charming, and she smiled, relenting to his persistence. "I suppose you're right. You do a fine job of that yourself, jumping off whatever great height suites your fancy."

That shut him up.

~ Eight ~

INCONSPICUOUS

Early the following day, Ophiera awoke to a soft rumbling sound. Her eyes remained closed as she recognized the feel of a now familiar bed at the very top of the mage's tower. Overindulgence from the night before left her groggy and resistant to rising.

The rumbling continued, and she became aware of a slight weight on her chest. As her mind caught up with her senses, she opened her eyes to find the source of the reverberations. Inches from her face, two giant blue orbs with narrowing pupils blinked.

Ophiera leaped up with a yelp, synchronized with an angry hiss from the now unseated creature. Mallow stared at her from the end of the bed, shaking her glorious fur with an indignant *mew*.

"I'm sorry, little one—you scared me," Ophiera whispered. She reached her unscarred hand out in a gesture of peace.

The cat assessed her fingertips but remained still as stone. Ophiera had mortally offended the creature and, for some reason, this caused her to feel pity for herself. She was good at scaring off most things without trying.

In a sudden shift of mood, Mallow leaned her head into Ophiera's outstretched fingers. Surprised by her warm, soft fur, Ophiera dug her fingernails into the thick coat, scratching as she went. The creature's purrs resumed, amplified, and Ophiera smiled in response. How could petting the little beast confer such joy on her? She half-heartedly blamed magic.

"I suppose you'll be joining us on our trip," she said to the creature. "I can't imagine Myronor leaving you behind."

The cat pulled away from Ophiera's caressing hand and looked up in question. Her inquisitive gaze matched her mage's as she dipped her whiskered chin.

Ophiera blinked. "Did you...just nod?"

Mallow bobbed her head again, and Ophiera swore she saw her nose twitch as if amused. Before Ophiera could confirm or deny her own sanity, the cat initiated a settling routine. Round and round, Mallow circled several times before plunking down in her lap. The warm weight felt oddly satisfying. She relaxed with Mallow, stroking the little black ears that looked too soft to resist. At least her touch was not offensive to the creature, Ophiera thought, as Mallow purred more still.

"Breakfast!" Myronor called suddenly from the doorway. Distracted by Mallow, she had heard no sound of his approach. Retirement had really softened her guard.

He held another food-laden tray, enough to feed a full tavern. Crisped sausages, chunks of bread, sliced apfelpoms with ruby skin still on and a few cups of a pale, opaque juice adorned the tray. His sky-blue gaze moved from Ophiera to Mallow several times over before fixating back on Ophiera.

"I asked her to come to wake you, not sleep on you. Though I'm surprised—and a bit jealous. She rarely approves of anyone's lap but mine." Myronor's voice held only adoration as he spoke of his familiar. He set the breakfast tray at the end of the bed and pulled up the rickety chair beside it as if in routine. "Go ahead and eat...I suppose you'll want to start our journey today?"

"The sooner the better, yes. But we should plan and purchase supplies first." She reached for a cup of juice and inhaled the invigorating scent of white yuzu. The alluring aroma of sharp citrus and sweet nectar was always her favorite, and she wondered how Myronor knew. She also wondered how it came into existence.

"So, how does this work?" she asked, gesturing to the tray of food.

"You put a piece in your mouth, chew, and swallow," he said with a smirk.

Ophiera's eyes rolled so hard she didn't think they'd make it back to glare at the mage. His smile widened even farther.

"Oh, you mean conjura magic? It's quite simple really; I convert my mana into sustenance. It's possible to convert other items into food as well, but that's more transmutation than conjura magic...and well...the logistics of that become complicated. You know, input-output ratios of mana to matter...It's simpler to conjure what you need, if you know the practice. Food can be quite difficult to conjure compared to something less complicated, like, well...a rock for example. A rock just has to be a rock, but food has to...Oh no...I'm boring you, aren't I?"

Ophiera blinked away the glaze over her eyes. Truthfully, she was more confused than bored. He spoke so fast she couldn't keep up with his words and process them at the same time. Her pride prevented her from admitting this though, so she pressed on in a new direction.

"I'm just thinking, will you be able to provide us with food for the journey?"

If Myronor's magic could ease the burden of sustenance, it would simplify their journey greatly. Ophiera knew all too well that hunger was an encumbrance of body, mind, *and* coin.

"Of course! I'm fairly efficient now, though I will admit, it took me years to master. I must have read the *Conjura of Nutriments* cover to cover over a hundred times. And there were many failures...disasters actually," said Myronor, smiling as he speared a sausage. He spoke as if telling a story now, slower and easier to follow. She found herself interested enough to listen. "It's a funny thing to convert mana to food—a lost art these days. Too much greed to sate and glory to claim by learning to conjure other substances instead. My mentor never had a knack for it, but personally, I rather enjoy it. I mean, is there a more philanthropic act than feeding someone? Providing them not only something they need but something they can enjoy?"

Ophiera found his thoughts quite profound. In the Cloister, food had never been treated as Myronor described; it was more of a weakness than a joy. Food was fuel and that was it, a minimal necessity. Only after she had left did she begin to appreciate the taste of real food. But old habits died hard, and in recent days, she found herself fasting without thought, or only eating because she knew she must.

She noticed him watching her as she dwelt on the past and pressed on. "I assume the same principles apply to water?"

"Surely, though it's not as fun," he said, resuming his smile. "Only so much you can do with water. Though I did learn to conjure a fairly strong ember whiskey...still not as good as what you find in the market. But why the questions about conjura?"

She thought it obvious and stared at him for a moment, waiting for him to laugh in jest. But he simply stared back at her with expectant curiosity. Did he not realize they would need to eat on their journey?

"Well, if you provide us food and water, that is far less to carry upon our backs. Saves us a bit of coin too, and time hunting or foraging along the way."

"Ah! I didn't even think about that...Makes sense though. Speaking of our carry," he said, as his eyes dipped down to her nightshirt. She wore the same tunic he had lent her the day before. It seemed the logical choice at the time, rather than sleeping in her leathers or nude. But now she felt self-conscious about her choice. "How do you manage to haul that armor around on a journey like this?" he said with a hint of teasing.

"I wear it," she said.

He chuckled softly. "Isn't it heavy?"

"The armor's weight is not a problem," she said with a hint of indignation.

He held up his hands in defense. "Ok, ok...Honestly, I was just thinking about the marketplace yesterday and wondering if, well...Would you be better off traveling without it?"

"No."

Ophiera protested before she even gave it a thought. But now that he mentioned it, did she need to be more careful?

She had never been proud of being a paladin, or her connection to the Cloister, but she also had never feared recognition. Her mind wandered to the bandits she encountered on the way to Feyralis. They may not have known she was a paladin, but the armor still had placed a target on her back. And if there was a target upon her back, it placed Myronor in danger too.

"I could transmute your armor..." Myronor began, watching her with caution. She must have looked angry. "You know, change the color at least. The gold is a dead giveaway."

His smirk, for once, looked off-putting. The mere thought of him changing her golden armor felt very much like a threat. Yet what other options were left? She could not leave her armor behind, yet it seemed to pose more risk as it currently stood. She wondered what the Cloister would have to say regarding the transmutation of adamantrium armor.

"Are you sure your magic will work on paladin plate?" she asked him, trying not to come across as too judgmental.

His eyes lit up. "And why shouldn't it?"

Not all knowledge lived in his library below, she thought smugly.

"The Cloister forged the golden armor from adamantrium, an ore born of the holy flames. Supposedly, the metal is indestructible, so I'm unsure how it will react to your magic."

Myronor rubbed his chin, his eyes distant for a moment. "Interesting...Well, I guess we can experiment a bit. What's the worst that could happen if it is truly indestructible?"

Ophiera was surprised at how much she truly detested the idea of anything happening to her armor. And yet, another part of her felt excited by the change. She loved and loathed the precious plate mail. But Myronor was right; the only way to know if his magic could work was to try. And yet the idea of tampering with her armor felt blasphemous. Round and round she argued with herself until she finally came to a decision.

"I suppose it's worth a try," she said. "Just please be careful."

"Don't worry, it's obvious how precious it is to you." Myronor sat back in his chair, stretching in a manner quite like his familiar. Only now did she notice he no longer wore the usual robes of deep blue. Rather, he'd donned a pair of black leather pants and a cream-colored tunic like the one she borrowed. Without the bulk of his layered robes, she saw he had a rather impressive physique for a bookish mage. Neither bulky nor lean, his build reminded her of the fishers in Iluka; a worker's frame. Broad-shouldered with lithe muscles, but as he stretched his hands high, she noticed they weren't calloused at all.

"I had an idea last night," he said, staring at the ceiling. "The closest port city from here is Cantheas, right? Iluka is just a couple of nights away from there. I say we rest in Iluka for a night or two before booking passage to Krysas."

Ophiera admitted it was a tempting suggestion. The idea of staying in her own home for a few nights before embarking on what could be a long and arduous task sounded divine. However, her duty must always come first.

"Do you not have responsibilities as Ambassador in Krysas? We shouldn't delay any more than we have already."

He shrugged before continuing in a distracted voice. "My duties begin when I arrive, no sooner and no later. A few extra days won't matter in the end." He smiled gently as he looked at Ophiera. "And it would be nice to say farewell to my father."

Berwyn. She had not considered Myronor's feelings on leaving Tanvik behind. So much of her life had been spent with nowhere to call home, she hadn't given thought to how he felt giving up his own. What would happen to this tower? To his belongings? Would he be able to return someday? At least Ophiera could return to her cottage in Iluka when all was said and done, but Myronor was uprooting the only life he knew. She felt a bit more sympathy for him now.

Regardless of the route, Iluka was *almost* on the way to Krysas. The Magistrate had told her to escort Myronor across the sea but did not specify the way. Continuing forward was all that mattered for her Oath, was it not? She peered at the scarred, runic patterns on her arm, stark against her skin. The constant reminder of her bondage always made her rebel.

"I like this idea, but let's see how the journey goes. I must admit that returning to Iluka even for a night would ease my ire for the task ahead."

The Cloister had laid claim to her life since her youth and was never a place to call home. The tiny oyster village, however, had been her own choice; her own home. And that choice betrayed her now. If only she had resisted that damnable shaman's pleas to serve as Iluka's Warden.

"I'm going to go pack a few essentials," Myronor said, his brow furrowed slightly. Did she offend him in some way? "Why don't you finish eating? I'll get Mallow out of your way."

To her surprise, she had forgotten about the little creature still lying curled in her lap. Warm and quiet, Mallow slept in a perfect ball of creamy fur.

"It would be a shame to wake her, wouldn't it?" Ophiera said quietly, running a finger behind one of her velvety black ears. The creature didn't stir.

Myronor snorted. "Don't let her fool you. She's just lazing...Mallow only truly sleeps in her crystal or in her armchair."

Mallow's ears twitched as she raised her eyelids to stare huffily at Myronor.

"Come now, you little scamp. Let Ophiera eat and ready."

When the creature did not stir, Myronor strode over to take Mallow from her lap. Ophiera tensed, unprepared for his sudden closeness. He leaned his shoulder against hers as his hands caressed the inside of her thigh to scoop up the cat. No one ever got this close to her, let alone *touched* her.

Warmth flushed her cheeks, and she looked out the window, trying desperately to rid her mind of the strange sensation. Why did it feel so overwhelming?

Oblivious to her struggles, Myronor made his way to the door with Mallow flung over his shoulder. "I'll start transmutating your armor if that's alright," he said without turning toward her.

"Just—"

"Be careful?" He turned to her and smirked. "I collected it from the riverside, remember? I swear I won't harm it now."

With Mallow bobbing over his shoulder, Myronor disappeared down the stairs.

Ophiera stared at the tray of food and found her stomach too full of nerves. Agitated, she left the bed to dress. This time she had brought her leathers to the tower room, though she had left her armor in the chest by the fireplace. She may have denied the weight to Myronor, but last night she had been too damn tired to ascend the tower in full plate.

The anxiety of her armor's fate sped her through the process of dressing. The dark brown leathers' function far outweighed their looks, in her opinion anyway. Laced from ankle to hip, the high-waisted pants fit her musculature like her own skin, yet remained flexible from years of use. The strapped leather top exposed her midriff, mirroring the shape of her gilded breastplate. Small leather plats hung from her shoulders, providing much-needed padding against the heft of golden pauldrons. Though perhaps by now, they were no longer gold.

Ophiera rushed down the spiral stairs, crossing the balcony and descending past the library to the main level of the tower. Upon entering the living space, she heard strange metallic noises coming from the center of the room. She wanted to look but also wanted to flee. What was he doing to her armor?

Myronor's back was to her as he handled the pieces of her golden plate over the large stone table. Most of the gilded pieces were piled to the left of him, while on the right she saw a few pieces she did not recognize. As she watched him pick up one of her scuffed vambraces, her heart jumped. No one outside the Cloister had ever before touched her armor, besides him. More than discomfort, the act felt violating—almost as vile as the thought of Myronor removing her clothing while unconscious. But she watched how Myronor maneuvered the golden plate with delicate precision, and it calmed her. With a wave of his hand and a glow of blue, the vambrace's bright golden gleam darkened to a deep, blackish bronze.

"Interesting color," she said.

He smiled, recognizing the praise. "I thought it might complement the violet of your eyes."

She shrugged off another of his strange comments, holding her silence as she watched. He took up her other vambrace next, repeating the process of transforming—no, *transmutating* her armor to the shadowy hue. He set it to rest carefully with the other.

"And this process doesn't change its properties?" she asked.

Myronor shrugged. "Not that I can tell—but you would know better than me."

Ophiera picked up the dark vambrace and turned it in her hands. It felt the same and even held a tinge of gold beneath the black, like a patina rather than paint. But there was only one test that really mattered.

With her Oath-scarred hand, she held the vambrace and chanted under her breath. The runes glowed brightly as she called forth her holy flames, directing them through the palm of her hand. The armor withstood the white fire just as it had before.

"You should really warn someone before you do that," Myronor said. His face appeared blanched in the light of the white flames and without a trace of a smile. She extinguished her hand immediately.

"Sorry," she muttered, setting down the heated piece of armor on the stone table. "I'll let you carry on."

Embarrassed, Ophiera turned her attention to the open chest, wherein her ragged pack still lay. She didn't mean to scare him. He had shown her such little fear and hesitation these last two days that she had almost forgotten she was something to be feared. Well, perhaps now his silliness would end. Perhaps now that he had witnessed a glimpse of the Aether, he would treat her like all the rest. Why did that idea feel both relieving and disappointing?

As a distraction, Ophiera pulled out her worn rucksack and began to take inventory. All her gear was still there—a knot of twine, a couple spare hammocks made of old fishing nets, a roll of canvas, plenty of flints, a few empty potion bottles, and a small but precious coin purse. Without need to carry food and water, her pack had ample space left behind. Rarely did she have this luxury of a void.

"We could find an alchemical shop," she said over her shoulder. "Potions will be expensive but useful on such a long journey. Especially now that we need not waste space on food or water."

"Rheta's Remedies is our best bet," Myronor said. "She usually gives me quite the discount."

Ophiera felt a foreign relief. Not only did he sound like his normal self, but preparations were falling into place with ease. Her initial dread of the trip slowly subsided. She turned to watch Myronor finish the changes to her armor. The mage was overtly silly and flippant, frustrating and pushy, but he was proving rather knowledgeable. Perhaps even helpful.

"I need to take care of one thing in the library before we head off," he said without glancing at her. "I'll leave you to your armor."

He ascended the stairs as Mallow pranced at his heels, leaving Ophiera in privacy.

With a sigh, she began donning her darkened plate armor. Though originally hesitant, she thought she might prefer the dark, matte luster to the ostentatious gold.

Her thoughts carried her through the muscle memory of equipping her armor, and without conscious thought, she finished moments later. She caught her reflection in the mirror above the mantle. If Myronor thought she looked intimidating before, she would be interested in hearing his thoughts now. As Myronor had intended with his choice of color, the dark bronze contrasted sharply against her lilac eyes and even more with her snowy braid. In her opinion, it was equally conspicuous as the golden armor, but at least it held no connotation to the Cloister.

Strange sounds and scuffs echoed down the stairs from the upper levels. What business did he have up there anyway? Perhaps he was packing some more personal effects. If he expected her to carry a bunch of books, he had another thing coming.

The former Ambassador, Myronor's mother, had never returned to Tanvik. All to serve a purpose above herself. Would he follow the same path? To never return? If so, he was handling the call of duty with far more grace than Ophiera ever had. Though when the Cloister had cast her fate, she had been little more than a child, without any real choice.

As Ophiera adjusted her open-handed gauntlets, a loud crash sounded above. She froze, focusing her hearing upward. Another bang and a hiss echoed down the stairs.

"Myronor?" she called.

When only silence returned, she grew concerned. The bookshelves were absurdly tall, weren't they? What if one had toppled over atop him?

Ophiera placed her claymore on her back out of habit and set a foot upon the spiral staircase. She called his name once more, but no one answered. The heft of her armor held no consequence against her speed as she bounded up the stairs.

The only light came from the windows above the balcony, casting the library in a dim, ominous glow. Again she called his name, but no one answered. Instinctively, she placed a hand on the hilt of her claymore and cautiously entered the room. She assumed the noise had come from the center study, and thus began walking along the inward spiral between bookcases. A sudden bang and a rustle of papers echoed in the massive room.

"Myronor!"

Why would he not answer her? She continued inward, along the single, continuously curved corner that served only to amplify her nerves. As she rounded the last section of the curve, Myronor rushed toward her. She nearly slashed the blur of blonde hair in two.

"What are you doing?" she growled. "I could have killed you!"

Out of breath, Myronor grinned. "Well, that's your fault. Who brings a sword into a library?"

Her heart stammered from the adrenaline as he calmly mocked her.

"What were you doing up here?"

"Nothing," Myronor said, before following her eyes to the tattered roll of parchment in his hand. "Oh...I was searching for a map."

"All that noise to find a map?" she asked.

"Seemingly."

"Why didn't you answer when I called?"

"Ophiera...were you worried about me?" His eyebrows raised as his grin widened. "I'm flattered, but what could possibly happen in my library? Unless...were you just lonely downstairs?"

Well, clearly her theory of him being frightened of her was wrong. Dead wrong. Her face grew heated with his teasing.

"I don't have time for your secrets or games," she said, turning away from him. "We're leaving for Rheta's now, whether you're ready or not."

~ Nine ~

ALCHEMY

Ophiera let Myronor take the lead to the potion shop. So far, he had taken her down several narrow alleyways, careful to avoid the crowds at the expense of time and distance. Despite her darkened armor, she thought it best to avoid the bustle of the main streets and he knew how to navigate the back streets better anyway. She had never needed an indirect path through the city before.

They walked through an empty residential street, along the gently curving alley. Only a single sign hung out above the street. A small painted board worn with age swung on a cast iron bracket, depicting a cauldron overflowed with bright flowers and straggling herbs. Where the paint had flaked off, the wood was left stained, the grain tinted by color. There were no words to indicate its name.

She was beginning to doubt his recommendation of an alchemician. Especially one that resided so far from the main market, and without so much as a shop name.

Myronor stopped below the sign, placing his hand on an unassuming wooden door. The window beside it held the vague outlines of bottles and vials, but so much dust had accumulated inside, the glass nearly mirrored the alleyway, obscuring what was inside.

"Here we are," Myronor said with a smile. He swung the door open and stepped inside.

Pungent odors rushed from the shop as if desperate to escape. Ophiera followed him over the threshold, dizzied by the strange aromas. She felt submerged in the herbal bouquets, sour fermentations, and acrid smoke—not entirely unpleasant, but quite overwhelming.

Every flat surface, whether shelf, countertop, or floor, was coated in a thick layer of benign dust. The dim light hid just how much grime Ophiera kicked up with her boots. Shelves of potions lined every wall and window, dirty but neatly stacked. And seemingly untouched. Was the shop even open?

Myronor strode over to the deep green granite counter, where he leaned lazily. A large leather-bound catalog of sorts lay open, and he began flipping through the thick pages of inventory. Like a cloud of smoke, the dust from the book clung to the air, but Myronor paid it no mind. She remembered the dust atop his shelves in the library and wondered if all scholars were this unkempt.

Leaving him to his routine, she gravitated toward the shelf in front of the window. The colorful crystal vials looked muted by the film of unkemptness, but their variety was impressive. A tall, narrow bottle caught her eye, containing a potion of an appealing shade of light blue. She smudged away the grime, hoping to reveal the label, yet she found the text illegible. It looked nearly as foreign as the runes on her arm.

Alchemicians rarely divulged their secrets, a long-held tradition in Tanvik. Whether wielded by mages or shamans or common folk, the power of alchemy was in the balance of formula and individual flare. As was common in most trades, differing means could lead to a similar end. Thus, in alchemical shops, potion labels often described an intended effect, not the ingredients within. Shop proprietors liked to claim uniqueness in their special brews—sometimes with truths so stretched, they touched falsehood. But it was obvious by the state of *this* shop that they were not relying on any gimmicky advertisements to sell their wares. In fact, Ophiera doubted they sold much at all.

A petite woman appeared from a back room behind the counter. Her head barely peeked over the worktop Myronor still leaned against. She had two wide-set eyes of swirling gold framed by dark chocolate curls. At first glance, she looked more like a doll than anything, and Ophiera thought she must be the shop owner's child. Until she opened her mouth.

"Myrny, you're back!" she cooed in a deep and sultry voice. She sounded like one of the old crones in the market, the ones who worked the side street stalls. Yet she looked younger than a maiden.

Myronor closed the hand-bound book and straightened up. His elbow had left an imprint on the dusty counter.

"Rheta, you're still here!"

The small woman shook her head of curls, adding to the illusion of her youth. When her gaze fell to Ophiera, however, her golden eyes narrowed to accentuate deep crow's-feet wrinkles. "I told you not to bring your dates here anymore, Myronor."

Dates? Ophiera found the idea of Myronor bringing "dates" here far more embarrassing than the assumption she was one.

"Come now, Rheta, play nice. This is my new traveling companion, Oph—"

"The Aspect of Retribution," Rheta interrupted throatily. "Under Magistrate conscription, again, thanks to you. Why the Magistrate decided on a paladin of her echelon still vexes me...and that damnable Oath offers her little choice."

The two appeared accustomed to taking verbal shots at each other. And to having conversations about people still in the room. Ophiera did not fully understand this type of combative friendship. Friend or not, the knot in her stomach tightened. No one outside the Magistrate and the Cloister referred to her by her true title.

"How do you know me by my echelon and Oath?"

Rheta turned to her with a sympathetic demeanor. "I deal in far more important matters than potions. Information is the true remedy for all ailments."

"Echelon?" Myronor asked, gazing between the two women.

Rheta rolled her gilded eyes. "Even with a tower full of books, you still know nothing. You're a regrettable scholar, Myrny."

"You know I only read for the drawings."

The two chuckled together, ignoring Ophiera yet again.

"But really, what is an echelon?" Myronor continued.

"To dumb it down for you, it's a ranking of a sort within the Cloister," Rheta said, looking to Ophiera. "Correct me if I'm wrong, but Aspect is your echelon, while Retribution is your Oath."

Ophiera nodded, impressed by the woman's knowledge. In an age when people barely even knew of paladins, this woman knew the inner workings of the Cloister. She wondered if this Rheta was why Myronor knew so much about her scars as well.

"And what do the rankings mean, exactly?" Myronor asked, looking to Rheta rather than Ophiera. She felt a sting in her pride.

"That is her business to tell," Rheta said gruffly, winking at Ophiera. "And speaking of business, tell me, what do you need?"

Ophiera answered before Myronor had a chance to open his mouth. "Basic potions for travel. Any tinctures or salves for wounds, diseases, or common poisons. And since you deal in knowledge, perhaps you have recommendations of what else we might need for our journey?"

The small woman smiled with pleasure. "Quick to defer to my expertise, unlike the idiot mage. I knew I'd like you, Ophiera. I'll gather a collection of my best."

Rheta bobbed out from behind the counter, curls bouncing as she grabbed a tan leather case from the floor. Inside, it looked more like a tackle box than a bag. She began selecting dirty potions from the shelves and placed them in the partitioned spaces. Ophiera realized far too late that the alchemician was preparing to stock them in extreme excess. She thought to her minuscule coin purse.

"It shames me to admit, but I doubt I can afford *all* that you are offering us. Neither the Cloister nor Magistrate provides much salary to paladins...none, in fact."

The title of Sea Warden did come with a modest stipend, but saving money was not on Ophiera's limited list of skills. She spent most of her coin at Iluka's tavern or paying the local children for silly errands.

"Don't fret, dear," Rheta said with a grin. "Myrny has a tab, and since it's his business that has you Oath-bound to this journey, it shall be he who handles my recompense."

Myronor rolled his eyes dramatically but smiled nonetheless. "Yes, yes, whatever it costs—as usual."

Again, Ophiera felt lost in a conversation between friends. Or perhaps business partners? She still couldn't place their relationship. He had mentioned a mentor earlier, but surely, he'd be far more respectful towards a teacher. Regardless, all she knew was they both knew a suspicious amount about the Cloister, Rheta in particular.

The Magistrate maintained their rule with secrets and exceptional care concerning their doings, much like the Cloister. They were also especially careful to hide any doings with the Cloister. She wondered how Rheta had secured her information if not from Myronor.

Ophiera felt suddenly distrustful of them both.

Handing the worn case to Myronor, Rheta smiled up to him, a full two heads shorter. "That should set you straight on your way."

"Thank you, Rheta. The tower is in your care now...Please be careful, especially with the library." Myronor took the potion case from her with a significant gaze.

So, they were here for more than just the potions.

Ophiera thought of his odd behavior and strange sounds in the library just before they departed. Her distrust was growing by the minute, but again, she held her tongue. This was their business, not hers. The less she knew, the better.

Rheta turned to Ophiera, gesturing between the potion case and their two packs. "Don't let this oaf make you carry anything other than your armor. He can transmute matter, you know—particularly good at making things smaller and lighter. Calls it *minimizing* or some flashy term."

"Rheta, you ruined my trick!" Myronor laughed. "I wanted to see Ophiera's face when I revealed that bit of magic."

Again, Ophiera did not appreciate being the subject of a conversation she could hear. When the two embraced each other, Ophiera turned away, uncomfortable witnessing the affection. So perhaps they were friends.

When the alchemician let go of the mage and turned her attention toward Ophiera, the paladin froze. The slight woman looked more threatening with her arms spread wide. She wasn't...She was going to *hug* her, wasn't she?

Ophiera's expression must have conveyed her mood as Rheta lowered her arms with a smile.

"Don't worry, I know better than to hug a paladin. But please, take care of him." She eyed Myronor, who slung the potion case over his shoulder and headed toward the door. "He may be an idiot...but he's an important idiot."

Ophiera nodded, confirming the duty already tasked to her. But as she turned to leave, Rheta stilled her with a gentle hand. "I know what the Cloister teaches you—what they put you poor things through." Her voice was barely a whisper, only for Ophiera's ears now. "But I promise there is more to this world than your Oath."

Rheta let go of her arm and darted behind the counter, leaving Ophiera dazed and alone in the shop. She turned toward the door and grew angry with the woman's bold words. If Rheta knew so much about the Cloister, then she knew that all Ophiera had in this world was her Oath.

Myronor stood outside the shop in the alleyway, waiting for her to join him.

"Well, that was productive!" he exclaimed, holding up the potion case proudly. In a flash of blue, Ophiera watched as the tan leather case shrank until it fit within his palm. She tried to hide her awe by scowling instead. "Damn Rheta—always ruining my fun," he muttered. He actually looked disappointed. "I can minimize your carry as well—lighten the load?"

She felt the weight of her bag, comfortable as always with the burden.

"No, thank you," she said with an edge. "I prefer to carry my own."

She turned her gaze toward the sky. Their preparations had occupied most of the morning. Without a cloud in sight, the midday sun hung high in the sky. They could still cover a good amount of ground before nightfall if they left soon.

To travel again took away some of her dread, particularly now that they might venture to Iluka first. The journey from Feyralis to Iluka typically took her five or six nights by foot, traveling at her own pace. But Myronor remained untested. This time, she must think ahead to keep her charge safe on the road. Intrusively, her thoughts fell back on the three bandits she had encountered outside Feyralis. There were likely to be others; more of the same vile anathemas of some unknown faction. She should have asked Rheta what she knew of the bandits wearing yellow bands.

Myronor cleared his throat, drawing Ophiera from her reverie. She turned to him, irritated.

"Shall we be off? Or would you like to brood some more?" he said with a standard grin.

A childish part of her wished to explain to him that her brooding was, in fact, planning for his inadequacies. But she held her tongue. They both needed to survive this journey.

"How far is the Southern gate from here?"

"Fairly close. And we can avoid the crowds by going this way." Myronor began walking down the narrow backstreet, glancing back at Ophiera to ensure she followed.

As they walked in silence, she gazed upon the old sod buildings and thatched roofs of the dwellings on either side. The spires of Feyralis were grand and colorful, yet the drab buildings here were where the people truly lived. It was a disturbing metaphor for the city itself, a facade of grandeur that shrouded the neglect within. A shiny distraction from the city of beauty and beast.

Myronor turned and began backpedaling down the alleyway. "What an interesting start to this journey, eh?"

"Leaving a potion shop?"

He laughed. "No, not quite. I consider the riverbank the start of our grand adventure, wouldn't you say?"

Ophiera chewed on her lip before speaking. "I would say that was closer to an end than a start. We both nearly returned to the Aether."

Again, his laughter echoed between the narrow buildings.

"Ah, but we didn't! I survived the plummet, a feat which I'm sure few can claim. And you survived your manasickness. That's what I would call an interesting experience...one worthy of reflection."

"You only survived because I happened upon you, nearly dead and about to be swept away by the river."

Myronor stopped in his tracks, clapping his hands together. "Exactly! Can't you see? It's much too convenient to be chalked up to the mundane chance of life."

"I haven't found any part of this to be *convenient*—but I do find it mundane to look back when we have so much ahead of us. Especially pointless if viewed through a lens of amusement rather than atonement."

She made to walk by him, away from his silly theories and stupid smile. But Myronor grabbed her shoulder to stop her, his head cocked in question. That same odd surge of overwhelming discomfort halted her step. She was beginning to wish he *was* afraid of her, at least enough to physically distance himself.

"Ophiera, can't you appreciate the circumstances? The exceptionality of fate that led to this moment. Even if you don't believe in destiny, is it not worth stopping and appreciating the beauty of life's strange path that we've now found ourselves upon together?"

The way he spoke somehow lacked his usual amusement. He was...serious.

She may have actually considered his words if she were less bitter. He requested an investigation into his mother's death; he was the reason she was conscripted again. This was his fault, not fate. She wondered, neither for the first nor the last time, what would have happened had she left him on the riverbank to die as *fate* intended.

"I cannot appreciate any of these strange paths, as you call them, because mine have always been preordained—out of my control and never ending happily. Backward or forward, shared or alone, *my* path, my fate, has been decided for me, and trust me, it has never been beautiful." She shook her shoulder loose, taking a step back from him. "I'm done entertaining this conversation at the expense of usable daylight. Lead the way to the gate or I will find it myself."

~ Ten ~

PARTITION

Solitude was, perhaps, the most consistent part of Ophiera's life. How she lived, how she traveled—everything was done alone.

And she preferred it that way.

The Cloister embodied isolation. In the very beginning, it had been difficult. But by the end of her first conscription to the Magistrate, she found isolation peaceful. Necessary even.

Over the years, the Magistrate had demanded her Retribution across nearly every realm of Tanvik. Thus, she had spent far more time traveling to and from than at any single place. She may not have chosen the destination, but the journey itself? That could be her choice. The one and only time she had a say in anything. Alone on the road, she was unburdened.

Now, she couldn't help but view Myronor as an intruder upon her sovereignty. A direct infringement on her again limited freedom. He served only as a burden and a liability—naturally lackadaisical and naive. Traits that could become reckless on the road. His nature also meant, somewhat unsettlingly, that he did not fear her. Unlike the crowds in Feyralis, Myronor held no wariness or prejudice against her. Such interaction alone lightened the burden of a charge. At least his general cheer was a refreshing break from repeated ostracism. But still, she would prefer to be alone.

Together, they walked at a brisk pace along the paved main road, leaving Feyralis behind them. The Slumbrous River paralleled their path and had slowly returned to sleep since the week before. If only Myronor had fallen from the wall today, she wouldn't have had to swim so far in that icy water. But then again, he probably would have died on impact without the swollen river to catch him. And given the choice again, would she have just kept walking?

As the river dwindled to a gentle stream, the surrounding countryside grew ever more bucolic. The snowcaps faded to bare peaks on the far horizon as the riverbank fell drastically in the water's absence. For less than a week, she had lain unconscious, yet the countryside had finished its transition from spring to summer. She didn't appreciate the sensation of time lost.

After some time walking, Myronor released Mallow from her crystal to explore alongside them. The familiar slowed their pace a bit with her incessant inspections. But surprisingly, Ophiera didn't mind. The curious cat enjoyed much of the world that she often ignored.

Hours into their journey, Mallow encountered a rather odd flowering herb. Ophiera knew the plant as shadeweed, named so for its resemblance to a vesper. The perfectly round and ethereal pappus mirrored the texture of Mallow's fur. The shimmering orb of pale green bobbed in the breeze, tempting the familiar to sniff the willowy seeds. The cat sneezed, blasting the achenes away, leaving only a stem behind. Her eyes, wide in shock, followed their journey in the wind. As the seeds grew distant, Mallow looked to Myronor defensively, refusing to take the blame for the occurrence.

And for the first time in what felt like many years, Ophiera laughed. Uncontrolled, she held a hand over her armored abdomen, entertained to the point of pain.

As they trekked onward, they passed several merchant carts and other tradespeople traveling to and from Feyralis. Myronor passed some time discussing the variety of goods available in the country-side. Though Iluka alone had mastered the art of oyster pearl farming, many other villages surrounding the capital held their own specialty crops and wares. He spoke of the textiles produced in Kav, a small sheep-herding town in the veld outside Feyralis. Apparently, that was where his favorite blue robes came from.

Listening to him talk was exhausting. He was like a living library; a comment or fact for everything, often with a story attached. Her continued silence and his own voice must have bored him at some point because he began turning their encounters into some kind of game. He asked Ophiera to guess what lay beneath the canvases of the passing wagons before postulating his own guess. She found it an odd game, since neither could win. Neither dared ask the trades-people to reveal their wares in the name of discretion; she feared they might look too closely at her armor, too closely at her scarred hand. Would they react the same as the people in Feyralis?

Thus far, none of the cart drivers seemed interested in the pair, acknowledging them only with a casual wave or tip of the hat. And though a few wary eyes fell upon her darkened armor and massive sword, Ophiera noticed their gazes held no animosity, only a cautious curiosity. So few people carried weapons in Tanvik these days, but the wealthier merchants often hired armed guards. She hoped that's what she passed for now. Still, every new encounter gave her pause, imagining the whisper of *anathema*. Did the people of Tanvik really view paladins as such now?

She often wondered if her soul was as black as those she returned to the Aether. The Cloister never made it clear if her Oath exempted her from the curse of her sins. But there was no denying she'd taken lives just like any anathema. Many in fact.

Maybe the people were right. Despite her best efforts to ignore these thoughts, she toiled away on them to pass the time.

They maintained their trek until the horizon exploded in the warm colors of sunset. Ophiera looked to Myronor, curious about the status of her charge. He still smiled, just as he had all day, even as the sweat beaded on his brow. When she considered his bookish lifestyle, she found his ability to keep any pace impressive. He appeared well suited for the road, or at least enthusiastic to be upon it.

Ophiera watched as he fixated on the setting sun now, his blue eyes reflecting the burning horizon. Like with Mallow, Ophiera found a strange fascination in watching him take in the sights. He acted as if existence alone made him happy—a concept that eluded her. His eyes found hers with the same look of wonderment he held for the setting sun. Ophiera broke her gaze from his, flustered.

"We should set up camp for the night," she said, searching the horizon. A larger patch of trees in one of the nearby meadows held promise for shelter and safety. "That wood will be suitable."

"Seems far off the road, wouldn't you say?" Myronor squinted exaggeratedly, searching for the location in the distance.

"The farther from the road we camp, the safer our sleep."

She led the way off-trail, through the tall grasses rustling against her armor. The sound reminded her painfully of the ocean waves against a hull; the sound of Iluka.

"You're just trying to get me alone, aren't you?" Myronor said with a sly inflection.

She flushed at his absurd accusation, ready to deny it. But she had learned his game of teasing and the only way to win was retaliation.

"It's true...I could bind and gag you without witnesses and finally have some peace and quiet."

Myronor laughed loudly behind her. "Ah, so you do have a sense of humor! I thought it sacrificed to your Oath."

Ophiera's heart iced as she continued to walk. Without turning to face him, she spoke in a voice devoid of jest. "You should not speak so casually of what has been sacrificed."

Few knew the requirements to become a paladin—the sacrifices the Cloister demanded. Perhaps she should not hold his ignorance against him. Only the kindled held the scars of reminder.

When Myronor finally spoke again, his voice sounded subdued. "My apologies. I don't understand much about the Cloister and their ways...but I want to."

She held her silence until they reached the edge of the wood. While she appreciated the apology, his interest in the Cloister vexed her. And often when something confused her, she simply ignored it.

"This spot is as good as any," Ophiera said, settling on a relatively flat area near a thicket of trees. Too shaded for the meadow grasses to grow in the small clearing, yet they were far enough from the young wood to avoid sleeping on shallow roots. She vaguely wondered how far she was from the tree where the three bandits were laid to rest.

She dropped her pack to the ground and Myronor followed suit in his own way, removing his miniaturized bag from his belt. With a glow of blue, the leather bag engorged, returning to its normal size once again. He tossed it gently upon the ground next to hers.

"Firewood," he said with a smirk as he meandered off along the end of the copse. "I read you can never have too much firewood."

Ophiera did not protest, as it allowed her to find some field stones and build a small fire pit in peace. As she went about her task, she looked to the distant road often, scanning for other travelers in the dim light. No one passed as the dusk faded. No one seemed to travel at night anymore. Strange. Why hadn't she noticed this before?

Soon, she gazed upon a field of dim stars against a velvet sky. Myronor dropped a small bundle of wood to the ground with a dull thud. "I can try to start the fire if you want to rest a moment."

Ophiera nodded, but watched him with skepticism. He pulled a set of flint stones from his bag, skillfully igniting the small pile of tinder he had prepared. Darkness crept over the camp as he coaxed the gentle flames to life, illuminating his self-satisfied smile. She had doubted his skills outside reading and writing, assuming he'd be more a hindrance than a help when it came to practical tasks.

But he appeared to have the campfire under control, and she found herself mildly impressed.

Free of duty for the moment, Ophiera began her turndown routine. As much as she cared for her armor, it was impossible to lie down comfortably with it on. Meticulously, she removed each piece of darkened metal plate, stacking them neatly in a ceremonious pile. Beside the armor, she unrolled her sleeping pad of layered furs and leathers. The smell of hides fatigued her immediately, along with countless memories of nights alone under the stars. This solitude, this freedom, had been her only joy for so long.

"Shall I minimize your armor? Hide it somewhere safe for the night?" Myronor said as he finished stoking the small fire.

Her illusion of solitude disappeared with his voice.

"Isn't tending to the true fire a better use of your magic?" she asked in deflection. Given recent events, she'd rather keep her armor very near her.

Myronor laughed. "Unfortunately, I'm not that kind of mage."

His words triggered a curiosity discouraged by the Cloister. A growing trend after spending the day with the mage.

"I admit, I know little of magic," she said. "It seemed your kind was rare before, were they not?"

"Hmm, not necessarily," he said thoughtfully. "I think we're simply more visible now. Mages have always existed; we've just become an integral part of Tanvik society recently. Nearly every Justicar on the Magistrate is a mage now, except for your friend Aleksander."

"He's not my friend," Ophiera said a bit more harshly than intended. But it was true; all positions of power were filled now by mages in Tanvik. Even the Justicar from the Southern Coastlands, a realm that held traditions of natural mystics rather than magic, had appointed a mage as their representative.

"How does one even become a mage?"

Myronor looked delighted by the question. "A mage is born. Usually with a specific affinity for a type of magic, but truthfully, some headway is possible in others through intensive training." The smile faltered on his face just for a moment.

"What is your specialty, then?" she asked. "You're quite adept at producing food. Conjura, you called it? Is that its own class of magic?"

With the return of his smile, Myronor conjured two hand pies from thin air. She thought him a show-off at first, but as he handed her the meal, hot and crisp, her gnawing stomach appreciated the demonstration.

"Yes, my affinity is for conjura and transmutation magic," he said. Ophiera nodded haphazardly, unwilling to admit she still did not fully understand the meaning of these words. Apparently, she could not fool the mage. "Transmutation is the ability to manipulate matter already in existence. Like the bag—I can change its properties, shrink it, expand it, change its color, but it must *exist* first. For conjura, it's more a conversion of mana to matter. It's a difficult magic to master, and many mages strive to convert their mana into more profitable things...like gold, or something they can sell. I'm best with food and water; something far more practical yet viewed as less valuable."

Ophiera thought she was finally beginning to understand. "But what does that have to do with the true fire?"

"It doesn't." Myronor chuffed before swallowing his bite. "See, I have little influence over the *energies* of Erum, like fire or lightning or sea. I can only manipulate that which already exists, or conjure something new, like food and water. I can't heal anyone or summon storms or manipulate flames. Though...I could experiment, I suppose."

Ophiera snorted despite herself. "Last time you experimented, you ended up dead on a riverbank."

"Dead?" Myronor said, staring at her mid-bite.

"Nearly dead," she corrected quickly, damning herself.

His eyes pierced hers, wordlessly interrogating her in the firelight. She looked away toward the flames, avoiding his gaze and the guilt she felt along with it.

She hated lying and was no good at it. But she found it imperative that he remain ignorant of her blasphemy. If he knew that she had seen his vesper, there would surely be questions, if not consequences. Myronor was an Ambassador, and she wasn't sure what obligation he held to the laws and taboos. She did know her actions would warrant punishment by the Cloister for using rites of another Oath. No good could come from him knowing what she saw.

She felt relieved as his gaze left her and returned to his meal.

They ate together in quiet until he turned to set up his own bedroll on the opposite side of the fire. She watched him for a moment, the itch of curiosity returning.

"Where does spanning fall? Is that conjura?"

With a heavy sigh, Myronor lay back upon his bedroll, staring up at the starry sky. "Not exactly. That's...unique. And difficult to explain." He looked at her with a grin that did not meet his eyes. "Aren't you exhausted? I don't know how you couldn't be, running us ragged today."

A typical joke, yes, but he revealed much by omission alone. She would not press where clearly barred.

"I'll have to pick up the pace tomorrow," she said, turning her back to the true fire as she readied for sleep.

The mage spent the entire day talking, yet twice now, he had hesitated to discuss his spanning magic. She wondered if there was a greater secret, or perhaps he truly did not know. Then again, when had she ever spoken of her own Oath or the holy flames? Perhaps she was being rude, asking him such questions.

"Is your exceptional stamina due to your Oath?" he asked from behind her. "Or simply conditioning?"

She'd thought their conversation had ended or maybe just wished it had. No one had ever asked her before about...well, *her*. And now that she was forced to reflect, she really didn't know.

"Perhaps both? The Cloister's training is intensive and unforgiving...but I know I couldn't have survived it without receiving my Oath."

Myronor's voice sounded hesitant over the crackling fire. "How does one even become a paladin?"

Her stomach clenched. She tried to stop her thoughts from going to a place she seldom visited. A painful path full of buried, burning memories.

"Paladins are made, not born."

Made sounded like too pleasant a word, but she could not think of a better one.

"Is it by choice?"

Her back was still to him. The warm true fire was nothing like the holy flames and yet it felt as if she were burning again.

"No."

She heard him shift in his bedroll.

"How? Of everything I've read, no one explains how someone becomes a paladin. It's maddening..."

If he thought the search for knowledge was maddening, she wondered how he would respond to the truth. The Cloister did not expressly ban their order from discussing the rites, yet no paladin ever spoke of it. No one desired to relive the day they were kindled.

"The knowledge you seek isn't pleasant," she said, turning to look at him across the fire.

He was perched up on his elbow, staring at her in that disconcerting way, as if studying her. She could see by the way his jawline was set though, her warning was pointless.

"I've found unpleasant knowledge is often the most important to seek," he said in a warm voice. "But I won't push you, Ophiera, especially if it causes you discomfort."

Few had ever considered her comfort. Speaking of the day she had gained her scars would cause her pain, yet his words compelled her. She did not owe the Cloister her silence like those under some other Oaths.

"I will exchange knowledge for knowledge," she said. She wasn't much of a diplomat, but she selfishly wanted her own curiosity sated as well. There had to be some incentive for reliving what she was about to divulge. "If I tell you how I received my Oath, will you explain more regarding your spanning magic? It doesn't have to be tonight...just someday...when you're comfortable."

Myronor smiled wide and nodded. "Deal."

~ Eleven ~

FLAMES

Ophiera drifted in and out of consciousness.

For days, she had lain alone in a dark cell. Naked and cold on a rocky floor that she had no recollection of falling against. Deprived of everything, she didn't have the strength to sit herself up. The only movement she could muster was to lick the moisture condensing on the stone pressed against her cheek. Her only sustenance since the ritual began.

Alone in absolute darkness, she teetered on the edge of death. This purgatory, she had been told, was a necessary preparation to survive the Sacramentum. The weeks of fasting and the years of conditioning prepared one's body and soul to accept the holy flames. All mortal connections were diminished to achieve closeness to the Aether, yet the goal was not to return. Many of the unkindled failed to resist the call. She could not remember how many of her brethren entered the Sacramentum before her. Few ever came back out.

She grew tired of swinging between life and death, like a pendulum of doom. At this point, she didn't care which side the pendulum landed, as long as it stopped. Alive or dead, she only desired an end.

Days into her confinement, Ophiera heard the door creak open. She thought it was a hallucination until she felt two sets of hands lift her from the ground without a word. She had no strength left to stand for herself or fight them off. They lifted her, supporting all her weight as they carried her out into a dimly lit hallway.

It took her eyes a moment to adjust to the brightness. The hands belonged to two priests who came into focus, wearing flowing robes of black. Ophiera lifted her head to see their ornate hoods completely obscured their faces in shadow, but they wore no veils like the clerics.

They began to walk, dragging her along the hall. She couldn't manage to hold her head up and let it fall limp toward the ground. It was strange watching her bare, dirty legs dragged across the stone floor. It would have been painful had she not been numb with the cold.

In the hall's light, her atrophied body came into full view. By Tanvik standards, one could barely consider her a woman, yet the Cloister held no such conventions. While most associated youth with health, such was not the case for the unkindled.

Her skin hung loosely over every protruding bone, covered in filth and grime. Dark hair hung in matted tendrils, swinging across her vision with every step the priests took. She tried to recall the color of her hair without dirt, but her mind fogged at the attempt. It didn't really matter. If she survived the rites, her echelon and Oath would be the only identity that mattered. And if she succumbed to the Aether, then she would be nothing at all anymore. The person she was would be no more, one way or another.

A light emanating from the end of the hall dragged her eyes from the ground. She had no idea where she was, but she guessed where they were going. The unkindled only saw the Sacramentum when they were ready to accept the holy flames. They only left after they received their Oath. And only those with an Oath of Sacrifice, like the two priests who carried her, knew the Sacramentum's location.

They served the Cloister, bound to silence by their brands, and thus could never speak of it.

As they approached, the light emanating from a large runic seal burned her eyes. The symbols churned across the split wooden door as if in a warning. While still supporting her weight, one of the priests raised their scarred hand. They did not chant, as their Oath demanded. But even bound to silence, they fulfilled their duty; theirs was the only Oath that could be evoked without the use of the chants.

Of the four Oaths bestowed by the holy flames, the Oath of Sacrifice was the only to require silence. The priests who received this Oath served the Cloister in ways Ophiera didn't understand. To her, *this* was their only role: to prepare and submit the unkindled to the Aether. Their rites were even less known than those of the clerics and paladins. Without words, the seal on the door reacted to the silent priest's scarred hand.

Slowly, the seal disappeared, leaving them in darkness yet again. The door creaked open, deafening in the silent hall. A blinding crack of light appeared, expanding as the doors opened wide. Ophiera's vision hazed as the light burned her eyes again, the pain shooting back to the base of her skull. She could not raise an arm to shield herself and instead pinched her eyes shut. The glowing red beyond her eyelids was little improvement.

The two priests pushed her into the chamber and let go. Unprepared to support her own weight, she fell hard against the floor. The doors slammed behind her, echoing for far too long. Beyond the pain from light and stone, she heard a rushing sound; neither comforting nor frightening, only foreign.

Ophiera cracked her eyelids, searching for the source. Tears streamed down her face as her eyes adjusted to the light. Before her lay a large stone dais, white and raised above the floor she lay against. The source of the noise emerged from the stone.

The holy flames. A blinding, roaring pillar of white fire. Pale and writhing, the burning geyser ascended out of the dais. She craned her neck upward from the floor, attempting to find the end of the column of wrath. But there was no end in sight; the flames climbed until she could no longer see their end. The vast room seemingly had no ceiling.

Despite the pain in her feeble body, she pushed herself up from the floor to a kneeling position. Trembling before the Aether itself, she watched, mesmerized but not afraid. The Cloister provided no instructions for the Sacramentum. Anytime she had asked, they had punished her. Now Ophiera searched the room for a sign of what came next. She only saw pale stone walls behind her and the pillar of roaring white flames before her.

What was she meant to do?

Ophiera gathered her strength and stood. Unsteady at first and with small steps, she approached the pillar. Her matted hair brushed uncomfortably against her crawling skin. Though the fire roared before her, the air lacked any warmth. Perhaps she was too close to death to feel anything anymore. Perhaps delirium overtook her as she watched the pale flames dance before her. She knew not what drove her to reach a trembling hand out toward the fire, other than a wish for any end.

Her life in the Cloister held only suffering. She wanted to escape this torture, either by death or duty, it didn't matter. The flames were the answer, were they not? She had nothing left to lose. And with that morbid thought, she thrust her right arm into the fire.

Pain as she had never known consumed her. The flames licked her arm, wrapping it in searing agony. Though the flames stopped at her elbow, the torment did not; pain radiated through her body, overriding any thought or regret she may have felt for her decision.

She barely recognized the scream that broke from her. Tears blurred the vision, but nothing could hide the sight of her own bubbling flesh. Her skin charred until only a blacken arm hung in white flames. Instinct begged her to remove herself, to salvage what was left of her broken body, but Ophiera held still. She needed the flames to take her. All of her. Whatever she had become was not worth preserving—this weakened, tortured girl. The holy flames would set her free in her purpose or in peace.

Her insides churned. Her vision blurred. She felt the pull of the Aether, consuming her soul until there was nothing left but pain. The tortured flesh of her arm began to crack and fall away in blackened ash.

This was it.

This must be the end.

She wasn't chosen for duty, and...that was fine. The relief of death was still a welcome outcome. Eventually, all of her would disappear into ash, just like all the others.

But something felt wrong.

The falling cinders revealed fresh skin that failed to catch fire again. Resistant to the fire, her arm yet burned even worse with pain. It was as if the flames themselves were trapped beneath her newly exposed skin.

Ophiera collapsed in agony, toppling over the edge of the stone dais. She cradled her arm against her chest, writhing on the stone floor. The burning pain in her arm worsened still and began to spread. Soon, every inch of her body burned as if she had thrown herself into the pillar of white fire.

The skin of her arm bubbled and rose. Deep red blisters appeared in distinctive patterns. Like the glowing runes on the door, the blisters wrote a message she couldn't know.

The torture was too much. The darkness enveloped her.

But to her dismay, Ophiera awoke again.

For a long time, she only remembered fevered dreams interrupted by black robes and a constant, unbearable burn. The fire was so deep inside her that it seared her very soul. Now, she wished for death, not duty. Wished the flames writhing within would consume her, not guide her. She needed an end that never came.

No one would tell her how long she struggled against the flames. Only when Ophiera recovered her mind did she remember that *surviving* the Sacramentum was the goal of the ritual.

She had succeeded and received her Oath. But only the priests could decipher the branded scripture of her echelon and Oath. So she lay in ignorance, wondering what duty the holy flames had bestowed upon her.

While the echelons and Oaths varied between the kindled, their fates were always the same. To serve the Aether. To serve the Cloister. In what manner was for the priests to reveal.

As an unkindled, she had admired the clerics, ascribed to serving the wounded with an Oath of Mercy. But the other prospective Oaths terrified her. The flames had not bestowed any kindled with Oath of Protection in hundreds of years. The mystery and unlikelihood of that Oath frightened her. And the life of a paladin, pursuing Retribution, seemed ill fitting. How could she judge if someone were an anathema? How could she become one herself in the name of the Aether? Despite her apprehension of Retribution, there was one worse Oath: the Oath of Sacrifice. She couldn't have her only purpose be serving the Cloister. She could never subject the unkindled to the torturous rites of the Sacramentum.

The day finally came when a priest arrived to read her fate. He arrived alone, his elderly face shadowed by an ornate hood. The sight gave her shivers, reminding her of the Sacramentum.

He came to stand beside her and grabbed her scarred hand in silence. She couldn't distinguish between anticipation and anxiety anymore; between dread and expectancy. Her soul still burned as he ran his icy fingers over the raised blisters on her arm.

The examination went on for ages and she flinched with every brush of his touch. His hand stopped on more than one occasion, only to re-read the same symbols over and over again with his fingertips. His hand began to tremble.

When he finally set her arm down, he walked away. She nearly screamed at him for not speaking the answer but remembered his Oath. He reached for a small piece of parchment and charcoal on the table by the door and began to write. His hands still tremored as he translated the glyphs into the common tongue of Tanvik, but his long sleeves obscured the result. He left the paper facedown on the table before departing the recovery room with a bow.

A bow? None of the priests ever bowed.

Ophiera wished he would have just handed it to her.

The table by the door seemed miles away from her recovery bed. But she needed to know. She placed her feet on the cold, stone floor and felt another surge of burning energy rattle through her. She wanted nothing more than to sink back into bed. But she needed to know.

Each step was agony, and she walked hunched to maintain her balance. White hair fell over her shoulder and she froze, examining it. She hadn't noticed this while in bed. It was common for the kindled to develop white hair after the Sacramentum. Expected even. Whether by the holy flames themselves or purely due to the stress they put on the body, the process of becoming kindled always produced strands of white. But none of the kindled she knew had completely white hair like this.

With clumsy fingers, she brought the scrawled parchment before her eyes. She couldn't focus for a moment.

Her knees gave way, cracking painfully on the stone floor as she collapsed. Tears fell down her cheeks as she read. They dropped onto the parchment, smearing some of the runes. But the translation of her echelon and Oath remained clear as day.

Aspect of Retribution

~ Twelve ~

THANKLESS

A melodic ballad woke Myronor from a fitful sleep. It was unlike any he had heard before, in verse and in song. He didn't need to understand the language for the sorrowful chorus to ache in his heart.

A beautiful, sad song.

With eyes still closed, he lay on his bedroll and listened. It was some time before curiosity forced him up.

The gray morning revealed Ophiera's empty bedroll. Her precarious stack of dark armor was also conspicuously gone. The melancholy lyrics flowed between the few trees. Mist hung low in the field beside the small wood. His bedroll lay dampened by the dew, but he didn't want to move from it. Myronor allowed the melody to embrace him again while studying the peaceful surroundings.

By some magic, Ophiera's tale of the night before had become song. Within foreign verse, he felt the aftermath of her suffering, a hollowness once filled with pain. Since Myronor had first laid eyes on the sodden, armor-less paladin, he'd been intrigued by her. Fascinated, even. He thought this draw was purely academic; he'd never met a paladin before, let alone one who'd saved his life.

When she awoke, he found the sorrow that clung to her violet gaze undeniably beautiful. But now he knew the source of her despair.

The clang of armor punctuated the rhythm of the song. Myronor looked to the woods, and watched as Ophiera appeared, framed by smoky mist, carrying a bundle of wood. As their eyes met, the music cut, and her lips stilled. She grimaced at him, averting her gaze. For a battle-worn paladin, she flustered incredibly easily. Myronor found it strangely satisfying to witness.

"Were you singing?" He asked. Obviously, it was her, but it was the tease he sought, not the answer.

She reached the blackened coals and dropped the bundle of wood, refusing to look at him.

"No."

Such a terrible liar. "So, I'm hearing voices?"

"I wouldn't be surprised if some madness took you," she said as her mouth quirked to one side. "Seems to happen quite often."

The fire crackled into life as Ophiera blew gently, feeding the flames. She rarely played along with his banter.

"So, it's preferable to think I've gone insane rather than to admit you were singing?"

"The evidence for one over the other is already established. You jumped from the wall in Feyralis—I call that insanity, yes."

He laughed, and relented. Her mention of the wall sent his thoughts away from the banter to the day by the river, when fate intervened. She could deny it all she wanted, but he held no doubt; fate brought them together for this journey. And now his curiosity demanded to see it unfold.

His insatiable need for knowledge had propelled him thus far through life. It drove him to apprentice in Feyralis, to become a scholar, and to learn more about the paladins. It was the only rea-son he accepted the position as Ambassador to Krysas. He needed to know *everything*.

The pendant around his neck was recognizable amongst the masses now, a symbol of the power Krysas had to offer. Tanvik saw the foreign nation as a source of prosperity, and yet they barely understood the kind of magic the mages of Krysas had mastered. As they had done in the past with Cloister, the people worshipped something that they didn't fully understand. But Myronor needed to understand all that crossed his path. Including the somber paladin tending the fire now.

But Ophiera's story remained difficult to understand. She spoke of the ritual with grace, unfaltering at even the most painful parts. And when she ended her story, she laid down for sleep without any further comments. How could anyone have survived that ordeal and talk about it with such apathy? The way she spoke of her own indifference to life or death chilled him. He wondered if she still felt that way now. Would she have preferred if *he* had left her to her fate upon the riverbank?

"You should dry out your bedroll," Ophiera said, crouched before the fire. "It gets musty otherwise."

Myronor didn't rise. "I didn't know the process to become a paladin was so...miserable."

Her eyes flicked from the fire to him, cold and calm. "Few do."

She returned her attention to the fire. The sight of the flames brought forth fabricated images of burning flesh and agony he could not comprehend. He had read about the paladin's Oath and assumed a person, not the Aether itself, branded the paladin. It was no wonder the Cloister kept such secrets.

"What does it mean to be an Aspect?" he asked, following the subject of secrets. He watched her tense, refusing to look from the fire.

"As Rheta said, Aspects are an echelon of the Cloister. For example, Aleksander is a Hand of Mercy...clerics are more often Hands. But the priests were almost always ranked as Keepers, with few deemed as Hands of Sacrifice." A sad smile broke her tension as she continued. "But like your spanning magic, to be an Aspect is something unique and poorly understood."

Even without her scars, Myronor would find her unique. But it did strike him at that moment that they at least held one thing in common. Neither asked for the power they were given. Yet the process in which Ophiera developed hers was far more torturous.

"Do you regret what happened?"

She continued to watch the flames in silence. He braced himself for the consequence of this question, suspecting he'd gone too far. But after a few moments, she sighed and looked toward him.

"Regret and retribution are at odds with one another. One stares backward, the other forward. Both carry the impossible wish to alter what cannot change. As the Aspect of Retribution, I have no choice but to move forward."

Wise words, Myronor thought, but her lilac eyes reflected a contradictory bitterness. He wished there was some way to take away her burden. But then he remembered he *was* the burden.

His presence alone must serve as a constant reminder of her Oath. He was the reason she resumed this forced service. Though it wasn't completely his fault. If only his mother knew what trouble her choices had caused.

"I'm sorry you've endured so much," he said. "Whatever I can do to ease the burden of this task, please tell me. I know we can make the best of this journey—perhaps even enjoy it."

Her eyes widened. How could someone so long-suffering look at him so softly now? The fleeting innocence faded from her gaze as quickly as it came, her eyes hardening like amethysts again.

"Completing my task as quickly as possible will be joy enough."

Eclipsed again by her duty, she turned her cold gaze to her bedroll and began shaking it out near the flames. Myronor thought her armor truly was the perfect manifestation of her ascetic nature. But he wasn't ready for her to retreat beneath the dark plate quite yet.

"Spanning magic is exceptionally rare," he said. "Seemingly undocumented in terms of magical manifestations."

Ophiera stopped shaking her bedroll, her expression soft again. "But you said your mother also possessed the ability?"

"Yes, but that's what makes it even stranger. Magic is often hereditary, both in ability and affinity...so wouldn't the trait have popped up earlier in my family tree? Wouldn't someone else have inherited it from my ancestors?" He snorted, frustrated. "It's strange to think the first manifestation occurred with my mother. But Pyra must have known something about it. When my magic awakened, she instructed me to keep our ability hidden. And to never span except in matters of dire need."

Ophiera remained silent for a few moments, but he couldn't tell what she was thinking. She just stared at the fire with a slight crease between her brow.

"And you broke this promise because of me?"

He should have guessed this was where her mind wandered. Her overworked sense of onus frustrated him, though it was not without charm.

"You were on the brink of death," he said, shrugging away her concern. "I considered that a dire need."

"My vesper—did you see it?" Ophiera asked with a frantic note.

"No, of course not. You're alive, aren't you? Like most people in Tanvik, I've never seen one."

He couldn't understand why she looked so...guilty. Her nature and Oath were often at odds with each other. But her reactions were always unexpected.

"You're right—it was a stupid question," she said. A frown pulled at her face. "Dry your bedroll—we're leaving."

Myronor recognized her blunt indication to move on and obeyed without argument. He shook out his damp bedroll near the fire, not having the heart to tell her he could have dried it the same with magic. She seemed like someone who needed a routine, and he didn't wish to break it further.

After packing up and traipsing across the meadow back to the road, Myronor called Mallow from her crystal. In a flash of light, she appeared and immediately began her exploration as they walked.

She happily chased any insect that came across her path—mostly swardhops and spring weevils this time of year.

For hours they walked behind the small cat, who failed to grow bored with her incessant inspection of the road. Ophiera watched with a smile that seemed uncomfortable. Myronor wondered if her facial muscles were simply unfamiliar with the motion. He couldn't decide which he found more entertaining, his beloved familiar or Ophiera's response to her.

"You seem quite smitten with Mallow," Myronor said.

Ophiera stared ahead at the prancing creature. "It's surprisingly pleasant to watch her inspect and explore. I can relate to her taking advantage of a few moments of freedom."

"Freedom? You make it sound as if I've kept her prisoner," said Myronor with a chuckle.

"Is she not captive to you and that crystal?" Ophiera said, staring at the shard bouncing on his chest. "She goes where you go, does as you instruct. I'm not sure how else to interpret that."

Her voice held no animosity, and yet her assessment felt like a smack in the face. He could never dream of holding Mallow captive as Ophiera described, yet her observations held merit. How could he explain the relationship between familiar and mage?

"Mallow is more my charge than captive—like I am to you. Well, except Mallow and I both volunteered for our partnership...so perhaps that's a poor example." He ran a hand through his hair, trying to find the right words. "Still, I care for Mallow. I keep her safe in this world until she decides to return to her own."

"Her own...?" Ophiera's expression fell to innocence again, incongruous with the dark, heavy armor.

Myronor knew it was dangerous to become fond of a mere expression, but he couldn't help it. He looked away before answering.

"The crystal—it's the link to Mallow's realm, Nijeka. It's a world outside of Erum...an alternate plane of existence."

"Mallow is not from Erum?"

Myronor smiled. He thought it obvious upon meeting the creature, but again, Ophiera's perspective surprised him.

"She's just a visitor. No one quite knows what draws the familiars to Erum or to a specific mage. But Mallow and I reached an agreement the day she appeared in my tower. While she is in Erum, I keep her safe. And in turn, she provides me company. She trusts my judgment when I ask her to return to Nijeka, but I assure you, she's free to do as she pleases."

It was strange how defensive his own voice sounded. Given Ophiera's past, he needed her to understand the difference between himself and the Cloister. He would never, under any circumstance, hold anyone against their will. And yet, was he not holding Ophiera captive to her Oath? It was by his request the Magistrate opened an investigation into his mother's death, the catalyst to Ophiera's re-conscription. Perhaps he was not as innocent as he thought.

"I understand your duty to her well-being, I suppose. It reminds me of the ancient Oath of Protection and those that served as guardians. But *her* reasoning vexes me still."

"What do you mean?"

Her lips pressed together, hesitant for a moment. "Not a day has gone by without me wishing I could free myself of Oath and Magistrate. So, I'm having difficulty imagining a scenario where one would *voluntarily* bind themselves to another's will. Mallow follows your command by her own inclination, but why would she bother if she's truly as free as you say?"

Myronor held his tongue a moment, trying to reason the subtle difference to himself first. What was the distinction between voluntary and forced servitude? Did it really only boil down to choice? He needed to understand Ophiera's perspective better before he could really answer.

"You bound yourself to the people of Iluka, as Sea Warden, to protect them, right? Is that much different than why Mallow might want a guide in this world?"

Ophiera frowned. "I see your point. But the people of Iluka and I had a mutual exchange. I protected them and in turn, they fed and housed me. But in this scenario, you're providing all three to Mallow. She exchanges some of her freedoms for safe exploration of a new world...but you...What do *you* gain from such an exchange?"

This conversation had become more difficult than he expected. But he enjoyed the challenge; it had been a long time since he had to explain himself so thoroughly.

"Well...I suppose companionship, mostly," Myronor said. "Her mere presence brings me joy."

"How?"

Her outlook saddened him, but what else could he expect? The Cloister isolated their disciples away from so much. He'd always disagreed with their teachings but was now beginning to despise their methods. They had burned Ophiera in more ways than the Sacramentum.

"It's simply pleasant having someone to come home to," he said solemnly. "You know, someone to talk to and look forward to seeing every day." When Ophiera still appeared confused, he continued with a new desperation. "I know Mallow's not exactly a person, but she's as good as...even better in some regards. But...I mean...don't you find it tiresome being alone all the time?"

Had she never felt that inexplicable pull toward another soul to comfort one's heart? Maybe he felt that way far too often.

"Solitude has been the only option given to me," she said stoically. Again, he was beginning to truly hate the Cloister for giving her these views. "But I think I understand your point. Her presence brings me joy for no particular reason. Even more, knowing she chooses to be here."

Myronor was relieved she no longer thought him a prison guard. Yet he began to wonder why he cared. He admitted to being arrogant at times; he simply never felt other people's opinions applied to him. People could think he was flippant or silly, idiotic or frustrating, and they were likely right, but it never affected his life or his choices. Then again, he never faced the same opinions as Ophiera faced. Only now did he think of his arrogance as a luxury.

The animosity the paladin faced in Feyralis proved how low the public's opinion of the Cloister had fallen. The paladins had become more myth than verity, kept alive by tavern songs and the occasional eyewitness. Even the clerics had become rare; but everyone knew of the Justicar of the Cloister, thus they couldn't be forgotten. Rumors had always surrounded the Cloister and their order, but lately, the doubt and skepticism had grown too commonplace. Myronor couldn't fault them.

He believed in *some* teachings of the Cloister. He believed the Aether existed, that inside every person was a vesper, and that reincarnation on Erum was likely. Murder was indeed a sin. But anathema? He was either agnostic toward or outright disagreed with nearly everything else in principle and practice.

It didn't help that the Cloister held an unequal amount of power in Tanvik. The Justicars of the Magistrate, five in total, represented the people of their realms based on region, not religion. But Aleksander, the Justicar of the Cloister, represented an empty realm both in population and following. The people of Tanvik had begun to question why one-fifth of the Magistrate's power was held by a dying religion. And why the other four allowed it.

Ophiera suddenly thrust out her arm, halting Myronor in place. He'd lost himself so thoroughly in thought that he forgot they were on the road. Before he could ask her what was wrong, the faint sound of screams cut through the air. Mallow scurried back toward the pair, ears flattened against her head. With a slight tremble, Myronor held the tethered crystal out for his familiar.

"Stay close," Ophiera said in a deadly voice. She handed him her pack roughly without a look at him. And before he shouldered it, she started off toward the scream.

Myronor tried to match her pace, but even laden in armor, she sprinted faster than he could ever hope to. To lighten his carry, he minimized her pack clumsily as he ran, following as close as he was able. He hoped she wouldn't mind.

Up ahead, a small outcrop of trees lay close to the road. The frame of an old wagon peeked out, only just visible past the cluster of trunks. A poor attempt to hide it.

Following another wave of screams and shouts, Myronor watched as Ophiera ran to the wagon. In one fluid motion, she pulled the claymore from her back. The sound of metal cutting through the air raised the hairs on the back of his neck.

He had no idea what was happening. Drunken fisticuffs at the pub were the worst violence he had encountered, and frankly, avoided. Now, he ran toward to the cluster of trees, trailing behind the paladin with a sword nearly the same size as her. She skidded to a stop on the road, giving him a chance to catch up.

"Stop!" Ophiera cried, facing the wagon. The threat in her voice caused everyone, including Myronor, to freeze.

Two middle-aged women in dirty clothes were on their knees in the grass, held in place by the threat of knives at their throats. A single man held both blades, towering over his hostages. His sneer faltered at the sight of Ophiera.

Against a spoked wheel of the wagon leaned a small child, her limbs bound tightly as she wept against a gag. She watched with terror as a second man attempted to bind a struggling boy, whose stubbornness showed in the wounds upon his face. Both men wore bright yellow cloths tied around their upper arms, a curious adornment, Myronor thought.

"Isn't it lovely when more sacrifices just show up?" the dual-bladed man's voice hissed. "You'll all fit into the wagon nice and snug."

Myronor had thought Ophiera threatening already, but something the man said unhinged her completely. She cocked her head until her cheek touched her shoulder. Under her breath, she whispered "the blades" to Myronor before facing the wagon again.

"If you seek sacrifices, then I seek Retribution," Ophiera shouted.

She spread her feet apart in a readied stance, her greaves scraping against the stones of the road. Her sword gleamed in the sun, poised to act. Only now did Myronor appreciate the worn condition of the great claymore. He wondered how many anathemas she'd claimed with it.

The man holding the two blades gestured to the other. With a sickening crack, the boy crashed to the ground, thrown with violence by the other bandit. Myronor feared for a moment the child would run or fight, only to cause more chaos. Yet he lay still on the ground, clutching his now obviously broken leg.

The approaching bandit withdrew another pair of curved knives. Ophiera flourished the claymore once again with a grace ill fitting such a cumbersome blade.

"Sweetheart, that sword looks a bit heavy for ya. Put it down and just come with us," the man said with a sneer.

Myronor found the bandit's delusion painful.

Ophiera twitched her sword ever so slightly toward the captive women, a message Myronor received loud and clear.

"My sword has always been burdensome," she growled.

With a whine of metal, she turned the point of her sword to the ground, grinding it between the road stones. A murmur of words crossed her lips, a familiar but unknown language. The man lunged for her, foolishly thinking he held the advantage.

Myronor flinched despite himself.

In a glow of white, the claymore burned for an instant before runic symbols appeared emblazoned on the ground. The pulsating glyphs surrounded himself and Ophiera, a barrier against the lunging bandit.

For a moment, time slowed. Myronor watched with the same horror as when he saw a beetle fly toward a spider's web. Ignorant of his own peril, the man sneered before the explosion of white fire. The intensity of the flames nearly blinded Myronor, but shock prevented him from looking away.

The man writhed for a mere moment. Before Myronor could blink, only ash remained, and a scream broke from one of the women held captive. The sound pulled Myronor from his stupor.

Using Ophiera's silhouette to hide the glow of his hands, he cast his transmutation on the captor's blades. The metal shrank and rounded in on itself until the knives resembled two large spoons instead. The hilts had retained their form, leaving the bandit none the wiser.

Ophiera wrenched her sword free from the ground, still burning white as she stalked forward. The loathing in her eyes should have frightened Myronor. He should have felt disgusted by the death she wrought before him. Yet he felt more awestruck than fearful.

The lone bandit pressed the false weapons hard against the women's throats. He looked desperate. "I'll kill them if you take another step, paladin!"

Ophiera advanced, looking at the two women. "Run now."

The women took notice of the spoon edges and seized their opportunity. After a momentary struggle against the distracted thief, they freed themselves. Immediately, they reached for the children, still near the wagon, bound and injured.

The bandit threw his now useless blades toward Ophiera in a tantrum of acknowledged loss. She let them bash against her armor without a flinch, never tearing her gaze from the man. Myronor held his breath as he watched. Her sword rose in a blur of metal as she descended upon the cornered bandit.

"What does *this* mean?" she growled, using her free hand to tug the yellow scarf loose from his arm.

"Handkerchief," the bandit seethed.

Ophiera pressed her sword closer to the man's neck, her teeth bared. Fury couldn't describe properly the look in her eyes. "Why sacrifices? What was your intention with these people?"

The man spat at her, trembling beside the blade. Ophiera closed her eyes for a moment, a look of disgust upon her pained face.

"You've already proven yourself an anathema—"

"Don't make me laugh!" he interrupted, still held under her sword. "Just because you send your victims to the Aether doesn't mean it's not murder. We're both the same, paladin, except my soul belongs to *me*."

Myronor saw Ophiera's beautiful eyes fill with hatred. The moment the revulsion turned inward, she dragged her sword from his neck in a blaze of white. A glimpse of ruby-red liquid slipped through the flames as the bandit fell to ash.

The sight of the man's throat opened for only a moment brought the carnage of Ophiera's actions to reality. Her other victim simply turned to ash in a death so quick it hardly registered as violent. Myronor knew Ophiera was a paladin, knew what her Oath demanded, and yet he had never truly understood what she was capable of until now.

Ophiera turned. He froze in place but she walked passed him without a glance. Following her path, his eyes fell and fixated on the glowing light before her. It was a sight he'd secretly wished to see, yet dreaded the circumstances required to see it. Above the ashen heap hovered a vesper; a manifested soul now freed of its vessel.

The luminescent orb was brighter than he expected. According to the Cloister, the shade of one's vesper reflected the life they lived, yet none knew the exact interpretations. For so long, only those of the Cloister witnessed the vespers as they enacted their Mercy or Retribution. It was still taboo for anyone else to witness death. Convention demanded he look away, but he couldn't tear his eyes from the glowing orb. It was beautiful, mesmerizing, and yet wrong.

A blackened web had been spun within the orb. No book had mentioned anything like this writhing corruption. The wrongness of its presence shook Myronor to his core. He thought the Cloister's description of anathemas was not so literal. Was the blight within the vesper the curse that came from committing murder?

Myronor watched Ophiera. How did she know? While it was obvious these men were nefarious, neither had actually committed murder before them. Had they truly done enough for her to judge them worthy of a death sentence? How could she judge innocence from guilt without sight of their vesper first, as proof? There were too many variables to make a swift judgment. Doubt now replaced his initial intrigue regarding the power Ophiera wielded. Had she ever judged wrong?

Statuesque, Ophiera stood over the wisp and began to chant. Her scarred hand lay over her heart, but despite her foreign words, nothing happened. Slowly, she turned to the ashes near the wagon, and Myronor's gaze followed to the second hovering vesper. Though the shade was different, the same dark distortion swirled within it.

Myronor struggled to process the events he had witnessed. Rarely was he overwhelmed by thought alone. As he gawked in a strained silence, Ophiera turned to the women by the wagon. One lay clutching the battered boy, both with the same shade of copper hair.

"May I heal his leg?" Ophiera offered gently to the woman.

She clutched her boy; her face draining of vitality.

"N-no! You're not s-safe."

The woman's terror forced Myronor to return to sense. No matter what she had done, Ophiera didn't deserve his or anyone else's doubt. He joined the paladin as a curtain of despair fell over her face. Even though Ophiera had saved her family, the woman remained fearful of her. The second woman sat beside her, fair-haired and heavyset and busy untying the young girl. The child had eyes only for Ophiera, a gaze of deep green without a trace of fear.

Taking a gamble, Myronor patted Ophiera's shoulder before bending his knee to address the children first. "I'm Myronor, a mage from Feyralis, and this is my friend, Ophiera, a paladin of the Cloister."

The little girl stared at him for a moment before looking at Ophiera.

"Your white flames were beautiful," she said, her voice pitched and sweet. "But mum says you're dangerous."

"Your mum is right," Ophiera said. The softness of her voice felt like a cool cloth on a hot day, soothing and yet startling. "But I can still help your brother."

The boy remained silent, biting his lip against the pain. Myronor examined the break more closely; it was unlikely to heal well without intervention. Ophiera studied the child with nearly the same expression of torment.

"Lucinda, dear...if she can heal him..." said the heavyset woman, a plea in her voice. Her eyes lingered on the agonized boy. A few moments of awkward silence passed; Myronor nearly shook this Lucinda. She acted as if Ophiera offered to break the child's other leg rather than heal him. How cruel and unfair.

"Please help my brother?" The little girl's sweet voice warbled with her trembling lip. At the words of the child, Lucinda shakily nodded her head in agreement.

Ophiera knelt beside the boy as his mother clutched him for dear life. Gently, she laid her hand upon the boy's leg, her scars hidden by the dark gauntlet. With eyes closed, she began reciting the strange tongue. Myronor recognized the incantation and recalled a sopping-wet paladin hovering above him. The reverie brought him a flash of heat in his chest.

A faint glow of golden-white light poured from her hand and into the boy. It resembled the holy flames, Myronor thought, and he wondered how the same power both destroyed and healed.

The ginger boy gasped as Ophiera chanted, and the mother whimpered as if she were in pain. When Ophiera removed her hand a moment later, the boy's leg lay straight and unbroken.

Some of the color returned to the boy's cheeks as he gazed at himself in awe. He scrambled out of his mother's clutches and onto his feet, his jaw still slacked in wonder.

"T-thanks," he breathed and smiled at Ophiera before turning to his mother. The copper-haired woman had fallen into hysterics on the ground, covering her face with dirty hands. "Mum, please stop crying—look! I'm fine!" He did a little jump, and Myronor had to cover his mouth to hide his smile. "It doesn't even hurt anymore."

As Ophiera rose from her kneel, Myronor saw she swayed with a fatigue he unfortunately recognized. The last time she healed someone, it nearly killed her, but Myronor's own injuries had been beyond a broken leg. He saw the early signs of manasickness...but did she?

"Is there anything else I can offer you?" Ophiera asked, addressing the heavyset woman.

Despite her son being healed completely, the copper-haired woman still watched the paladin with terror in her eyes. And yet Ophiera still offered the family more.

"My lady, you've done more than enough," the second woman said, coming to stand. She placed the little girl on her wide hip and stood beside the boy. "You saved my wife and our children from..." Her words choked, despite her apparent composure. "I can't thank you enough."

Ophiera fell silent, struggling against something within. Her eyes darted to the ashen piles, to the cart, to anywhere but the woman's eyes.

"Did they take the oxen?" Myronor asked, pointing to the wagon. "I'm afraid we can't provide much help in that regard, but we can send someone along if we meet them upon the road."

The boy looked excited for a moment. "Don't worry. Those men cut Brambles loose, but I can find him. He likes me best."

"Nuh-uh! He only comes when *I* call him!" cried the little girl, struggling against her mother's hold. After her mother set her down, the little boy and girl ran to the road and began calling the name Brambles into the meadows.

It amazed Myronor how the children appeared so untraumatized by this experience. Their parents, however, showed the signs. Lucinda was still in pieces on the ground, while the heavier-set woman stood hunched and wary. He imagined watching their loved ones mistreated was more traumatic than if they had received the blows themselves. His thoughts flitted to Mallow. Truthfully, he would gladly take any amount of suffering for his familiar. He wondered if this concept was as foreign to Ophiera as companionship itself.

"If there is nothing more I can do for you," Ophiera said quietly, turning away from Lucinda's hysterics. "We will take our leave and allow you to recover from this ordeal in peace."

"Wait—" the other wife said. "At least take some of our crop, as thanks. I can't imagine what would have happened if you hadn't..."

She still couldn't say the words. No one in Tanvik could. Even Myronor struggled still with the concept of death, moments later. He had just watched Ophiera kill two people. He saw their vespers, saw their lives, as despicable as they were, end before his eyes. Perhaps he understood Lucinda's hysterics a little...but only a little.

The heavyset wife lifted the canvas of the cart and pulled from within it a basket of chokecherries. Their color reminded Myronor strongly of the blood flowing from the man moments ago, and his stomach clenched. But Ophiera's face fell as she gazed at the fruit. Myronor admitted he did not know Ophiera well, but she wore her thoughts clearly on her face. Her despondent expression was one of unworthiness.

He stepped forward and took the parting gift. "Thank you. Please stay safe on the rest of your travels," Myronor said, waving his goodbyes to the family.

Ophiera paced ahead of him, far too quickly considering her fatigued state. He was about to suggest they slow down, but the tension kept him silent. Obediently, he followed, becoming winded rather quickly.

She glanced back to check on him, revealing streaks of tears down her lightly freckled cheeks. The sight ached his chest worse than their pace.

"You were amazing," Myronor said through deep breaths. He meant every word, but they sounded empty even to himself.

"Please don't," she said.

"Don't what?"

"Patronize me!" If she had slapped him across the face, it would have felt less painful. "I killed two people while traumatizing an innocent family," Ophiera said shakily. "There is nothing amazing about what just happened."

She continued her intense pace and pulled ahead of him without another word. He guessed the best thing he could do for her now was to remain silent. Maybe it was best for them both.

~ Thirteen ~

FEAR

Hours after their departure from the family, Ophiera still fretted over her decision to abandon them on the roadside. Lucinda had made her distress clear as day and the best help Ophiera could offer was to remove herself from their presence. The woman hated her nearly as much as the bandits, it seemed. Her duty, her Oath, was to Retribution, nothing more. That was justification enough for leaving them, wasn't it?

Myronor remained silent still. She had traumatized him along with Lucinda. Everyone feared her in the end, and the mage was no different. She had expected this outcome, knowing his jovial nature could not withstand witnessing her Oath fulfilled. But even in knowing the outcome, the silence depressed her. He would no longer speak to her casually. No more questions or jokes; only enough courtesy to hide the fear.

It felt strange to be disappointed by a lack of conversation. On the bright side, the silence afforded her a chance to brood. A favorite pastime.

Since leaving Iluka, she had claimed the souls of five anathemas. The blackened corruptions lacing their vespers hadn't been the only commonality between them. What did the yellow armbands indicate? Were they all a part of the same faction? More importantly, why did thieves require sacrifices? An empty threat? A misnomer for slaves?

The bandit's final words rang over and over again in her mind. The truth of them burned in her chest. She knew she wasn't any better than an anathema. The only difference between them was she had no choice in becoming what she was.

"Ophiera, can we take a break?" Myronor asked. His breathless voice broke through her stormy thoughts, but she refused to look at him. "We've been at this pace for hours."

She hadn't noticed the time or distance that had passed. But now she saw the color of the road looked different in the warm tones of an evening sun. They had nearly completed the day.

"We may slow, but we shouldn't stop until we're ready to camp," she said, still looking ahead. She wasn't ready to see Myronor's fearful eyes quite yet.

The mage heaved a great sigh. "It's close enough to dusk—we can just camp early tonight."

"The sun hasn't even touched the horizon—we can still make a good amount of distance if—"

"Ophiera, please," he interrupted. Her name sounded strained on his lips, forcing her to slow down. "You're exhausted. Between using up your mana and this absurd pace you set, you're running yourself—*us*—ragged. We have plenty of time to make it to Krysas. Let us rest. Or at the very least, let *me* rest."

Ophiera stopped in her tracks. He was right. Caught in a whirlpool of self-loathing, she had failed to recognize her own weariness. How could she keep her charge safe if she could barely stand? If she could no longer wield the flames without injury?

His well-being should have been her priority, but instead, she had wallowed in self-pity at the cost of his safety. She always knew she wasn't fit to carry a charge.

"Fine. We can set up camp in that thicket," Ophiera said, eyeing a patch of trees up ahead.

She hadn't noticed the dark clouds on the horizon until now. They wouldn't have long before the downpour began. This day was cursed, she decided.

"Whatever you say, as long as I can sit down."

She swore she heard a smirk in his voice.

In this area of the countryside, the Severed Wood encroached greedily on the surrounding farmland. The patches of thickets and woods grew larger, blotted against the fields in equal proportion. She looked at the landscape with bitterness.

On her way to Feyralis, she had covered the distance from here to the city in less than a day on her own. Slowed by Myronor and distractions of duty, this journey would take thrice as long if they kept this pace. Nothing was going as it should. She hated being slowed. She hated everything at the moment.

Ophiera led them to the edge of a small wood, scanning for a path, or at the very least, a break in the trees. These woods were older, compacted with undisturbed growth. Eventually, she found an opening—an old game trail that led into the dense, murky trees.

Splotches of lichenous moss covered most of the thick and gnarled trunks, textured in buttermilk and sage on blackened bark. The ground was thick and spongy with decaying debris. A few patches of bright orange mushrooms, colloquially known as blazecaps, spread across the forest floor. At night, they would glow like fire, drawing curious creatures to their poisonous spores, both beautiful and deadly.

She found a small clearing that was just large enough for a fire. No bedrolls would be needed tonight, she thought, looking to the sky through the tree clearing.

"It will rain soon. But I have a canvas in my—" Ophiera froze mid-sentence. What had she done with her pack? Her heart raced at her idiocy. In all the years she had traveled, she had never lost her pack.

"I have your bag here," Myronor said, taking a small pouch from his pocket. Ophiera watched it in his hands, avoiding his eyes still. "I minimized it though—figured you couldn't be mad if I was the one carrying it."

With an azure glow, the tiny satchel returned to full size, worn and dirty as always.

Why could she do no right today?

"I'm sorry." She sighed. "I didn't mean for you to carry it all this time."

It was only when she reached for her bag that she really *looked* at Myronor. He had tied his hair in a loose ponytail, revealing flushed cheeks glistening with sweat. She had expected the exhaustion after his complaints, but she hadn't expected him to smile.

"It was worth the carry just to see your expression when you'd thought it lost." He laughed loudly. "Even Rheta couldn't have ruined that."

Ophiera blinked stupidly. Indifference would have made more sense than his laugh. Was he so unfazed by what had occurred mere hours ago? And if that was the case, why hadn't he spoken to her since?

"How can you joke after today?"

"What, the business with the bandits?" Myronor asked, sobering slightly. "We saved a family from a terrible fate. That hardly seems a reason to be mournful."

"I killed those men—you witnessed it. My Oath, the holy flames, their vespers..." Ophiera clutched her bag so tightly her knuckles hurt.

Myronor shrugged. How could he shrug?

"Don't you...fear me now? Don't you hate me?"

Again, he laughed. It was enraging and relieving at once. "Don't take this the wrong way—because you are *absolutely* terrifying when you're angry—but I doubt I'll ever fear you, Ophiera." He smirked. "You've saved my life. And another four today. How could I ever fear a savior?"

Stunned, she felt a flush of anger cross her face. "Why haven't you spoken to me for hours then, if not because of fear?"

"I was struggling to keep up with your pace," he said with a scoff. "You think I could spare a breath for conversation?"

As always, the mage had a frustrating way about him. Regardless of his demeanor, Ophiera felt eased at the return of conversation. She let out the breath she didn't realize she held and began pulling the extra supplies from her bag.

While she always carried a few spare hammocks, she had packed only a single canvas cover. At the edge of the clearing, Ophiera found a triune of trees the proper distance apart. Tying knots like Berwyn taught her, she fastened the two hammocks to the trees in the shape of an arrowhead. She had to keep them close together to accommodate the canvas tied above. It provided suitable coverage despite the odd layout.

As she turned back to the clearing, she saw Myronor drop a pile of wood. He stared bewilderedly toward the hammocks behind her.

"Are those rubyfin nets?" Myronor cried. He crossed the small clearing in a few fast paces and plucked at the hanging weave with childlike satisfaction.

Too easily she had forgotten Myronor was from Iluka. Again, she could do no right.

"Berwyn traded them to me ages ago," she said.

As Myronor examined the hammocks, Ophiera began the fastidious process of removing her armor. She tucked away the pieces beneath her chosen hammock, piling them neatly away from the rain. Without her armor, the exhaustion of the day truly hit her; armor, guilt, and anger were efficient at keeping fatigue at bay.

"You hung them so close together," he said with a chuckle. "What are you planning to catch with them?"

She felt her face burn and turned away from him, toward the pile of wood. At least his stupid jokes proved that truly nothing had changed between them. Still, she hated that she could control the holy flames themselves, yet not her own expression.

"If you'd prefer to sleep in the rain, you're welcome to move yours," Ophiera said, pulling some flint from the small pouch in her leathers.

"Oh, come now—it was a joke. Try to laugh!"

"I require something to be funny in order to laugh," she called over her shoulder, kneeling to build the fire.

The mage only responded with a stray chuckle.

With two strikes of her flint stones, the orange flames sprang into life. She blew on the true fire, watching it overtake the dry pieces of wood. At least they could keep warm for a bit before the storm hit them.

"Have you ever used the holy flames to start a—what do you call it—true fire?" Myronor asked, watching her closely.

"No."

"Why not?"

She sighed. Did he do anything but joke and question? Still, Ophiera found it better than the silence. "That would be outside the purpose of my Oath."

Behind her, she heard the sounds of him readying his hammock. Though his magic made no sound, she noticed the air felt different when he cast. As if to prove her right, she heard the thud of his pack on the ground and the soft sound of his bedroll unfurling.

"Have you ever *tried*?"

Ophiera watched the orange flames in silence. Funny enough, she had never really thought of the true fire as similar until his mention. The holy flames were their own entity and held their own purpose; like Myronor and herself, they might both look similar with two legs and two arms, but that was where it ended.

"No, and I don't plan to. I've only ever seen the holy flames turn people and objects to ash...and they seem to never have an effect on other living things, like the grass or trees."

"Hmm...interesting. I'm still curious to know more about how your rites work. Like the chants and those glyphs on the ground."

She smiled to herself. He was always curious. And if she had learned one thing about Myronor, he would not relent until she answered him. But discussing her powers, her holy flames...Well, she hadn't really done that before, had she? It took her some time to find the right words.

"Well...all of the kindled from the Cloister carry the holy flames within. For the rites of Retribution, we call upon them, both from within ourselves and from the Aether itself. The runes channel the power of the Aether beneath Erum, using our mana within as guide."

She sat down beside the fire now, nearly winded from the lengthy explanation. Well, lengthy by her standards.

Myronor dropped down beside her. "So you serve as a conduit for the holy flames, in a sense? And the Aether?"

Ophiera nodded. "They're one and the same."

"And the healing rites? Those are the Aether too?"

She dropped her gaze to her scarred hand, flexing instinctively. "I believe so, but...truthfully, I don't really know. I'm...well, I'm not supposed to know those rites, let alone use them. I only know they work best with a physical connection. I call upon the holy flames from the ground when I fulfill Retribution. But when I evoke the Mercy rites, it's as if I call upon the soul within to fix itself. I don't know if that's even correct, but that's what it feels like."

She fell back into a silent reverie of a time she hoped to receive an Oath of Mercy. After the Sacramentum, the Cloister forbade the kindled from learning skills beyond their Oath. The holy flames had deemed her soul worthy of Retribution and nothing else. But a younger version of herself had rejected the rules of the Cloister. At least for a time.

The forest turned dark quickly. The thick trees and incoming storm siphoned away the daylight faster than she expected. The fire before them provided most of their light now. And warmth. Which made Ophiera sleepy.

"What is the Aether exactly?" Myronor asked quietly.

She was too tired for that particular question. It's not as if she hadn't thought about it before. She used to question its intention, its purpose—even its very existence. Why would such a power exist? Only to demand recompense for souls lost to its embrace? Did it even demand anything, or was it all conjecture, interpretation by the priests of the Cloister? She surely didn't have an answer. And she had stopped toiling over the question a long time ago.

"I don't care what the holy flames are—it does not change their purpose, demand, or burden."

A distant rumble beckoned her eyes toward the sky. A habit of futility. What use was seeing the storm clouds if you could do nothing to stop them? Still, she watched the sky as the thunder rolled over them again.

"Want to eat something before the storm?" Myronor asked.

She nodded, thankful for the change of subject.

Myronor opened his palms while blue light streaked through the air. In a matter of minutes, he had conjured a feast of a meal. Between them, he placed a large roast of beautifully marbled meat, crispy yams, a few rolls of bread, and even a small, neatly iced cake. Never before had she experienced such luxury while on the road, in quality or quantity.

"Are you expecting guests?" she questioned. But even in her mild protest, the aroma of the feast perked her spirits.

"A good meal fixes a hard day." Myronor smiled.

The mage provided two unique commodities—sustenance and sympathy. Despite his happy expression, she could see the act had worn him down. He breathed in short, rapid breaths and his face appeared waxy in the firelight. Like her own, his mana was limited, and the act of conjuration seemingly cost much. This meal had taken much of his energy and her appreciation for it became caught in her throat.

Together, she and Myronor ate in contented silence, interrupted occasionally by the rolls of thunder. Each rumble put her on edge, waiting to hear the rain begin. But as long as it was dry, they would stay by the fire and enjoy. She was happy to ignore the inevitable for the moment.

The first bite of the roasted boar was nearly enough to restore her spirit. By the time they were ready for the cake, she thought she might burst. But the sweet and heavy confection would be worth any burden. Only after departing the Cloister had she discovered proper food, and sweets were always her weakness. She devoured the cake like a starved animal.

"Hold...very...still," Myronor said, his tone low and serious.

Ophiera tensed immediately, her eyes sliding to her claymore by the hammocks. What had he seen? If anything approached their camp, she would have surely heard it by now.

Myronor reached his hand to her face. His thumb gently grazed her nose before pulling away.

"Frosting." He laughed as he stuck his thumb in his mouth. "The grace of a paladin, I see."

Her heart fluttered with aggravation. Mostly.

"You shouldn't do that. I thought there was something seriously wrong."

Myronor's only response was laughter, as usual. She couldn't hear the start of the rain over his amusement. But when she felt the droplets—so sparse they left one to question whether they had fallen at all—she knew their time ran short.

The sky opened in full a moment later. Not even the thick canopy of the forest could halt the onslaught of rain.

Myronor was first to abandon the fire, but Ophiera was first to reach the hammocks. She hopped gracefully into her bedroll lain across her hammock as the mage struggled to balance on his own.

The light from the fire faded as the rain extinguished it, leaving only dim embers behind. Their shoulders nearly touched in the darkness as he finally lay still in his hammock, situated at last.

It would have made more sense for Myronor to place his head on the other end of his hammock. Then, they would have had more room. And his face wouldn't have to be this close.

She turned her attention to the storm above, studying the flashes of lightning in distraction. They created beautiful silhouettes against the broad leaves and branches of the thicket. The tension in her shoulders softened as she watched, listening to the soft pitter-patter of thick droplets drumming on the canvas above. Rolls of thunder didn't startle her but rather induced a sort of tingling sensation on the back of her neck that trickled down her spine like the rain itself. Her whole body relaxed in the midst of the storm.

"I don't sleep well in weather like this," Myronor murmured. She could feel his warm breath mingle with the cool, stormy air.

"I find storms quite peaceful," Ophiera said. "They remind me of Iluka."

"Ah, of course *you* do," he said with an audible smirk. "Perhaps that's the reason storms put me on edge. A simple consequence of being the son of a fisher. Weather can mean life or death out at sea."

The rain had a strange way of making people reflect, and Ophiera was not immune. How was it that Myronor, the mage she was tasked with escorting, had ties to Iluka? She knew if she asked he'd blame it on fate. Or had his answer changed since seeing her Retribution?

"What were the chances we both hail from Iluka?"

Myronor shifted next to her in the darkness, and she knew without looking he'd turned to face her.

"I don't believe it's due to chance," he said. "I told you fate wove our meeting and intertwined it beyond Iluka."

So today hadn't changed his odd outlook. But maybe she could. "Or perhaps I merely made a poor choice in choosing Iluka as my place of retirement."

Myronor laughed, and she glimpsed his smile, flashing like the lightning. "What made you settle in Iluka?"

Yet again, more questions. And yet again, she found herself compelled to answer him.

"When I first gained my freedom—well, my retirement from the Magistrate, I traveled. The idea of a permanent home was never an option—a lifestyle beyond my comprehension. But as I wandered the Southern Coastlands, I stumbled upon Iluka. And never left."

"But why the Southern Coastlands? There's nothing but sand dunes."

"Precisely," Ophiera said. It felt strange to recollect her past decisions. "I was desperate for two things: solitude and the ocean. It was wonderful, alone under the stars, drifting to sleep beside the waves every night. My Oath...well, it's quite useless without people around. I can't seek Retribution without *someone* to retribute. But in one particularly rough storm, I decided, against my better judgment, to find a room at the inn in Iluka."

"Against your better judgment? Finding an inn seems a fairly harmless act."

Ophiera sighed, a moment of bitterness tainting her peace in the storm. "The mob in Feyralis was unusual, yes...but the family today was not. No matter the village, it always played out the same. After I entered a tavern, the room would fall silent. The chatter might resume eventually, only to be filled with questions and pointed stares. It's true most in Tanvik don't recognize paladins, or any of my order. But they know of the Cloister, and someone in armor carrying a sword was rare enough to cause a stir. I was either a paladin or an anathema; neither was welcomed. More often than not I was told to try the stables. *If* I could manage to get a meal, I was always placed in a corner far away from the other patrons. There I could eat, like some beast on display, while they waited with bated breath for me to leave. It was never a pleasant experience."

Myronor watched her through the darkness, his own exhaustion drawing on his face. She shouldn't have let him conjure such an elaborate meal. She shouldn't have pushed him so hard on the road earlier.

"What happened in the Iluka, then?"

"Absolutely nothing," Ophiera said as she smiled. "I walked into the tavern, but the room kept its chatter. When I inquired about a bed, the old barkeep, Yelena, smiled and told me I could have my pick between two rooms. I remember...there was a large table of anglers, several drinks into the night already—raucous and merry. A man from the table approached me at the bar and I assumed the night was about to be ruined. But he introduced himself as Berwyn and asked if I would join the table. In exchange for my meal, he asked I tell them news and stories acquired on my travels. I agreed, mostly out of shock. It's still one of my fondest memories. That night, I was neither paladin nor stranger."

"That's how it should be everywhere. I don't understand this fear surrounding paladins..." Myronor trailed off, sounding frustrated.

Ophiera was now the one to laugh. "Everyone fears the unknown and paladins have become such. Half cast to myth even while the Magistrate still employs them. Though I would think a mage would hold more mystery than a paladin. Has no one ever expressed fear of your magic?"

Myronor was silent for a moment. "Mages dominate Tanvik's culture now, ever since allying with Krysas. And Feyralis has more mages than any other city, though we're still the minority of the population. There are entire institutions dedicated to magic— libraries, scrying halls, and imbuement shops. Magic has weaved its way into the very culture of Feyralis, even if only a few possess that type of mana themselves. Perhaps that is why I have never known the persecution you face. It must be difficult to contend with."

When she was younger, it had been. She had found extreme difficulty in accepting her treatment by others. Her bitterness grew over time, but eventually, that disdain turned inward. If the world viewed her as something to fear, then surely they were right.

"There is justification for their persecution," she murmured. "They are right to fear what I am and what I must do."

"You can't possibly think that woman's response was appropriate today. You saved her family and healed her son, yet she treated you no better than the bandit. At least *I* appreciated it when you healed me." Myronor chuckled, the sound oddly comforting amid the ongoing storm.

"But the woman was right," Ophiera said. "The holy flames are dangerous and thus, I *am* a danger. I kill, regardless of the justice it serves. I'm no better than the corrupted souls I claim. I'm the same as that bandit."

Ophiera sighed, closing her eyes. It was strange putting her anxieties into words. They felt more real, more true, and it caused her heart to clench. She could do no right.

"You're wrong," he said. She felt him shift beside her, his warmth permeating through the breeze. "They're wrong. Everyone is wrong. Well...the little girl was right...your flames are beautiful, Ophiera. And so are you. Like this storm, a force of nature so exquisite cannot possibly be cursed."

Silence fell between them. She had no response to such strange words. Did he wish to tease her or simply anger her for his own amusement? Or perhaps he expected her to swoon because he'd called her beautiful? The most terrifying prospect of all was that he truly meant any of it.

She turned away from him in her hammock and closed her eyes in a plea for sleep. "You forget that even the wisest of fishers still fear the storm."

~ Fourteen ~

CONSEQUENCE

By midday, the sun burned Myronor's shoulders as he trailed behind Ophiera. The humidity left behind by the night's rain lingered, clinging to the hot air and weighing down his breaths. Yet again, he wiped the beaded sweat from his brow and wondered why leather pants were somehow more acceptable for travel than a breezy robe.

He assumed his clothing was far more comfortable than the darkened plate armor of his companion. Yet he observed, with equal amusement and annoyance, that Ophiera barely glistened with perspiration in her armor.

This morning she had answered him only in nods, without uttering a single word. Her eyes purposefully darted from his, avoidant but never cruelly. Myronor wondered if he had overstepped last night by calling her beautiful.

Like with books, he usually grew bored of people quickly. But his fascination with Ophiera hadn't diminished as he expected. Instead, it had grown. She was unlike anyone he'd ever met before. Duty overshadowed her luminosity, but like the corona of an eclipse, failed to hide it in full. Unfortunate experience had forged her light into a dark soul, one tainted by suffering, not by sin as she believed. He found himself needing to know more about the woman obscured by contradictions.

Myronor's hope for an enjoyable journey fell short again today. The sweltering silence between them promised a day no better than the last. He hoped they wouldn't encounter any more trouble on the road, but the heat was trouble enough at the moment. They had hours of travel ahead and already his shirt clung to him.

His internal grumbles were silenced by curiosity at the fork in the wavering road ahead.

"Which way to Iluka?" Myronor asked.

The paladin slowed a pace, allowing him to catch up beside her.

"Technically either. But we will go left."

"Why?"

Myronor had learned quickly that Ophiera never volunteered information. But he required a constant stream of answers. It's why he loved books. All information was laid out before him, to peruse at his discretion. If one book didn't provide what he sought, he merely found another that did. People were more tedious than books, especially stoic paladins. They required coaxing, prompts, and interpretations. Still, he did not mind the process of pulling answers from Ophiera. Her thoughts were quite distinct from any book he'd ever read.

"The left is the more direct and well-traveled route. It follows the main road through the Severed Wood. The right is less traveled, and can barely be considered a road. More like a trail. It briefly traverses through the Severed Wood, past the Pellucid Falls, until it edges between the forest and the Sloughmire swamps. Locals call it the marsh road."

As unexpectedly as he had hoped, she had volunteered a wealth of details this time. Perhaps as he learned about her own habits, she also had learned of his; namely his questions.

"Pellucid Falls? I didn't see that on my map. Or the forked route, for that matter."

"You have a fairly useless map then," Ophiera said with a smile. He was momentarily stunned, the tease alone lifting his spirits. It seemed the silence this morning was simply her default; he misread her solemnness for standoffishness. He'd have to make note in his journal later.

Still, the map he possessed was fairly new. The Magistrate commissioned it after he accepted the position of Ambassador. It should have held all official routes throughout Tanvik. But he knew better than to say this out loud. He refused to mention the Magistrate now; not when Ophiera's mood had finally brightened.

"Thankfully, I've you as a guide," he said. "Have you seen these falls before?"

Her eyes unfocused for a moment. "Once."

"But I thought you traveled this route often?"

She sighed and pointed ahead. "Of the two paths before us, one is a direct route with a well-tended road, while the other is a run-down path that adds half a day to the journey—*if* conditions are good. Surely even you can guess which I frequent."

"Only half a day to see something as beautiful as a waterfall?"

She frowned for a moment. "It was never a priority."

"Well, it is now—we're taking a detour."

Already, he imagined standing beneath a cascade of violent, cold water, washing away his stale sweat.

"Didn't you hear the part about it barely being a road? And this is not a time for sightseeing," she retorted. "We're already behind because of your pace and that business yesterday."

He was not about to be thwarted by her misplaced sense of duty.

"When would be a good time, then?" She went rigid, with lips pressed together, but he kept the pressure on. "I likely will never return to Tanvik, so this may be my last chance to witness these glorious falls."

He couldn't tell if her armor rattled from her pace or her anger.

"Fine," she finally said harshly. "Have it your way."

Her greaves clanged as she strode ahead. Before Myronor could celebrate the win too much, Mallow, who had witnessed the entire conversation with wide eyes, darted between Ophiera's legs. Sweetly mewling, the familiar rubbed against the darkened greaves. The little traitor.

He watched as Ophiera scooped Mallow from the ground and placed her upon her pauldrons. Somehow, the familiar's presence did little to detract from the paladin's intimidating stance. Both creatures were, after all, wildly dangerous. And exceptionally alluring.

At least he remained consistent with his preferences.

As Mallow settled, Ophiera spoke in a softer tone. "For the record, I'm only agreeing to this because we will be less likely to encounter any people on the road less traveled." She turned to him and her eyes narrowed in threat. "But I truly hope you have no deadline to meet in Krysas because it is *I* who will receive punishment."

"You act as if we were committing a crime!" Myronor could not believe she continued to fight him on this point. "We're still heading toward Krysas after all."

Despite the worried crease on her forehead, a small smile tugged at her lips. "Just promise you won't jump from the top the moment we arrive."

"The last time I leaped from a great height, you ended up in my bed for several days, so the idea is still tempting."

She stopped upon the path while Myronor pulled ahead, too amused with himself to recognize the overstep. His glee became guilt when he heard a hiss from Mallow, who stared back at him with a warning glare.

"To think how simple my life would be had I just left you on the riverbank!" The genuine anger in Ophiera's voice brought him an unfamiliar discomfort.

She had risked her life to heal him, only to discover he himself was the reason for her conscription. And even with that bitter knowledge, she continued to keep him safe on their journey.

Regardless of his own growing infatuation, the last thing he wanted was for her to resent him.

"I'm sorry, Ophiera. My comment was in poor taste. It was a tactless way of telling you I would jump off any height again if it meant our paths would join as they have now." Myronor hoped his apology conveyed his intentions better than his first attempt.

"I didn't..." she began, shaking her head, flustered. "I've just never met someone like you before...and I still can't decide if that is good or bad. I don't know how to comprehend your flippancy or triviality...but that does not mean I regret how events have transpired. I shouldn't have said I would have left you on the riverbank —it was unkind and untrue."

Myronor blinked stupidly. The volunteered elaboration of her thoughts, without his prodding, left his heart warmed. It felt like the rare occasion when Mallow willingly jumped into his lap without coaxing. Though he felt proud to earn even the slightest affection of the fickle, glorious creature, he was not delusional enough to over-interpret its meaning.

While his attraction to Ophiera grew beyond academic interest, he accepted she would always view him as a burden. And rightly so. Yet she claimed to hold no regrets. She was a constant contradiction.

He wondered if there was no way to break the Magistrate's hold on her. Or better yet, to break her Oath entirely. Tempted to ask, he again held his tongue. Today, he had tasted his own foot well enough.

"I promise I won't jump off anything," Myronor said with a smirk. "Unless you tell me to, of course."

They remained silent until they arrived at the fork in the road. The sun faded in the dense trees of the Severed Wood. And while the thick greenery helped to cool the air, it stifled any chance of a breeze.

Not long after they entered the forest the paved stones eroded to little more than gravel, leaving only an uneven path before them.

Even Myronor could see the road was not intended for anything more than light foot traffic.

Large puddles remained after the night's storm and in the thick mud, walking seemed rather treacherous. At least for him. Ophiera marched on as Mallow's head bobbed on her shoulder, appreciative of the ride that kept her paws clean.

He idly wondered how many carts and travelers had suffered this unforgiving path, but he said nothing to Ophiera. There was a chance she might interpret his musings as regret, and he would not risk it.

Hours passed before the sound of the waterfall finally filtered through the trees. The low rumble seemed distorted by the ancient forest, but as they approached, it became so clear that Myronor began daydreaming of the cool water. This daydream, of course, involved Ophiera joining him for a desperately needed swim. Already he pondered ways by which to persuade her.

The water fell thunderously as the path cornered ahead, and Myronor spotted an opening in the canopy where sunlight and the cloudless sky broke through. As he quickened his pace, Ophiera met his stride, and he could sense her own anticipation to finally see this glorious detour. Even Mallow's eyes shone wider than usual as she clung to Ophiera's shoulder.

As they turned the corner of the path, the forest opened dramatically before them. They stood upon the edge of a crystalline pool amidst the thick trees. The fathomless depth held a cerulean hue, unnaturally blue against the dark rocky shore. Perfectly mirrored in the clear, placid pool, the falls stood on the opposite bank. The narrow cascade was impossibly tall and fell with a torrent of white, frothing energy. Myronor's tower in Feyralis was a mere stump in comparison. He was quite pleased he had promised not to jump.

"There," Ophiera said. Her tone indicated she still resented the lost argument. But her eyes were wide with wonder as she gazed at the cascading water.

Myronor pulled his tunic over his head and untied his leather pants. The cool air by the water felt wonderful over his bare, overheated skin. By the time Ophiera had taken notice, he was completely nude.

"What in the name of the Aether are you doing?" she growled.

He had never seen anyone so flustered by bare skin before. "How else do you swim?"

At the edge of the pool, he dipped a toe into the water. The heat of the day caused the water to feel frigid by comparison, but Myronor shivered with relief. He pulled off the leather strap binding his hair back, shaking his locks loose as he turned to Ophiera. She stood cross-armed, pointedly staring away from him with a frown. Mallow reflected her stance with eyes narrowed.

Such moody creatures.

With a deep breath, he turned back and dove. The cold rush ignited all of his senses in unison, an overwhelming sensation of pleasure and pain. From beneath the surface, he could hear the muted pounding of the waterfall crashing into the pool. After enjoying a few moments of weightless submergence, he surfaced with a gasp. On the shore stood his two companions, posed identically.

"Come on!" he called, treading water. "Mallow can watch our gear...Right, my little minion?"

Mallow gave her armored steed a bump with her head. Ophiera understood the message and removed the familiar from her pauldron. She placed the cat on the ground and scratched her under the chin. Both continued to ignore him.

"Do you fear water or just nudity?" he shouted.

Even at this distance from the shore, he saw her pauldrons shake against the taunt.

"Should I drown him for both our sakes?" Ophiera said to Mallow, loud enough for him to hear over the falls.

Myronor watched as the paladin meticulously removed her multitude of armor pieces. Each piece was stacked neatly next to

Mallow by the shore. He found a strange enjoyment in watching her routine, like a bird building its nest.

When she only wore her leathers, she glared at him. "Turn!"

He laughed, but faced the other way, nonetheless. "I'm not a pervert!"

Myronor swam out a way, allowing her space. He heard a gentle splash, barely audible over the roaring falls. When he turned, he saw nothing but the faintest ripple across the placid water. Mallow sat alone on the shore with a pious glare beside the pile of armor. His gaze returned to the water.

Nothing. No movement, no bubbles.

"Ophiera?"

Only the thunder of the falls responded.

"Ophiera!"

Without warning, he felt a rough hand weave through his hair. Yanked back, the cool skin of his shoulder met another's, warmer and soft. His moment of fear transformed to a thrill. Her warm breath brushed against his ear as her bosom pushed against his back.

"You dare accuse the Sea Warden of fearing water?"

In an instant of foresight, he took a deep breath. It was nearly too late as she pushed his head under the water, holding it there for a moment with a terrifying force. For a fraction of a second, he thought she might actually drown him, to rid herself of him where no one could find him. But she let go rather quickly.

As Myronor surfaced, he took a relieving breath and watched as she swam away. Long strands of pure white swirled in her wake. Before she had decided to drown him, she also loosened her braid. Priorities.

Watching her swim was surely worth the pain of getting her into the water. She moved gracefully as if she were born in Iluka, not merely a transplant. Never before had he seen her hair down, swirling around her like the white flames she wielded.

With a triumphant grin, she waved her scarred arm, holding a small cake of soap.

"I'm going to wash," she called. "Then we're leaving!"

A moment ago, she casually tried to drown him. And now, he found it quite unfair she'd decided to run away so quickly.

"We're not leaving until I've had *my* retribution!" he yelled to her.

With a deep breath and a powerful kick, he tore toward her through the water. When he had built enough speed, he poked his head above the surface to see her reaction.

Her bright eyes widened, but she did not hesitate to whirl around and bolt for the shore closest to the falls. She might be the Sea Warden of Iluka, but he was born and bred by the sea. As a child, he'd spent more time in the ocean than on dry land, and the speed at which he gained on her served as evidence.

Still, she was fast. Much faster now, being pursued. As he closed the distance between them, he felt deafened by the falls. A body length away, he cursed to himself as her scarred hand emerged and slapped hard onto the flat stone edge. She turned to him, back against the rock with a breathless smile.

"I'm safe!"

He had never seen her light-hearted and, for this reason, lacked a reply. Instead, he swam closer.

A moment of alarm crossed her face. "I touched the shore...That's the rule, right?"

"I don't know what game you're playing, but the only safe place is *out* of the water."

She pressed herself back against the rock defensively but did not flee.

The thundering falls drowned out any sensible voice left in his head. He boxed her in, placing his arms upon the rock behind her. They were close, so close he could see the flecks of azure faceted within her violet eyes—the source of their jewel-like sheen. Her lips were parted, allowing the escape of her rapid breaths.

How could someone be this painfully alluring? Her look of apprehension only furthered her dichotomy, both threatening and innocent.

"I think I deserve retribution after you nearly drowned me," he said, inches from her.

The worry crease on her brow smoothed and rose, incredulous now. "That *was* retribution, for your snark," she said.

"So we've begun a cycle of vengeance now?" He could feel her breath against his lips, his heart pounding against his chest. "When does it end?"

She watched him, her eyes boring into his as her breath quickened. Were her thoughts as impure as his?

"I don't know," she breathed. "I suppose it can't."

The sorrow in her voice told him she no longer spoke of their little game. He leaned closer, desiring to draw her sadness away with his lips. But she disappeared beneath the water before he could blink.

He reached for her, turning against the rock in his search, but felt nothing. Only a few effervescent bubbles and cold water fell between his fingers.

Looking toward the falls, he saw her surface, astonished she held her own against the onslaught of water. She waved the bar of soap again before diving underneath the foaming falls, this time resurfacing behind the veil. The distorted outline of her body was barely visible through the veil of water. But had he not been looking for her, she would be nearly invisible.

Disappointed, he watched her a moment, wondering if he now was, indeed, a pervert. The past times he had seen her nude did nothing to stir his desire; she'd been hypothermic and unconscious or disorientated with manasickness. She had been in need then. But now, he found he was the one in need. Heat spread throughout him, despite the coldness of the water.

Definitely a pervert.

A plunk in the water caught his attention. Bobbing in the water, he spotted the bar of soap. He smiled to himself, appreciating her generosity as he washed.

He truly missed having a companion. Mallow was the perfect familiar, but Ophiera was different. Her duty-driven nature was admittedly taxing, but it also made her exceptionally trustworthy. And trust was a difficult thing to come by these days.

He turned his gaze to Mallow, an instinct calling his attention. The rush of water deafened any sound, but he saw her hackles raised high in defense. Something was very wrong.

A man and a woman were walking along the dirt road, pointing down toward the pile of armor and gear.

"Ophiera!" Myronor called, but she didn't respond. It was impossible to hear anything over the roar of the falls.

There was no time to waste. He dove, swimming full force across the pool to where the newcomers approached. As he surfaced, Mallow's hissing replaced the roar of the falls. While he was confident he could handle these two strangers alone, he wished Ophiera had heard his shouting. An invincible paladin was always good for a potential confrontation.

"Good afternoon," Myronor said as he exited the water. The two intruders looked at each other, confused and discomfited. Why did nudity make everyone so uncomfortable?

"Your armor?" the man asked.

The question felt accusatory, and now Myronor understood why Mallow acted so defensive at their approach. Something felt wrong about the way their eyes darted between him and the armor.

"Yes, it is...but surely I don't need to put it on to convince you to leave."

Words alone seemed to threaten them little. The woman took another step forward. Lucent blue light emanated from Myronor's palms in warning, pulsating in the surrounding air. Both strangers stared, blanching slightly. As they turned silently back to the road, he saw a flash of yellow on both their arms. Recognition tickled the back of his mind, but Myronor was far too preoccupied with ensuring they walked away.

As he watched their departure, the woman pointed out into the pool. His eyes followed, finding a blur of white shooting across the water. The two strangers broke into a sprint up the road, disappearing into the trees.

Myronor heard a splash from the shore and knew Ophiera had finally reached him. As he faced her, he saw all her modesty had disappeared, now replaced by fury.

"Who were they?"

He felt shocked by her anger. Shouldn't she be glad he scared them away without need of her Retribution?

"Does it matter? They're gone now."

She stood before him, sopping wet and naked, yet he kept his eyes on hers.

"Did they have yellow cloths tied to them?"

His stomach sank. "I believe so."

"Damn it all," she growled as she grabbed her leathers. She dressed in frantic speed as she eyed her armor next. "We might catch them if we hurry!"

"They're long gone, Ophiera. I don't understand—"

"Exactly!" she snapped, unhinged and cruel. "You understand little!"

He watched her for a moment, completely at a loss. This wasn't Ophiera blowing off steam. He had truly enraged her.

"That seems unfair—"

"Don't you dare talk to me about fair!" she interrupted. "I should have never gone swimming, never let my guard down. My Oath requires Retribution! If they were anathemas, then I...but, I know you don't understand."

He didn't. He really didn't. But he was scared to admit it. And like a predator on the hunt, she read his fear and pounced upon it.

"You can't understand. You've been too busy locked up in your tower, reading your books, and laughing your life away with no concept of responsibility or consequence!" She threw her arm out, pointing after the fleeing bandits. "I have already claimed five of this yellow-banded group! Do you honestly think those two are innocent? I have my Oath to uphold, and yet you let them go!"

He stared at her, confused. This rage was unlike any he had seen from her. It hurt him in ways he could not understand. Ignoring her questions, Myronor began dressing in silence. Anything to distract from his growing guilt.

"Don't you understand?" she continued in a strained voice. "They know our route now. They know we're here! They will send others after us! After *you*!"

He paused with his shirt in hand. "Why would they come for me?"

Throwing her hands up, she pulled at her hair with a cry of fury. He recalled her tantrum against the statue in the Magistrate and braced himself for the worst.

She took a few deep breaths before turning to him, cold and composed. "You are *my* charge!"

He wished she did not sound so furious when claiming him as hers. Was he truly such a burden?

"If something happens to you..." Her voice cracked with emotion. "Do you know the consequences I face if harm comes to you?

"I...didn't realize," he managed to mutter. The apology was on the tip of his tongue, but he swallowed it.

She stood shaking a moment before the coldness overtook her eyes, her features stone again. "I tire of explaining basic concepts of survival in this world to one who claims such intellect."

She bent over her armor pile and gave Mallow a gentle stroke, but her hand trembled still. The cat leaned so hard into Ophiera that the beast nearly lost her balance. Though Ophiera's expression softened, her voice still shivered as she whispered, "At least you have a sense of responsibility."

Ophiera pulled her armor on, despite the loose, damp tangle of her hair. Without a word or glance, she started toward the path, expecting him to follow.

~ Fifteen ~

AFFLICTION

Myronor had remained uncharacteristically subdued since Ophiera's outburst at the Pellucid Falls. Last night, they had camped in utter silence within the Severed Wood. It was not as though he had acted cold or childish, simply distant. He had gone to gather firewood and still conjured them a meal without uttering a word. As Ophiera settled into her own bedroll, she saw he wrote in a tattered journal by the firelight. His hair fell like a curtain, blocking his eyes from hers.

As was her way, Ophiera sank herself into a cycle of frustration and guilt. Though she had preached of consequence, she now realized that shouting at Myronor had been a thoroughly thoughtless act. She had taken out her anger at herself on him. And now, this solemn version of the mage distressed her.

She felt utterly conflicted. How could one be justified in thought, but guilty in action? She was unsure what to say or do to ease the tension. In the past, she had always sought silence, yet now the quiet sat ill with her.

Today, however, was a new day, and she hoped following a good night's sleep, they might leave the dark cloud behind them. But as

Myronor dried the dew from his bedroll near the fire, his shoulders remained slumped and his eyes unfocused. Without Myronor to distract her, the yellow-banded visitors of yesterday occupied her thoughts today.

Why had the two bandits only questioned and fled? Perhaps they feared an encounter with Myronor? She was far more threatening than the mage, and that alone never thwarted their previous attacks. If their only goal had been to obtain information, what could they possibly have been seeking near the falls? Was their camp somewhere nearby? Or worse...did they seek her out? Were they now being followed?

Unfortunately, no alternative route existed now, short of a cross-country trek through wild terrain. Ophiera knew what manner of creatures lurked in these woods. Rarely did anything dangerous approach the road, but within the forest, the risk of being hunted outgrew that of becoming lost.

Fed, in part, by the very same Slumbrous River, the marshes of the Sloughmire would be waterlogged this time of year. Even Ophiera dared not cross the swamps when the waters were high. Many had drowned in the deceptive scum ponds, or worse, become inextricably trapped in the muck, only to be slowly devoured alive by murklouses. She always found it disturbing how the Cloister considered such suffering to be a natural death. The murklouses didn't commit murder when they picked the flesh off their victims with their skittering claws; they couldn't help their nature. Anathemas had a choice though. But where did that leave her Retribution?

Why had she agreed to visit the falls anyhow? Between the encounter with those yellow-banded individuals and her failure to uphold Retribution, she regretted the risk. She had taken off her armor despite her better judgment. In more ways than one.

Swimming in the pool beneath the falls was the closest she had come to joy in a long time. In the water, she wasn't the Aspect of Retribution, but rather one of the kids that swam and played off the pier in Iluka. When she thought of Myronor closing in behind her, her heart stammered. Who in their right mind *enjoyed* being chased? But she had, for some reason.

When he caught her, she had enjoyed that too. But something about him changed; the chase no longer felt like a game, but something more real. Games didn't have consequences, but what she feared Myronor wanted did indeed. He had been so close to her, with only water separating their bare skin. The mere memory of that moment was too intense, even now as she walked the trail. She wished she could dive back into the cold pool again. But reality sobered her better than any amount of cold water. At this moment, he kept his distance. And she guessed he'd stay that way from now on.

Morning sunlight penetrated the canopy as the trees thinned, and soon Ophiera stepped out of the dense wood.

A cool morning breeze played across her face as the marsh came into view. She thought it odd how quickly they reached the edge of the forest, but admitted it had been a very long time since she last traveled this route.

When the wind ebbed, the stillness of the air tugged violently at her senses. A putrid smell filled her nostrils, and her body recoiled instinctively. The Sloughmire always smelled of decay, but *this* was something foreign, something fouler. Yet when the breeze blew again, the stench disappeared.

A thick veil of morning mist still clung to the low quagmire, a gray blanket obscuring the swamp beneath. As she examined the shrouded marsh, she sensed something unknown and yet disturbingly familiar. The scars on her arm began to itch with anxiety.

"Everything ok?" Myronor said, stopping beside her.

The deep tenor of his voice cut her tension. She hadn't heard him speak for so long.

"I'm not sure yet," Ophiera admitted.

He shifted uncomfortably as she scanned the murky landscape again.

"It's impossible to see anything through that mist," he said quietly. "If we keep moving, whatever it is may reveal itself."

Normally Myronor acted the curious one. She thought for certain, by his nature alone, he would be compelled to investigate further. But he merely walked away.

He continued along the dirt path that now ran between the wood and the marsh. Vacant and cold, this version of the mage was painful to watch. As she followed, she regretted wishing he acted any differently from the carefree oddity she had awoken to in the tower. Then the revelation struck her.

She was the problem. She had always been the problem.

The shaman of Iluka used to lecture her about her interactions with others. Ophiera used to wave off the criticisms as another silly tease. But the truth was now obvious. She was repellant by nature. She constantly pushed everything and everyone away in order to hold true to the duty-bound path of the Cloister and Magistrate. Even when she was free of their control, her nature remained impervious. Nothing else mattered but her Oath. Her flames dealt death, but her personality destroyed spirit.

"Ophiera!" Myronor's voice called.

He stood at the edge of the path closest to the marshlands and stared at something below the road. When she reached him, she followed his gaze to a small patch of marshland adjacent to the road. They stood double their height above the mist that was beginning to clear. Through the thin vapor, Ophiera witnessed why her senses had screamed in warning.

The once lively marshlands had decayed into nothing more than vitreous muck. Hollow, gray reeds collapsed dead below the mist. From the vile mud emerged rotten corpses of various creatures. Dead anurolas, murklouses, and silt fish lay blackened and rotten. Those were just what she could recognize, as the rest became indistinguishable in decay. Now she knew the stench that battered her senses.

"What could have caused this amount of death?" Ophiera asked breathlessly, her mind reeling in disgust.

Myronor looked sickly. "Some kind of disease? I have never seen or heard of anything like this, in either book or tale."

The mist parted farther, revealing more of the blackened landscape. It had spread like a plague throughout the swamps. She scanned back to where they had emerged from the wood, tracing the path of the darkness. The trees that touched the marsh were sparse and lifeless. She couldn't believe she overlooked it as they left the Severed Woods. It was as if the marsh had begun to strangle the very forest.

Ophiera felt sickened. "Surely news has reached Feyralis? How could a blight like this go unseen?"

Myronor shook his head. "I'm not sure which is more disturbing...Has it gone unnoticed or purposefully neglected? I can't imagine Eliana ignoring a plague in the Sloughmire; she might hate the swamps, but she knows their value."

Ophiera was caught off guard again by the informal way Myronor referred to the Justicar of Feyralis. She wasn't sure about the Justicar's views on the Sloughmire, but Myronor was right about something. Eliana, despite her harshness, was a strong, capable leader. If she knew anything about this plague, she would have at the very least made the people aware.

"Wouldn't the Justicar of Quargonia know as well?" Ophiera asked. "This is the border of her domain."

"Again...I'm not sure which scenario is more disturbing. But if I had to guess, I doubt any member of the Magistrate knows this is happening in these marshes."

Ophiera caught the stench of the air again as the breeze faltered. She raised her hand instinctively to her mouth and held back a gag. "We should leave immediately. I'm uncomfortable sleeping anywhere near this rot. And we have to tell someone before this spreads. How long do you think it's been this way?"

Again, Myronor shook his head. "It looks widespread, but it's impossible to tell if this happened overnight or over years. Where is the nearest town or village?"

Ophiera's heart sank. "Isyath is on our path—a day and a half if we travel with haste. We can send a courier from there to Feyralis with a warning."

"Assuming they haven't been affected by whatever this is. I don't want to think about what this disease might do to the crops and water supply downstream."

"Let's move then," she said with a tremble in her voice. If Isyath had fallen to this blight...But no. If a village had succumbed to something like this, the Magistrate would have surely investigated. Isyath had to be there.

"I'll follow whatever pace you set to get away from this abhorrence," Myronor said with a half-cocked smile.

She returned the expression. "You may yet regret that."

Ophiera started jogging, her armor clanking gently with her rapid stride. Beside her, Myronor kept pace, and both remained silent, focusing on their breathing. Whatever sickness had struck the land, she prayed it would not reach Isyath before they did.

The Sloughmire was one of the Five Realms of Tanvik. Its principal city, Quargonia, lay at the center of the swamps, far from their path. Like the Southern Coastlands and Feyralis itself, a Justicar represented the Sloughmire on the Magistrate. The current Justicar of Quargonia, Moysent Frenzel, was one of the longest-serving Justicars on the Magistrate. Ophiera had spoken to her a handful of times when she was conscripted, usually to be tasked with Retribution against fugitives hiding in the swamps. She always seemed sharp for her age, quiet but caring. She would never let this kind of plague go unchecked. So then, why had no news made it out of the swamp?

Ophiera quickened her pace to match her questions.

Maybe no one *had* made it out of the swamp. This path, the marsh road, had been traveled less and less over the years. The improvements of the main roads and construction of more left these old trails obsolete. Still, at least a few people must have traveled this road in recent weeks. What happened to them?

For hours, all Ophiera heard were her worried thoughts and heavy steps. The silence of the marsh felt as deadly as the plague itself. Their footfalls sounded oddly synced as they focused on vacating the dying swamp.

Once the sun had passed its zenith, Myronor broke the silence in a panting voice.

"Ophiera...I'm sorry...for my blunder...at the falls."

His breathless apology surprised Ophiera. And guilted her.

"There's nothing to apologize for," she said, her voice strained as she took deep breaths. "I never explained my worries regarding those yellow-banded men...I didn't tell you I encountered them before. And I was mad at you for convincing me to take a swim...For allowing them to escape...For not knowing exactly...Well, you get the point...My anger was unjust and misdirected...So I'm the one who should be sorry."

Myronor chuckled, and for once, she felt relieved rather than annoyed. "Well, all will be forgiven...if you admit that...you had fun swimming at the falls."

"I won't deny it was fun...But I'd also argue...most actions deemed fun...are also foolish."

A moment passed before the weight of her own words sank in. Yet again she'd culled the spirit of enjoyment.

But Myronor laughed. The sound replaced her guilt with embarrassment, and soon she joined him in laughter. They tried to keep pace as they both struggled to breathe. It relieved so much of their tension that it was worth the sacrifice of air.

After their outburst, they only slowed in intervals to catch their breath and sip some water. But then it was back to their quick steps, fleeing the diseased lands. The marsh remained unchanged as they passed by, black and rotten as the rest. Across the path, however, the Severed Woods suffered more and more decay as they progressed. Dead trees now lined the forest's edge, dark and bare. She could not tell if they had become infected or had simply been strangled out of a water source. Regardless, nothing now remained but dead wood toppled over in a weave of thick, impenetrable trunks.

Ophiera had never before felt so trapped upon an open road, decay on either side. The only path was forward, and even that she dreaded; Isyath had to be there.

Exhaustion began to set in as the sun touched the horizon. Luckily, the edge of the blight was in sight. The decaying rot clashed violently with the lively marshland at the border between the two. Tendrils of death and decay swirled within the vibrant green, seemingly spreading through the veins of water into the very land. Like ink spilled on parchment, it was both a disturbing and welcoming sight.

"We won't be able to escape the *sight* of the blight by nightfall," Ophiera breathed. "But at least from atop that mound near the woods, we can see what will become of this place in the dark." She gestured to a plateaued hill ahead, a steep incline topped by a few strangled trees.

Myronor nodded his agreement.

Their trek up the steep hillside seemed nearly impossible after the day's journey. Reaching the top at last, they both collapsed in exhaustion, rolling onto their backs. They lay there together for a moment, heaving heavy breaths, and savoring the first real break of the day.

"I'm impressed you kept up," Ophiera said finally.

Myronor had no breath for laughter and only smiled sheepishly. "I want nothing more than to accept your compliment, but I must admit...I cheated a few times."

Slowly, he levitated only an inch above the ground, while his hands emanated a soft blue light.

"So you can fly too? Is that conjuration or transmutation or another hidden talent?"

"Transmutation." He chuckled. "Similar to the charm that nearly caused my demise in Feyralis. I transform the air beneath me to propel my step."

"And you did not think to cast it upon me?" She chuffed jokingly. "I'm hurt."

Myronor lowered himself back to the ground and rolled onto his side, propping himself above Ophiera. His nose hovered inches from hers, and she could see every bead of perspiration on his face. How could he look *more* handsome exerted? But he was almost as close to her now as he had been by the waterfall. She grew wary of his intention and hoped this was still a game.

"You know I'd never try to hurt you," he said, suddenly serious.

Ophiera choked on a breath. "It was a—"

"A tease, I know. But for once, I'm serious...and I need you to know," he said, still far too close. As if reading her discomfort, he stood abruptly. "I'll get a bit of wood for a fire."

~ Sixteen ~

TARRY

Ophiera felt dazed, and not just from their day-long run.

While Myronor gathered wood, she prepared the bedrolls, though it seemed pointless. She wouldn't sleep tonight.

The blackened marsh loomed ominously a distance away. She feared what dangers nightfall would bring in such a place. After all, it seemed no one had brought news of this plague to the world. But neither she nor Myronor had the energy left to travel any longer.

After a quiet, exhausted meal around the small fire, the skies above blackened. Both moons were out tonight, and though they shone brightly in the sky, the marsh absorbed all light, leaving them in inky darkness. They needed only to get through the night. Tomorrow, they would travel through untainted lands and reach Isyath—where they could finally secure a quiet night's rest.

"Did Rheta provide any stimulant potions?" Ophiera asked quietly.

From his boot, Myronor extracted the minimized potion case and expanded it with a gentle glow. By the light of the fire, he searched among the minuscule bottles until he found what Ophiera requested.

Myronor chuckled as he handed her a vial. "It's labeled 'Rheta's All-Nighter.'"

The potion looked yellowish, with a chalky consistency. She popped the waxed seal of the small vial, observing the concoction. It looked rather unappetizing. She brought the bottle close to her nose. It smelled of bright citrus and mint, pleasant enough to convince her to drink. The aroma matched the flavor as she consumed the tonic in a single gulp. The lingering texture, however, caused her to smack her tongue several times.

A warm buzzing sensation radiated from her tongue outward to her limbs, reaching the tips of her fingers with a tingle. She'd forgotten how intense stimulant potions could be. Suddenly, she felt alert and more wakeful than she had felt at the start of the day. Unfortunately, the potion did little for her physical fatigue and only amplified the ache of her legs and feet.

"I'll take first watch," she said, standing from the fire with a stretch.

"Wake me if you need to swap," he said with another grin. "I've heard sleep-deprived paladins can be quite cranky."

Myronor yawned exaggeratedly before lying on his bedroll and despite herself, she smiled. Either she was beginning to appreciate his teasing or the stimulant potion addled her mind. But as she moved to the edge of the hill to begin her watch, her smile faded.

The stars and moons shone brightly, yet the darkness felt more suffocating than ever. Only the crackle of the fire met her ears. The silence felt disturbingly foreign in a once lively marsh. Despite the green swamp nearby, there were no croaks of the anurolas—a usually deafening chorus. She recalled how peaceful she found the faint blue glows of the majflies, yet only blackness blighted the marsh now. Had everything died in the Sloughmire or simply fled before the blight?

As the firelight faded, she checked again on Myronor. Asleep, his tranquility looked too much like before, as if his vesper were about to come crowning from his chest again. The thought caused her heart to jitter. A side effect of the stimulant potion, surely. Searching for another channel for her anxiety, she began to hum quietly into the silent night. When Myronor did not stir, she thought it safe to sing aloud.

The familiar lyrics calmed her spirit and though she knew the words by heart, she never knew what they meant. She couldn't remember exactly where she had learned the song—it seemed to be the same language as the rites, yet the Cloister had always discouraged music. Like most of her memories from before she was kindled, it was likely not worth remembering.

Time meant little as she sang softly to herself, the melody shepherding streams of thought to and fro as she stood guard. One recurrent image kept floating across her mind—Myronor's eyes burning through her as he cornered her near the falls. Every time the intrusive vision came to her, she placed a cool hand on her cheek to calm herself. The strangeness of him and his gaze without fear. Something else was present in his eyes that day, something that permeated into his behavior of late. She dreaded its meaning.

The Cloister had sheltered her, but she wasn't naive. She had observed for herself how the people of Tanvik conveyed *affection*. She had also witnessed how people conveyed *possession*. Not even the Cloister could keep her sheltered from the possessive nature of people—the few who felt entitled to someone simply because they wanted them.

The only time she had ever been kissed was by force, at the Cloister of all places. And in the end, the priests punished her as equally as the assailant. But what she saw in Myronor's eyes by the falls wasn't covetous; it was wishful.

Ophiera wondered what it would feel like to be kissed by someone with desire rather than claim. Her thoughts grew fuzzy as she imagined Myronor's lips against her own. He'd probably smile. She wondered how *that* would feel.

But she shook herself back to reality. There was no future in whatever would come from such an act. The futility of their situation made it easier to push aside the disappointment she felt.

A sudden movement in the darkness caught Ophiera's attention. She stopped singing and halted her breath to listen. For a moment, she thought it had been a trick of her eyes. But then, the rotted marsh undulated again.

"Don't stop," Myronor called out sleepily. "I was enjoying your voice immensely."

"Something is happening in the marsh," she whispered. "Come, tell me what you make of this."

Her eyes did not leave the horizon as she spoke. The movements increased in fervency, a crescendo of vibrating masses. Within moments, the once still, black marsh had transformed into a sea of black waves that seemed to absorb all light. Whatever this disturbance was, it seemed far enough away from them to pose a threat. But even at this distance, she didn't feel safe.

She grasped the hilt of her claymore as Myronor came to her side.

"What...are they?" Myronor asked, his voice inflected with disgust.

Shadowed creatures had begun to emerge onto the road. Dark in the pale moonslight, they crawled from their abyssal marsh, fanning out in jerky, unnatural movements. Some looked like anurolas hopping, small but broken. Others were larger, vaguely resembling the silhouettes of familiar creatures found in the marsh and the wood. When she saw a two-legged mass nearly the size of herself rise from the muck, her lungs collapsed. All the bones had gone missing from her limbs as her skin crawled. For the first time since leaving the Cloister, she felt true terror.

"Whatever they are, even my flames could not eradicate them all. Quickly, up into one of the trees." Ophiera motioned to Myronor, indicating the largest of the trees atop the plateau.

In a flash, he had minimized their gear, placing the tiny bags on his belt. As she knelt to boost him to the lower branches, she saw only the dead fire as evidence of their presence.

Without question, Myronor stepped upon her hands and pulled himself gracefully up to a thick branch. He saddled himself upon the bough before reaching a hand down to Ophiera. She gripped his arm, realizing too late the weight her armor would add. It mattered not as she watched his hand light up in blue and felt the weightlessness of his spell gently lift her. It took her a moment to regain her balance on the thick limb. Turning back toward the marsh, Ophiera watched in horror as masses of the strange creatures poured forth onto the road.

"Should we have gone into the woods?" Myronor asked.

Ophiera turned to him with a sad smile. "The edge of the wood here is dead, likely killed by the same vileness that claimed the marsh. I don't imagine we'd be any safer in there, but at least from here we can see what's coming for us."

"Maybe they won't come this way at all," Myronor said with a hopeful smile. "The way they move, I can't imagine them making it up this hill."

Ophiera prayed he was right. She shifted on the bough, facing out toward the Sloughmire now. More creatures poured from the blackened bog, the variety of shapes and sizes more apparent from the higher vantage point. Her stomach churned at the sight.

The screeching began shortly after.

Wails of horror pierced the night. The sounds varied as much as the creatures themselves. Snorts and croaks, cries and growls. All the noises emanating from the marsh were vaguely familiar yet devastatingly wrong.

"What in the Aether could cause this kind of horror?" Myronor asked. The fear in his voice broke Ophiera's own.

She couldn't afford to be terrified when she had a charge to protect.

"I don't know. But I do know they only crawled out of the muck when the sun had set. Perhaps with sunrise, they'll disappear again. We just have to remain unnoticed until then." Ophiera dropped her gaze to their shadows on the ground. In the bare branches of a dead tree, they might as well be on display to the night. She questioned her choices now; was up here really safer than on the ground?

"I can help with that," Myronor said. He reached a beckoning hand to her. "Come, sit in front of me. It's easier to maintain if we're close."

"Maintain what?"

He patted the bough before him with an incredulous look. "A spell, of course."

Still feeling as if she'd missed some critical point, the movements of the marsh encouraged her forward. She placed her claymore against the center trunk, leaning it against another branch for stability. As she did so, she watched the creatures again. They fanned outward as if seeking something.

Ophiera kept her back to Myronor as she sank onto the branch. Before him, she saddled the limb uncomfortably in her armor. A flash of blue caught her eye.

"Hold this," he said, handing her a small vial. In the moonslight, she couldn't tell what color the potion was, but she did see it shimmered.

"This is a potion, not a spell," she said sarcastically.

He sighed heavily before scooting closer to her. Even through her armor, she felt his warmth pressed against her back. "I'm going to put my arms around your waist," he said.

"W-why, exactly?"

"It will be easier to maintain if we're as near as possible."

"Can you just tell me exactly what—" A scream of demonic anguish cut her question short. That call was nearer to them than any others had been. The monstrosities were getting closer.

She leaned back into Myronor and felt his arms fold around her armored waist. His hands glowed a soft blue across her abdomen, and she watched her armor quiver as if heat rose from it. She turned her gaze to the ground, examining the shadow of the tree. In the light cast by the dual moons, she saw no silhouette of her and Myronor embracing—only shadows of empty branches strewn upon the ground.

"How long can you maintain this?" she asked, turning slightly to find his eyes closed tightly in concentration.

"Holding you? Oh, I could do that a very long time," he said with a smirk.

"The spell," she hissed as quietly as possible. With the sounds of the marsh creeping closer, she feared their conversation might be heard.

"Well, that's why I gave you that mana potion," he said with his eyes closed. "I should be able to make it through the night, but I'll let you know if I need that."

Ophiera faced forward again, frowning. Myronor had already cast his magic to run here, and conjure a meal. She didn't know the limitations of his mana or when he might be in threat of mana-sickness. As she turned the vial in her hand, she wondered how the mana potion could even work. How could she know so little of her charge and his power? Surely Myronor would be glad to answer her questions, but now was not the time. He needed to concentrate.

From her vantage, Ophiera had a clear view of the abandoned campsite, the marsh road, and the distant swamps, both dead and alive. Whatever monstrosities now prowled the darkness, they had thinned as they vacated the bog. Some had fanned out in their direction, drawing ever closer.

Ophiera had never encountered anything like the chaos that now surrounded them. And yet, something about the blackness gave her some feeling she knew she'd felt before. Maybe *feeling* was the wrong word. It wasn't fear or disgust, it wasn't even an emotion. More like a sensation; an awareness she couldn't place.

Myronor set his chin on her pauldron without warning. Goose-bumps broke across her skin as his breath danced across the nape of her neck. This also caused her to feel something quite different. Something quite foreign. Something she also needed to ignore.

The hours slowly passed in the darkness. Periodically, she would turn to check on Myronor. His spell kept them well hidden, but she saw the toll it began to take on him. She felt the tension growing in his arms and wished the laugh lines around his mouth were creased in a grin instead of concentration. Such a serious expression wore oddly on his face.

"You've been quite squirmy," he whispered. "Why do you keep turning?"

"I'm ensuring you haven't fallen asleep," she whispered back, elbowing him gently in the ribs.

His soft chuckle close to her ear sent shivers down her neck. "I would enjoy nothing more than to fall asleep with you in my arms. But alas, I doubt I could keep us invisible while asleep. A shame really."

Another dark beast shrieked into the night, closer still. Her heart jumped, but for more than one reason.

"This is no time for your jokes," she chided quietly. "The beasts are drawing near."

The weight of his chin lifted from her pauldron, and she felt his breath against her ear. "Who's joking?"

Heat flushed through her, but the cries of the marsh kept her anchored in reality.

"You should be. And if you're not...you're a greater fool than I thought," she whispered.

Chuckling again, his grip tightened around her waist, both alarming and exhilarating. The growls sounded so close, surely the creatures were on the road below them now. But she couldn't take her eyes away from Myronor's hands, wrapped around her. Thrill overtook caution and excitement danced with fear. Her heart drummed as if she were about to go into battle.

"Why is it so foolish to desire to hold you?" he said, with lips against her ear.

Swallowing hard, she found her voice tense. "It's foolish to desire anything from me but Retribution."

"Ophiera, you're not only your Oath," he whispered. "Can't you see that by now? You are so much more than scars and duty."

He pressed his lips softly against her neck. The sensation was overwhelming, with warm breath and soft skin on hers. She'd never let someone touch her like this; no one ever dared. And yet she was thrilled that Myronor, of all people, had dared.

A shriek of a creature sounded nearby, shattering their fragile moment with reality. Ophiera turned her gaze toward the road and watched as a massive, blackened beast began to scale the steep plateau.

"It approaches from the road—on the hillside now," she whispered.

"It will find nothing but a cold fire," Myronor said.

All thoughts of their conversation left her as she glared at the disgusting beast rising slowly over the ridge. Survival replaced all other concerns.

Atop the plateau, the creature lumbered in the darkness. Squelching noises escaped with each heavy step. In the dim light of predawn, the creature's silhouette became more than just a smear of black against the night.

The front legs were taller than the rear, and a high mane sat upon its back. From its blunted snout, broken tusks protruded grotesquely, covered in blood or dirt. Though bulky in frame, the creature walked on spindly legs that moved as if attached to puppet wire.

With an overwhelming feeling of disgust, she realized its entire body writhed unnaturally, like a sack of venomous snakes. She watched in disbelief as it rooted through their fire pit with wet, squealing breaths. To her dismay, she realized many of the wagons they had passed upon the road were smaller than this beast.

"What is it?" Myronor whispered.

"It *was* a troynt...but now..."

Ophiera hadn't seen a troynt since she had been first conscripted by the Magistrate. Similar to the sandy boars along the coast, troynts were monstrous cousins from the deep forest. The blight had claimed endless wildlife, but a troynt? Either this was an unlucky beast, or the plague had spread deeper into the Severed Woods than she thought.

With a yowl unlike any other, the troynt called into the night, deafening and anguished. Ophiera felt Myronor squeeze her against the reverberating cry. Respondent howls and croaks and squeals in the distance signaled the creature to leave. It ran down the hillside and past the road, fleeing from sight into the uncorrupted marshlands.

As Ophiera followed the retreating beast with unblinking eyes, she saw masses of blackened creatures returning to the swamp. Relief spread through her; so they would return to their graves with the dawn.

Though the sun still lingered below the horizon, the predawn light illuminated the landscape well enough to relieve Ophiera.

"I think they're receding back to the swamp," she said hoarsely. "We're likely in the clear now."

She watched as the wavering air disappeared from her body with the end of Myronor's spell. His hands remained firmly around her waist, but now he slumped against her, breathing erratically.

"What's wrong?" she asked.

"C-can I have that mana potion?"

Ophiera placed the vial in his upturned palm with a new sense of urgency. He had overspent himself and now fought against the weakness. With one hand, he popped the cork and brought his trembling hand to his lips. Ophiera's eyes followed, her chin on her shoulder as she watched him drink the potion. He took a few deep breaths with his eyes closed, but when he opened them again, his expression relaxed. He stared at her with a sheepish smile.

"Don't do that again," she said.

"What?"

"Drain yourself like that!" she hissed, anger now heating her face. "You should have told me it was too much or asked for the potion sooner."

"Don't look so worried," he said. "I might start to think you actually care for me."

She turned away from him, mad at him and at herself. His arm still held her around the waist, the sensation curbing her anger.

"Thank you," she murmured, slightly embarrassed. "For keeping us hidden."

"Ah, it was nothing," he said, though his chuckle sounded weak.

"We must get to Isyath and send a warning to Feyralis."

"After what we just witnessed, I don't know if a warning is good enough. If only I had an affinity for fire magic, I'd set this whole place ablaze in our wake."

Ophiera shared his sentiment. Whatever this plague was, it needed to be cleansed.

"Let's get going then," she said and shifted against his grip. Myronor loosened his hold of her and quickly dropped to the ground. With a glow of blue, he landed without a shred of grace. She was about to tell him to stop casting, but he turned to her with a smirk.

"If you jump, I'll catch you."

"If I jump, I'll crush you," she said tersely. She knew he wouldn't have the mana left to lift her down, potion or not. She retrieved her claymore from against the tree, but before she turned back to jump, a haunting squeal cut through the air.

Below, Myronor stiffened and turned to face the same monstrous troynt rising again over the hill. It stalked toward the tree, a disgusting mass of rotting flesh and mangy fur. Its skin had peeled away in places, revealing slabs of putrid muscle and rotted bone. The black corruption of the swamp oozed from its mouth, and from its eyes, milky white and dead.

Death lingered within the beast, impossible and yet undeniable.

"Quickly, back up!" Ophiera cried, reaching her hand down to Myronor. But he only stared ahead, wide-eyed with panic. He took a step backward, stumbling over the roots of the tree. His back slammed against the trunk as he slumped to the ground, and there he stayed, slouched, staring, and shocked.

The creature took a sickening step toward him, its milky eyes focused on *her* charge. Suddenly, Ophiera's panic became fury. She gripped the hilt of her claymore, white-knuckled and trembling with anger. She pointed the tip downward and jumped toward the approaching troynt. Stabbing as she fell, she landed hard on the back of the creature, piercing its ribcage with a horrible scrape of steel and bone.

As Ophiera dragged the blade downward, she heard the beast's roar of agony until her feet slammed into the ground. She stumbled, holding onto the lodged claymore for stability. No blood came from the gaping wound. Instead, she was met with the overwhelming stench of rotting flesh and despite herself, she retched.

Pulling her sword from the rotten beast, she staggered backward against the stench, away from where Myronor lay. As she gained her footing, the creature turned to face her.

Ophiera knew there was no time to flee, but she needed to get the creature away from her charge. She dragged her sword in the dirt as she moved away from the tree, the creature's gaze following her. At least it no longer wanted Myronor.

With a piercing squeal, it charged. She didn't have time to make a proper stand, and instead dodged the barreling beast. Exhaustion made her sloppy, and in her evasion, she fumbled her sword. She heard the creature's squelching steps as it rounded on her for another attack. Coming back to a stand, she kicked her heels in deeply behind her and lifted her arms, preparing for the attack.

Myronor shouted her name from somewhere behind the monster, but she barely heard him over the beast's ragged, putrid breaths. As it swung its great head toward her, the creature's breath felt like a deadly breeze. She nearly gagged again before gripping hold of the protruding tusks. They were slimy and vile, coated in blackened ichor that burned her skin to touch. Her greaves dug into the rocky ground as it began pushing her backward toward the edge of the hillside, thrashing as it went.

Ophiera began chanting the incantation, her words rattling against the strain. As if aware of her intention, the monster responded with a desperate thrash. Her unscarred hand lost its grip, but it mattered not. As long as her Oath-bearing hand held tight, she could finish the incantation.

A sudden and sharp pain in her abdomen interrupted her chant. As she and the troynt continued to thrash together, she felt an unnatural throbbing from the wound. Straining to breathe, she struggled to finish the chant as they neared the edge of the plateau. A flurry of white flames erupted from her hand and, in an instant, the pale wildfire engulfed the monster. She stumbled forward through a cloud of ash.

The sun broke the horizon, coinciding with a fresh stab of pain in her abdomen. She fought to stand, placing her hand over the wound.

She had gotten sloppy. Stupid even. Had she ever been injured like this before?

The pain overwhelmed her, forcing her to collapse to her knees. She watched through blurred vision as Myronor ran to her, golden hair falling around his horrified face.

"Well, I think we're evenly matched now for idiotically jumping off things."

A groan was all she could manage in response. She pulled her hand away from her abdomen, revealing crimson blood mingled with blackened ichor. She felt it ooze beneath her armor, warm and sticky and on fire.

"Y-you're injured?"

"I'm as surprised as you are," she said through gritted teeth. Nothing had ever penetrated her armor before, and she still felt the shock of it. She attempted to stand, but the wound screamed in pain, causing her head to swim. She couldn't find the strength to stand. What the hell was wrong with her?

"Ophiera—we need to remove your armor now!"

Myronor reached for her and began undoing the clasps of her breastplate as she kneeled. The wound radiated a pain unlike any she had experienced before. Through the dazed agony, she saw a trickle of smoke rise from her armor as he tossed it aside.

"What...is that?" she said, as the air seemed to vacate her lungs. The smoke now poured from the hole in the armor, surrounded by glistening blackness.

"I don't know, but it ate through your armor, and it consumes you, too!" His voice was shaking as he laid her against the ground. Even though he was gentle, the wound burned through her insides. She looked to her abdomen and saw through torn leathers a dark contamination festering in the puncture.

"How do I stop this?" he pleaded, full of fear.

Was the wound truly so dire? As she felt the burning travel toward her chest, she knew it was. Darkness threatened her vision as claws crept up her spine. It was as if something had ahold of her throat, determined to wring out every last breath.

"G-get away," she commanded in gasps. Even as he backed away, she saw terror marring his face.

In an act of pure instinct, she placed her runed hand atop the one that held the wound and began chanting the same words she had used against the boar. With a scream of agony, she released the holy flames from her hand onto herself.

The pain of the flames was just as she remembered from the Sacramentum. Only this time, her flesh did not char. Smoke rose, but it was the ichor that burned. When the fumes stopped, so did her flames. The pain lingered, but her skin remained unburned. She wished her leathers could say the same. A fist-sized hole had seared through them, framing a deep puncture wound that now flowed red.

"You've purged it," Myronor said in a shaky voice, gently peeling back her torn leathers to inspect more thoroughly. "But this wound is still a problem."

Nothing had ever penetrated her armor before, and it was not for lack of effort. Yet this ichor had allowed the tusk to pierce her plate and wound her as never before. This alone shocked her far more than any amount of blood lost.

"Rheta...?" she said, trailing into silence as a dizzying wave crashed against her.

Myronor pulled the potion case from his boot, enlarging it with shaking hands. He began to rifle through the countless potions within.

"Damn it all—I told her she needed to start labeling the tops of her potions," Myronor groaned. Even through her pain, an amused snort escaped her. "Ah, here—this one looks like it's applied directly to the wound." He held out a small jar for her to see.

She reached for the jar, willing to try anything to stop the bleeding.

"I'll do it—your hands are filthy." He pushed her arm away and she hadn't the strength to fight him.

Moments ago, he was frozen with fear, yet now his hands were steady as he dabbed the salve on her wound. It stung enough to distract her from his touch, but only just.

After he dressed the wound in scraps of linen from her bag, Ophiera attempted to stand again. Myronor offered to help her, but as he said, her hands were still filthy. She swayed the moment she stood but Myronor steadied her by the elbow.

Weakened as she felt, there was no time to waste. Her dark breastplate still held traces of the smoking ichor. She heard the sizzling sounds near the tusk-sized hole, the edges of which revealed the original golden sheen of her armor. The dark ichor had eaten away the metal, leaving behind pockmarks and jagged edges. She bent with a hand to the ground and chanted again to call upon the cleansing flames.

Whatever the ichor was, the holy flames worked effectively against it. She turned back, looking to the blackened marsh in thought. Was the ichor from the troynt the cause of the marshland's decay? If the Aether was effective against it, maybe she could...But no. Even if she were fully rested, she could never call upon enough of the Aether to cleanse the extent of its spread. This problem was far beyond her power, and far beyond her duty. All she could do was hope beyond hope that the tiny village of Isyath had yet to see the darkness they had only just survived.

~ Seventeen ~

HOSPITALITY

"An inn sounds too good to be true after last night," Myronor said as he searched the horizon ahead.

Thinking about their destination, Ophiera felt the same sense of relief. "The marsh has been clear of the blight so far today, so Isyath must be untouched. And we'll arrive well before dark."

The promise of a soft bed and strong drinks kept Ophiera's pace quick, even in the face of utter exhaustion. Neither had slept the previous night as they huddled together, waiting out the screams of the blackened creatures.

Ophiera's wound had quickly healed thanks to Rheta's unction, adding an illusion of time passed since the ordeal. At the start of the morning, she had felt a stabbing pain with every step, but now it had dulled to discomfort. The salve had worked as well as any the shaman in Iluka had made.

"You've stayed in Isyath before?" Myronor asked.

"It's been years since I've passed through. But I've stayed there more often than anywhere else."

"Good drinks?" he asked with a smirk.

"Yes, but that's not why. Isyath sits at the crossing of the marsh road and several other of the old paths. The first and last way station near the Sloughmire. And the innkeeper there is nearly as well-informed as Rheta."

"You know them well?" Myronor eyed her.

She took a deep breath, considering. "I don't know anyone well. I've just known him the longest."

The conversation ended as breathing again became the priority. The border of the Sloughmire was green and vibrant now, rich with tall reeds and noisy wildlife. She feared this beautiful land would soon succumb to the hellish pestilence they had left behind. The Southern Coastlands and Feyralis shared borders with this realm, leaving them vulnerable to its spread.

The Cloister needed to be informed almost as urgently as the Magistrate. She was the last kindled to leave the Cloister with an Oath of Retribution. And there was no possible way she held enough power to cleanse the Sloughmire. But perhaps there were other weaknesses to exploit, other ways to coax the Aether into destroying the plague on the land. Surely the priests could find a way, couldn't they? Surely the Chaplain would take this threat seriously, wouldn't he? She hoped it was only exhaustion that fueled her doubts.

When they finally arrived at Isyath, the sun teased the onset of nightfall with a bloodred sunset. It looked as beautiful as it was disconcerting.

Isyath was more a way station than a village. The only structures were the inn, a stable, and a few pieced-together shanties, sometimes inhabited by a handful of colorful vagrants, more often abandoned. The courier's shed sat next to the stables, but Ophiera couldn't tell if it was occupied at the moment. Isyath shared their courier with a few villages of the Southern Coastlands, including Iluka. If the innkeeper kept to his habits, then he'd never send a courier on the marsh road, blight or not. Too dangerous, and not enough places to pick up news along the way.

Isyath was a place to pass through, a crossroads of new and old paths. The first and last stop through the Sloughmire for those on their way to Quargonia. The last place to turn around, or head south into the coastlands.

A hand-painted sign swung in the breeze outside the familiar inn, and Ophiera smiled. A single indigo flower, painted with accents of yellow and white, looked just as vibrant as she remembered. Beneath the flower, a dark, curvy script read: The Lonely Iris.

Luckily, the stables sat empty, and Ophiera guessed they'd be the only guests tonight. She swung the dirty wood door wide and stepped into the small tavern, overwhelmed at once by a wave of nostalgia.

Sparse tables and chairs were cobbled together, worn and empty. She doubted more than a single table had ever been occupied in the establishment. If it had, she'd never borne witness.

Lush green plants filled every windowsill, spilling over as if a tangled jungle encroached through the glass. Many bloomed brightly with the season, while others vined across the walls, unguided and unpruned. She used to have their names, scents, and uses memorized but now she only recognized a few. From the rafters hung dried herbs and more flowers, including a lone, preserved iris suspended in the center of the room.

Behind the bar stood a massive man, tall and wide. He wore his auburn beard braided artfully over his bulging midriff. His skin had the texture of worn leather, engraved heavily around the aged dark eyes. His coal-like gaze moved to the door as he wiped a mug with a dingy rag.

"Lass!" he boomed. His thick arms opened wide. "Where ye been all me life?"

"Lotus!" Ophiera smiled, swelling with relief as she reached the bar. "It's been too long."

Myronor followed her lead, quietly inspecting the establishment as he joined her at the bar. She clasped the barman's arm tightly in greeting. They kept hold until one of them winced, and even though Lotus wore thick bracers adorned with silver vines, Ophiera always held out longer.

"Yer gonna break me arm one of these days," Lotus shouted, shaking his arm out with a grin. His face fell as he eyed her up and down suspiciously. "The hell happened to yer armor?"

Few could hold a candle to Lotus's charm, and she was glad to see he hadn't changed. But her smile faltered as Myronor stuck his hand out in greeting, taking claim for the blackened armor. Before he could open his mouth, Ophiera intervened.

"Myronor did it," she blurted, pushing his hand away, down to the bar. "He's the newly appointed Ambassador to Krysas and my new charge, courtesy of the Magistrate. I needed to keep a low profile, so he helped me darken the armor."

If Lotus had played their little game with Myronor, he'd certainly break the mage's arm. Luckily, Lotus feigned ignorance and continued to wipe his cups. Most would have taken offense, but the mage simply smiled as he looked around.

"I love what you've done with the place," Myronor added. "You must *really* like plants."

"The way I understood it, ye had retired," Lotus grunted, again ignoring Myronor.

"Me too. But you know how the Magistrate works. I'm officially conscripted...again." She did not mean to growl as she spoke, but the way Myronor's eyes darted downward, she knew she had failed.

"So, they brought ye back to serve as some politician's bodyguard?" Lotus said huffily. "Idiots...Waste of yer talent."

The massive man turned to the keg and filled two steins with his oaken mead. He had spent years perfecting the recipe using bog honey from the apiary out back.

The first mug dropped in front of Ophiera with a thud, and after a momentary pause, the other before Myronor. Charming *and* capricious; that was Lotus.

"Waste or not, the Cloister deems me Oath-bound to oblige," Ophiera said, raising her stein in salute.

She hadn't realized how parched she had been until the sweetness touched her tongue. Myronor followed suit, and the two didn't stop drinking until the mugs lay empty. As Ophiera set down her hollow stein, she noticed Lotus watching them with one eyebrow raised.

"Is my room available?" she asked, cutting off whatever question brewed behind his dark eyes. They would get to that business in a moment.

"Aye..." Lotus's bushy eyebrows furrowed as he looked between Ophiera and Myronor. "I'm sure ye remember, there's only one bed...I got room in the stable for yer charge."

Ophiera rolled her eyes up toward the rafters, wondering if she would regret her next words. "One bed is fine. We've had a long journey."

Myronor snorted into his empty cup, confirming her regret.

"'Nything for ye, lass," Lotus said, sounding skeptical. "Long journey, eh? Ye both look rough...actually, downright horrible. What in the Aether happened?"

His eyes swept over the layers of sweat and grime caked on her hands, settling on the dark circles beneath her eyes. Exhausted or not, she needed to tell Lotus of the blight on the Sloughmire. But while there would always be trust between them, something strange was happening in this region. She needed answers from Lotus of a different sort.

"We came by the old marsh road," she said calmly. "Have you any news about the route?"

His eyes darkened. "Truthfully, yer the first folk that've come from that way in—oh, say, two months maybe?" He paused, scratching his beard. "Not unusual though. No one travels it 'nymore and many didn't before either. With the main road mostly paved now, well...figured that's why nobody has come from there lately."

"Two months?" Ophiera whispered as her heart sank. The empty stein trembled in her hands as she thought of all the death gone unnoticed. Lotus's giant hand took the stein from her and set it down. He bent low, meeting her eyes with a cocked eyebrow.

"Lass...ye know ye can tell me. What happened that got ye so spooked?"

She felt Myronor's eyes upon her and her breath stalled. No words would come as she thought of the two-legged monstrosity she hoped she'd imagined. But if two months had gone since anyone left that road, then...how many souls had been lost to the plague of the marsh? How many had become monsters like the troynt?

"There's something wrong in the Sloughmire," Myronor began. Whether he sensed her distress or merely enjoyed hearing himself talk, Myronor described their journey to Lotus while Ophiera collected herself.

As the mage spoke, Lotus's face grew darker. His carved features became more pronounced, a terrifying look seldom seen on the man's face. At least Ophiera knew this was the first Lotus had heard of such trouble from the marsh road. It was of little relief.

When Myronor described her battle with the tainted troynt, Lotus glared at her. His eyes dropped, lingering on the hole in her breastplate. There was an uncomfortable silence as Myronor ended the story.

"Now it makes sense why ye both look like hell," Lotus said gruffly. "Lucky for ye, the courier's here. I'll get her goin' to Feyralis by way of Iluka after I get ye settled."

Ophiera opened her mouth, about to explain that she and Myronor were also headed to Iluka. But Lotus cut her off before she could speak.

"And don't ye dare suggest going with the courier. Ye know damn well she's faster than ye without armor running for breakfast. Now, head upstairs and I'll bring ye some supper and more drink."

Ophiera nodded, appreciating how Lotus showed his understanding. She silently led Myronor through the dining room to a small staircase in the corner. At the top of the stairs sat a single room with a familiar wooden door.

It was just as Ophiera had left it.

The room was small. A straw-stuffed bed filled most of the space. Normally, the skylight above the bed provided light during the day, but the room was dark in the evening. Half-burned candles remained by the bedside, just where she left them years ago.

Ophiera reached to light the candle, uncomfortable with the darkness after their evening near the marsh. She heard the door close behind her and twitched despite herself.

"One bed is fine, huh?" Myronor said, his eyebrows raised to the ceiling.

"You can sleep in the stables if you prefer," Ophiera said over her shoulder. She had begun removing her armor, desperate to be relieved of its weight. Neatly atop the corner chair, she stacked the pieces in an old habit. Though the new hole in her breastplate annoyed her beyond reason.

"No, no. I just never expected to share a bed with a paladin," he said slyly. She could hear the tease in his voice, and it did nothing to help the burn rising in her face. There was only one way to win with him.

"If you're uncomfortable or incapable of sharing, we can duel for the bed; loser takes the floor," Ophiera said, resting her claymore in the corner.

Myronor laughed, shaking his head in defense. "That won't be necessary."

Relieved of the weight, Ophiera sat on the edge of the bed wearing only her leathers. Lotus's inn always felt like a haven, but after what they had just encountered, that feeling couldn't be truer. She thought back to the many times she had rested at the Lonely Iris as she untied her muddied boots. This was not quite how she had imagined her return to Isyath.

The plague of the marsh was a threat beyond her comprehension. She had fought off her fair share of violent wildlife, but never a creature hanging between life and death itself. The ichor had damaged her armor, the only desecration the plate had ever taken in her employ. And the beast had injured her—a rare occurrence.

While she had often doubted the golden plate was *truly* indestructible, she questioned if Myronor's transmutation had weakened the armor. But she quickly shook that idea off her mind. Instinct told her that either the pestilence itself or the Cloister's armor was at fault. What worried her the most, however, was the state of the Sloughmire. How had it gone unnoticed for months, even by Lotus?

A gentle splash roused her. She turned to watch Myronor conjure water into a large bucket with a struggle. The mana potion only helped so much, it seemed, and he'd restored little during their travels.

He pulled a soap cake and a few scraps of cloth from his bag and dropped them in the bucket. Her own grime and staleness felt even more apparent now. She examined the damaged bodice and the signs of struggle coating her body. She was absolutely filthy.

Before she could ask, he placed the bucket before her, handing her a damp cloth. She thanked him with a nod.

First, she attacked the blood caked beneath her fingernails. Then the grime coating her arms, highlighting her runic scars. Her leathers were a lost cause; they would never be the same again. She hadn't realized how much she'd bled until she began cleaning it away.

Several times over, the cloth was saturated with filth and rinsed away in the clean water. When she had finished cleaning around her nearly healed wound, she realized Myronor had been observing her with a strained expression.

She recalled their conversation in the tree and felt the heat rise again in her face. Myronor opened his mouth to speak, but a knock from the door silenced him.

"Come in," Ophiera said, relieved by the interruption.

Lotus entered the room bearing a tray laden with stacks of flatbread and two enormous bowls of vegetable curry. The overflowing mugs of oaken mead frothed and jiggled as he carefully placed the tray on the rough dressing table.

"Got yer favorite here, lass," he said proudly.

"It smells amazing."

The mere aroma of rich herbs and stewed vegetables in a spicy sauce was nearly as satisfying as actually *eating* what Lotus cooked. It was true Lotus was no mage, but he performed magic in the kitchen.

"'Nything for ye, lass," he said again with a smile.

She noticed on the tray sat a small vase carrying a goldencress bloom, a habit of Lotus's to complete every meal with a flower. The intense yellow of the delicate petals, however, brought to Ophiera's mind something far less enjoyable.

"Do you know anything about a group of bandits wearing yellow armbands, by chance?"

Lotus's face fell, and Ophiera could sense his rage flooding the room.

"Aye."

"Who are they?" She asked, perhaps a bit too aggressively, because Lotus's expression continued to darken.

"They're called the Vespula Brotherhood."

"What kind of name is that?"

"Dunno. But if 'ny other than ye, lass, mentioned that name in this establishment, I would throw 'em through the wall."

She tried to keep her expression nonchalant. "Do you know where they come from? A hideout? A camp?"

Lotus cocked his head to the side, an expression far more dangerous on him than on Myronor. "Why ye askin', lass?"

Now she was the one to cock her head in challenge. "You know better than anyone else *why*. My Oath requires Retribution, and if they are anathemas, then I must—"

"No," Lotus said, moving to the doorway. "I won't send ye to yer death, lass. Leave 'em be, ye hear? Focus on the task at hand. Them's yer words."

Ophiera snorted in annoyance. "My death? Lotus, when have I ever—"

"I know yer tougher than a slab o' cheek meat. But that lot is somethin' else. Somethin' *even* the Aspect of Retribution can't handle right now."His eyes lingered on her armor as he spoke.

The use of her title sobered Ophiera. Lotus never called her by the name the Cloister had given her. With this final warning, Lotus strode from the room, shutting the door angrily behind him—moody as ever.

Nothing—truly nothing—frightened that man. And if Lotus refused to provide her any information about these bandits, she feared what it must mean.

"So...you plan to go after these Vespulas now?" Myronor asked with no hint of a smile.

"I was gathering information on a continuing threat to our travels," she said defensively. "Besides, you heard how unhelpful Lotus was—I wouldn't even know where to start looking for them."

His blue eyes saw through her feeble excuses. "That death swamp posed more threat to us than these bandits have, didn't it? Why are you fixated on them?"

"I am not *fixated*," Ophiera said tersely.

She wasn't. A feeling deep in her gut told her this Brotherhood was responsible for more than they let on.

"The five of their faction I've run across have been anathemas, so it's reasonable to assume the remainders are as well. They will continue to besmirch the Aether unless someone—unless *I* end them."

"But your Oath—"

"My Oath demands Retribution against the likes of them," she spat.

What did he or Lotus know about her Oath? More than anyone else, but not more than herself, the one who bore the burden.

She took a deep breath, recognizing the question in Myronor's eyes. "But I am bound by the oath of our journey first and foremost. Which is why I was simply looking for information."

Myronor stood abruptly, and she thought he made to storm out of the room. But instead, he carried and placed the tray of food between them.

"Can we just agree to have a moment in which we do not discuss your life in peril, past, present, or future?" He ran a hand through his hair, his brow knit tightly in frustration. "Each time I close my eyes, I see you wrestling with that demon or bleeding on the ground. I don't want to think about this Brotherhood too, knowing they've tried to best you more than once. I just need a moment's peace—not another threat to consider."

Ophiera sat silent a moment. She didn't understand how her fight against the troynt affected him more than her killing two men. Like Myronor, she found herself tired as well. But this had been her way of life—a never-ending string of violence and exhaustion. She'd been used to feeling tired of everything, all the time, well before her retirement. It disturbed her how quickly she fell back into the cycle.

"Why don't you call Mallow out a bit?" she suggested, finally collecting her thoughts. "She's always a welcome distraction."

Myronor smiled sadly, nodding in agreement. Soon Mallow appeared from her crystal, enticed by the new location. As usual, she first inspected every corner of the room, interrogating at great length each strange object in the small chamber.

As she wandered nearer and nearer, Ophiera offered her the remains of her bowl of curry. She wasn't sure if the spices sat well with her kind, but the familiar seemed to thoroughly enjoy Lotus's cooking.

The distraction had been a success. Myronor seemed a bit more chipper. His smile widened each time he stroked Mallow's sumptuous coat. They sat together like this, slowly decompressing from the last few days with food, drink, and Mallow's company.

Eventually, they readied themselves for bed, and Ophiera stretched out on the straw mattress, still in her battered leathers. The bed was nearly as familiar as her own back in Iluka.

She glanced over to see Myronor, yet again, removing his clothes without warning. In addition to her normal embarrassment, though, she found herself quite distracted.

Myronor claimed to be a scholar, but his physique suggested otherwise. With his back to her, she saw now why he was able to swim so fast. He still reminded her of the young fishers in Iluka, yet the mage didn't lift a finger to be blessed with his physique. Lucky bastard.

He turned abruptly and caught her gaze with a smirk. Flustered, she spat, "I hope you're not planning to sleep nude."

He snorted. "I don't know where your mind is, pervert. I'm changing into clean clothes for sleep." From his pack, he tossed a familiar tunic to Ophiera. "In case you wish to do the same."

Begrudgingly, she accepted.

"Turn around."

He watched her far too intently. "And what if I don't?"

For someone who wanted a moment's peace, why must everything be a fight with him?

Ophiera pulled the tunic on, overtop her leathers. He raised an eyebrow in question, but she kept her glare on him in silence. In an act like a contortionist, she undid her leathers under the cover of the oversized shirt.

Myronor still stood bare-chested, his own shirt still in his hand, observing the entire ordeal with a smirk.

"Ah, so you *can* do magic."

Exasperated, she refused to respond and instead pulled one of the hand-knit blankets up over her shoulder. A light floral scent imbued everything Lotus made, and the blanket was no different. She really missed the Lonely Iris.

The bed shifted with Myronor's weight. It only occurred to her now that she had never shared a bed before. It was only after she had left the Cloister that she had even had a proper bed.

His words from the previous night echoed in her mind. *I would enjoy nothing more than to fall asleep with you in my arms.* Why did that pop into her head now? The logistics seemed awkward, sleeping while being held. Borderline uncomfortable. Foolish even. Yet her stomach twisted at the mere thought.

"Ophiera?" he whispered.

"Hmm?"

"If you knew the Brotherhood's location, would you really seek them out?" he asked solemnly.

She paused a moment in consideration.

"Yes."

He sighed heavily, without amusement. "And you think I'm the fool."

~ Eighteen ~

DISTRACTION

Ophiera awoke early to find Myronor deep asleep, limbs draped haphazardly as gentle snores escaped him. He had slept like a freshly caught rubyfin, flopping and flailing around most of the night, despite his stillness now.

The peaceful expression he wore caused her to watch him for some time, just to ensure he drew breath. She was only concerned because he was her charge—that was all. For the same reason, she covered him gently with a blanket before quietly leaving the bed.

Maybe she was the fool between them after all.

Curled into a ball between their pillows, Mallow watched Ophiera dress. Despite being in the safety of the inn, she needed to feel the weight of her armor today. Sleep had done little to chase away the horrible visions of the Sloughmire. Her pride took longer to heal than the wound itself, and the armor at least provided a feeling of security. As did her claymore.

Myronor continued to sleep, undisturbed by her actions. She couldn't decide if she was stealthy or if he slept like a boulder. It didn't hurt to let him sleep longer, especially with Mallow to watch him. Quietly, she unlatched the door and snuck silently downstairs.

As usual, the tavern was completely empty. She often wondered if it really qualified as a tavern, given the general lack of customers. The Lonely Iris was more like Lotus's home, which he occasionally opened up to a rare guest. She was likely his most frequent customer, even if she never paid.

A dreary gray dawn broke through the windows, but the plants transformed the muted light into a warm glow. Each time she visited, the place seemed a bit more of a greenhouse and a bit less of a tavern. Ophiera perched herself on one of the low stools by the bar and listened to the ruckus back in the kitchen.

A moment later, Lotus plowed through the archway behind the bar. As he caught sight of Ophiera, he faltered and nearly spilled the breakfast tray held in one hand.

"Damnit, lass—ye can't do that to me," he muttered, free hand over his heart. "I don' have the constitution for it 'ny more."

"I didn't want to disrupt you. I know how you get when people go back there."

"Aye, aye, ye got me there," Lotus said and shook his head. "I know yer an early one, so I whipped up a little somethin' special."

He slammed the tray in front of her. Charming and capricious, but never graceful. The stack of round, crispy cakes had nearly toppled over on three small clay pots. One held warmed bog honey, another clotted cream, and the final, macerated chokecherries. Emotion stung her throat and hunger panged her stomach as she took in the sight.

"Pancakes?"

"Aye." He beamed. "I still remember ye as that wee little thing, dirty and ravenous on yer way to the Cloister."

"Thank you, Lotus," she breathed, taking in the aroma of the delectable treat. The first bite always reminded her of the first time she had tasted the sweet honey layered between yeasty cakes.

Ophiera hadn't met her eighth year when the Cloister had plucked her from the streets of Feyralis. The robed cleric had persuaded her and several other street urchins to come with them, promising shelter and food and a life of meaning. None of the children knew what they would sacrifice in exchange. Sometimes Ophiera wished she had trusted her instinct, and stayed far away from the charming cleric and his silent priests.

Their new life had begun immediately. Crammed into a small caravan, the priests drove the oxen hard. Ophiera remembered how sick the motion and stale air had made her. Looking back, they must have traveled the marsh road then, as it was the fastest way to Isyath from Feyralis. The Cloister's caravan damaged a wheel along the way, and they were forced to stop in Isyath for the repairs.

Ophiera remembered her naive excitement, hoping to stay at a real inn like the traveling merchants. But her hopes had rapidly disintegrated as the silent priests ushered the children into the stables, forcing them to huddle upon the ground for the night.

A cleric instructed the barkeep to provide them no food, only water—the start of their training to live without. But Lotus refused to house anyone under his roof without providing. The man's heart was bigger than his belly. During the night, he snuck trays of pancakes out to the stables. It would be the last meal for many of them.

Now, each time she passed through Isyath, Lotus prepared this specialty for Ophiera. He had done so much for her over the years. And yet withheld from her what she really needed now.

"Why won't you tell me about the Vespula Brotherhood?" she asked.

He rolled his eyes up to the rafters and heaved a great sigh. "I knew ye wouldn' drop it."

"Then just tell me and I won't bother you further," she said.

"I'm still not gonna tell ye where they be, but I'll tell ye what I know about 'em." Even though the hour was early, Lotus reached for two clean steins and filled them with mead.

"These Vespulas, they're *not* bandits. There're rumors...evidence even, that they're dabblin' in things no one has a right to dabble in. It goes deeper than jus' some raiders with a bit o' magic. Like most of Tanvik, they renounced the Cloister...but they've taken it further and desecrated the Aether purposefully as well. They torture and kill without hesitation. Word is they take sacrifices fer their rituals to some new god, something in opposition to the Aether. The Magistrate knows their numbers are growin'...the Justicar o' Feyralis will sort it out soon, don't ye worry, lass."

This was not what Ophiera had hoped to hear. Especially the hesitancy in Lotus's voice when he spoke of Eliana. How could Eliana know of the Vespula Brotherhood and not have tasked Ophiera with dispatching them? She was the Magistrate's executor of Retribution, but they'd conscripted her to investigate the murder of a diplomat. Her Oath was better suited to deal with the Vespula Brotherhood, not to investigate and escort. So if not Retribution, exactly what was the Magistrate doing to combat the Vespula Brotherhood?

"Lotus...I may have caught the Brotherhood's attention," she confessed. "I claimed five of their faction for the Aether already. And two others encountered us but fled. I fear what they may know of my route, my charge... What if they followed us here?"

Laughing, Lotus slapped the counter. "Lass, ye need to stop bein' so *dire* all the time. They prolly just fled 'cos between ye and that man upstairs, well, yer quite an intimidating pair, ya know? And here? Ye know I can handle meself. None have taken this inn yet, and they won't 'nytime soon."

She truly wanted to believe him, but could only play with the swirls of honey and cream smeared across her empty plate.

"Come help me in the kitchen, lass," Lotus huffed, escaping behind the archway behind the bar. "We can keep chattin' while I get today's curry goin'."

Ophiera gazed up at the attic, where she presumed Myronor still lay fast asleep. He would be safer there than venturing into Lotus's kitchen, that was for certain.

For some time, Ophiera helped Lotus prep his seasonal curry for the day. Together, they ground spices and chopped vegetables while Ophiera recounted her experiences since leaving Iluka. Lotus was always a good listener, oohing and grunting throughout, but never interrupting. He particularly enjoyed her recount of the tantrum against the statue in the Magistrate and had laughed for far too long at Myronor's solution of a stiff drink.

"Aye, so the lad has brains, after all," Lotus said, wiping a tear from his eye. "Thought he seemed a bit vacant, meself."

And there it was. Lotus had begun his signature tactic for acquiring information. Rather than asking directly, he always provided his opinion and banked upon the other person to volunteer their own in agreement or argument. Usually, Ophiera refused to entertain his little sleuthing games. But she felt the need to say her thoughts aloud, more for her own sake than his.

"He's naive but not stupid. He constantly smiles like a fool, but he did save my life. And despite this business with the Magistrate and knowing I can burn someone alive with a few words, he's been...very kind."

She wondered if "very kind" described his actions of late. Did she only see kindness in his eyes when he cornered at the falls? Was holding her throughout the night in the death marsh only kindly? Were his words too when he claimed her more than her Oath?

"I still don' like the way he looks at ye."

Ophiera chuffed. "I did think him a pervert at first. But the only look he has is one of question or of laughter. Besides, you've seen what I can do with a claymore if he tries—"

"Ye know what I mean, lass! I'm sayin' ye should protect yer heart, and a claymore won't help with that."

Ophiera remained silent, her heart churning like the curry bubbling in the pot. Her heart had no business in this matter. He was her charge—a duty—a task she never wanted. When she thought of something happening to him, it was her Oath that rebelled against the notion. Not her heart.

Then why did her chest ache now as she remembered his vesper?

Without a word, she walked out of the kitchen, hoping Lotus hadn't seen her face. She hadn't told Lotus she saw Myronor's vesper. And now, as she paced through the tavern with worry, she wondered *why* such an act was taboo. If that beautiful, pale blue orb hadn't shown itself to her, where would she be now? Traveling alone to Krysas, still Oath-bound to investigate the former Ambassador's death most likely. Would she have had to escort a different Ambassador? Or would she have had to go alone? Neither prospect felt right. But knowing she would soon be traveling with Myronor again did.

She cursed Lotus under her breath for making her think such things.

Restless, she decided Myronor had slept long enough. Maybe seeing him would put an end to these silly thoughts. She stopped her pacing and climbed the stairs to the attic room. As she reached for the door handle, she noticed the door itself was ajar. She knew she'd latched it shut this morning.

Caution gripped her as she pushed the door open to find the room empty. The bed lay askew, though the room remained otherwise normal. But Myronor was nowhere in sight.

Her heart began to thrum with panic.

In a creamy blur, Mallow leaped out from under the bed, mewling as frantically as Ophiera felt.

"Where is he, Mallow?" Ophiera asked. The desperate cat jumped up on the mattress. Her black paw dragged at a piece of cloth strewn across a pillow.

Ophiera's vision blurred as she snatched the strip of cloth and marched downstairs. "Lotus!"

"Lass?" The burly man bustled out from the kitchen, gawking at her hand and shaking his head. "Wha—No, lass, no..."

Between her scarred fingers, Ophiera held out a cloth of goldenrod yellow. As yellow transformed to white, caught aflame by her runic arm, the ashes fell to the ground.

~ Nineteen ~

GLOAM

A deep chill consumed Myronor in the darkness. His wrists ached, sticky with blood as tight bonds cut deep into his skin. Through the foggy thoughts, he remembered. Cursed, concussed, or drugged, it didn't matter—someone had incapacitated him at the Lonely Iris. He remembered Mallow hiding from sight just before everything went dark. Next, he awoke bound and beaten in the icy cold. At least his familiar had escaped. But what about Ophiera?

Sudden screams brought him to awareness. He tried to look for the source, but the darkness suffocated him. He hated the dark. It felt too familiar. Too much like the forbidden space he traversed when he spanned.

He had told Ophiera that spanning was instantaneous travel, but he had lied. He didn't want to tell her of the dark place he had to cross, the suffocating in-between he hated so much.

Concentrating, he thought of the Lonely Iris and tried to call upon the power he swore to never use to return him there. But nothing happened. Whatever material constrained him seemed to consume his mana and block his magic, leaving him utterly helpless.

He struggled against his bonds, but they wouldn't budge. In the process, he felt the minimized potion case still within his boot. At least he had gotten dressed before his assailants had arrived. Normally, the concoctions would aid him now, but without the use of his magic, he might as well have left them at the Lonely Iris.

A callous, feminine voice called out from a distance. "Bring them to the altar!"

Myronor's mind spun, his thoughts tangling over the terrifying cries. Both his skull and heart felt as if they might split. Where in Erum was he, and why was there an altar?

Suddenly, the darkness broke into a slit of light. He was slow to recognize the open tent flap before him. Beyond, he saw a dusk-colored sky.

Two figures entered the tent. One, wearing black robes, held a pale lantern. The other wore similar garb of bright yellow, and both approached him. Up close, he saw they both wore tabards with strange adornments. At first, he thought them decorative, but as he studied them, they looked vaguely like runes or glyphs.

The black-robed figure held the lantern to his face and without warning, struck him hard with a closed fist.

"You stand before the Reverend," she hissed. "Show your respect." Her voice was the one he'd heard only moments before. Something about it made his skin crawl.

"Technically, I'm sitting..." he said with an aching jaw. "And tied to a post, mind you, so you'll forgive my lack of a curtsy."

She struck him again. And again. Each blow sent fresh shock waves through his already aching skull. He wished she would hit him harder and relieve him of his consciousness. The beating continued until his mouth flooded with blood that dribbled down his chin.

"Enough, Marvena. He needs to be alive for her to come."

The voice of the yellow-robed man was high-pitched, icy, and unnatural. Myronor's vision blurred, but through the haze hung a gaunt face, drained of vitality in the lantern light. The putrid yellow of his robes did him no service, highlighting each of his sickly features.

Myronor laughed.

"I fail to find the humor in your situation," the Reverend said, icy and disgusted.

Myronor spat a mouthful of blood to the floor before smiling up at the man. "No one even hit you and yet your face is absolutely ghastly."

He seized Myronor by the hair, adding to his growing list of aches.

"Ah, well, we were just prettying you up to see your paladin friend."

Myronor felt his stomach turn. He spat more blood, this time into the sickly face of the Reverend. "Where is she?"

The Reverend chuckled, wiping the blood from his face with a claw-like finger. He licked his hand as if it were crimson honey, savoring the taste with rolling eyes.

"Well, that's the question...Hopefully she'll be here, soon enough. We're counting on you to draw her to us."

Though his heart sank, Myronor held his composure. "Joke's on you; she won't come for me."

The Reverend laughed, a cold, pitched cackle. "You scholarly types are always poor liars. Whether you want her to or not, she'll come. She's bound to you by powers she can't deny. She'll come, even knowing it means her death. It will be quite the show, I assure you."

Marvena peeked her head through the tent flap. "Reverend, the sacrifices are in place...Shall we begin?"

"I suppose." He simpered, releasing Myronor's hair. "I will be back for you once your friend arrives. To think, our task will end so soon; the Mistress will be pleased, Marvena. Very pleased."

"What could the Vespula Brotherhood possibly want with her?!" Myronor screamed, his rage cracking his voice.

The Reverend froze at the entrance to the tent. "You may know who we are, but it will do nothing to stop what we've already begun." He took another step outside but hesitated again. "Marvena—I changed my mind. Bring him with you. Let him witness exactly what we want with her."

As the Reverend left, Myronor felt rough hands behind him, untying his binds from the post. It was too much to hope Marvena had removed them completely. With his wrists still tied together, Marvena yanked on the rope connecting them. He fell face-first into the dirt.

"Get up," she hissed. She yanked the rope again, digging the binds further into his skin.

Myronor struggled to stand, only to be dragged out of the tent on unstable legs. He fell again outside.

"I said up!"

Another blow to his face, another fresh mouthful of blood. Pained and tired, he stood again. One of his eyes had begun to swell, blurring his vision. As he took in the sights before him, he wished he had gone completely blind.

Throughout the dark clearing stood dozens of people adorned with yellow armbands. Their gazes fell on a massive, black stone altar in the center of the clearing. It was too dark to see anything beyond the altar but dead trees. They were in the woods, but that was all he could discern.

Near the altar stood three people, distinct from the rest. Bound and beaten, all three wept as the Reverend approached. An elderly woman and two young men in farmhand clothes.

Marvena's voice slithered by his ear. "The Reverend wants you to pay attention. He wants you to understand how futile resistance is against us."

Dread filled his heart as he watched the scene unfold before him.

"Brothers and sisters!" the Reverend cried, and the crowd cheered. "Today we offer these souls to the Void and into the embrace of Aud!"

The crowd's jeers drowned out the sobs from the three bound people by the altar. Myronor couldn't look at them. Not only was he helpless, but pathetic too.

"Tonight, I claim these souls for Aud and in exchange, the Abyss Mother will provide me the power to destroy her enemy: that which is born of the Aether!"

The crowd cheered in unison. "May the Void consume us all!"

Myronor's very soul turned to ice, his mind fogging in panic and dread. His thoughts filled with the family they'd saved on the road. Was he about to witness their fate had Ophiera not intervened?

The Reverend grabbed one of the young men by the binds and dragged him to the altar. He was screaming but Myronor couldn't hear him over the crowd's chants.

"May the Void consume us all!"

The Reverend held the man by the hair, pinning him over the stone altar. With a flash of silver, the Reverend slit the man's throat and blood poured over the stone like a waterfall.

Myronor retched and turned away, only to feel cold fingers yank him forward by the hair.

"Pay attention," Marvena said, nearly giddy. "You'll miss the good part."

She held him, facing forward to the altar. The young man's body lay slumped over the stone as the crowd grew quiet. From his corpse rose a brilliant green vesper, illuminating the vacant eyes below. It was a horrifying and beautiful sight. The vesper held no trace of blackened distortions—only pure, beautiful vitality. This shade was nothing like the corrupted vespers he'd witnessed Ophiera claim. But before his very eyes, the shade changed. Rather than disintegrating into the ground as the other vespers had done, this one began to turn black.

With a loud crack and a shockwave in the air, the darkened vesper collapsed in on itself, leaving but a tendril of dark smoke behind. Myronor watched, horrified, as the Reverend inhaled the fleeting smoke through his nostrils. His mind was going blank as the air grew heavy. He couldn't draw breath. He couldn't understand.

A dark sensation washed over Myronor, the same sinister feeling he'd had in the dead marsh. A sensation he'd encountered even before that. In the dark place. An all-consuming, blackened vortex that threatened his very soul. All souls.

Only a moment of silence passed as the oppressive atmosphere lifted. The crowd cried in celebration.

"Hail Aud!" the Reverend roared over the crowd in a triumphant voice.

Tears flowed down Myronor's face as he collapsed to the ground. He heard Marvena's taunts, but barely felt the tug on the binds or the kicks to his gut as she tried to rouse him. He couldn't move. He couldn't do anything but watch as the Reverend pulled his next victim to the alter to repeat the process.

His mind shut down in a blur of numbness.

Only when Myronor was tied again to the post in the tent did he regain some of his awareness. He wished he hadn't.

Three innocent people had been murdered before him. Three pure, beautiful vespers turned into blackened smoke. And the crowd...the crowd...they *cheered*.

These were not bandits. They were fanatics. A cult of anathemas, gathered in terrifying numbers, committing atrocities he couldn't comprehend. He *felt* the powers the Reverend drew upon, the familiar darkness from a place never meant to be seen.

Ophiera had been right all along. She had guessed they would use him against her. She thought the Vespula Brotherhood was likely responsible for more sins than she knew. He should have never doubted her.

Now, his only hope of escape was Ophiera. And yet he desired for her to never set foot here. Not when they so desperately wanted her dead.

Blood trickled from his mouth onto the ground in a rhythmic drip. He was so useless. He couldn't do anything to save the sacrifices, to save himself, to save Ophiera.

Perhaps his idea of a linked fate had always been naive. The vision of Ophiera, chanting above him on the riverbank, flooded his mind. Something about this moment connected him to her in a way he could not explain. She was *meant* to find him, *meant* to heal him, *meant* to journey with him. She was meant to be with him. But now they were destined to die together instead.

Despite the encroaching darkness, his thoughts still lingered on Ophiera. He desperately pictured her face. Not the fierce face she wore in battle, but the soft, beautiful expression she wore while swimming in the falls or playing with Mallow. With a pang of longing, he thought of holding her through the night in the dead marsh and the words he had confessed to her there.

He wished he had confessed more. He wished he had told her of his mother and the mess she created. He wished he had told her his true intentions for becoming the next Ambassador. He wished he had told her that, despite her warnings, he was falling in love with her. He thought they had time, but he was wrong, so terribly wrong.

~ Twenty ~

RETRIBUTION

Voices yelled outside of the tent, pulling Myronor back to an agonized wakefulness. Dim sunlight leached in through the cracks in the canvas, and many voices melded together in the ruckus.

"Get the mage!" someone yelled. "She's here!" cried another. The words nudged his memory as important. But he couldn't navigate the haze of his mind to know why.

Two figures entered the tent; Marvena and a stranger.

"Get up!" an unfamiliar man yelled.

But Myronor couldn't move. The shock from last night still clung to him, paralyzing him. Then a swift kick to the gut broke his palsy. Black spots filled his vision as the wind vacated his lungs.

"Don't!" Marvena said. "We need to get him to the clearing alive. She's almost upon us!"

She? Who was coming? And why did Marvena sound both pleased and terrified?

He heard screams in the distance, far beyond the tent. They evoked a vision of white hair and amethyst eyes into his mind.

"Get him up before the Reverend becomes angered!" Marvena spat.

Myronor felt himself lifted, untied from the post, and forced to stand. The mana-draining bonds still dug painfully into his wrists, and his legs gave way as he tried to move. The two Vespulas cared little as they dragged him from the tent.

The bright morning light was disorientating, filtered by countless branches of dead and dying trees. The encampment looked more disturbing in the daylight than at night. A decay had taken this part of the forest just like the Sloughmire. There was no green anywhere in the wood—no leaves, no ferns, no plants. Gray gnarls of branches reached toward a feeble sun that could not free them from the blackened ichor oozing from their bark.

Roughly, his captors dragged him through rows upon rows of tents he hadn't seen the night before. There must have been over a hundred people living in this camp. How could such a large faction have gone unnoticed?

He smelled ash on the air before his captors stopped. Shouts and clashes of metal rang out in the distance. With a struggle, he raised his head to see the crowd of Vespulas, weapons drawn.

An uncontrollable urge to call to Ophiera overcame him. He needed to warn her to stay away. As desperate as he was to see his dear friend one last time, he wished she had never come.

Myronor fell at the robed feet of the Reverend, dropped by his escort. The yellow color of his robes looked even more putrid against the gray, dead forest. The Reverend moved behind him, and he felt thin fingers scrape across his scalp, grasping his hair. The cold steel of a blade touched his throat and visions of the blackened altar stalled his breath.

"Let her through!" called the Reverend. His hands shook with manic excitement against Myronor's throat and scalp. Meanwhile, he felt ready to purge at any moment.

The crowd obeyed, parting with weapons still drawn. Framed against the frantic scurry was an exquisite sight, one that soothed Myronor's soul yet tore at his heart.

Ophiera marched toward him, a vengeful purpose in her gait. Her drawn sword shone brightly with flames, illuminating the crimson splatters across her face and armor. Even through the pain, he found her terrifying and beautiful.

"Welcome, Aspect of Retribution!" yelled the Reverend, almost in a cackle.

The paladin stopped when addressed by the title so few knew. Her violet eyes darted through the crowd, assessing her surroundings with destructive intent. But when her eyes found his, they told a very different story. Myronor's heart sank. Neither of them would leave this place alive.

"Greet your friend, rude little mage!" the Reverend scolded him as he pulled painfully on his hair. The knife left his neck, only to slice his cheek with a sharp pain and a warm trickle of blood.

Myronor smiled sadly at Ophiera.

Her eyes were stone as she spoke the words he refused to hear. "Let him live and I will submit."

"A trade?" the Reverend replied.

"My life for his."

"No—" Myronor shouted, but a swift kick landed hard against his stomach, silencing him without breath.

"A negotiating paladin. How impressive!" The bitter man took his knife and cut the bonds that had torn at Myronor's wrists. "I accept."

The confusion that fogged Myronor's mind eased without the bonds. But to his detriment, his mana remained nearly depleted. He was still completely helpless, surrounded by enemies. The reverberating clang of a sword thrown to the ground only served to further his self-pity.

"Restrain her and remove her armor!" the Reverend said before kicking Myronor once more. "And make sure to gag her; can't have her chanting now!"

As Myronor fell to the ground, he watched the crowd converge on Ophiera. The flurry of activity blocked his view as injury and fear kept him facedown in the dirt. Through the frenzy, he caught glimpses of what they were doing to Ophiera. The sight destroyed Myronor's very soul.

Ropes had been wrapped tightly around her bare arms, where they had removed her gauntlets and vambraces. She stood, stretched taut between two dead trees with a thick leather gag across her defeated face. Several people roughly tore the remaining armor from her, tossing the dark pieces unceremoniously in a pile on the forest floor.

The number of times he had watched her carefully remove that armor, only to see it so crudely thrown about, sent him into a fury unlike any other. But Ophiera's eyes found his own and he could almost hear the words within them.

Run.

Someone grabbed him by the hair and dragged him upright.

"Move!"

He recognized Marvena's voice as she threw him to Ophiera's feet. The crowd laughed, stalking around them like starving creatures. Marvena brought a knife to his throat.

So, they had never intended to let him go. Ophiera stared at him with a sickening self-loathing in her eyes. Myronor chanced to speak, knowing this might be his last chance to tell her. "Ophiera! I'm sorr—" But another kick to his ribs interrupted his plea.

Ophiera screamed through her gag.

The yellow Reverend sauntered to her and spoke in a low voice. "I failed to mention, paladin...We never intended to kill the mage. Our Mistress needs him alive—even if barely."

Mistress? Did he mean Aud? And why did they need him?

The Reverend drowned her furious screams with a call to the crowd. "I have been chosen by Aud herself to usher in the Void!" The crowd jeered, yellow armbands shaking in solidarity. "Today, *I* provide the greatest gift to the Abyss Mother! Today, she will feast upon the soul of the Aether itself: the Aspect of Retribution!"

The Reverend grabbed Ophiera by the throat, staring at her as if she were a newfound treasure. Gently, his thin pale lips kissed her forehead. Myronor cried with disgust, matching Ophiera's own violent thrash.

The Reverend staggered backward from her with a hand clutched to his face. A few in the crowd gasped as a trickle of blood fell from his lips. Myronor wanted nothing more than to cheer her well-placed headbutt, but he kept silent.

The Reverend again approached Ophiera, holding his curved knife to her chest. With a flick of his wrist, he cut one strap from her leather top, where it fell loosely to the side, exposing the top of her breast.

She growled as the crowd cheered and laughed.

"Not that, you say?" cackled the Reverend. His frenzied eyes fell on the pile of armor on the ground. "The Cloister has kept the secrets of their so-called paladin's plate well hidden. Brethren, did you know *true* adamantrium armor cannot be destroyed? The metal born of Aether, unadulterated, is resistant to all magic, all weapons. But against the gift of Aud, the Cloister is nothing!"

The Reverend gesticulated methodically in the air above her armor, chanting in a vile, unknown tongue. A moment later, a shred of darkness appeared in the air above the armor. The tear sent a shock wave through the encampment, similar to what Myronor had felt the night before as the vespers imploded upon themselves.

Black, ethereal tendrils descended from the break. The dark tentacles searched blindly, neither liquid nor solid, moving toward the armor in jerky movements. As a dark ichor dripped from the appendages, Myronor felt sick with recognition. The vileness before him was the very same as in the Sloughmire.

The tendrils caressed the armor greedily, covering it in the viscous, vile substance. Smoke rose and a putrid smell stung his throat.

Myronor watched in horror as Ophiera's armor disintegrated, forming a dark stain on the ground.

Muffled screams of pure agony escaped Ophiera's gag, piercing his heart. He watched a piece of her die before him. As quickly as they had appeared, the blackened vines receded into the portal as it closed. Even the crowd appeared relieved by their retreat.

"The gift of Aud *will* defeat the Aether!" the Reverend cried to the cheers of the crowd.

Myronor did not take his eyes from Ophiera, who hung limp as if they had killed her already. He couldn't let her give up. The potion case still pressed against his ankle; if he could only get to it, maybe he could find something, anything to save them.

After the jeers subsided, the Reverend returned his predatory gaze to Ophiera. "For my next trick, I won't require the Abyss Mother's power. Not yet. There are so many other ways to destroy a soul."

Before the words registered in Myronor's mind, the Reverend had rushed him. Yellow robes blocked his vision as the Reverend struck him hard in the jaw. Marvena held his head in place by the hair, forcing him to take the brunt of the blow. His vision swam as he felt the warm gush of blood in his mouth, draining sickeningly down his throat.

Ophiera screamed through her gag, more agonized than when her armor had been destroyed. Another kick to the stomach and Myronor could not help but cry out in pain. Blood sprayed from his lips to the ground and the crowd laughed as Ophiera shrieked. He wished he could die just to end her pain as much as his own.

"Tsk, tsk...The paladin is doing a poor job of upholding her Oath." Another kick came to Myronor's ribs, and he felt a revolting crack. He gasped, but failed to draw any breath. "Why aren't you taking Retribution for this?" Another fist to his jaw caused him to black out for a moment. "Or this!" A knife dragged along his back, slicing through shirt and flesh as warm blood soaked him.

They said they needed him alive, but he couldn't survive much more.

The beating stopped suddenly, and the laughing crowd quieted. Their jeers died, replaced by quiet murmurs. The hand that held his hair dropped him to the ground.

Back against the dirt, he felt relief for a moment. He could die here now, couldn't he? But he could no longer hear Ophiera's screams. He forced his eyes to focus on the trees before him. Ophiera hung limp, strung up and silent through her gag. But the runes upon her arm glowed white-hot.

Without a chant, waves of power emanated from Ophiera before the runes suddenly ignited. Bright white flames overtook her arm and, as if awakening, Ophiera screamed through her gag as the fire slowly engulfed her. Myronor watched the flames reach her leathers, burning them from her, along with her bonds. Her screams never stopped.

Paralyzed, the crowd watched as the blazing form of Ophiera dropped to the ground. She rose slowly, engulfed in pale flames that only revealed her jewel-bright eyes, amethyst against the white. She continued shrieking with an anguish that could have shattered glass, but it only struck his heart.

"Ophiera..." Myronor whispered, barely audible even to himself. She turned her gaze to him, still laid out in the dirt at her feet. He recalled the charcoal sketch in his library. A being of white flames, whose eyes held both pain and triumph.

Without looking away from him, she dropped her hands to the ground, and the world quaked beneath him. Fissures of pale flame opened and spread from her hands like a web of fiery fault lines. The white fire rose from every rift, engulfing the crowd as panicked screams and the smell of burning flesh and ash filled the air.

If Myronor burned along with the Vespula Brotherhood, it would be a fair price to pay. But no flames reached him where he lay. With considerable effort, he pushed himself up from the ground. While he watched the world burn around him, beneath him remained still. Only then did he notice the emblazoned barrier of runes surrounding him. Even in her wrath, Ophiera protected him.

Myronor watched as fiery crevices chased down those attempting to flee. One by one they turned to ash, torched by white flames. A whimpering noise nearby pulled him from the destruction. The Reverend lay on the ground, holding one charred arm clutched to his chest. But he couldn't escape Ophiera's judgment.

Her flames pulsated with each fateful step toward the Reverend. The ground ignited behind her with every footfall, her anguish no longer expressed with screams, but with flames.

"M-mercy!" the Reverend cried.

Ophiera grasped the man by his throat, and sizzles of burning skin hissed through the air. The Reverend screamed as she dragged him upright. But unlike the others, he did not immediately burst into flame. She drew out his suffering with purpose.

"I'm not Mercy," she seethed, her first words spoken since igniting. "I'm Retribution."

She touched her lips to his forehead, repaying his previous violation in a white-flamed kiss. His high wails went on longer than the others. But in the end, they all became ash.

Myronor stared in reverence at the fiery being before him. The brightness of the flames seared his eyes, but he refused to look away. He felt no fear, even after witnessing the destruction. Her eyes only left his when she sank to the ground.

"Ophiera?"

On her hands and knees, her form convulsed. New flames erupted from the surrounding ground.

"I-I—can't—stop—" she screamed.

The ground quaked worse than before, but his protective circle remained. She still held some control at least, and Myronor wracked his mind for some way to extinguish her. He felt the potion case in his boot again and did the only thing he could.

"Hold on!" he yelled, feeling the stabbing pain of broken ribs.

He knew Rheta wouldn't fail him as he searched for something useful. Ophiera's cries of agony were distracting, more painful than any injury he had suffered. The ground shook even harder, as if she were building power rather than spending it. Tears began streaming down his face, distorting his frenzied search. It was as if her cries burned him like the flames had not.

A small white vial caught his attention. Unique amongst the rest, the label read, "Don't get burned."

Myronor drank the potion and recklessly stepped from the safety of the runic circle. The white flames had no effect on him, and he stumbled to where Ophiera lay. Instinct compelled him to pull her from the ground, forcing her to stand against him, away from the ground opening beneath their feet.

He held her even as she fought to pull away, and it caused him pain beyond the physical toll. His ribs and heart ached as she screamed. His skin began to burn where he held her. And he hated what he was about to do to her, but it was the only path he could see.

"I won't let go, Ophiera," he said, feeling the heat emanating from her. "If you can't control this, then we both join the Aether! So try—try to get ahold of this—for me."

He knew no potion could withstand the holy flames for long. But his risky challenge must work. She'd proven time and time again that she would always protect him—even from herself.

Ophiera slowed her thrashing until only agonized grunts escaped her. When she had stilled completely, Myronor held her gaze along with her inflamed body. Her tears evaporated before they fell, but he watched them pool in her terrified eyes.

She never broke her gaze from his. And slowly, the heat and flames subsided. In his arms, she no longer felt like formless energy, but corporeal and tangible. Her white hair fell loose around her bare flesh, and she collapsed against him as her pain turned to sobs.

Myronor held her close as she shuddered, unwilling to let her go. He needed to feel her, to hold the proof that she was real. Her sobs eventually stilled, and she looked up at him with tear-filled eyes. She was more beautiful than ever, covered in ash. He wiped the moisture away from her cheeks as he held her face in his hands.

"That was incredible," he said with a rasp.

There was nothing in all of Erum as exquisite as her, even amidst the glorious devastation. Though the holy flames had disappeared, they left behind hundreds of vespers. Over endless piles of ash, the shades glowed throughout the ashen forest. The afflicted trees had also been claimed in her wrath, leaving them out in the open.

Her lilac eyes went even wider as she looked around, taking in the scene. "I don't understand—"

But her raw voice cut off suddenly. Myronor barely heard the whizzing sound before her eyes unfocused and her body jerked. He watched in horror as blood poured from her mouth, covering them both in crimson warmth.

Myronor couldn't comprehend what had just happened. He looked down in panic and saw a thick arrowhead protruding from her bare chest. It had missed his own flesh by a hair. His pale tunic was now stained red with her blood.

He saw a figure drop from a spared tree in the distance, falling in a glow of blue light. A mage. Protected from the carnage below by nothing more than their distance from the ground, the sole survivor of Ophiera's wrath now fled, a blur of black and yellow with a crossbow slung along her back. He recognized Marvena.

Ophiera collapsed to the ground, rasping and gurgling as blood poured from her chest.

"No...no!" Myronor's frantic screams pierced the now silent forest. He could not think of anything to do other than hold her. As he collapsed to the ground with her, he pulled her limp body into his lap.

"Tell me what to do!" he sobbed, barely able to understand his own words.

She reached a hand to his chest, trembling over his heart. He held it as a weak smile crossed her lips. But her hand went limp within his and the jewel-like shimmer left her eyes.

The world broke.

Myronor broke.

Ophiera was gone.

He searched his mind for hope, grasping in desperation. But he found nothing. Nothing but her lifeless body in his hands. His very soul was being torn to pieces, his heart stammering against his ribs as it shattered.

Ophiera was gone.

He couldn't breathe. He couldn't think. He only felt. And no person could withstand this agony.

A bright light cut through his tears. He opened his eyes despite the fear of what he knew shone so brightly. Where the arrow protruded, Ophiera's vesper emerged. But there was nothing similar between hers and the others he had witnessed.

Her shade was dazzling. Swirls of shimmering gold against the white glow, bright as the holy flames. Pure, untainted radiance.

A fresh wave of grief crashed against him. His own heart stopped with the proof Ophiera was dead. Yet her vesper did not leave her body. It hovered like a dome of brilliant light. He couldn't breathe as he watched a small coil of light stretch out from her vesper. The tendril of purest white probed the air as if searching. It drew toward Myronor. When it reached him, the vine of light embedded itself within his chest. Warmth embraced him, spreading through him as if mending his very soul back together.

He watched as another tendril, blue in hue, emerged from his own chest. The azure stem wound its way around the white, intertwining in a beautiful weave until it reached the center of Ophiera's vesper.

The connection overpowered his mind. Images he didn't recognize flashed before him. It only took him a moment to realize these were memories. As if it were pulled from his own mind, he remembered climbing into a covered wagon on the streets of Feyralis as robed figures coaxed him along.

In another flash, he fell—beaten, starved, and endlessly punished in a darkness that never broke.

Now, he held a massive sword in hand, his arms shaking with the weight. He couldn't drop it, no matter what; his life depended on holding that sword.

Another flash. He lay on a cold, wet floor with nothing but despair, desperate for his life to end. Then burning. Endless, torturous burning.

The memories blurred together and incoherent thoughts melded with jumbled emotions, but none were joyous. It was only suffering until one memory stood out with a sense of hope. He clung to it like a raft in a storm and saw his own body laid crumpled on the riverbank. A blue orb rose from his chest, similar to how Ophiera's vesper had just behaved. A pair of hands, one marred with symbolic scars, pressed against his chest. Muffled words in a language he didn't understand coaxed the orb back into his body.

Emerging from the visions, Myronor opened his eyes and saw the connection of blue and white light had dissipated. The white orb sank slowly back into Ophiera's chest, just as in the memory. And in utter disbelief, he watched her torso rise and fall with breath. A new pump of red blood spilled forth from her wound.

Myronor couldn't explain.

He held her tightly and felt a dim vitality pulsate through her. Without thought, only instinct, he had pushed himself to the brink. Mana, Aether, life, it didn't matter. Everything he had left, he now poured into spanning them to safety.

~ Twenty-One ~

TETHERED

Waves crashed gently in the distance, a soothing rhythm that broke against the nothingness. Ophiera vacantly listened to the sea, unfeeling, unseeing, and uncaring. Everything was numb.

Was this what the Cloister meant by the peace of the Aether? If so, she would be content to spend her eternity like this, listening to the waves and sleeping in numb tranquility.

But there was another sound within the surf. A familiar rumble that she felt more than heard.

Mallow?

Ophiera recalled the arrow. She recalled the pain as it tore through her heart. The white flames had hurt worse, she admitted. But neither death nor holy fire reached the threshold of agony reflected in Myronor's eyes as she died.

In the end, she could not wholly protect him from harm. But at least he had remained alive.

If she were dead though, how could she hear Mallow's purrs now?

Ophiera had instructed the familiar to remain behind and search for Myronor if, by chance, he had escaped. She'd assumed the Vespula Brotherhood would not accept her trade, but there were few other choices. It was the only option that granted the slightest chance of Myronor's survival.

In the end, it worked out for the best. She was dead, along with countless anathemas she'd claimed in her blaze of Retribution. She wondered if there were any innocents caught in the swath of annihilation. She hadn't inspected the shades before the arrow. Was Mallow too close to her cataclysm? Did the beautiful creature become a casualty of whatever power had overtaken her?

Watching Myronor beaten within an inch of his life broke her as nothing else had. All she remembered was her pain turning vengeful, burning as she swore Retribution against the Reverend and anyone else who harmed him. The next she knew, her entire body was aflame. And the endless Aether from within Erum was at her disposal.

Ophiera didn't hesitate to use the newfound power to destroy all who stood in her path. She had no limit anymore, no longer needing mana or a chant to bend the holy flames to her will. She channeled the flames as if she were the Aether itself.

The purring intensified, magnifying her guilt. And now her chest ached with the weight of loss. Despair further disturbed her numbness.

With a soft mewl, a rough tongue grazed her cheek. Strange. How could she feel anything if she were dead? Hesitantly, she opened her eyes.

Déjà vu overtook her as she viewed the brightly lit surroundings. The faded blue walls were familiar, as were the driftwood beams in the thatched ceiling. Painfully familiar, in fact. Was the afterlife so kind as to bestow her own cottage upon her?

"Ophiera?"

A soft voice called her name, and she feared the implication. Had she failed to save him, after all?

"Say something, please."

She felt a warm hand take her own. His touch held too much sensation, too much emotion to bear. He was real.

"Am I dead?"

"No..." Myronor said, in a voice like a laugh mingled with a sob. "Not anymore."

He was squeezing her hand harder now, skirting a line of discomfort. She dared not look at him. Was she truly alive?

In this realization, she felt no relief. With her free hand, she searched for the arrow wound, the fatal shot taken by one of the survivors.

Bandages obscured the aching spot, wrapped tightly around her entire torso. In a flash of recall, she relived the sensation. The blood had pooled in her chest, weighing down her every breath. Her heart ached, unable to beat with the arrow skewered through it. The moment of death had been a relief from that horrific sensation.

"I should be dead."

"Don't..." he muttered.

He brought her hand against his lips and held it there. The reality of this affection, of his warmth and touch, forced her to look upon him.

Myronor was beaten beyond recognition. His bright eyes were bloodshot and swollen. The wounds of his imprisonment were evidenced by endless cuts and bruises along his face and hands. Even his fair hair had lost its luster, now hanging drab and limp over his slumped shoulders.

Her heart ached thinking of what he had endured, wishing she'd found the camp sooner. She reached with the hand he held to feel how real he was. As she cupped his cheek, he smiled and it served as the ultimate proof he lived.

"How badly are you injured?"

"Not nearly as badly as you...you were..." The words choked away in his throat.

"How are we *here*?" she whispered.

"He broke the rules." A deep, amused voice boomed from the doorway. "But I'm sure Pyra would have approved of it."

Instinctively, she and Myronor pulled away from each other. She felt caught, only now aware of how they had held each other. Why had she done that?

"You're early," Myronor said. He rose to greet his father, embracing the burly fisher.

Ophiera tried to sit up, but Mallow pounced on her shoulder, pushing her down into the bed with a glare.

Berwyn laughed, revealing his relation to Myronor. "The little monster says you need rest, and I reckon she's right. We're glad you're back amongst the living, Warden."

Ophiera nodded her thanks, but his words made her question again. She remembered her death. Myronor had held her, sobbing and desperate, the anguish on his face proof of her demise. Yet she still lived. Injured, yes, but alive. Or was she?

Myronor strode with a limp to a far window where a fragrant sea breeze entered. As he reached the far side of the room, overwhelming fatigue hit her. She grabbed her chest in discomfort, feeling the pain of her wound in full. It felt as if Myronor himself jumped upon her heart.

He turned, horror dragging on his face as he rushed back, prying her hand from the bandages.

"What's wrong?" Myronor asked with frantic hands. But as quickly as it had begun, the pain subsided.

"I-I don't know—but I'm fine now. Just a moment of pain. Probably from healing."

"Unfortunately, Warden, you've done little healing," Berwyn said, and crossed his thick arms. "The shaman hasn't been here. Offshore with the deep-water vessels for auxis season, you know."

"Well, neither of us is dead yet, so we must be doing something right without her," said Myronor with a sad smile. "Perhaps sleeping has always been the answer to a speedy recovery."

"Then I best let you rest, Warden. Whatever you need, just let us know." Berwyn nodded with consolation before heading back toward the door.

Myronor joined his father to walk him out. But as he crossed the threshold to the next room, another bout of pain shot through her. She grunted against the intensity of the ache, trying to breathe. Was the arrow still lodged within her?

Again, Myronor rushed to her side. And again, her pain fled the instant his hands were upon her. Myronor watched her, his eyes reflecting her own confusion regarding this strange phenomenon.

"I'm going to test something," he said cautiously, "but you may feel pain again."

She nodded.

Myronor walked backward across the room, his eyes fixed on her as he hobbled. All seemed normal until he stepped beyond the threshold and the pain pierced her again.

"What's happening?" Ophiera asked through a clenched jaw.

Again he returned, and the pain dissipated. Myronor sighed, unwilling to meet her eyes. "I fear you may hate me if my theory is correct..."

Hate him?

Despite her guilt and fears over what had transpired at the camp, she did not for a moment regret her choice to come for him. She reached for his arm and shook him weakly.

"I walked into a trap to save you...I'd be foolish to hate you after such an ordeal."

He laughed sadly. "I don't know what you were thinking..."

"I was thinking of keeping you alive. At any cost. And here you are, as I intended, yet I know I should *not* be..." She squeezed his arm in a plea. "Tell me, what is my consequence for avoiding death?"

Myronor remained silent.

In search of her own answers, she reached a hand beneath her bandages. Myronor's eyes flashed with disgust but he didn't stop her as she felt the hole in her flesh, still open—still bleeding—and still fatal.

Impossible.

"Am I...going to become one of those things? Like the troynt, rotting away while still alive?"

Her fear seemingly prompted his confession.

"After the arrow—your vesper," he choked. "It left your body—at least, it started to, but behaved very oddly..." He wiped his face with his hand, steeling himself to continue. "I know this sounds crazy, but your shade...it attached itself to me. I could feel you—I was you...or something I don't quite understand. Once your vesper returned to you, your life force came back and clung to my own as if...linked. I can't fully explain how...but I can feel my life intertwined with yours, and yours with mine."

This explanation was...unexpected.

While her mind still held doubt, her gut knew he spoke the truth. The connection—she felt it now. A quiet current ebbing between them, unseen and undeniable. She searched her memories and discovered images of a life not her own. Of times out at sea on a rubyfin boat or buried in books written in languages she didn't know.

She didn't understand what had happened to them. But a part of Myronor's explanation confused her still.

"Why do you think I would hate you for this?"

He looked away from her, revealing more bruises and cuts. "When our vespers connected...I felt *everything*. So much of it remains garbled and nonsensical...But I *felt* the crushing weight of your Oath, clear as day. The bitterness and anger you hold for unsolicited servitude...the toll of unfairness...the pain, the guilt..." He ran his hand through his hair, this time gripping a bundle for composure. "I didn't understand it before. But now that I've felt it for myself, I know you must resent me for binding you to another fate you didn't ask for...for binding you to me."

So, she had been spared the freedom of death by yet another force that bound her will. This time, Myronor himself. Ophiera tried to hate him as she hated the Cloister and the Magistrate. But she could not muster even a sliver of animosity. All she felt was...relief.

"My Oath and the Magistrate have already bound me to your fate. One more tether couldn't change that much between us, could it?"

He finally looked at her, his eyes matching the calm sky beyond the window. His gaze always discomforted her in a way she did not understand. But now, as he ran his knuckles across her cheek, she felt his intentions behind the pale stare. And this time, she wanted what he did too.

"Even your words are beautiful," he said.

In sudden grief, she turned her face away from his hand. Her damaged heart was fickle too. Suddenly, she hated the way he looked at her, with reverence rather than the scorn she deserved. As if the fire that burned her entirety hadn't been painful enough.

"There is nothing beautiful about the abomination I've become...about what I did."

He let out a disbelieving breath. "Surely you don't refer to the flames?"

The moisture welling in her eyes surprised her. Soon, tears ran down her cheeks, and she found herself unable to speak. But Myronor's gentle touch surprised her more, wiping away her tears with a trembling hand.

"Ophiera, you were magnificent. Without your flames, the Brotherhood would have killed us both."

She cried silently, unable to hold back the overwhelming thoughts of the encampment.

What had she become? What had she done? What was she now?

Myronor came to lie beside her. She didn't know why she let him wedge against her and wrap his arms around her. But the unfamiliar closeness didn't make her nervous. All pain from her wound disappeared as she pressed against him, sobbing with a different ache in her chest.

She cried for a long time. Throughout it all, Myronor simply held her, letting her cope with what had happened in the only way left to her. She broke into pieces against him.

Eventually, she exhausted herself to a mere sniffle. And as she faded to the edge of sleep, Myronor shifted away.

"Please don't go," she breathed.

Her words sounded foreign even to herself, but she didn't care. Without question or teasing, Myronor relaxed back against her. The warmth of his presence comforted her very soul. It felt as if her life depended on him being near, as if his arms were the only thing holding her together anymore.

* * *

The sea had always brought Ophiera peace of mind before. She admired how it held freedom and power in perfect balance. Nothing could truly tame the sea, and while it served as a provider, it remained ever indifferent to the plights of the living. She used to see her own reflection in the dichotomy of the ocean. But now, as she gazed across the cerulean horizon, she simply felt lost out at sea.

Every morning since arriving in Iluka, she sat on the small dock by her cottage, watching the water. Often, she hung her legs over the wooden edge and dipped her feet in the warm water, just as she had before. She watched for ships on the horizon, one of her favorite pastimes in her retirement. Yet despite her best efforts to convince herself it was the same, everything had changed.

On the surface, she appeared placid, but a tumultuous current raged beneath. Bitter with diffidence, angered by change, and frightened of herself, she found no peace here, even in the sea.

Death lurked within the unhealed wound in her chest. Yet by some unknown arcana, she sat here alive. Her heart harbored both life and death; a duality felt every time she looked at Myronor.

In her desperation to save him, she had unintentionally awakened something terrible within her. A flamed entity of death and destruction. A monstrous being of unchecked and unlimited power. Her mind had lingered on the Vespula camp incessantly since arriving in Iluka.

How had she cast the flames wordlessly? How could she have destroyed so many souls without judgment first? Had innocents burned on her pyre of vengeance? If her soul didn't bear the burden of corruption before, it did now. She was certainly an anathema.

The guilt threatened to consume her.

And yet, every time she traveled this path of compunction, she reached the same conclusion. The arrow *should* have claimed her. It would have been for the best. But like most of her existence, the best outcome was not what came to pass. The only path now was forward.

Neither she nor Myronor was in any condition to continue their journey to Krysas. Her cottage dock was as far as Ophiera could walk before becoming winded and fatigued. The deep ache in her chest went far beyond her mortal wound when she strayed too far from Myronor.

The new connection kept her constantly aware of the space between them. She struggled to come to terms with the limitations of the tether. The farther she distanced herself, the more she suffered, but like a muscle, the link strengthened and flexed. The first day she spent on the dock ached her chest; but the next day, she only felt a pull. And the next day, a gentle tug to let her know Myronor was not by her side. Still, she didn't understand *what* had happened between them.

Ophiera needed answers. She needed the shaman to return to Iluka.

The village shaman always accompanied the deep-water boats on riskier voyages. Storms and monsters alike threatened ships in the waters of the Lucent Strait. The shamans of Tanvik practiced a craft unique to the coastal villages: hydromancy. They channeled the power of the waters to both heal and destroy. Similar to a paladin, a shaman could give or take life. The difference was, again, in choice; the shamans chose their own path.

Regardless of what had occurred, Ophiera remained Oath-bound to escort Myronor to Krysas and investigate his mother's death. Yet her confidence had faltered under wounds and weakness.

She knew her Oath was not befitting to take on a charge. Even less so now. She gazed upon the runes of her arm, knowing they'd acted on their own in the encampment. Igniting and consuming her in flames before she even knew what happened. Never again could she risk losing control like that. She saw only one choice left to her; deny herself her own power. At least until she could get rid of it or learn to control it.

"You don't look very happy."

Myronor's warm voice hit her like a gentle wave, pulling her from her brooding. He wore his blue robes again now that they were unable to travel. They suited him best. She felt more at ease as he sat next to her, though she couldn't speak. Her voice felt lost more often than not these days.

Even though the tether allowed them to distance themselves now, a constant yearning for his presence lingered. The changes to her heart and soul were too vast, and they'd happened too quickly. She couldn't cope with the constant flux. The desire to be close to another was foreign on its own without the confounding tether. Had she always felt this way about the mage? Or was it purely a consequence of their mysterious bond?

Myronor dropped a bindle into her lap. She hadn't even noticed he carried one. He smiled at her gently before lying back on the dock, absorbing the sun. His bruises and cuts were highlighted in the daylight—more obvious and more terrible. More proof of her failures.

"Berwyn dropped those off," he said, smiling with eyes closed. "Freshly baked this morning."

Unwrapping the cloth parcel, she found a handful of enormous muffins. The familiar scarlet berries had burst during their bake, accompanied by the aroma of chokecherries and white yuzu. Berwyn always knew her favorites. She blamed the salty air for the sting in her eyes.

"I wish we could just stay here," Myronor said. Now his pale eyes pierced her as he lay on the dock, looking as pained as she felt.

She wondered if he truly felt this way or merely reflected her own emotions through the tether. Still, his words forced her imagination. What if they did stay in Iluka? A mage and a paladin deciding to live in a tiny fishing village sounded like the start of a terrible joke.

A blemish appeared on the horizon. The auxis boat was returning with its catch and the shaman, bringing with it a cold reminder of reality.

"I cannot break my Oath," she said. They were her first words spoken today. "Once we are able, we must continue onward to Krysas."

Myronor wrinkled his brow. "Will you be able to return here to Iluka when your Oath is fulfilled?"

She knew he referred to the tether and the same concern that plagued her own mind. The thought had kept her awake the last few nights. Even as she lay next to Myronor, basking in the peace of his closeness, she knew it was wrong. Her emotions were no longer her own. Nothing was. Her soul belonged to the Cloister, her Oath to the Magistrate, her armor to the Brotherhood, and now her heart seemed lost in this strange connection.

"We'll see what the shaman knows," she said in a solemn tone. "Perhaps there is a way to break our tether."

Logically, she knew this was the easiest solution. But every time she thought of it, her chest ached.

"If a way exists to break this...perhaps there is a way to break you of your Oath as well?" Myronor said.

Ophiera remained silent for a moment. In the past, she would have called this blasphemy. But whether due to exhaustion or the tether, she considered the prospect.

"According to the Cloister, death is the only means to break an Oath. And only if the paladin has reached atonement. Though the Cloister also claimed my armor was indestructible...so it's difficult to know what is true anymore."

In her mind's eye, she thought back to the encampment. Again, the uncontrollable pain of flame and destruction intruded on her composure. The power began with her Oath, she knew that; but how and why? It frightened her how quickly and willingly she'd annihilated all who threatened her charge. She never wanted to feel that dangerous again. She never wanted this Oath, period.

Myronor sat up suddenly and placed his arm around her. Tears flowed down her face as he pulled her against him. Had she ever cried so much in her life? His embrace felt frustratingly wonderful, a comfort she did not trust. But she gave in to the pull of the connection and pressed herself against him.

"I think I can find a way to break you of your Oath. In Krysas, I'll inherit my mother's personal library, as well as gain access to the Consortia's foreign knowledge. I know we can find a way for you to be free of all burdens, not just me."

Myronor stared sadly at the water.

"The thought of being free of you causes me pain beyond words," she said, her voice wavering with tears shed. "Yet I desperately want what you offer...I don't know, nothing makes sense anymore."

"The shaman will have some answers," he said encouragingly.

Ophiera watched the ship on the horizon grow incrementally as it neared, the only hope for the answers she so desperately sought.

~ Twenty-Two ~

CONSULTATION

The *Equinox* arrived just before sunset, carrying the auxis catch and the village shaman.

Ophiera knew the mystic well during her retirement. Their roles as shaman and Warden were integrally linked within the village, embedded in the rich culture of the Southern Coastlands.

Shamans served as unofficial leaders, advising and directing Wardens in protecting village interests. Together they had served the people of Iluka, but never had Ophiera needed her guidance so desperately.

Ophiera stood with Myronor at the shore of the village pier. Her cottage lay on the outskirts, and the trek here had sapped nearly all her regained strength. Against her pride, she leaned on Myronor for support, collecting herself before the shaman arrived.

As the shaman disembarked, Ophiera straightened up, defiant. Kaikora wore her bronzed, ombre dreadlocks loose with the sea-salt-saturated ends falling between her wide shoulders. She stood unusually tall, broad, and scantily clad; a half-naked giant of rippled muscles etched with dark tattoos. The wavelike designs crossed her torso and arms in seaweed-green swirls that ebbed and flowed with her musculature. On her neck, she wore a yoke of gnarled rope and sea glass, the only article of clothing above her waist. It barely covered her chest, exposing her ample torso to the elements. On her wide, curved hips hung a low loincloth crafted from nacreous scales that reflected the sunlight like the surf.

The moment her bare foot touched the wooden planks of the dock, Kaikora targeted Ophiera with a gray gaze. The shaman held a trident of sea glass and silver, which she banged thrice upon the wooden dock. "Warden! I was not expecting you back until tomorrow!"

Myronor snorted. "Is this the sight in action?"

"She does possess the gift...but this is merely a lost bet."

As Kaikora approached the shoreline, more fishers disembarked from the ship. When they recognized their Warden, they called their greetings with surprised smiles.

Though weak with injury, Ophiera tried to hold her head high as she waved back. She did not deserve their welcome after abandoning them under the Magistrate's conscription.

As the two clasped hands, Kaikora pulled Ophiera into an embrace. The shaman squeezed her wounds, testing what the sight had likely shown her.

"You return as half the person, without sword or armor," Kaikora said. "What happened?"

Ophiera groaned. "Too much...as I'm sure you've *seen*."

The shaman studied her a moment as if she did not recognize her. She assessed Ophiera's black tunic and leather pants with an inquisitive glare. They were the only clothes she had that sat comfortably on her wound.

"I've seen nothing," Kaikora said, shifting her gaze to Myronor instead. "But I see now you brought Berwyn's son along with you."

"Oh come, Kaikora—don't tell me you forgot my name," the mage said with a smile.

Ophiera hadn't realized Myronor and Kaikora had overlapped in their time in Iluka. But now that she dwelt on it, foreign memories of an adolescent shaman bubbled in her mind. It seemed...they hadn't gotten along in their youth, but Ophiera dropped the thought quickly. She hated *feeling* something that was not her own.

"Name or not, you fell to a similar fate as the Warden...yet only your body has suffered," Kaikora said. She turned toward the road. "You two have been quite busy. Come—let us have this discussion in my home."

Kaikora stalked away, greeting villagers as she made her way up the winding path to a large hut set atop the hill.

Ophiera and Myronor followed, passing along the sloping paths in the crisscrossing dunes. The distinct landscape of the Southern Coastlands led the people to build their abodes upon stilts, especially close to the water. Raised homes proved sturdy against the frequent storms and left the land as undisturbed as possible. But there was still a smattering of traditional sod homes, Ophiera's cottage included, that rested within the sand.

Kaikora's long strides carried her along the path, leaving both Ophiera and Myronor behind at their injured pace. The shaman's uniquely round hut was one of those few structures without stilts— another tradition of the Southern Coastlands.

When she and Myronor stepped inside, the shaman had already set a kettle upon the central hearth. Nearly the entirety of the shaman's abode was a deep, sunken sitting area, open to the sand it was built upon. A wooden boardwalk circumvented the room, housing shelves of endless clay pots, tattered books, and other sundries. Near the door, a hook on the wall held her trident upright, next to her traveling cloak and bag, covered in dust.

Kaikora sat beside the hearth in the circular den. She barely fit on one of the reeded pads strewn across the sand. The hearth was more of a fire pit, built from ornate stones and dusted with sand. The entire one-room home was illuminated by the sun cascading in from the smoke vent in the roof above.

From a large clay urn, Kaikora scooped a mixture of dried leaves and herbs into the now steaming kettle. She didn't turn to greet them but smiled as she spoke.

"So, why have you returned so quickly, Warden? You said the Magistrate would hold you hostage for as long as they could."

"I haven't returned," Ophiera said moodily. "My task for the Magistrate remains unfulfilled. How I ended up in Iluka so soon...Well, that's what we're here to discuss."

The shaman stretched her thick, long legs out before her. Ophiera wondered how many days she had been at sea, only to now deal with her problems.

"Grab three mugs from over there and come tell me of your troubles," Kaikora said, gesturing to a shelf packed with pottery.

After the shaman poured them all a cup of herbaceous tea, Ophiera began recounting the events since she first left Iluka.

She glossed over certain details—perhaps too many. Such as Myronor's vesper on the riverbank. Again she played it off as her healing rite gone awry, which it had. She didn't want to lie, but simply omit, though both actions felt the same now. She just couldn't bring herself to talk about vespers, not after what had occurred in the encampment.

When Ophiera began telling the shaman of the blackened plague in the swamps, Kaikora hissed under her breath.

"So you know of this then—the ichor or plague or what have you?" Myronor asked, reading her response.

Kaikora shook her head. "The Phratries have tales of such a blight. But finish your story first. We will discuss when *all* of your problems are out on the table."

She should have guessed the shaman would have some knowledge of the blight. But Kaikora was even more stubborn than Ophiera. The only way to learn more about the taint of the Sloughmire was to finish her tale.

When Ophiera reached the part of their journey that ended in Isyath, her words disappeared. She couldn't voice the frantic fear that came with finding her charge kidnapped. She didn't want to discuss the fight with Lotus as he begged her not to go. The memories burned in her throat, but no words would come.

Myronor cut in and began to describe his captivity with the Vespulas. Though he held the wounds as evidence, Ophiera didn't know exactly what had happened to him during his imprisonment. She didn't want to ask him to recount such an experience, for her sake as much as his. But as he spoke, she learned of the bonds that had sucked away his mana, the sacrifices he watched die, the transformation of the vespers stolen from the Aether, and the beatings he had endured.

He had been mistreated and abused in the two days he was held. Yet since their return to Iluka, he had only ever smiled at her. Was he truly not suffering that lingering horror that followed such trauma? Or was he hiding it, focusing on her wounds instead?

Her worry for him was quickly overshadowed by his revelations of the sacrifices.

Myronor's had been the first uncorrupted vesper she'd ever witnessed. And never had she *watched* an anathema take a life. His description of the vespers imploding in dark smoke and corrupting the Reverend was borderline unbelievable. She couldn't tell if this was what normally happened when someone committed murder, or if it was a consequence of the sacrificial rites evoked by the Brotherhood. She barely had time to contemplate the implications of his experience before he began telling of her own capture.

This part of their tale was too fresh still. The wound remained open, quite literally, in fact. She didn't want to listen to him describe the destruction of her armor. Her precious, golden armor. Even now, it felt as if she were missing a limb, or some other integral part to her whole. And it was something she could never get back. She wondered how the Cloister would interpret her loss of the artifact; had any paladin ever lost their armor? She was sure the answer was no.

Myronor had just begun to discuss his torture; the last act of the Reverend before she...

"Just when I thought they would kill me, I saw...Ophiera...Ophiera, your arm..."

She looked down and saw the scarred runes glowing bright without will or chant. Panic overtook her and she closed her eyes, willing herself into restraint. The consequences if she succumbed to this power were too terrifying to consider. An eternity passed in her silent battle against herself before Kaikora's voice broke her concentration.

"Open your eyes, Warden."

Ophiera cracked one eye open, half expecting the room to be in flames. But she only saw Kaikora's smug grin and Myronor's sweet smile. No burning hut. No terrified stares.

"Kaikora, I don't know what's happening to me..." Ophiera's voice broke as the shaman shook her head.

"Ophiera, you've always been a bit...dramatic," Kaikora said with a husky chuckle. Ophiera failed to find the humor in any of this. "Like I said, when all problems are out on the table, we will discuss them. For now"—she turned to Myronor—"continue...and tell me how she transformed."

Myronor had not spoken yet of her transformation in the encampment. But Kaikora *knew*. She knew what Ophiera was capable of becoming. How? Her tongue turned bitter and dry.

The mage continued with details of the massacre in the encampment. Ophiera refused to listen. She had lived through it once already; she didn't need to hear it retold too. She didn't want to hear how many she killed or how close she came to killing her charge. She didn't want to hear the adoration and the pain in Myronor's voice. She wanted to scream to drown out all the things she didn't want to hear.

"Ophiera—you have not been truthful," Kaikora said with a glare.

"About?" Ophiera murmured, returning to the conversation.

"You saw his vesper, didn't you? The day you found him on the riverbank."

Ophiera didn't have the energy anymore to fight Kaikora's nature. The shaman would always find the truth.

"Yes."

Myronor leaned toward her with eyebrows raised. She averted her gaze.

"By the sea..." Kaikora stared in joyful amazement between them. "You performed the rite of Birzhan...by mistake?"

"The what?" Myronor said, whipping his eyes to Kaikora.

"The soul-binding ritual."

"How?" Ophiera asked.

"You have laid eyes on a vesper of the living. Seeing a vesper is rare on its own...so few of us are there the moment a person passes to the Aether. But you saw a vesper that didn't return to the Aether. By your intervention, Myronor's vesper returned to its vessel, forever altered. Now imagine this happening twice. You have seen each other's souls in the absence of death. It is an unthinkable rite in our times."

"Our times?" Myronor asked pointedly.

Kaikora leaned in with the teapot and refilled their cups before speaking.

"The shamans retain Tanvik's history and the tales of the first peoples. The mother clans practiced strange mysticisms and the rite of Birzhan was a rare but powerful ritual. The binding of two souls was difficult, but once bound, they formed the ekatma—the one soul. The ritual required one to sacrifice themselves, dying with the intent that a chosen other would view their vesper before revivifying them with risky spells or rites. Once revived, the returned soul would witness the other soul undergo the same death and revival. The key was those being bound must see each other's vespers and live. Two ekaths linked as ekatma."

Ophiera's thoughts tripped over themselves in endless questions. But in her silence, Myronor asked them first.

"To what end? Why risk death to become soul bound?"

A hesitancy lingered on Kaikora's stern features. She looked to Ophiera with gray eyes of implication before addressing the pair.

"Ekatma are immortal."

Ophiera choked on her tea as if to prove Kaikora wrong. But as she felt her injury throb with her coughs, she knew the shaman spoke the truth. She had walked about for days with a hole through her heart.

"Can you elaborate?" Myronor asked.

How had Ophiera ever found his incessant questions a burden? She was thankful he pushed while she merely reeled.

"The two souls are tethered to each other, rather than to the Aether. One cannot die while the other lives, no matter how grievous the injury or sickness or age. The mother clans used the Birzhan ritual to form alliances between clans. Two chieftains, linked in immortality, became a formidable union. I'm sure you can fill in the details on your own as to why. But some tell of more romantic motives...to bind themselves in the name of love."

Love.

Ophiera turned the word over and over again in her head. That word did not exist in the Cloister, and neither did *immortality*. When faced with so much newness, she could only fall back on what she knew.

"What consequence does this hold over our fates? On my Oath?"

Kaikora watched the orange flames in the pit, drinking her tea for a moment. "I cannot say."

In silence, the three companions digested the implications of this knowledge. While Ophiera found comfort in knowing the condition they both suffered now, the idea of immortality disturbed her. The fatal wound in her chest proved the point, but the consequences of such a fate felt too far beyond present concerns.

If soul-bound leaders of the ancient clans continued on with separate lives, regardless of distance, then perhaps Ophiera and Myronor had hope. She imagined a scenario in which Myronor remained Ambassador in Krysas, and she returned to Iluka. But the bond protested this idea, squeezing her chest uncomfortably at the mere thought.

Kaikora's tea helped quell the growing knot in Ophiera's stomach. It tasted of lavender and winesap, with something sharp she could not quite place. But whatever it was had a profound effect on her mood.

"Feeling better?" the shaman asked with a laugh. "My own blend—a must when I return from the deep-sea voyages. Does wonders for the stamina, doesn't it?"

"This would be an exceptionally useful brew to take with us to Krysas," Myronor said, only half paying attention. He was staring into his cup attentively, studying the contents.

Kaikora shifted her gaze to Ophiera. "My tea will provide little help if Ophiera refuses to use the holy flames again."

The taunt stung Ophiera as much as the shaman's knowing assessment. Damn her and damn the sight. Ophiera could only glare at her.

"An Aspect that refuses their gift is quite useless."

Myronor looked to Ophiera as understanding dawned on him. She hadn't told him her intentions to avoid the flames. However, he didn't question her and instead turned a frosty eye to Kaikora.

"Perhaps it would be more productive if you shared your knowledge of what's happening to her instead of mocking her choices."

Unfazed, Kaikora turned to Ophiera. "What did the Cloister tell you of your brands?"

Ophiera found the shaman's temperament a constant frustration. But she would swallow her pride in order to understand.

"Very little," Ophiera said, unable to hide her temper. "When they read my scars as Aspect of Retribution, I didn't know what it meant. I had learned of the other echelons before my kindling: the Hands and the Keepers. But I had never heard of an Aspect until the day my Oath was branded. The Chaplain, the priests, well, everyone at the Cloister seemed...disappointed with the results. They wouldn't speak of it—told me to focus on mastering my Oath and ignore the echelon."

Kaikora nodded slowly. "Well, they did not tell you the truth. Perhaps they've lost the knowledge or simply were fearful of it. It has been centuries since an Aspect has been born of their flames, so long they've forgotten its purpose. It was once believed an Aspect was the embodiment of the Oath possessed. And the truth is more literal than figurative."

"Literal?" Ophiera asked. "So, I really am nothing more than my Oath after all."

Kaikora chuffed. "Again with the melodrama. You know better than I that when a paladin receives their Oath, they absorb a small portion of the holy flames to wield and manipulate. Your mana. But the true power of an Aspect is to control the source; the Aether itself as it flows beneath our feet."

The shaman's explanation fit with the events at the encampment. Never before had Ophiera summoned without chants or limitations. She had called forth the endless fire without tiring, but she also couldn't stop herself. Her awakening was as if a dam had broken; the Aether flowed through her unabated. But when all was said and done, she struggled to drop the floodgate. Myronor's reckless behavior forced her to extinguish it, but had he not, she wasn't sure how long she would have burned.

Even now, she felt the Aether beneath the ground. It called to her, whispering faintly, though she did her best to ignore it.

"Why would the Cloister keep this from me?"

A wave of pity crossed Kaikora's gray gaze. "All the Cloister knows is the brands of the Aspect appear in times of great upheaval. They simply fear what your presence means for the world order. Their order. By keeping you in the dark, the cowards could keep their heads in the sand."

Great upheaval? World order? These words were too weighted, and Ophiera felt her mind buckle beneath the truth. "I would have preferred to remain in the dark. I do not want this power that I cannot control."

"In the end, you controlled your flames in the encampment, and just now today. Besides, your ekath may serve you well if he is willing to help."

"Of course," Myronor said instantly. "I would do anything to ease her burden."

Ophiera's heart clenched at his words. If by "helping," he referred to his idiotic behavior, she refused to accept.

"Well, I've helped solve the mystery of soul and flame," Kaikora said. "What next?"

"The blight," Myronor said. Ophiera felt relieved he'd taken the lead on a different subject.

"Ah...yes," Kaikora said. Her face fell to a frown. "Don't worry about it."

"What?" Myronor snapped. Ophiera had never heard him so angry before. She preferred his laugh.

"I said don't worry about it."

"How can you say that after we told you how far it had spread? It was in the Brotherhood encampment, Kaikora! They're responsible, aren't they?"

Kaikora wouldn't look at either of them. "That is a problem we cannot solve here and now. You've sent word to the Magistrate, and I promise you, I will inform the Phratries. That is all we can do for now. I find there is a larger problem than the blight." The shaman's gaze pinned down Ophiera again, a slight smile returning to her lips. "You're a paladin without sword or armor."

"I'm aware." Ophiera grimaced, tiring of her inadequacies being brought to light. "But those are irre—"

"I wouldn't call them irreplaceable," interjected Kaikora, predicting her words. The shaman maintained her silence, along with her parsimonious reputation, and provided no elaboration.

Ophiera's patience waned, and she refused to play this game of bait and switch anymore. She held her silence, waiting for the shaman to elaborate.

"What could replace the adamantrium armor?" Myronor inquired for her.

"You cannot replace what never was." Kaikora smiled sadly. "No armor or weapon the Cloister possesses now is made from genuine adamantrium. When the Cloister lost the source of the Aether-ore, they smelted down the armaments that remained. They created alloys, combining the adamantrium with other precious metals. The sacrifice was quality for quantity—though the quality still surpassed any other armor in Erum. You noticed the wear of your blade, the signs of age on your armor; you knew what you wore was destructible all along."

Again, the information left Ophiera speechless. She had been taught by the Cloister to treat her armor as if it were more valuable than her life. Of course, she had noticed the wear and tear, the slight dents and scratches throughout her claymore and armor. But she never considered anything deeper than suspicion. Now the shaman told her the golden plate had never been real?

Her entire existence had been turned into a mockery within a single conversation. She came here to find answers regarding the hole in her heart, not to have the entire organ ripped out and shredded before her by the shaman. What other falsehoods had the Cloister fed her? And why did Kaikora know more of her order than she did?

"So, my life is a deceit?" Ophiera said in a quivering voice. "What else about me is fraudulent? My Oath? Is that also a lie? Am I nothing?!"

Kaikora had the grace to remain silent for a moment, allowing Ophiera to collect herself. Her scars burned with threat, but no flames flared from her. Watching Myronor flinch at her every word helped her control the anger.

"Ophiera," the shaman said in a stern tone. "You are still the Warden of Iluka; that will not change. You are still the Aspect of Retribution; that will *never* change. You remain everything you were before, simply unrestrained by some of the lies. You are more now, Ophiera, not less."

The shaman's words nearly echoed those of Myronor's own claim. In the Sloughmire, he told her she was more than her Oath. More? She didn't want more. That's why she retired in the first place. She wanted to avoid her Oath, to avoid the Retribution demanded from her. She grew tired of the killing, even if justified. But her Oath...her Oath still *had* to be real. Or else, the lives she claimed in the name of the Aether would make her worse than the worst anathema she'd ever crossed. Then everything she'd done would be...

No.

She couldn't think like this now. Not when so much changed around her; she needed to uphold her Oath. Something had to be consistent—truth and law—and that was her Oath. She clung to it in the storm of revelations. She must escort Myronor to Krysas. She must discover the fate of Pyra, and enact Retribution if she judged so. To do this, she needed her armor and a weapon.

"What do you propose I do about my armor?"

Kaikora smiled. "I suggest you find a new set."

"How?" Myronor asked, his own impatience apparent.

"Not from the Cloister," Ophiera said through gritted teeth.

"Why not?"

"Because no one knows where the Cloister is located," Kaikora cut in. "Not even the Phratries, and especially not the Cloister's own disciples. The Hands that leave the Cloister to uphold their Oaths only return by the draw of the Aether when their time is near."

"Exactly," said Ophiera. "So I'm still wondering where you think I'm going to find armor and a sword half as good as the set the Brotherhood destroyed."

Kaikora smiled. "The Phratries have evidence that one of the first Aspects was laid to rest in a tomb north of here. Buried within the rainbow cliffs, along with their armor, ages ago."

Never before had Ophiera heard of a paladin entombed. Then again, it seemed she knew little of the Cloister. But Ophiera did know the shaman meant her words. And as frustrated as she felt, the prospect of replacing her armor provided a flicker of hope.

"So we head to the Cliffs of Eidolon?" Myronor asked.

"We cannot do anything until we've healed," Ophiera replied.

"Not a problem," Kaikora said.

"I find the hole through my heart quite problematic," snapped Ophiera.

Kaikora laughed throatily. "Between my winesap tea and a salve of shadeweed and ink kelp, you'll heal in no time. Plus, now that you are an ekath, well...I'm sure you've noticed how the tether draws you together. The closer you are, the faster you will heal."

The shaman handed Ophiera a burlap satchel of the same lavender scent as the tea. Leaning back, she stretched a long, muscular arm to a small shelf behind the sunken den. She returned with a small clay pot with a wobbly lid. Ophiera took the gifts, understanding their cue to leave. Myronor stood first, stretching with a wince in his blue robes.

"One last bit of guidance," Kaikora said, stretching her legs before the fire again. "The Birzhan ritual originated overseas with the mother clans. Many have forgotten, but Tanvik's first people originated from the Shole deserts of the Orbolas continent—west of Krysas. Surely some of those who remain there will know more about ekatma."

"Such as how to break the bond?" Ophiera asked. Her chest tugged uncomfortably.

"That is beyond my knowledge."

"Yet the secrets of the Cloister are not?" Ophiera clapped back.

"You never asked, so I didn't tell." Kaikora shrugged. "Who has more responsibility in that scenario, hmm?"

It was true.

Ophiera never asked. And as always, everything that had gone wrong was her own fault.

~ Twenty-Three ~

AMELIORATION

Ophiera and Myronor left the shaman's hut with their parting gifts. Neither the bag of winesap tea nor pot of unction was heavy, but Ophiera felt weighed down as they departed.

Finding out her armor was not what she had believed felt nearly as damning as watching it melt into nothing. Kaikora said not to worry about the black ichor, but how could she not? What was to say that same substance couldn't just melt a new set of armor too?

Kaikora claimed the tomb was that of the first Aspect. Did this mean the armor she spoke of was pure adamantrium? Ophiera didn't understand how the tomb could be outside the Cloister's knowledge. It all felt too convenient and too outlandish at the same time.

The sun now set as the pair walked silently through the village, heading back to Ophiera's cottage. The discussion with Kaikora had left Ophiera feeling ignorant beyond words. Ignorant of the powers of Erum and of herself.

As they passed the village dock, Ophiera saw the *Equinox*, empty of fishers and cargo alike. The homecoming bustle was over now and most of the village celebrated at the tavern. What a lovely, normal day—for them. To think, if she hadn't been conscripted, she would be in the tavern now, joining in the festivities before beginning her nightly patrols.

When she and Myronor finally arrived at her cottage, Ophiera placed the tea and salve on the side table in the small kitchen. She felt winded by the trek and took a moment to collect herself. What a frustrating feeling, this weakness.

Myronor hovered behind her, silent and distant. A tension had built between them throughout the silent walk, and now she hesitated to face him.

If she hadn't witnessed his vesper on the riverbank, he would not be bound to her now. The fate of serving as her anchor to life would have never fallen to him. Ekatma, that's what Kaikora called them. She had forced this fate on him, like the Cloister had forced a fate on her.

He should have hated her. He should have blamed her. But the tension she felt through the silence was not one of repulsion. Their connection—their ekath—reverberated with something unfamiliar.

"Shall we?"

Ophiera peered over her shoulder, confused. Myronor had already pulled his robes over his head, undressing on a whim yet again.

"Shall we *what*, exactly?" she said, unable to hide her shock.

He laughed in a familiar tone, the one usually reserved for a joke at her own expense.

"We should apply that salve as soon as possible, shouldn't we? But I can't really reach my back..."

Bare chested, he lifted his arms and turned, revealing his carved back and bruised ribs.

Ophiera hadn't seen him without his robes since arriving in Iluka. He always slept in his robes, or changed out of sight; she should have known how out of character it was for him to act coy. She knew he had been beaten, had *watched* as it happened, but she didn't know the full extent of his injuries. He looked as near to death as she felt. Before, he'd assured her he was fine. This was not fine.

A hollow pit formed in her gut at the sight. Without words, she snatched the clay pot from the table, leaving the loose top behind. She dipped her scarred fingertips into the viscous paste, noting the aroma of ink kelp.

With his back still to her, she applied a liberal amount of the now tingling salve. The rough gash where the Reverend sliced him had already begun to heal, but the sight still churned her stomach. She doubted any amount of salve would prevent this from scarring. His beautiful, muscular back was marred forever by the Reverend. Ophiera had taken Retribution against the wretched man, but it didn't feel like justice enough.

"Turn around," she whispered. The ache in her chest stole her voice. He did as she said, arms still up to reveal his ribs. She winced at the number of healing contusions blanketing his beaten ribcage.

She tried to suppress the visions of the Reverend beating him near death. She tried to forget his cries of pain or how the blood sprayed from his lips or the way he curled in on himself when it stopped. But she couldn't. Every time he winced or grunted, her rage grew. Every injury was a testament to her failure. If her hands were not on him, she would have burst into flames again.

After Ophiera had covered his ribs in salve, she *sensed* his relief. It disturbed her how clearly this knowledge—no, feeling—came to her through the ekath. She wondered if he felt her emotions as well. Did he sense the rage shaking her hands as she daubed the last broken rib? Or the guilt of her failures on display beneath her fingers?

Myronor lowered his arms and held an outstretched hand to her, indicating the jar of salve. "I can reach the rest myself. I don't want you to feel uncomfortable."

So he did sense her mood. But perhaps he misinterpreted.

Ignoring his outstretched hand, Ophiera began applying the salve to his bruised abdomen. Her vision of him kicked over and over again faded, instead replaced by a heat that burned her cheeks. She ran her hand along a bruise, just above the intimate parts of him, and...by the flames, was she the pervert all along? Her thoughts were...not right. She shook, reminding herself she was touching him for penance.

After retrieving more salve from the pot, she made her way up his chest, a safe distance from distraction. She covered the plethora of scrapes and bruises there before finding his face.

Only now did she notice how intently Myronor watched her. His very soul was linked to hers now, and yet she couldn't bear his eyes. The blue, interrogative gaze saw too far through her now. But the location of his next injury promised relief.

"Close your eyes," she mumbled.

He obeyed without a word.

As Ophiera applied the balm to his facial injuries, she studied his features at leisure. A gash above his eyebrow looked deep, likely to scar much like his back. At least the bruises on his jaw had faded. Hopefully, with the salve, they'd disappear by the next day.

He sighed as a slight smile played across his lips. She had the desire to run her fingers across them as well, though they were not injured.

"Hold out your hands," she said.

"Am I allowed to open my eyes now, Warden?"

"No."

He obeyed again with a smirk.

She dabbed around the still raw imprints where his wrists had been bound. The bonds had temporarily sapped him of his power, exploiting his weakness. If the Brotherhood was in possession of items that could take away a mage's power, no wonder they also knew how to destroy her armor.

Avoiding her bitter thoughts, Ophiera spent too much time inspecting his hands. He truly was the son of a fisher. Strong yet soft, large but dexterous. She imagined all the times, throughout their journey, these hands had acted upon her. He had cast spells and patched wounds. He had conjured meals and wiped away tears. He had saved her life twice now, but at what cost? His very soul was now bound to her fate; a fate no one deserved.

Those same hands suddenly wrapped around her own, embracing them in warmth. He squeezed, and the hollow pit in Ophiera's gut bubbled with something new. The ekath tugged first, drawing her to him before his hands began to pull. Everything drew her to him, but she couldn't give in to these false feelings.

"Done," she said, taking her hands away. She had resisted the draw.

Before Myronor opened his eyes, she turned away, placing the pot back on the kitchen table. A few steadying breaths were required before she could face him again.

Once composed, Ophiera turned back to find Myronor standing inches from her. Still bare, he watched her incredulously, negating all her efforts to calm herself. As his arm reached behind her, she froze. Her heart hammered clumsily as she feared his intentions. As his golden hair brushed over her shoulder, she wondered...Was it fear she felt? Or something else?

He stood back, holding up the little pot in his hand.

"I believe you still have a hole in your heart," he said with a sad smirk.

"How could I forget?"

She was impressed with herself for keeping her voice so calm. In her mournful assessment of Myronor's injuries, she had somehow forgotten her own.

Ophiera reached to take the pot from him, but he pulled it away from her groping hand, smirking yet again.

"I'll do it. You won't be able to reach your back."

Hesitant at first, the constant pull from beneath the wound begged for her submission. She lifted her black tunic over her head as she turned, revealing her bound back to him. Pale linen remained tightly wrapped around her torso, covering her back and bosom.

Ophiera held her arms out as she had every other time they changed her bandages. Myronor's steady, gentle hands peeled back the linens that wrapped around her chest. She still felt flustered standing bare before him.

As the bandages dropped, the cool air soothed her wounds and caused her skin to bump up. She shivered slightly at his touch between her shoulders. The wound was still tender, and the salve stung, causing her breath to hike a moment. But as he ran his finger from the wound down her spine, it surprised her how comforting his touch felt.

"Turn around," he said.

She covered her breasts with her unscarred arm and did as he asked. But with a jolt of sorrow, she realized they had stood similarly when the arrow pierced her. With that image in mind, she feared treatment of this wound might be too intimate for her. And too painful for him.

"I can do it," she said, reaching for the pot with her free hand.

He pulled the salve away from her grasp again and instead took her hand in his own, holding her steady.

"Please," he said in a wavering voice. "I could do nothing before..."

He pressed her hand against his chest, where she felt his racing heart. The tether connecting their souls quivered, revealing the foundation of his pain. And she could not deny him.

She left her arm across her chest, exposing the wound without exposing herself in full. As he applied the salve upon the gaping wound near her heart, she saw his jaw tighten. His eyes glistened with mourning and something more...intimate. Though her skin still shivered, she felt warmth flood her cheeks.

He lifted his hand and, in a flash of blue light, held clean linens. As if in an old habit, she turned away and held her arms out again, happy to be relieved of the intimacy of his eyes. He wrapped her chest several times over and, with one last tuck of the bandage, her dressing was complete. And yet he still stood close behind her.

Suddenly, his bare chest pressed against her back. From behind, his arm draped over her shoulder, and he placed a trembling hand over her wounded heart. His other arm came across her waist, pulling her against him. In his embrace, she felt his whole body shudder as warm tears fell to her shoulder. His breathing grew erratic as he sobbed against her.

His raw emotion shattered her heart beneath his hand. Yet the intense rhythm of vitality seemed to calm him some.

His tears still fell as he held her with an iron grip. As if he feared she would disappear. The guilt, the terror, and the loss played across her heart as if they were her own.

This is my fault...all my fault.

And she realized the guilty thought was no longer hers alone.

As if a floodgate had opened, Myronor's emotions bombarded her, jumbled by painful thoughts and visions of the encampment. The ekath connected them beyond a tether.

The hollow pit now filled with burning, pushing out despair and replacing it with a fiery need. A need for *him.* A need for Retribution. Her scars tingled dangerously, simultaneously reminding her of terrible power and her duty to her Oath.

Regardless of the ekath, her path was far from Myronor's in this world. Until Pyra's death was resolved, her Oath remained unfulfilled. And once her Oath was fulfilled...they had no future. Perhaps he sensed the way her heart now slowed as it became stony with purpose.

When his breath finally steadied, Ophiera gently removed herself from his grasp.

"You are convincing me you are indeed the pervert I suspected," she said, her voice forcibly light.

"You often mistake first aid for perversion." He chortled. But even beneath the beautiful, familiar laugh, she saw the pain in his eyes.

A pain they both shared now.

~ Twenty-Four ~

APPRAISAL

The last time Myronor swam in the ocean, it felt very different now. As he lay on his back, buoyant and lazy, he knew it wasn't the sea that changed. Only *he* had changed.

Between the ekath and the shaman's interventions, Myronor and Ophiera had recovered at a remarkable pace. Few signs of their ordeal remained after only three nights of tea, salve, and sleep; three wondrous nights of recovery in Ophiera's cottage.

Neither had left the other's side, even whilst they slept. Not intertwined like some of the spicier tomes Myronor owned back in his tower and not even embraced; they had simply lain beside each other, occasionally hand in hand. Despite everything, they were some of the most peaceful night's sleep he'd ever had.

When awake, they drank the shaman's tea and reapplied the salve several times a day. Each time Myronor smeared the salve across her arrow wound, his own heart ached. Each time her fingers danced across his own injuries, something else ached. The ekath tugged constantly, and though he willingly submitted himself to the call, the boundaries of her heart lay clear. Distant.

Now nearly mended, Ophiera's Oath drove her to continue their journey as soon as possible. Myronor, however, never wanted to leave Iluka again. On his back, bobbing in the gentle surf off the shore of Iluka, he remembered why he loved his home.

The Brotherhood and their encampment had sapped away his curiosity about the world beyond. He felt too exhausted to think of next steps—at least for now. But regardless of what he wanted, Myronor could not bring himself to ask Ophiera what would happen if she broke her Oath and stayed in Iluka instead.

He had *felt* the fear in her heart during the discussions with Kaikora, as if it were his own. The pain of the Cloister's betrayal, transferred through the ekath, had been enough to deter him from mentioning Iluka or her Oath at all while they recovered. But while Ophiera's body healed, he felt her spirit begin to fester. The weight of all the recent change was too heavy on her now bare shoulders. Reluctant as he was to leave Iluka, Myronor had accepted that Ophiera needed the armor from the tomb. It was the simplest of her vulnerabilities to solve at the moment, though he still questioned the shaman's guidance.

According to Ophiera, those baring Oaths outside of the Cloister only returned when it was time to succumb to the holy flames. He wasn't sure exactly *when* this was meant to occur; when the kindled fulfilled their Oaths? When they reached old age? Or were they summoned back by the holy flames themselves? Regardless, he understood why it was strange that a tomb even existed. And so near Iluka? He read the doubt etched between Ophiera's brows every time they discussed it. And yet, if she trusted the shaman's words as truth, Myronor should as well.

To prepare for their journey to the Aspect's tomb, Ophiera insisted that Myronor acquire some sort of weapon to defend himself. At first, he disagreed completely. His magic was powerful enough and frankly, more suited to serve as a determent rather than combat. But every time he protested, Ophiera would point out the fading marks of the Brotherhood's bonds around his wrists. Eventually, he couldn't say no to the anguish in her eyes.

As usual, Kaikora provided. After a discussion with Ophiera, the shaman offered to craft a weapon for Myronor and even train him to wield it. He protested again, trying to ensure whatever weapon she gave him he could figure out on his own. Magic was one thing, but the physical act of hurting another person, the visceral feeling of causing bodily harm—that was beyond him. It was best to leave those types of situations to Ophiera. Only after Kaikora explained that her own trident served as both weapon and conduit for her mysticisms did he hesitantly agree.

Myronor opened his eyes now, feeling the sting of salt water and sun. He desired a few more moments of his peaceful swim, but from the corner of his eye, he saw the shaman descending from the village. She carried a burlap-wrapped parcel under her arm, likely the reason for his peace being disturbed. The trident remained in her other hand, and even from this distance, the sea glass prongs shined a pale green in the sparkling sun.

He swam beneath the surf toward the dock where Ophiera held her usual vigil. She wore the cream-colored tunic he had lent her ages ago. Her dark pants were rolled just above the knee where the cerulean waters touched her calves. And as he watched her gently kick her legs in the sea while she fixated on the horizon, he glimpsed the past; a beautiful, carefree Warden of Iluka. Was this how she had spent her retirement before the Magistrate had conscripted her? Before her Oath forcefully chained her to him and his mother's cause? These thoughts occurred more and more frequently, but he was becoming rather adept at pushing them from his mind. There was no changing the past—and no sense in worrying about it.

Mallow napped next to Ophiera, having spent the afternoon frolicking in the sands. As if she had dropped from the sky, the cat splayed with contented, closed eyes. Again, he appreciated the otherworldly look of both creatures on the dock. He swam until he reached the edge of the small wooden pier and heard Ophiera speak.

"Is that the weapon for Myronor?" she asked curiously.

"Yes, though I am surprised he is not with you," Kaikora's voice boomed.

The shaman had not seen him beneath the waves. Something must have distracted her. With aid from his magic, he splashed up violently from the water, lifting himself onto the dock. To his disappointment, the shaman remained forever composed.

"By the flames, cover yourself," Ophiera said, averting her eyes from him. "Kaikora doesn't need to see that..."

As one should, he swam without clothing. Myronor pulled his blue robes from the dock with a devilish smile, dragging them roughly over his head. "You see what Kaikora is wearing? Or rather, the lack thereof? I think you, my prude little paladin, are the only one with a problem—"

Suddenly, he found himself facing the bright afternoon sky as he fell backward. And pain shocked him as he collided violently with the dock. Ophiera had dropped him swiftly with one swipe of her arm. He had to laugh at the violence of his companion. It was strange how her prowess for fighting bothered him so little, yet he held an aversion to it himself.

As he sat up, rubbing his tender back, Kaikora hefted the heavy parcel into his lap. "It's a quarterstaff. Should help you channel your magic, as well as defend yourself."

As he carefully unwrapped the burlap, he revealed a staff that matched his height. Gnarled and weathered, the pale driftwood contrasted handsomely with dark leather adornments. Atop sat the largest Iluka pearl he had ever seen, a fist-sized blushed and spherical stone. Kaikora's craftsmanship lingered on every surface, a testament and tribute to her skills.

"It's beautiful," he said, coming to a stand.

Kaikora acknowledged his comment with a nod, forever humble. "When do you plan to depart for the tomb?"

"Thanks to you, we could leave tomorrow," Ophiera said, still gazing out at the sea. "The sooner the better, obviously, but I would appreciate it if you showed him how to wield the staff first."

"Oh, come now, it's a stick. How hard can it be?" Myronor said. To prove his point, he swung the driftwood staff wildly.

"Warden, shall we show him what a 'stick' can accomplish?" Kaikora asked quietly. She wore a smug grin as she walked toward the patch of sandy beach beyond the dock. The corner of Ophiera's mouth twitched before she stood, shaking the seawater from her feet.

A duel between a shaman and paladin; the idea piqued Myronor's curiosity. Though he learned best by reading, he accepted some skills required real-life demonstrations to learn properly. For this, he would happily play pupil.

"I'm yours to teach, Warden," he said with a slight bow to Ophiera.

Her eyes rolled above her twitching scowl. The exact expression he had hoped to see. And feel. The ekath made teasing her even more enjoyable.

"First lesson is how to hold it," Ophiera said. A scarred hand swept across his vision, leaving only his empty grip behind. In the blink of an eye, she had deftly seized the staff from his grip. She bit her lip in a triumphant smile and turned away. He wanted the staff back just so she would do that again.

Smitten, he followed her down to the beach where Kaikora stood waiting. Ophiera took her place, ten paces apart, facing the shaman. As their eyes met, the air grew heavy. Did he sense something unsettled between them? Myronor realized this moment might go far beyond Kaikora's original intention to train him.

With a shrug, Myronor plunked down upon the tufted sand dunes. In preparation to watch whatever score was about to be settled, he conjured himself a drink. Kaikora took notice and scowled.

"You will observe *for now*," she said. "But this isn't for your entertainment. Ophiera will show you how to wield the staff, then you and I will work on channeling your mana through it."

Myronor nodded in agreement, taking a deep drink of his conjured beverage. A mixture of white yuzu and brine mint was perfect to combat the heat of the sun.

Kaikora's pearlescent loincloth shimmered as she flourished her trident. Meanwhile, the paladin grimaced at the staff before gracefully twirling it about. She looked to be weighing its movements. With a pinch of guilt, he realized what a poor substitute a stick must make for her claymore.

"Fire and water meet again!" Kaikora shouted, brushing her tendrils of liquid bronze hair over her shoulder. "It's been a long time since we've danced."

"Be gentle—I had a hole in my chest not so long ago," Ophiera said with a challenging smile. Another expression enhanced by the ekath.

"On my mark then."

Kaikora stood low and primal, holding her trident pointed forward while resting on her forearm. In response, Ophiera placed her feet firmly apart in the sand, standing straight and tall. She held the staff with her scarred arm behind her body, pearl pointed downward. The confidence with which she stood was breathtaking —especially wearing his shirt. He knew, regardless of what Kaikora insisted, he was about to be entertained.

"Begin!" Kaikora barked.

The shaman was the immediate aggressor. Motionless, Ophiera held her ground as the gigantic woman barreled toward her. Myronor felt his nerves prick at her lack of reaction. Why wasn't she moving?

Just as the shaman was upon her, Ophiera swung her stick upward with a quick and precise jerk. She held the sea-glass trident at bay with the stick—no, the *staff*—lodged between the prongs. As Ophiera twisted away, she brought the trident down to the sand with her own weapon and aimed a kick at Kaikora's legs. The shaman dodged, disengaging with a backward roll. When she came to a stand, her excess of bare skin had picked up a dusting of white sand, as had her trident.

Ophiera resumed the same stance as before, stoic and staring down the shaman. Myronor had never witnessed her fight without armor. Free of the bulk, she moved like Mallow hunting a beetle; a graceful predator. Without flames, armor, or Oath, she fought free of the Cloister's burden. She fought for fun and he much preferred this style.

Kaikora crouched low again, preparing for the next spar. But first, she yelled to Myronor. "See how close I came before Ophiera countered? It's quite the advantage to keep your maneuvers subtle, or hidden until the last possible moment."

Ophiera glanced toward Myronor, and he smiled at her, as he usually did. But through the ekath he felt something new behind her lilac gaze. Whatever it was, it brought him an inexplicable sensation of comfort.

Without warning, Kaikora charged in a second furious attack. This time, she caught Ophiera distracted and pressed for the advantage. But Ophiera recovered and recalculated, maneuvering the staff quickly between her hands to halt the trident mere inches from her chest. It looked as if Kaikora was really trying to stab her. Myronor's stomach clenched. When had this spar had turned serious?

Locked in a forceful stalemate, Kaikora pressed forward as Ophiera held her ground. The shaman called to Myronor again, her voice strained with effort. "Now, if the Aspect would actually use her power, she could channel the flames and be free of this situation."

Myronor wished bitterly that Kaikora would stop taunting Ophiera over her decision to suppress the flames. While he agreed with the shaman that this precaution was unnecessary, he respected Ophiera's choice. The shaman didn't have to feel her fear of losing control at every waking moment. But the ekath ensured Myronor felt it all.

Ophiera's arms shook under the full force of Kaikora's might. But he saw the burn behind her eyes. With a quick, forceful thrust, Ophiera drove the staff upward, dislodging the trident with it. The sudden change in direction shifted Kaikora off-balance. Ophiera disengaged, but didn't retreat. Instead, she dropped low and swung the staff in one fluid motion, sweeping Kaikora's legs out from under her. The shaman fell, landing hard on the sand.

Kaikora lay still in the sand a moment before a deep laugh resounded against the waves.

Myronor surged with pride. Ophiera didn't need the holy flames to defend herself from Kaikora. And though he of course appreciated the skills she possessed, he couldn't help but stare at the way her body moved as she fought. Without the plate mail, he could see every curved muscle contributing to her grace and power. He didn't want her to think him a pervert, but watching her perform like this tested his resolve.

"And you requested that *I* be gentle!" Kaikora exclaimed as she stood, knocking sand from her backside. "It's your turn now. Show the mage how to properly attack with that weapon."

"I prefer a weapon with an edge," Ophiera complained as she studied the blush-colored pearl adorning the top of the staff. "But then you'd truly be in trouble, wouldn't you?"

Kaikora nodded with a grin. "I'm ready whenever you are."

The shaman barely finished her words before Ophiera charged.

The paladin looked petite compared to Kaikora. The shaman stood poised like a wall of muscle, braced for her opponent's charge. With a forceful swing, Ophiera aimed for her legs. But the shaman had clearly learned her tactics.

The trident moved to block the first strike. For such a brawny woman, Kaikora moved with unbelievable speed as she dodged and parried Ophiera's continued attacks. At each exchange, Kaikora blocked with ease and he could feel Ophiera tiring through their link.

Ophiera shifted her grip on the staff and he instantly recognized the position; it looked as if she held her claymore. She danced around the shaman, pressing the attack until she found a hole in the shaman's defense. In a tiny miscalculation, Kaikora blocked a little too high and, with a swift jab to the chest, Ophiera broke through violently. Knocked back, the mountainous woman stumbled and gripped her chest. Ophiera faltered and lowered her weapon as worry mingled with the sweat across her brow.

"Are you trying to match my heart to yours?" Kaikora asked, smiling with threat. "Now, it's my turn to demonstrate the advantage of actually using one's mana."

Myronor recognized the shaman's hydromancy before her eyes transformed. Her stone-colored eyes became the reflective, placid pools he remembered from his youth.

Defeat washed over Ophiera's face and she cast the staff to the side. It landed in the sand with a sad thump as water began pooling around her feet.

The shaman called forth the sea, pulling the bubbling water up through the sand and flooding around Ophiera. Violent waves of crystalline water surged, eventually lifting her from the ground. Myronor tensed as she became engulfed in an orb of swirling ocean. She took one last breath before becoming completely submerged in her liquid prison. He found it strange to see her surrounded by water, rather than white flames. She looked peaceful floating in the sphere by comparison.

In his childhood, he had witnessed Kaikora's water bending at sea, but never on land. She must have called the water from the sea to the beach, and naturally, he had questions. But his intrigue soon turned to worry as time passed. She wasn't releasing Ophiera.

Myronor rose from his sand dune and approached the shaman. Why was his heartbeat quickening? And did he feel out of breath?

The ekath reached for him, dragging at his very soul. And he knew Ophiera was drowning.

"I've seen enough," he said, trying desperately to keep his voice steady. The shaman glared back toward Myronor with mirrorlike eyes.

"Do you not wish to test the immortality of the ekatma?" she asked, smiling at Ophiera. Peaceful before, Ophiera now thrashed against the bubble. She could not break the surface.

"End it now, Kaikora!" he yelled. "She's drowning!" But again, the shaman only smirked, ignoring him. The panic pressing in against his chest was too much to bear. He felt Ophiera slip closer to the Aether. Just as she had that day in the encampment.

"I said that's enough!" he spat. Blue light flashed from his hands as the globe suddenly crashed around Ophiera. She hung suspended in the air for a moment before crumpling onto the wet sand.

Over Kaikora's cackling laugh, he could hear Ophiera's gasps and coughs. He ran to her. Strands of white hair had come loose in the water and covered her face as she breathed deeply. Unable to help himself, he took her face in his hands, wiping the water and white locks aside.

"Are you alright?" he asked, praying the pure terror he felt did not show on his face. She nodded, but her eyes hardened as she glared at the shaman.

"Are you satisfied with your test?"

Kaikora's stare returned to gray, but her expression remained unreadable.

"The mage knew you could not die yet still interfered," she said with a shrug. "I'm more impressed that he overpowered my spell."

Myronor still held Ophiera, unwilling to let go. There was no smile on his face as he turned to Kaikora. "It is not about death, but suffering! We've been through enough without drowning her to prove a point."

Hadn't Ophiera been through enough? Hadn't he? He had watched Ophiera skirt death too many times, but now with the ekath, he *felt* her suffering. How could Kaikora act so callously?

Ophiera's chilled hands grasped his own, and she squeezed gently before pulling herself upright. "She is right, Myronor. We need to know the limits of our...of this." She turned to the shaman. "Though I'd appreciate a warning next time."

He could not believe Ophiera agreed with Kaikora's methods. She was willing to risk her life to test a theory. And for the first time since he'd met the enigmatic paladin, he grew angry with her. Did her own existence mean so little? Did she not realize what her suffering did to him now?

"I'm going to change clothes," Ophiera said, standing from the wet sand. "You two should continue training without me."

Without so much as a glance, she left for her cottage. Myronor felt her emotions weakening as she walked farther away. A numbness spread within her that had little to do with drowning.

He felt the shaman place a hand on his shoulder.

"She is complicated," Kaikora said.

He knocked her hand off him, turning on her with anger. "Perhaps she would seem less so if everyone was not out to hurt her...especially those who claim to be her friends!"

Kaikora laughed, a seemingly inappropriate response. Now Myronor understood why Ophiera bristled whenever he laughed at her.

"I know you care for her in ways beyond the ekath. She feels it too, but..." she said. The shaman rarely hesitated in conversation, and he wondered what was so difficult to say. "The concept of any bond beyond her Oath is so foreign to her, that it feels wrong. She will need time to adjust."

"I don't care if she ever adjusts or reciprocates. She can break the ekath for all I care. I just wish she would value her life as much as I do."

Kaikora smiled. "You've grown up since your days on Berwyn's boat. Come, let us continue to train."

Myronor felt little desire to learn how to use the staff at this moment. He never shook easily, but his stomach had yet to unknot after feeling Ophiera drown. The tightening and draw of the tether as she distanced from him wasn't helping either.

"Mallow?" he called toward the docks. The sunbathing familiar's ears perked at the noise, but the lazy creature refused to move. "Mallow, can you go keep Ophiera company?"

That got her attention. The cream-and-dark-blue familiar rolled onto her feet with a luxurious stretch before trotting up the path to the cottage.

He plucked the staff from the sand and tried to hold it as Ophiera had. Kaikora appeared before him, ready to begin.

"This isn't imbued?" he asked.

"No."

"How can a weapon have magical properties without formal imbuement?"

"You refer to the imbuteria arts practiced in Krysas?" she asked. He nodded. "Then you know imbuteria only works on materials capable of being infused with magic in the first place. What do you think makes those materials so special?"

Though mages in Tanvik had only recently begun to explore the art of imbuteria, the mages of Krysas had mastered the skill long ago. Some materials were stronger than others, and certain materials were preferred for specific enchantments. The manner in which Kaikora had phrased her question seemed to suggest enchantment might be even more complicated than Myronor thought.

He shrugged, beckoning her to continue.

"The material must contain power first. Any combination of the endless sources of mana found on Erum. My trident, for example, is embedded with prongs of sea glass. Storms and sea and earth converged to form this precious stone, making it exceptionally powerful." She pointed to his staff. "Life and sea formed that pearl and the wood. Cultivated and nurtured, all of the energy that was poured into the formation of a precious gem remains within."

"And how does this aid in channeling magic then?" he pressed, trying to hold the staff as Ophiera had.

"The material lends you its strength, conserving some of your mana. Try a spell channeled through the staff and feel the difference."

The first spell that came to mind was a transmutation on Kaikora —payback for what she had pulled earlier. But he was becoming less bitter as they spoke. Besides, the laws of Tanvik forbade any transmutation of a person. To transmute an object required a very different approach than transmuting a living being with a vesper. Years ago, Tanvik negotiated an agreement with Krysas banning transmutations on the living. So instead, he thought to try to channel conjura magic through the staff.

In a moment of concentration, he focused on his forte. The largest cake he had ever attempted to conjure materialized into thin air. Bright purple frosting covered the three tiers of perfection, decorated in iris flowers, sugar, and white spires of shining frosting. It was painfully obvious what had been on his mind as he conjured it, but even this extravagance had cost him half the mana with the staff in hand. Thus, he used his excess to float the cake in the air, just like he had with his feet in the marsh. It looked out of place, hovering before him on the beach.

Kaikora laughed as she dipped a thick finger into the pale frosting, smacking her lips. "Quite delicious!"

"Why is this not common practice amongst the mages of Tanvik?" he said, examining the blushing pearl. "I feel like all mages should have a staff or something to channel with."

"The people of Tanvik refuse to remember the old ways and have yet to master the new," she said. "The mages refuse their history, while attempting to relearn it from a foreign country."

"Couldn't you teach them?" Myronor said. Kaikora would make a fortune selling these staves to mages in Feyralis. With enhanced mana, the mages of Feyralis could enact real change, do some real good for the people.

"Some knowledge is best left to be discovered, not taught. Just like many skills require failures to truly master. And some truths must be reached slowly, on one's own time, rather than being thrust upon them."

Myronor felt Ophiera's approach before he heard her. And at that moment, he knew the shaman's words were no longer just for him.

"I see training is going well," Ophiera said, dressed now in a fresh linen shirt and pants. She felt calmer; more like herself as she eyed the hovering cake. Mirroring the shaman, she dipped a finger in the frosting and sucked her finger. Myronor's heart teetered on edge at the sight.

"What troubled you before?" Kaikora asked, watching the paladin.

Ophiera's brow wrinkled in a moment's pause. "Nothing," she said, but the shaman would not relinquish her glare. "I'm just eager to get my own proper weapon."

She was a poor liar, even without the ekath telling him so. Something much deeper had troubled her, even if she suppressed it now.

"Well, we've trained as much as he needs," the shaman said. She relaxed her stance. "You should leave tomorrow."

"We will. I fear what consequences await me if I do not fulfill my Oath soon."

Though he smiled at her, his heart sank slightly. The damnable Oath.

It was simple for him to push their obligations from his mind, to fantasize about a life without duty. It was especially easy at night whilst he slept by her side, imagining an existence in Iluka together. Yet her duty held priority, and he knew that was how it must be. Though Myronor viewed her as much more than her Oath, he wondered if Ophiera would ever see beyond the brands the Cloister had left on her.

~ Twenty-Five ~

QUANDRY

The next morning, Ophiera and Myronor departed in darkness, hours before dawn. The shaman knew their intentions to leave that day, and thus Ophiera felt no need to say goodbye. Kaikora *knew* everything, after all.

Her growing sourness toward the shaman had little to do with her choice of an unsociable departure. Nothing at all.

Either way, Myronor didn't seem to mind slipping away quietly. She knew he was already hesitant to leave Iluka, but supposed it was easier abstaining from any goodbyes, especially with Berwyn. It wasn't as if she wanted to leave either; it was simply that she must.

If there was even the slightest hope for her to acquire a new weapon and armor, she had to seize it. She needed armor to fulfill her Oath. And she needed to fulfill her Oath in order to return to Iluka. To return to her retirement.

Unfortunately, those were the only clear paths before her now; everything else was chaos.

Ophiera feared what fate would befall her and Myronor once they reached Krysas. Would the ekath be able to bear the separation that must come? Bound to each other, yet bound to the wills of others first. Which held precedence: her Oath or the ekath? She could not break her Oath without penalty of extinguishment—at least that was what she had been led to believe. But the Cloister had lied about many things, things Kaikora *knew* all along.

Despite her resentment toward the shaman, even Ophiera had to admit Kaikora never lied to her. Withheld? Yes. Evaded? Yes. But never lied. Did the Cloister then knowingly lie about her armor? If they were willing to perpetuate that falsehood, how many others did Ophiera live her life by?

"You seem rather preoccupied," Myronor said in a warm voice. He walked beside her, using his staff as a walking stick rather than a weapon. He looked less mage-like dressed in his traveling clothes, but the staff gave him away as something more than just a man.

With a sigh, Ophiera ignored his comment and pulled ahead of him in the sand, leaving his curious gaze behind her. She didn't want to discuss the storm brewing in her heart.

The sun may have risen a few hours ago, but it was still too early in their journey to discuss what was on her mind. The choices they must face, and the ones she had already made for them both. She wasn't ready to say out loud the conclusion she had reached.

They simply needed to keep moving.

Ophiera heard the familiar *mew* of Mallow exiting her crystal, no doubt coaxed out by Myronor as distraction. The little familiar pranced ahead of them in the sand and began her signature inspection of all things new. The sight tore Ophiera's thoughts away from the future and back to the present.

The coastal dunes looked peaceful in the morning sun. Long grasses and pale grains broke through the coastal dunes, dancing in the sea breeze. Mallow prowled in the grasses, threatening the peaceful view with her interest in the wildlife. The cat batted at the small red geckos that clung to the reeds of grass. But the lizards quickly learned the familiar was only so tall. Once they were out of Mallow's reach, she gave up; the lazy creature couldn't be bothered to jump, after all. Bored with the geckos, she tried to claw several crabitas out of their sandy dens. She managed to scare a few out and chased them, skittering toward the surf. But that was where the pursuit ended; the familiar dared not step a toe into the sea.

While Mallow served as a wonderful distraction until the late afternoon, Ophiera inevitably fell back into worried steps. The beautiful landscape would transform into tougher terrain eventually. And she doubted Mallow would enjoy herself this much again, at least until they returned.

Ophiera vividly remembered the rocky sandstone shores leading to the Cliffs of Eidolon. Years ago, when she first saw the swirling reds and oranges and yellows of the treacherous cliffs, she found them breathtaking. She had always wanted to return someday. Though perhaps under different circumstances.

After she retired from the Magistrate's service, the first task she took on for herself was to explore the Southern Coastlands. A nomadic hermit, she wandered up and down the coast, trying to hide from the world while searching for peace of heart.

Her Oath demanded she uphold Retribution, not seek it out. And so, she reasoned, by staying secluded along the coast, away from people, she might never need to perform her duty again.

A loophole, at best.

Still, the Magistrate and the Cloister had granted her request for retirement and thus, her Oath had remained unbroken. But she couldn't shake the feeling that she was being punished now. What if all the recent changes were the seeds she'd sown for trying to change her fate? She'd avoided her Oath for most of her retirement but now had become the embodiment of it. Was the flamed monstrosity she'd become in the camp her tithe for her disobedience?

"Are you going to spend the entire journey brooding?" Myronor asked.

Ophiera took a deep breath before answering. "I'm not brooding."

He laughed.

Mallow scampered ahead of them, sensing the tension and leaving it far behind her. Ophiera wished she could do the same.

"You said it would take two nights to reach the cliffs, right?" Myronor said, coming to walk beside her now. "That's a long time to keep your thoughts to yourself. You could, oh I don't know, talk to me instead?"

"About what?" she asked with a sigh.

Myronor chuckled again. "Well, how about you tell me what worries you?"

Like her Oath demanding Retribution, the ekath demanded honesty. She didn't wish to discuss her Oath or armor or any of her thoughts with him right now. But...he lived his life in questions, so why couldn't she?

"What will we do when we arrive in Krysas?" she asked quietly.

"I suppose we'll want a bite to eat and a strong drink. I know Krysas is infamous for its herbaceous wines—"

"You know what I mean," she interrupted. This was why she didn't want to talk, but again the ekath forced her lips to move. "You and I have separate duties. Duties that preceded this tether. How do we reconcile those responsibilities when we are bound to each other by magic neither of us understands?"

"Do you worry this much about the sun rising?" he said, smiling at her as if actually expecting an answer. But she only glared in silence. "Ophiera, I understand your concerns—trust me, I share them. But what will worrying do for us *now*? Surely, what will happen in Krysas has little effect on our current task of retrieving your armor and weapon?"

Ophiera grimaced. He wasn't wrong, but he wasn't completely right either. It was an overly simplified answer for an overly complicated situation. She remained silent, still conflicted as he spoke again.

"There is no sense ruining today with the problems of tomorrow. We will deal with our situation when we come to it, just as we always have."

Her heart felt the comfort of his words, the reassurance that in the end, things would work out. But her jaw clenched at the absurdity.

"*Always?*" she snapped. "We've barely escaped with our lives several times over now. The riverbank, the Sloughmire, the encampment...It hardly feels like we've dealt with anything successfully."

"I mean, safety and success are often at odds with one another," he said, still smiling. "The whole 'you have to break eggs to make a cake'...Well, *I* don't have to break eggs, I don't even need eggs...but you would, so you get the point."

She did get the point; she *had* to break things to succeed. She needed instruments of violence to fulfill her Oath. She needed to burn a person alive to cleanse a soul. But Myronor, he simply succeeded. His power was one of creation, not of destruction. He provided, while she only claimed. And like everything else in her path, she would destroy him, by accident or on purpose, in order to succeed.

"The point is you would be better off without me," she muttered.

And there was the conclusion she wanted to avoid. The thought that had been plaguing her since Kaikora tried to drown her to prove a point about her soul. It wasn't fair that Myronor was stuck with her as ekatma, bound to her violent life and her darkened soul. Her task was to protect him, but how could she protect him against herself?

Myronor stepped before her, halting her step as the smile faded from his lips. "How could you say that?"

She dropped her gaze, staring down at her blackened leathers and her poor excuse for a weapon dangling from her hip. The machete she borrowed from Berwyn was nothing compared to her claymore, just as her leathers were nothing compared to her armor. She grew tired of the constant reminders of her inadequacies.

"I only say the truth," she said, her voice gaining volume and speed. "The situation has changed; I can't protect you without flames or armor or sword. And there's no guarantee I will get any of those things back soon. I think..." She swallowed the lump in her throat. "I think we should go our separate ways as soon as possible. Perhaps the link can accommodate our distance now that we're healed. Perhaps Berwyn or Kaikora can escort you to Krysas. Our future lies on two different paths regardless—"

"Stop, Ophiera." He took a step closer. She kept her head bowed, unable to look at him. "I don't want you to protect me. I do want to help you fulfill your Oath, but not for my or my mother's sake. I want to help you so you can be released from this absurd task and all others. My decision has nothing to do with this tether or the Magistrate—it's simply my choice. I *want* to be on the same path as you."

Ophiera's face grew warm, matching the hue of the pearl set atop Myronor's staff. Doubt nullified her fluster quickly. "The ekath compels you to say such nonsense."

"You're wrong again. I felt this way long before the Brotherhood took me captive. I told you already I thought our meeting was fate. Our paths are the same and I still would have it no other way."

She didn't know how to respond. A conflicted pain squeezed her chest. Before the encampment, before she had *died*, she had been willing to sacrifice her life for him, hadn't she? Since the day she had laid eyes upon his vesper, it would seem. What if viewing his vesper alone had bonded them? What if everything she felt for him this entire journey had been nothing more than a consequence of her actions? Of her horrible, heinous actions...all in the name of her Oath.

"It was not fate," she said, raising her eyes to meet his. "Fate would not be so cruel as to bind your soul to one such as mine."

"How could you say that to someone who has seen your very soul?" he said in exasperation. "Your shade was—"

"Don't!" she yelled, taking a step back. "Regardless of what you saw, I know what's inside me. I'm nothing more than what the Cloister took and replaced with white flames and violence. Fate has bound you to someone who will bring you nothing but despair. The best way to protect you is to stay away. And I swear I will find a way to break this bond so you're no longer forced to share my fate."

Her words struck him across his beautiful face, and the pain was too much for her to bear. With a hard step, she began walking up the beach again, leaving him behind.

He didn't follow her right away. She wondered if she'd broken him, just as she broke him at the Pellucid Falls. Maybe he'd head back to Iluka as he should. But once she felt the pull of her heart, she knew he began following her again. Like a leash, the ekath dragged him along, furthering her guilt. No one else deserved to walk this path of failure with her. Especially him.

The day progressed to evening in painful silence. Like all travels through sand, their progress was more consumptive than productive. The terrain acted as a leech, draining their stamina and slowing their progress. And Ophiera knew it would only become worse as they approached the Cliffs of Eidolon.

When the tide receded back to the ocean, they moved to walk along the surf. The flat, saturated beach accommodated the waning strength in their legs. And while their stamina had clearly suffered during their recovery in Iluka, she knew the ekath bolstered their constitution now.

The terrain began to shift as they finished the last leg of their trek for the day. Where before lay smooth dunes, now sat boulders of florid sandstone, protruding through the tufted grasses. Small alcoves of painted rocks smattered the beach, breaking the monotony of the sandy surf. A preview of the rainbow cliffs. Tomorrow would see the sand turn to rocky coast, a most beautiful but treacherous shore.

When twilight settled, they made camp between two dunes that had just enough rocks for a small fire pit. Myronor enlarged their bags without a word and began arranging the colorful stones in a circle. That was usually her job when they camped.

"I'll gather wood," Ophiera said, turning away from the ocean to begin her search.

She needed a moment to compose herself, anyway. Their earlier conversation still weighed on her uncomfortably. Plus, the idea of making camp without her armor made all other routines feel disjointed. She had grown used to performing her turndown while Myronor gathered wood. The removal of her armor had always been near therapeutic, relieving the weight on her spirit just as much as the carry. But now she only felt burdened with no relief in sight as she gathered material to burn.

The dunes only provided brittle branches of driftwood, dried seaweed, and reeds for a fire. The lowland portion of the Severed Wood was visible in this distance, but she saw no reason to venture there now. A small fire tonight suited Ophiera just fine. In fact, she held little desire to see fire again, true or holy. But she couldn't let Myronor grow cold in the night.

When she returned, Myronor had just finished minimizing their packs again. Her heart stammered as she saw the bedrolls. Side by side, he had laid them out to form one, large sleeping pad beside the fire.

Since their escape from the Brotherhood's encampment, they had slept together. It was platonic—purely in the name of sating the ekath and strengthening their recovery. It did not differ from when they had shared a bed at the Lonely Iris, or at least that was what she told herself.

She'd thought they would resume their previous habit of lying on opposite sides of the campfire now that they were healed. But there seemed to be no going back to how things had been before.

Myronor took the bundle of kindling from her and began to build the fire. Useless again, Ophiera sat on the edge of the bedroll. When the sparks of flint caught the tinder, she lay back, preferring the sight of stars to flames tonight. She gazed up at the clear, darkening sky, familiar and vast. Her feet grew warm with the crackling fire, and the crashing waves served as a metronome for her heart. Slowly, she calmed.

Myronor dropped beside her, lying back until they lay shoulder to shoulder. The feel of him beside her brought her comfort at the cost of her calm. Even without the ekath she could feel the tension of the unresolved. But they both remained silent, watching the coruscating stars in the velvet sky.

"May I ask how you came to be in service to the Magistrate?" Myronor said quietly. He watched her from the corners of his eyes.

Despite their spat, Ophiera was unsurprised to find his first words to her a question. "There's not much to tell."

He shifted. "How were you chosen?"

"I wasn't." Even without the ekath, she knew he found this answer unsatisfactory. She took a deep breath. "The Cloister always abides by the Magistrate's request for conscripts. Usually, Hands are the only echelon permitted to leave the Cloister. But the former Hand of Retribution who had served the Magistrate was called back to become the next Chaplain of the Cloister. And there were no other paladins born of the flames, except me—so I wasn't chosen, I was simply a last resort."

"No other kindled bore Retribution as their Oath?"

She shook her head. "The Cloister has so few disciples these days. And the unkindled...Well, most don't survive the Sacramentum. Those who had were nearly all branded with Oaths of Mercy and Sacrifice. My former—the Hand of Retribution—had gone to the Sacramentum shortly before I did, actually. And he was conscripted immediately. That left me as the only bearer of Retribution in the Cloister. And when he returned as Chaplain, he sent me to the Magistrate in his stead."

"But you're not a Hand...you're an Aspect. How does that work then, that you were conscripted?"

She shrugged. "The Chaplain decided I must leave and the Aether allowed it, so it must not have mattered. Like I said—last resort."

Myronor turned over on his side, facing her now. "What binds you to the will of the Magistrate? Is it magic or simply the fear of consequence?"

Ophiera frowned. "I don't know...Both, I suppose. If I disobey the Magistrate, I disobey the Justicar of the Cloister. Disobeying the Cloister is considered a breach of Oath, and thus, I would be subject to extinguishment." It sounded weak, even as she said it. But it was the rule she had lived by since she could remember. Was this a lie as well?

"Extinguishment...Is that different from death?" Myronor asked.

The endless questions were becoming trying. She'd already spent the day with worries and ideas exhaustively bouncing around in her head. But like poison drawn from a wound, speaking to Myronor about these things she seldom considered felt slightly relieving despite the pain.

"Potentially worse. We are submitted to the Sacramentum again for final judgment. If the Aether deems our Oaths fulfilled, our atonement reached, then our souls return to the Aether for reincarnation. If we abandoned our Oath, our vespers burn for eternity in the Aether."

Myronor shifted again, discomforted by the revelation. But it was a reality Ophiera had had to live with since surviving the Sacramentum. At least an Oath of Mercy was easy to gauge in terms of fulfillment; you either healed someone or you didn't. But the Oath of Retribution demanded her to do the very thing she was seeking vengeance for: murder. She knew how the Cloister interpreted her destruction of the corrupted souls, but to her, wasn't murder simply murder? Regardless of the reason, she claimed a soul. She fulfilled her Oath, but at what cost to herself?

"It seems unfair to judge anyone so harshly for a fate given without choice," Myronor said.

"*Fairness* is not a part of the Cloister's vocabulary."

After a moment of contemplation, Myronor sat up to throw another bundle of seaweed on the fire. It smoked a bit, but the smell was pleasant and the warmth comforting. The sea breeze was becoming chilled without the sun.

Myronor lay back beside her and took her scarred hand in his. Over their recovery, he'd developed a habit of tracing the runic scars with his thumb. But after such a discussion, his actions felt more meaningful than a simple fidget. Her chest ached.

She didn't want to enjoy the feel of his soft hands on hers; she didn't want to slide closer to him or lay her head on his chest. She didn't want to find comfort in the rise and fall of him beneath her, nor the musty citrusy scent of his travel shirt. She didn't want to feel solaced by just being close to him.

Still tracing the scars of her hand between them, Myronor pressed his lips against the top of her head.

"Will you tell me of the day you left the Cloister?"

She didn't want to tell him. "Why?"

He spoke in a murmur, his lips still moving against her snowy hair. "When you...When this link formed between us, I saw and felt many of your memories. They were chaotic and choppy, but most of all, they were painful. I can't fully understand what I saw, but I want to. I want to understand your burdens. We share them now, whether you like it or not."

Ophiera closed her eyes, remembering the last day she saw the Cloister. Though she didn't want to tell him, the ekath tugged at her heart until she would comply. After a few moments of struggling against herself, she took a deep breath against him.

"I'll tell you...but like everything else, it's not a pleasant tale."

~ Twenty-Six ~

JILT

Rattles from her armor echoed off the mountain peaks as Ophiera shivered. She had done her damnedest to hold still and silent, but the cold permeated everything in the Cloister. Hours ago, she received the command from the Chaplain to wait outside the barracks, fully equipped. But otherwise, the notice provided no further guidance.

Today was the first time she'd donned the ancient golden armor. Even during her training, she wasn't allowed to use the *real* armor. Instead, she had worn sets made of dark iron, pockmarked and rusted. It held twice the weight but at least the dark iron armor had fit her. The new-to-her adamantrium set was too large for her frame, allowing the frigid breeze to penetrate and linger beneath. She wouldn't have cared about the fit if she could just stop shaking.

Since sunrise, she had stood in place as instructed, awaiting whatever task the Chaplain demanded of her. Her role within the Cloister had always been confusing. The Hands left the Cloister and the Keepers stayed, but no one knew what an Aspect did. All served the Aether, but it was impossible to fulfill an Oath of Retribution within the walls of the Cloister. So Ophiera had been told to train. And train she did.

She worked endlessly, day in and day out improving her combat forms with a claymore. She used to study in the Archives more often, but now only read the scrolls pertaining to Retribution. The lesson had been hard learned, but now she knew there was no changing her fate.

As she watched the light of day disappear behind the snow-covered peaks, the Chaplain still had not appeared. Her legs shook with fatigue and cold, but fear of punishment kept her standing in place. Like the Cloister itself, the surrounding mountains held no pity. The bare peaks provided little shelter from the elements. Even if it had been only slightly warmer, she desired nothing more than to return to her tiny room in the barracks. But she resisted the temptation to abandon this vigil. If they ordered her to wait, she would wait.

The purple light of dusk clung before the night when the Chaplain finally approached. Two priests flanked his side in silence, obeying their Oaths of Sacrifice. The Chaplain shared her Oath of Retribution. Yet, unlike her, Uzziel reveled in his allotment. Since the Sacramentum, he had wholly embraced his fate while she had only fought hers.

As unkindled, Ophiera nearly considered Uzziel a friend. But once he was kindled as a Hand of Retribution, the Magistrate immediately conscripted him. It was the happiest she had ever seen him. She should have known there were no friends in the Cloister.

Now, Uzziel had become the new Chaplain of the Cloister. Most Chaplains served their Oaths for decades before being appointed. Meanwhile, Ophiera, the only Aspect of Retribution, remained in perpetual training. While he had found his place at the top, she still floundered at the bottom.

The Chaplain, as he must be addressed now, stood before her. He looked as ostentatious as the heavy gilded armor he wore. Her eyes darted around his features, avoiding his uncomfortable hazel gaze.

The set of his strong jaw twitched with authority, clean-shaven and unblemished. Not a single hair fell out of place from his tight braid. His plait was of black and white, twisted in a mesmerizing pattern. She had always been jealous of his hair.

"You've been conscripted," the Chaplain said with a tone too similar to disgust.

Ophiera blinked twice, processing the words. "By the Magistrate?"

"Obviously," he said. It was as if he scolded her. "They require a paladin now that I've been relieved."

"I...I didn't think...I'm honored, Chaplain."

"Don't be."

That stung. She tried to remember when he began to hate her so much. She thought it was after their last spar...the one where he claimed something more than victory from her. They had both received the punishment and shortly after, he was kindled. That was when everything changed.

"When do I depart?" Ophiera asked, keeping her composure.

"Now."

She couldn't help her eyes from going wide. "But I've not prepared, or packed—"

His mirthless laugh silenced her stutter. She nearly yelped as his hand grasped her jaw, forcing her face close to his. The memories of his previous transgression churned her stomach more than his laugh.

"You have nothing to pack," he growled. "Everything here, including yourself, belongs to the Cloister."

His words felt like a slap. "Y-yes, sir."

"These priests will escort you from the Cloister immediately. After that, you must head to Feyralis and submit yourself to the Magistrate."

Confused, Ophiera began, "Uzziel, I—"

"You dare?" he shouted. She cringed against his commanding voice as if struck.

"My apologies, Chaplain."

He let go of her jaw, finally.

"Seek out the newly appointed Justicar of Feyralis, Eliana Diamont. She is expecting you, as is Aleksander, Hand of Mercy—our own Justicar."

Ophiera nodded, not daring to speak.

"Represent the Cloister well. Obey Aleksander and uphold your Oath."

"Yes, sir."

"Remember, the Aether is unforgiving to those who betray the gifts given. Abandon your Oath, and face extinguishment."

The threat in his voice frightened her more than the mention of extinguishment. Before she could compose herself, the two priests were upon her. A burlap sack flung over her head and shoulders cast her into suffocating blindness.

"W-wait—how will I know how to return to the Cloister?"

"You won't. Not until the holy flames themselves summon you for the final judgment."

Without another word, she heard the stomps of his greaves grow distant.

The priests pushed her away and though they were gentle enough, Ophiera felt like a prisoner. They guided her quite a way in the darkening cold before pushing her into a carriage, or what she assumed to be one. Wherever they had placed her, at least she'd finally escaped the chill. But the smell of spoiled grain had permeated the burlap blind and began to nauseate her. The carriage lurched forward, only furthering her queasy discomfort.

She pined for fresh air. If she could just peek out, perhaps a break from the scent would save her stomach. She also wanted to know where she was exactly. Though the cart or carriage she was in now drove away smoothly, she couldn't hear anything pulling it along. What kind of animal pulled a carriage in silence?

Still, she knew better than to remove the hood. How many days had she spent in confinement for her past disobedience? The starvation, the broken bones, the humiliation. Eventually, it had become enough to break her into submission. Perhaps that's why they'd conscripted her now; she was ready to obey.

Hours passed in blind silence, or perhaps only moments. Without sight, her other senses felt...off. For some time, she doubted if the carriage moved at all in her disorientation. Her head swam with a sudden onset of pressure in her ears. Eventually, she fell into a fitful sleep. Had she imagined the hands dragging her elsewhere? At least she could hear the oxen now. Between her dizzied mind and the strong odor of the hood, time became jumbled.

Ophiera did not know how much time had passed before she felt the hood dragged from her face. A pair of icy hands pulled her roughly onto the ground. Weak with exhaustion, she stumbled trying to stand herself upright, her greaves clanking in the dark.

She stood on an unfamiliar dirt road, surrounded by dark woods. She couldn't see beyond the thick trees, but she smelled something sour on the air. The only light emanated from the lantern hung on the carriage illuminating two starved oxen. One wheel was a different aged wood than the others, proving this was the original caravan that claimed her for the Cloister.

She felt sick.

In silence, the priests returned to the wagon. They did not glance in her direction as they turned the cart and left her alone on the barren road. They returned to the Cloister, taking with them the only source of light.

Ophiera's breaths sounded shallow in the dark. The faster they came, the more her control slipped away. Soon, she heard the rattles of her own armor again.

She had wished for this day, every day—the day she could leave the Cloister. So then why did she feel so utterly abandoned now?

She held no memory of her parents and therefore had never felt their absence. But now, alone on the road, the emptiness of desertion consumed her. It pained her in ways she had believed herself incapable of feeling since the kindling. The prickling in her eyes and tightness in her chest felt foreign now; wrong.

To quell her growing panic, Ophiera began reciting the meditations the clerics had always suggested. After a few shaky verses, though, she abandoned the farce. The meditations had rarely worked before and they wouldn't start now. But the rhythmic repetition of the words reminded her of song, and the mere thought of music relieved some of her tension.

She was alone, with no one to chastise her for singing now. Slow to start, she hummed one of the few songs in her memory. The melody carried her distress away, at least enough to bring her some clarity. It was a strange feeling; the first time her own choice resulted in anything but punishment.

She latched on to the freedom. And her armor stopped shaking.

She had not endured the Cloister's trials and trainings only to stand helpless in the dark now. What had been the point of the suffering if she simply gave up? Yes, she was alone, abandoned, without even a direction. But a reasonable step forward would be in the opposite direction of the priests.

Ophiera took a step forward in the dark with a new decisiveness born from the ashes of her trepidation. Wasn't it better to move forward in the wrong direction than to remain paralyzed by what remained behind? Despite standing all day in the cold, she felt energized again. Never before had such simple choices belonged to her, without correction, judgment, or punishment.

As Ophiera walked the dirt path, the dark woods thinned into marshlands. The sour smell grew stronger, but not in an unpleasant way. Even the air felt different from the Cloister. As she walked the night slowly turned to morning without a moment's rest. She didn't have food or water anyway, and if she stopped, she wasn't sure she could start again.

As the sun reached its zenith, a crossroads appeared in the distance—the first sign of others since the priests had stranded her. She wasn't sure if the small settlement was abandoned or not.

Throughout the night and morning, she hadn't met another person on the road. Perhaps no one lived wherever she was in Tanvik.

The village turned out not to be abandoned after all, but she dared not call it a village anymore. Other than an inn and stable, there was nothing of substance. Yet the place held an odd familiarity as if conjured by a dream.

A rough wooden sign hung above the inn, bearing a painted blue flower. The delicate hues of indigo and butter yellow appealed to her. She read the neatly curved letters and realized the flower must be the inn's namesake—the Lonely Iris.

As she entered the establishment, the stark difference between interior and exterior struck her. Greenery seemed to cover every square inch inside, complementing the empty wood tables.

A giant man towered behind the bar, a question held in his dark eyes. He had a beard of deep auburn, ornately braided against a bulging belly. And Ophiera was struck by a rare itch of recognition.

"Aye, ye're far from the Cloister. What can I git ye?" His voice reverberated, deep and kind.

She wanted to ask for water; for anything to eat. But she had been taught the values placed on goods outside the Cloister. At least the priests and clerics hadn't left her without knowledge, but they had left her without coin. So, she asked for the only thing she could afford.

"Directions to Feyralis, please." The growl of her stomach interrupted her, and the heat of embarrassment flushed her cheeks.

The bartender's mouth twitched in amusement. "Take the right fork toward the marsh road. Rough road, but I'm sure ye'll be fine. Follow that until ye hit the main road—it'll lead ye straight to Feyralis. Maybe four or five nights by foot."

She nodded, trying to hide her disappointment. Four more nights without food, water, or shelter—far worse than she had expected.

"It's a long road ahead for an empty stomach," he said with a gentle smile.

"I agree, but I have no coin to spare." It hurt her pride to admit that all she had was her armor and sword.

Again, the man's mouth twitched. "I'd be willin' to trade services if ye don't mind giving me back a break."

She stared at him for a moment. "I don't understand."

With a bark of a laugh, the bartender continued. "If ye move some bags o' grain for me, lass, I'll give ye food and drink in exchange. Then ye can be on yer way to Feyralis."

The Cloister provided no guidance other than to uphold her Oath. How would Retribution factor in here? Would they consider such an act a bribe, or instead a service to the people of Tanvik? Also, how *would* she eat? And where would she sleep? The Cloister had beaten obedience into her, yet sent her off into the world without counsel. Frustrated, she pushed aside the veil of the Cloister's rubrics and made yet another decision.

"I would be happy to help with any tasks you may have for me," she said.

"Aye. How about ye eat first since ye're already here? Path o' least resistance and all." The man patted a giant hand upon the bar before disappearing through an open doorway behind him. He returned moments later, carrying a steaming bowl in his large hands. The dish placed before her filled the air with an aroma unlike anything she had experienced before. Her mouth watered oddly.

"I'll get ye some water—ye Cloister folk don't handle the mead too well at first."

Ophiera didn't know what he meant by *mead*, but frankly, she didn't care either. The bowl before her held more food than she was allowed over several days at the Cloister. Hunger overrode patience, and she tested the first spoonful. A single bite carried more flavor than anything she had consumed at the Cloister. And at that moment, she understood the term *famished*. Not only from her night-long journey, but from years of deprivation. As she shoveled spoonful after spoonful of the spicy dish into her mouth, she wondered if that had been the Cloister's intent. They fasted more often than not. And when they could eat, it was typically bland. She couldn't long for what she'd never had, but this food was worth longing over.

The barkeep returned with the water, eyeing the empty bowl. He laughed. "Ye know, I thought I recognized ye. And how ye just put away that curry proves it."

So the dish was called curry. She needed to remember that. But more importantly, how did he recognize her? She cocked her head, mouth too full to speak her query and he laughed again.

"Ye was much younger—hair was different too. Ye was headed up to the Cloister with the other wee ones. Fed ye pancakes, remember?"

Ophiera dropped her spoon with a clang. The reverie of a broken wheel, of a carriage stranded in Isyath, shook her. It was a bizarre sensation—realizing she had carried the memory of this man all these years, yet didn't know it until now. She seldom thought back to her life before the Cloister had claimed it.

"You're Lotus...right?" He nodded with a smile. "That was the first time I ever tasted honey. The last time, too."

Lotus laughed so hard the mugs rattled above his head. "I still got lots o' bog honey. Ye can help me with that, too."

He beckoned her back to the kitchen with a wave. Clumsily, Ophiera scraped every last remnant of food from her bowl before following him.

And from there, the day passed in a pleasant blur.

She helped Lotus move the bags of grain while he talked endlessly, covering all topics of past, present, and future. He was like a living tome, full of news and knowledge. He told her of the surrounding country, the path to Feyralis, and even suggested contacts within the walls of the city. The constant stream of conversation was foreign, but pleasant. The Cloister had always been a silent place, but Lotus spoke in excess and even answered her questions.

After she moved the grain, she offered to join him as he tended the stables. She continued offering her help with any task, including chopping wood and weeding the small garden behind the kitchen. Subconsciously, she looked for an excuse to stay.

Ophiera was quite certain more herbs and flowers existed within his small plot of land than throughout the entire Cloister. And the way Lotus tended the plants...She had never seen anyone treat another living entity with so much adoration and kindness. He crooned as he trimmed dead leaves, and sang encouragement to open blossoms. The man held a temperament rarely found at the Cloister and she wondered if all the people of Tanvik were as kind.

Dusk fell before they returned to the kitchen. Ophiera inspected the ingredients lining Lotus's wooden shelves as he led her to the main tavern. She had never seen half the sundries he stored, and even more hung from the ceilings.

"Lass, ye helped me more today than a bowl o' stew and some honey was worth. Why don't ye stay the night in the attic room and we'll call it even in the mornin'?" He pointed toward a rickety staircase in the back of the tavern.

"I should get heading to the Magistrate...I've delayed too long already and taken up too much of your hospitality," she said apologetically.

"Nonsense," he said. "It's not healthy to travel fatigued and underfed. The Magistrate doesn't know when ye left the Cloister and so they don't know when to expect ye. I won't tell if ye won't; what happens in me bar, stays in me bar."

He was right. No one knew when she had left or when she'd arrived. The last time she had slept was the cart ride from the Cloister, and she could hardly consider that rest. More like a hallucination.

She accepted his offer with a timid nod, and Lotus seemed pleased. After a mutual exchange of pleasantries, she made her way upstairs, unsure of what to expect.

The size of the bed surprised her at first. An upgrade from the scant piles of straw and leathers found back in the barracks. In the corner of the room stood an ornate washbasin, and with a feeling of pure joy, Ophiera realized she could remove her armor and bathe, unwatched and undisturbed.

Afterward, as Ophiera lay down for sleep, she stared at the exposed runes branded upon her arm. The sight of the scars turned her heart turned bitter with purpose.

She wasn't made to do chores. She must obey the Cloister and the Magistrate now. She must fulfill her Oath. That had been the purpose of her existence; the reason for her suffering. But wasn't helping Lotus a greater service to the people than Retribution ever could be? She turned away from the thought, again reminding herself that she served the Aether first. And the Aether demanded recompense.

~ Twenty-Seven ~

TRIUMPH

A bright sunrise greeted Ophiera the next morning. The sea reflected the transition beautifully, the waves shimmering from indigo to gold. It was as if she had been transported back in time. How long had she spent traveling this coast alone, hiding away from duty? The familiar sights and sounds brought her a much-needed calm—especially after the conversations from the night before.

Myronor snored gently beside her through the breaking dawn. She watched him carefully, glad he regained some peace after her tale last night. He said he wanted to understand her burdens, but it felt more as if he took them upon himself. She hated the guilt and pity she detected through the ekath before they slept. Perhaps she had finally convinced him that a life bound to hers was more doom than fate.

When Myronor finally awoke, they packed their bedrolls and continued on their journey. He remained uncharacteristically quiet, yet Ophiera felt nothing alarming through their connection. It was a solemn, but comfortable silence—one she welcomed.

Hours passed as they traversed the bright sandstone beaches preceding the Cliffs of Eidolon. A cloudless sky had damned them to a hot day of travel—well beyond what the sea breeze could quell. The stony shore provided little shade and even Mallow quickly grew tired of the beating sun. She mewled at Myronor until he fished the crystal from his sticky shirt, providing her escape. Abandoned in the sweltering silence, Myronor and Ophiera pressed onward.

Her dark leathers boiled against her skin, reminding her yet again of her missing armor. The shiny, reflective surface had done wonders against the heat. Even after Myronor transmogrified the metal, it retained this strange quality. Regardless of whether it had been crafted from pure adamantrium or not, the armor was still special. And she missed it bitterly.

Shortly after the sun had peaked, Ophiera sensed Myronor's struggle to bear the heat. Though he did not voice his need for a break, she decided it was time. A tall boulder near the water provided the only shade, and so she led them down toward the shoreline. Uneven barnacles covered the rough stones, darkening the vivid layers of ancient, compressed sand. Recently submerged, the rocks were cool and wet to the touch; a blessed relief.

Myronor conjured water and they both drank greedily until the skins had been drained. After they had cooled off enough to allow for hunger, Myronor spent a moment rummaging through his pack. He finally pulled out a bundle of chokecherry muffins, courtesy of Berwyn, and smiled as he handed her a treat.

Myronor's smile truly matched Berwyn's while holding a chokecherry muffin. When Berwyn wasn't out at sea, he had always shared his latest creations with Ophiera, claiming the need for an unbiased taste tester. Most fishers enjoyed their quiet downtime onshore, but Berwyn needed to stay busy, much like herself. She admired that about him.

Day by day, the similarities between father and son grew more obvious. Before she thought them opposites; Berwyn was a quiet and gentle man with a strong work ethic and utmost respect for the precepts of the Southern Coastland's culture. Meanwhile, Myronor never stopped talking, actively challenged most social constructs, and rarely took anything seriously. But the more time she spent with Myronor, the more she realized their core values were the same. They both had the same, endless capacity to care for others.

"I didn't realize you knew Lotus for *that* long," Myronor said, catching her eye.

Ophiera hadn't realized how long she had been staring at Myronor while musing about his smile. She looked away, confused by her own action and more by his question. Was her friendship with Lotus truly the first question to come to mind regarding her tale last night? She thought he'd be more curious about the Cloister; more about the Chaplain or the secretive nature of the order. Why didn't he ask why the Cloister remained hidden, even from their own disciples? Maybe she just wanted to know the answer to that.

But Lotus?

She wondered if he could feel her thoughts, reminiscing about Berwyn, and assumed her mind was on Lotus instead? Or perhaps he recalled something from her mind? The ekath left her questioning his every action and every thought, and it was becoming exhausting.

"Lotus has been the most consistent person in my life," she said, trying her best to be honest. "My first year under the Magistrate would have destroyed me were it not for him."

The first few years of enacting her Oath had been a dark and cruel time of adjustment. With food and stories, Lotus had been the only light and had stayed her heart from despair countless times. The Lonely Iris served as her only respite from her Oath until she ultimately retired. It was hard to hide anything with the ekath, but she hoped Myronor couldn't feel the tightness in her throat.

"I don't think he liked me much," Myronor said with a snort.

"His likes and dislikes change on any given day. But he gave you a drink and didn't force you to sleep in the stables. That's about the closest to approval you could get from him."

Myronor chuckled. "I doubt he'd approve of anything that's happened since."

Ophiera's heart sank. For all Lotus knew, she and Myronor were dead. She wished she could tell Lotus everything that had happened. She wished she could go back to how things were before. But it was probably for the best he thought her dead; he said he'd never forgive her anyway for leaving.

Her eyes stung now, in addition to her throat.

"What happened between you two?" Myronor said gently. "I mean, after the Brotherhood captured me?"

The overplayed innocence of his question raised her suspicion. Had he glimpsed the argument from her memories? Or did he feel her sorrow now? Maybe she was right to question everything now that they were linked. If he already saw what happened between her and Lotus, there was no sense in hiding anything.

"A lot of what happened after you went missing is a blur. I was so furious, and things happened so quickly...we both said some regretful things. He tried very hard to stop me from going after you."

"Why?" Myronor asked, again feigning innocence. If he knew the answer, why was he making her say it?

"He said if I found you, I'd find death too. And that if I died, he'd never forgive me."

"Well, he wasn't wrong," Myronor said calmly as he stared out at sea. "But I doubt he meant the latter. You could destroy every plant in his garden and I'm fairly certain he'd still worship the ground you walked on."

Ophiera smiled sadly. "I don't know. I hurt him deeply that day. And Lotus knows how to hold a grudge better than his ale."

Lotus *had* been right about everything though. He had been right about Myronor, right about the Brotherhood, and right about her choices involving both. Now she was left wondering if she should have listened to him. What would have happened if she left Myronor to fate with the Brotherhood?

If she had listened to Lotus, Myronor's soul wouldn't be bound to hers now. The Reverend claimed to need him alive, so at the very least, he wouldn't have died. If she could go back to that moment when Lotus tried to stop her, could she have even listened to him? Could she have let Myronor go?

"What in the world is that in the water?" Myronor said abruptly. His voice came across as near cheerful as he craned his neck out to sea.

Ophiera followed his gaze, her heart jumping as she saw what had caught his attention.

Jade scales breached the surface of the water, reflecting the sun in a blinding shimmer. As they writhed and splashed, it was difficult to tell just how many of the creatures danced gently beneath the surface of the water. But Ophiera had seen these beasts once before.

"It looks like a pod of ippomares."

"The horse serpents?" Myronor jumped to his feet and reached for Ophiera's hand. Before she could pull away, he dragged her up the rocky shore, closer to the splashing creatures. The pod still swam a distance off the coast, but from where he stopped, the individuals were now distinguishable in the mass of scales.

Five serpentine bodies writhed in the water. A head breached the surface, vaguely resembling a horse's in shape and size. The creatures were an iridescent, opaque green color, slick and camouflaged beneath the water. Their eyes were coal black with no whites and fathomless as the depths. Two slitted nostrils flared as they surfaced, spraying the sea as they exhaled. In place of a horse's mane, the ippomares bore a golden dorsal fin, tracing the length of the creatures' otherwise limbless bodies.

With eyes wide, Myronor watched the ippomares writhe and call to one another in eerie wails. Reminiscent of a whinny, their calls carried oddly over the crashing waves. Ophiera stiffened as Myronor placed an arm around her shoulder and squeezed with excitement.

"My entire childhood I watched these waters hoping to see an ippomare, you know? The fishers talked about them all the time, but even out on my father's boat I never saw one. By the time I left for Feyralis, I was convinced they only existed in books."

Ophiera shrugged under the weight of his arm. "I've only ever glimpsed them once before, and they were not playing like this."

As if aware of her words, the largest of the creatures turned its dark gaze toward them. Ophiera felt certain their presence alone would spook the animals, but to her surprise, the serpentine horse continued its dive, slapping its tail upon the surface of the water.

She didn't understand their odd behavior. Not that she was an expert, but what she knew of ippomares was from the fishers of Iluka. And they were the most reliable source. These creatures were usually found far offshore, over the deepest trenches of the Lucent Strait. They were known for their playful demeanors and were a good omen for safe waters. But why would they travel so close to the shores of Tanvik now?

"I'm going to greet them," Myronor said, releasing her shoulder and tearing his boots from his feet.

"Are you insane?"

"Likely," he said with a flash of blue. His clothes fell away from his body. "But I can't let that stop me."

Before Ophiera had been given the chance to blush at his nudity, Myronor had leaped from a jutting rock out into the ocean. She swore under her breath, removing her own boots, in case she needed to intervene. But unlike the mage, she couldn't magically disrobe. By the time her feet were bare, Myronor had nearly reached the pod.

Annoyed at the number of laces on the blackened leathers, she accepted the futility of her actions. It wasn't as if she could do much to protect him against such a creature anyway. She refused to wield the flames and only carried a machete now. Kaikora had already proven the immortality of their bond. Perhaps observing from the shore, safe from drowning, was the best way to protect him now. More proof that Myronor's safety was dependent on her distance from him.

Ophiera watched as the creatures tensed with his approach. Myronor swam with incredible speed and grace, his loosening hair flowing behind him. He stopped a few arm's lengths away from the ippomares, breaking the surface with a grin. She hated how beautiful he looked in the surf.

In flashes of blue light, he conjured globs of ink kelp floating before him. Ophiera thought the ippomares would surely flee from his spell, or maybe she just wished they would. But instead, the largest of the ippomares approached Myronor, sniffing cautiously through slitted nostrils. Its head was half the size of Myronor himself.

Myronor nudged the ink kelp forward in offering while treading against the waves. She held her breath as the ippomare chomped on a tendril, fearing his hand was in the way. But after it swallowed the first bite, the remaining creatures approached with expectation. Like an overexcited child, Myronor conjured more of the seaweed and observed as they ate greedily before him.

Myronor turned to shore. "Come on, Ophiera! They're friendly!"

The ekath pulled her toward the surf but she resisted its drag. They may have found *him* harmless, but anything with a pulse tended to find Ophiera threatening.

She sank down near the water's edge, hanging her feet over the rocky shore into the surf.

The ippomares continued amusing themselves, diving and surfacing around Myronor. It was like they were putting on a show, perhaps, of gratitude for the meal. She still couldn't believe his first instinct was to jump in the water and swim with the horse serpents. For as intelligent as he claimed to be, he made some idiotic decisions. Yet he always remained carefree, as if no burden was too heavy for him.

Before, she had found this trait obnoxious, but now, she found it rather endearing, even admirable. The Brotherhood camp had been a traumatic experience for Myronor, and yet he pressed on as if it didn't affect him. She knew it did; she felt it every day through the ekath. But he made an effort to forget. At times she wished she could be more like him.

Eventually, Myronor swam back to the rocky edge where Ophiera still sat, feet cooling in the water. Murky clouds had begun to encroach upon the sky, blocking the sun out in gray favor. As he pulled himself from the water with a spell, he looked more alive than he had in recent days. Invigorated and healed in a way beyond what Kaikora or the soul link had managed.

"That was fun!" he said, shaking out his wet hair.

Ophiera smirked, refusing to look at him nude. "I'm glad you enjoyed yourself."

"You could have too if you tried."

"I don't want to be sticky with salt water for the rest of the day."

"You know I'm a mage, right?" he said, his head thrown back in a laugh. She didn't understand until he had conjured a shower of fresh water, dousing himself and splashing Ophiera in the process. She stood to shake off the water, feeling her annoyance rise. But with another flash, they were both dried instantly.

"I always forget the problems of the world don't apply to mages," she grumbled.

Myronor continued to smile, unfazed. Thankfully, he donned his pants again before speaking. "Come now, what's the point of traveling all over the place if we can't have a little fun?"

In any other circumstance, Ophiera would have dropped the issue. Perhaps due to the ekath or pure frustration, she needed Myronor to understand what she still struggled to reconcile.

"The point? We're on this path to replace my armor. You know, the set which was destroyed by a cult of anathemas that wished to sacrifice me to some dark power. We still don't even know what their intentions were for keeping you alive or why they sought us in the first place." She took a breath, unable to stop the words and worries pouring from her mouth. "Once we're finished with this little side quest to a supposed Aspect's tomb that not even the Cloister knows exists, I must escort you, whom my very soul is now tethered to, across the sea to investigate your mother's death. That's all without mentioning the power of the Aspect that I cannot control—the flames that frighten me more than the blackened ichor of the swamps, which we're just apparently ignoring for now on Kaikora's instructions. Oh, and that doesn't include the lies of the Cloister, revealed by Iluka's shaman, who never once mentioned her knowledge of the Cloister or my echelon throughout my entire time serving as Warden." She finally took another breath before finishing her point. "My *entire* existence has been turned upside down in a matter of days...so forgive me if I find it difficult to find any joy within this mound of tribulations."

Ophiera's nostrils flared as she breathed, having never felt so winded from simply speaking. The rage and bitterness still clawed at her chest, begging to be released in full. She had only scratched the surface of her ire with her rant. But she held back the beast of resentment as Myronor's understanding eyes met hers. Still without his shirt, he placed his hands on her shoulders, squaring up to her.

"I know you bear the bulk of the burden between us," he said gently. "But the burden remains the same, regardless of whether you're enjoying yourself or not. It's as useless as worrying about the sea being salty...which I suppose you did, actually..." He laughed, shaking his head. "Still—these problems aren't within your control, but letting yourself enjoy life is."

Whether by link or words alone, he again steered the conversation to his favor. Ophiera found him slightly more convincing without a shirt on. His warm hands melted away her angst, and she wanted nothing more than to let go and give in to the comfort he offered. And yet, she couldn't.

"What you fail to understand is that I've never had control of anything...my Oath, my self, my fate...my heart..." She stared at the ippomares, still frolicking in the waves. "How can I enjoy anything in a life that has so rarely been mine?"

His hand slid from her shoulder and danced up her neck. She didn't understand the movement until she felt his thumb skate affectionately across her jaw. He tipped her chin up, forcing her to meet his eyes.

"Ophiera," he whispered. "You have to try."

The damn connection tugged at her chest, intensified by the feel of his hand still cupping her face. She should—at the very least—be able to remain in control of her own emotions, but even that escaped her.

Still, hadn't she just admitted to herself she wished she could be more like Myronor? Maybe he was right...maybe all she needed to do was try.

"Watching you tame an ippomare was mildly entertaining," she said with a defiant tone.

He leaned in closer to her. Was he really about to...But as his lips pressed against her forehead, she felt embarrassed for misreading his intent.

"Good try!" Myronor said before releasing her and stepping away.

The absence of his touch felt...disappointing. She shook herself to her senses, aided by Myronor pulling his tunic back on. Without that distraction, she could think properly now.

"Let's move on," she said, looking to the sky. "We should reach the cliff base before dark."

"You managed a whole thirty seconds of fun," Myronor chided with a chuckle. "I would wager that's a record."

Like a child, Ophiera stuck her tongue out and turned to pull her boots on. When she turned back, Myronor had tied his hair back in a twisted, elegant knot. The link thrummed with a strange approval.

They continued along the rocky coast, keeping the sea close, at least by sight. Soon, the waves began to fall far below their path, independent of the tide. The elevation increased steadily as they walked along the edge of the sea, and before long, the stony terrain lost all traces of sand.

Traversing the weathered stones became more arduous as they progressed. Ophiera noticed that, if Myronor's attention wandered for even a moment, as it often did, he easily lost his footing. Continually slipping, he managed to catch himself with his staff at each falter, saving his handsome face from the hard stone.

Ophiera had no such troubles.

Following his advice, she turned the trek into a game—a fun challenge to reach the Cliffs of Eidolon without losing her footing a single time. She had traversed these rocky shores many times over and always enjoyed the test of her skill. There was even the added benefit of not having her armor throwing off her balance. The only silver lining to its absence she could find.

"Is there no spell to keep your feet from slipping?" she asked Myronor, leaping gracefully from rock to rock.

Myronor chuffed a laugh, nearly out of breath. "I assumed you'd tell me to conserve my mana or some such nonsense."

"Isn't that what your staff is for?"

He laughed again. "Fine, you win." With the glow of his hand on the staff, his boots rose a few inches above the rocky terrain. He began walking on air with a smug expression. "Happy?"

"Ah, so again, you could have saved us both some struggles yet chose to only help yourself," she chided, remembering his spell in the Sloughmire.

Myronor laughed. "I dare not call your method a struggle—hopping around like some sort of mountain goat. But I can cast it upon you as well if you insist."

She bounded to another rock, landing perfectly balanced on one foot. "Don't waste your spells on this goat—I'm just fine."

"Are you mad I called you a goat?" he asked, throwing his head back with a chuckle. "I was just surprised a paladin could be so graceful."

She glared at him, and though she knew she fell for his bait, she couldn't help herself. "I can traverse these shores faster and more gracefully than you, even with your cheating boots."

He grinned and it nearly stopped her heart. "Let's find out, shall we?"

Without a warning, Myronor bounded forward, sprinting on the inches of air separating his feet and the rocks.

Ophiera let loose a cry of outrage at the cheating mage before dashing after him. She took powerful strides, unburdened by armor, across the rocky shore. At least the brutal conditioning of the Cloister would serve a greater purpose today. She couldn't let the mage win a simple footrace.

Her footing stayed accurate despite her speed, never missing or overshooting a landing. She advanced on Myronor quickly. Too quickly. With a smile, she realized the hovering boots could not gain much momentum. While she continued to gain speed, Myronor had already reached his maximum.

Her victory was guaranteed.

Perhaps Myronor sensed her surge of triumph, forcing him to glance behind him. A flash of shock crossed his face as he realized she had gained so much on him. But his surprise quickly shifted to a grin. Blue light flashed again, and he rose farther above the ground.

It seemed a waste of energy to Ophiera—moving up rather than forward. Perhaps he thought she meant to tackle him? The cheat would deserve it. But as Ophiera's attention again turned forward, she saw the reason for his tactic.

Ahead, a low delta cut deep into the rock, flowing gently out to sea. The wide mouth of the canyon river was nearly five of her body lengths across and dropped even farther down to sea level. While Myronor would glide effortlessly above the ravine, Ophiera needed to find another solution. And quickly.

"If you admit defeat, I'll ensure you don't fall to your death!" Myronor called down to her as she continued to run toward disaster. "I'll even carry you across in my arms."

Ophiera accepted the challenge with a snort. With a single quick glance, she had found her mark. A massive stone had toppled over long ago and lay tilted toward the sky, like a ramp. As she swerved toward the slope, she concentrated wholly on her stride, calculating her sprint up the inclined rock face. The delta loomed ominously below, reflecting the gray clouds in a near metallic sheen. If she fell, it would be to meet the Aether.

Nearing the end of the incline, Ophiera leaped at the very last moment, pushing off hard with one leg. Her momentum carried her forward, but she kept her limbs swinging, propelling her through the air. True weightlessness was a feeling seldom achieved, but as she launched herself across the river, she felt absolute freedom. Free from all burdens, even gravity itself.

With the ball of her foot, she caught the edge of the opposing cliffside. Pushing her momentum forward, she rolled from the edge and planted her feet back onto gritty sandstone. The landing had barely slowed her now continuing dash.

She chanced a look over her shoulder to find Myronor dumbstruck. He watched her with both fear and admiration, disbelief and pride wrapped up in a grin she craved to see. It was an expression she found herself wishing to see more and more as time went on.

Of late, it felt as if she had lost everything: her will, her armor, her soul, and perhaps her heart as well. It was peculiar how the loss of so much weighed so heavily upon her and yet...

As she slowed, allowing Myronor to catch up, she found the answer to her question.

Despite what Lotus had predicted, and what fate befell them or what the future held, she wouldn't change any of her choices. Like Iluka, Myronor had been her choice. She chose to save him on the riverbank, chose to go after him when he was taken from her. He was just as much her choice as Iluka had been for her retirement. She could never regret her decisions in regards to him.

The difficulty came in the choices to come. But knowing she would always choose to save him over anything else brought her some peace about the future. The trouble was, eventually, she must save him from herself.

~ Twenty-Eight ~

AWAKENING

"I didn't want to waste my mana," Myronor said with a roll of his eyes. "I could have pulled ahead at any time."

The pair had just finished setting up camp at the base of the stratified cliffs. Ophiera had unashamedly gloated over her victory and, for once, the mage became defensive. She understood now why he had needled her so often in the past; this was...fun.

"You seemed unconcerned about mana when you jumped from the wall in Feyralis," Ophiera said, as she unrolled her furs on the ground. "Or in the Sloughmire, when you charmed your feet. Or—"

"Or when I held you throughout the night, keeping us invisible?" He interrupted with a grin. Her face grew warm at the mention of that night. She guessed that was his intention. "The truth is I've learned a thing or two from you. Saving my strength is just one."

Ophiera snorted. "Learning something from me? That's the funniest thing you've said since our meeting."

With a quiet thud, Myronor dropped his own bedroll next to hers. "Come now, I've always been funny. Even you must admit that."

"I will admit that a person may be funny and irritating simultaneously."

As she lay back on her bedroll, she felt the hard bedrock through the thin padding. Tonight would be a rough sleep. The ocean sounded distant from their place amongst the rocks, and tomorrow, they would have much farther to climb.

Myronor lay down beside her. "Training in matters of irritation is standard for all Feyralis mages."

Though she grinned, his words made her realize she still knew nothing of Myronor's own path to becoming a mage. Despite the many questions he'd asked, he very rarely volunteered information of his own. When the ekath formed, he had seen her memories, and she now tried to recall some of his. Blurred, disjointed images of Rheta and the tower, of endless books and blue light. There were many flashes of Eliana Diamont and the Magistrate's halls. But the most compelling parts of the foreign memories were the feelings associated with them. She felt the pride, the challenge, and the disappointment in so many of his reveries.

"How did you become a mage?"

Myronor stared at her, his brow raised in surprise. "Well...like I said before, mages are born."

"How old were you when you knew?"

He bit his lip, feigning shame. "I was what one would call a late bloomer. Most mages demonstrate magic, in one capacity or another, before the age of ten. I was thirteen or so."

"How did it manifest?"

He watched her suspiciously. "Why are you suddenly so curious?"

She shrugged, avoiding his gaze. "I don't know...maybe I learned a thing or two from you too...like how to ask endless questions and not mind my own business."

His laugh echoed off the surrounding stone. "I see, now you're the funny one."

"You're not the only one who has memories that don't belong," she said quietly. "I want to understand too."

He smiled so warmly that the stony ground no longer held a chill. "I suppose you know already it happened in Iluka."

* * *

Even as a child, Myronor rarely felt sad. The day his mother departed for Krysas, he shed no tears. Even later, he felt little in regard to Pyra's absence. Of course, he missed his mother, but he knew her choice was for his benefit in the end. At least that's what she told him. And what he continued to tell himself. Her reason must have been important enough for her to leave him and his father on their own. The only sadness he felt was for Berwyn, who suffered greatly in Pyra's absence—even a year after she left.

Myronor had kept himself occupied, but Iluka was quite boring for a thirteen-year-old boy with an inquisitive mind. While many of the villagers worked the oyster beds, Berwyn had carved out a market fishing the rubyfin schools off the Southern Coastlands. Any fish remaining after feeding the town was salt cured and shipped for sale in Feyralis. The business was not as lucrative as the oysters, but it provided them with a comfortable existence.

Since Pyra had left, Berwyn trained Myronor as a fisher, which served as some distraction. He had always learned quickly and was eager to prove himself. Already he had surpassed his father's height, though he had yet to fill out his gangly limbs. He preferred his hair short for working on the boat, keeping his pale locks just above his eyebrows.

Near the end of rubyfin season, the boats always traveled farther from shore, seeking the last of the migrating schools. Recently, though, their expeditions went much farther out into the Lucent Strait than expected. Myronor paid no mind—he loved being out at sea, the longer the better. Berwyn, however, held a constant crease of worry between his eyebrows of late.

The night before the last voyage of the season, father and son sat down in their stilted cottage. In the center of the village, the three-roomed abode was cozy with a combined kitchen and living space, as well as two bedrooms; one for each of them.

Together they ate a humble meal of boiled sun tubers and grilled rubyfin. Myronor sighed, poking at the fish with his fork in annoyance. He grew tired of the same meal every night, though his father remained quite contented. Berwyn had already inhaled his plate of food, which now sat empty, as he watched Myronor carefully.

"You're staying in the village tomorrow, son."

Myronor dropped his fork. "Why?"

"The shaman says rough storms, and you still got your land legs," Berwyn said. He stood and brought his plate to the washbasin. As if that were the end of the discussion.

"How am I supposed to get sea legs if you won't take me out on rough seas?"

Berwyn sighed. "There will be plenty of other voyages. Weed eel season starts in the small moon's time."

His father slapped a massive hand on his boney shoulder before retiring to his bedroom. Myronor sulked alone at the table, staring at his full plate. He had barely held an appetite to begin with, but now his gut was filled with disappointment.

Had he not proven himself enough this last year working on the boat? Had he not earned his father's trust?

The hurt he felt was beyond the emotional capacity of a teenage boy. So, like any young person with a sharp mind and ambitious spirit, he had turned his angst into rebellion.

Before the sun rose, Myronor arranged the pillows and blankets in his bed to resemble his sleeping body—an old but effective trick. When he arrived at the village dock, he found it empty at such an early hour. As only a youthful fisher could, Myronor hoisted himself without ramp onto the *Mistral*, his father's pride and joy.

The boat was as familiar to Myronor as his own home. He quickly stowed away in the small storage hold below deck. It was unlikely his father or any crew members would set foot in the hull until they needed the nets and buoys. By then, they'd be far out at sea. By then, it would be too late to turn back.

Patience was not a typical virtue of anyone his age, but Myronor fancied himself anything but typical. He sat quietly in the hold, wedging himself between a stack of folded nets and the hull as a precaution. There, he waited in the cramped darkness until he heard the familiar thump of the ramp, followed by boots on deck.

"Aye, Kaikora! Glad you could make it."

He recognized his father's voice greeting the new village shaman. Myronor had only met the young woman a few times, but she was close to his own age—only three, four years his senior. So his father welcomed her aboard, while Myronor had been forbidden?

More interesting was why a shaman was needed to sail today. She had warned of the storm, yes, but a shaman only went to sea on the long voyages.

"I hope to be of help," she said in a deep tenor.

Berwyn laughed. "Always helpful to have a shaman on board, especially for tasks like today's!"

His father had said storms were expected, yet now he spoke of some task. Which was it? Come to think of it, Myronor hadn't seen a cloud in the sky while boarding the boat. Usually, the storms could be seen miles from shore, but some moved in quickly, he admitted. The conversation above provided no more clues, leaving him to stew in his own skepticism.

Myronor waited patiently as the crew loaded onto the boat. He only began to feel a bit restless after he heard the call for departure. But once the ship groaned with speed, he calmed again. He had to wait until the crew came to gather the first nets before exiting the hold. If they were too close to shore, his father might throw him overboard to swim back to Iluka.

After some time, his toes lost all feeling, and the air tasted stale. Yet he heard no calls for the nets. This was far longer than usual, even for the end of the season. Would the storms prevent the crew from fishing at all today?

But rough seas always accompanied the storms and, for now at least, the boat remained steady. Nothing today had made much sense, but rather than feeling alarmed, Myronor simply became more curious.

Unable to remain cooped up any longer, Myronor snuck from the hold to the deck to investigate. As he climbed the ladder, he didn't hear the expected shouts from the spotters. Nor the gossip or jabber from the crew. Below the hatch, he hesitated.

Was there perhaps some reason his father did not wish him to sail today? Some mystery he ought not to be involved in? Like most teenagers, Myronor absolved his guilt by placing blame on his father—Berwyn should have told him the truth from the beginning.

Myronor gently pushed the deck hatch forward and peeked through the narrow crack. Surprisingly, the rear deck was entirely abandoned, with only a blue, cloudless sky visible above.

"Ready yourselves!" Kaikora's voice boomed. Myronor guessed she was near the forward bow, beyond his sight. "The navarra approaches!"

Strange; he had never heard that word. Was it some new fish they aimed to catch today? Was that why they didn't need the nets? Though why then would Kaikora's assistance be required?

Myronor rose to the deck.

As he had guessed, Kaikora stood at the bow of the ship, surrounded by a sparse crew. Her tattooed arms were spread wide as she breathed in a strange rhythm.

Myronor watched, mesmerized, as a wall of water rose before the ship. The glassy, wavering sea distorted the horizon and for a moment, he feared the wall would crash down onto the ship. He had never witnessed the shaman's hydromancy like this before. He had always assumed her mysticisms were more parlor tricks than anything.

Now, he watched as she continued to raise a barrier of the ocean around the entire ship. Like a protective veil, it made him feel as if they were submerged. Fortunately, the sky above stayed open and clear.

Myronor's mouth went suddenly dry. Did he imagine the dark shadow passing behind the water wall? He studied the crystalline barrier and saw the distortion again, this time near the bow of the ship. Kaikora stood unmoving, holding her spell as a serpentine head appeared behind the wall. A pair of deep yellow eyes searched, confused by the barrier of water. With fangs bared, the sickly pink mouth opened wide enough to swallow a man whole.

He stood paralyzed as the crew began to call to one another, their words muffled by fear and sea alike. What in the Aether was this beast?

"Myronor!"

The tone of the call broke his paralysis. As Myronor unglued his eyes from the monstrosity beyond the veil, he found himself nose to nose with an equal terror. Berwyn bore down on him, his face the color of chokecherries.

"Of all the blimey times to disobey me!" he yelled, grabbing the boy by the shirt. "Get below deck, now!"

With surprising force, Berwyn tossed his son aside. The impact on the deck hurt less than the shock of his father's action. Never before had Berwyn yelled or raised a hand to him. And...had he been carrying a weapon?

Berwyn hurried away without a backwards glance, a harpoon in hand and thick rope trailing behind. A handful of the crew followed suit; each with a harpoon connected to a tendril of weathered rope. They all fell in line behind Kaikora.

The serpent snapped and hissed, unable to penetrate the water wall. A wail of fury rippled through the veil, gripping Myronor's spine in its call. Every muscle in his body twitched with the need to flee from that sound. Yet he could not find the strength to lift himself from the deck. He didn't know anything so terrifying could exist in this world.

"On my signal!" Berwyn called to the crew. After a loud whistle, ropes snaked through the air as the crew hurled their harpoons.

The barbed weapons sliced through the water wall, penetrating the serpent's dark scales.

The navarra roared in pain and thrashed against the barrier wildly, still unable to penetrate the water. But the ropes tightened, and soon the wrathful creature was pulled and pinned against the water wall.

"Aim for the third eye—the gray between the yellow!" Kaikora yelled in a wavering voice. Her muscular arms shook violently as if struggling against the weight of the sea itself.

Searching for the third eye, Myronor spotted the small gray area between the two angry, yellow orbs. It didn't look like an eye at all. It was smaller than the others, and barely visible, camouflaged against the dark scales.

They were doomed.

"Clear the way!"

Myronor turned to watch the other deckhands back away, clearing a path to the serpent. In one graceful lope, Berwyn hurled a spear with a velocity unlike any of the others. The rope followed a perfect trajectory, arching through the thinning veil of water. His father's spear met its mark, sinking deep into the skull of the beast, directly between the eyes.

With a writhing wail, the beast fell.

Myronor finally found the strength to stand a moment later. He and the crew stood frozen, watching in disbelief as the riggings disappeared beneath the surf.

"Cut the ropes!" bellowed Berwyn.

Myronor understood the fear in his father's voice and felt stupid for not realizing the danger sooner.

The weight of the sinking beast would be enough to capsize the *Mistral*.

Kaikora dropped the water wall as she collapsed to her knees. The crew frantically hacked the running lines, but already the boat had begun to tip with the weight.

Myronor noticed a neglected attachment nearby. From his boot, he pulled his fishing knife and moved to slash the rope. The bundle quickly uncoiled, the feed whipping over the ship's side. He couldn't cut the rope as it dragged, but he could cut somewhere within the bundle. He worked up a sweat trying to sever the connection, but the rope's ends finally frayed. A victory that was tragically short-lived.

One brief glance at his father's horrified face was all he saw before the rope tightened around his ankle, yanking him down to the rough deck. Before the stars left his eyes, he was dragged overboard. Berwyn's cries were instantly muted as he plunged beneath the water.

The stinging, salty ocean flooded his nose and mouth as the serpent's corpse dragged him down. All light disappeared within moments, replaced with panic as the pressure of the depths squeezed his ears and chest. Despite his worry, Myronor couldn't help but wonder if this was poetic justice. Did the navarra know its last act would be retaliation? Drowning the son of the man who killed it?

Myronor wasn't sure if he'd drown first or be crushed to death by the weight of the ocean. It was difficult not to reflect on his life while holding on to it by a thread. His life would be cut short. He wondered how his mother would react when she received word. She probably wouldn't care; she left after all. He hadn't realized how bitter he felt toward her until now that he was alone in the dark. Berwyn never spoke ill of her, even though he suffered from her absence more than anyone.

An image of his father took over the darkness in his mind. He would be completely alone now. The thought caused Myronor more pain than the pressure of the depths. He knew his father too well; he would have nothing left but guilt and blame if his only son perished at sea.

Myronor needed to find a way back to that boat. For his father's sake, he needed to survive.

Suddenly, a glowing light pierced the darkness. But...it shone from below. Was this the light of the Aether, coming to reclaim him? Was this why he felt so strange? Strangely...alright, given the circumstances?

He gazed down at his own two hands, as one does when questioning their existence. A blue glow emanated from his palms, a painfully familiar hue. Pyra's hands had shone the same when she performed her spells.

This was magic.

Myronor had all but given up hope that he possessed the talents of his mother, but the blue light was proof. He was a mage too.

Instinct overrode any remaining fear. He pictured the deck of the *Mistral* with every fiber of his existence. The only place he wished to be.

And suddenly, inexplicably, the crushing pressure disappeared.

As Myronor opened his eyes, his hands still glowed, but the light shone differently in this new darkness. Oppressive, yet vacant. If not for his deep, rasping breaths, he would have believed himself dead. But he was alive and somewhere...different.

A sensation of trespass shivered through him.

Foreign sounds reached his ears, barely registering in his senses. They were not muffled, or distorted, simply...beyond his comprehension. Though he couldn't see anything but darkness, he *felt* as if a world surrounded him. Every sense tingled with recognition, but he remained utterly veiled. An intruder in the dark.

And he was not alone.

A presence lurked, distant, but disturbed by his arrival. It remained far away for now, but aware and...curious?

The desperate need to flee thundered within his chest. He needed to get back to the boat. He needed to be anywhere but here.

A streak of light broke the darkness before him, momentarily blinding him. The tear expanded, revealing a familiar ship deck and the ocean horizon. He could see the crew holding Berwyn back as he raged, desperately reaching over the boat's side.

At the sight of his father, Myronor reached a hand through the rift and felt the warm sea breeze dance between his fingers. The entity lurking in the darkness now approached with more fervor, as if alarmed by this new disturbance. Without a moment's hesitation, he leaped through the portal, away from pursuit.

His knees smacked hard against the wooden deck. The smell of brine flooded his nostrils, the air uncomfortably warm after he'd been so cold.

"Myronor?" Kaikora's voice carried over the commotion surrounding Berwyn.

As Myronor trembled against the deck, he found himself unable to stand. He felt like purging, and a cold sweat broke over him. His mother had explained this once to him; manasickness. Overuse of his newly found power had exhausted him; as if a near-death experience wasn't enough.

He heard footsteps cross the deck. Rough hands lifted him up and forced him into a bone-crushing embrace. The guttural sounds of his father's sobs scared him nearly as much as that dark, unknown place. And soon, Myronor mirrored his father's tears. Only when he felt his own despair purged from him did he pull away from Berwyn.

Kaikora stood nearby, eyeing him with a blank gray stare. She looked as exhausted as he felt. He wondered if the shamans experienced the same drain on their mana as mages did. A question for another time.

"How?" she asked.

A good question, Myronor thought. "I don't know, magic? I was in the water, and my hands...it was just like my mother's hands."

"No. How did you return from the darkness?" Kaikora held his gaze but somehow stared beyond him.

Myronor's swollen eyes hid his shock. He didn't know how the shaman could know what had transpired, but it left him distrustful. If his mother had taught him anything, it was how to withhold knowledge to his advantage; to play dumb.

"You mean the depths? I was deep in the water, I felt the pressure and the darkness, but then suddenly I was not," he said, turning his attention to his father.

Berwyn patted his son on the head, buying into his act of ignorance and sarcasm.

Kaikora's brow furrowed as she glared at him. But to his surprise, the shaman turned to Berwyn. "We must return to shore and perform the rites."

Berwyn nodded before shouting orders to the crew for their return sail. After the others had busied themselves preparing to sail home, his father placed an affectionate hand on the back of Myronor's neck.

"Looks like today was your last day on a fishing boat, son."

* * *

Myronor watched Ophiera closely as he finished his story. He'd studied her expression in depth throughout their entire journey, and hadn't stopped now, even whilst he spoke.

When he first met the paladin, she rarely smiled. In fact, she rarely showed any emotion other than a solemn annoyance—most often directed at him. But that had changed as they traveled. She had begun to smile more, and slowly, over their journey, she let him see beneath the armor.

Since the ordeal in the encampment, they had grown even closer. But her somber moods had also grown deeper and more damaging. A rift was forming in her heart, filling with her duties and hesitancies and worries. He didn't know how to stop the doubt from consuming her. But tonight, as he spoke his tale to her, her amethyst eyes held none of the worries—only the curiosities.

"I'm sorry you went through that," Ophiera said, her voice quiet. "It must have been extremely traumatic."

Myronor smiled sadly. It was true; for so long, he had regarded the navarra as the most traumatic experience of his life. Yet now, the memory of Ophiera's lifeless body in his arms overshadowed any despair he'd faced before.

Never had his own existence felt so dependent upon something else. *Someone* else. When the arrow had pierced her heart, his world had shattered along with it. It was easy to blame the ekath, but he had fallen apart long before her vesper appeared. He didn't need the strange connection to bind his heart to Ophiera. Now the rift he felt building between them scared him more than the navarra too.

"There's one thing I don't understand," Ophiera said.

Drawn to her voice, he laid down his head on the bedroll beside her. "Which part?"

"How could you suffer such an ordeal with that beast yet act so terribly reckless with the ippomares?"

Myronor laughed. "You say that as if a navarra and an ippomare are similar threats! I can assure you, they are not."

Her returning laugh plucked at his heartstrings.

"I think the truth is you are simply incapable of learning anything outside of a book," she said.

He knew that to be a flat-out fallacy. He'd learned so much from her on their journey. Not all were pleasant lessons, but he wouldn't trade them for anything. But the moment was too light-hearted to admit such to her.

"I would argue," he began, "that I simply don't let past blunders hinder my future enjoyments."

"Exactly...you don't learn."

Together, they laughed. It was almost as beautiful as her singing voice, made better by the fact that he caused her joy. Without conscious thought, he took her hand in his own, needing to feel that happiness through the link. She laced her fingers between his and squeezed, though her laughter faltered.

"Do you go to that dark place every time you span?" she asked.

It felt as if the air had been sucked from his lungs. He didn't want to discuss that place, but her grip steadied his voice. "I do. But I never loiter."

"And that's the reason your mother made you swear never to use your power?"

"Yes."

Ophiera turned her gaze to the night sky. It looked as if she read something amongst the stars. She pursed her lips in a way that returned some heat to Myronor's chilled body.

"How did Kaikora know? About this other realm?"

He was impressed by how quickly she made the connection.

"I've asked her several times—back then and in recent days," he said with a sigh. "But in standard form, Kaikora has avoided any direct answers."

Ophiera snorted. "If the flames had not turned my hair white, Kaikora certainly would have...The damned shaman."

He felt the flare of frustration from her and wanted to stamp it out before it spread and burned her mood.

"I like your white hair," Myronor said.

"Don't mock me."

"I wouldn't dare," he said with a chuckle. "The color is quite appealing...It reminds me of the first snow at the end of autumn."

She blushed in the firelight, reflecting his description aptly.

Ophiera said no more and instead continued watching the sky. Myronor followed her lead, gazing upon the bright stars hovering in the endless dark. He was glad to still have her hand in his.

How silly it was that a man his age hated the dark so much. But ever since his magic had awakened, he had feared the dark. It was easy to maintain his promise to Pyra—nothing could draw him back to that dark place voluntarily.

Except for Ophiera.

Twice now he had traversed the dark realm to save her. And in those moments, he had felt no fear of the place itself—only fear of losing her.

"I barely understand our own world," Ophiera said, her breath fogging in the cool air. "And now I've come to find others exist.

Mallow's home and your dark place. I wonder how many others there are."

He much preferred when she asked questions in lieu of silence.

"Scholars have debated for ages," he said. "The mages of Tanvik know of Nijeka well enough, even if familiars are rare. My guess is there are many realms of existence beyond our own—likely wondrous and beautiful."

"Or filled with endless turmoil..."

Myronor ran his thumb against her palm, hoping to quell the sadness in her voice. The Oath scars felt rough against his smooth, pampered hand.

"Beauty and turmoil can coexist, can't they?"

"Perhaps." She shrugged, but her eyes grew cold as she interpreted his meaning. "Or perhaps they negate each other—leaving behind only a dark, empty void."

And like an earth shake, the rift between them opened anew. He felt the link shift as Ophiera's thoughts spiraled downward, muting any joy they had just shared. Though her hand remained in his, she suddenly felt far away.

"But *you* are both," he said, throwing caution to the wind. "Beautiful and tumultuous...That's far from nothing."

She closed her eyes, and he felt her heart recoil through the link. "I'm simply what the Cloister made me."

"Not to me."

Her hand tightened around his but despite her touch, his heart now felt suddenly cold. Though he could not read her thoughts, he felt the mood of them. How could she still deny the bond that was clearly between them?

He had fallen in love with the most beautiful and frustrating person in all of Erum. And she was slowly slipping away from him.

~ Twenty-Nine ~

ASCENSION

The cold stone beneath Ophiera pressed painfully against her side. Despite the crisp air of the early morning, she didn't feel cold.

Myronor lay warm and heavy against her back with an arm draped over her waist, and his hand over her heart. Strands of golden hair fell over her shoulder and familiar snores tickled her ear. The sensation of him cradled around her felt undeniably wonderful. So much so that she wished it could be real. But she knew his affections were misplaced by the ekath.

After sailing to Krysas, she would break the bond and prove it. And whatever this was, whatever they were, would end. The thought grieved her, but she had promised to protect him, and freeing him from her fate—her soul—was the best way to do so in the end.

Until the time came, Ophiera knew she should keep her distance. But the ekath became harder to fight as he continued treating her as if he cared. Last night, she felt the affection of his words more than she heard them. And yet she still doubted them, even with his warmth pressed against her now. How could she distinguish truth from the ekath?

The Cloister held no warmth—a deficit that extended far beyond the weather. It wasn't a place of care or nurturing, but training and duty. The only physical connections she experienced were those during training, and none were enjoyable. She was beaten most of the time. And once, a different sort of physical misconduct.

The thought disgusted her now more than ever. Uzziel had always been her sparring partner before they were kindled, and he had always won. The day Uzziel decided to claim his victory with a kiss, taken from her by force, the action held no warmth either. She hated every second of it. And when they were caught, the punishment received had destroyed any chance she'd desire physical intimacy again.

But with Myronor...something had changed. Despite the conditioned fear of consequence still lingering in her mind, she could not ignore the way his touch affected her. Each breath that tickled her neck sent heated shivers down her spine. His hand was resting against her racing heart, protective and warm. Only a few scraps of linen and leather separated them, and yet she wished for less.

As if Myronor had sensed her thoughts, he pulled her closer with a snore. To her surprise, he buried his face in the crook of her neck. The warmth of his nose and lips pressed against her made her face grow hot.

She wiggled against him, hoping to wake him gently. Instead, he groaned as his hand fell from her heart to her breast. Her entire body felt hot suddenly as he enveloped her, caressing her through the leather bodice. The sensation was overwhelming, and in a moment of panic, she coughed loudly.

Suddenly awake, Myronor removed himself from her, rolling back onto his bedroll. The chill morning air cooled her quickly, bringing her back to composure.

"Sorry—" Myronor said through a yawn. "Didn't mean to encroach last night."

"At least we stayed warm through the night," she said, feigning nonchalance.

In need of distraction, Ophiera searched with half a mind for her pile of armor. The pang of disappointment after realizing its absence stung a little less today. If Kaikora was to be believed, her lack of armor might be remedied before nightfall.

She stretched, stiff from the hard night's sleep, and stared up to the rainbow cliffs. The local nickname for the Cliffs of Eidolon referred to the chromatic rock that reached the sky. The sandstone of reds and oranges swirling with spots of dark, bluish granite created a masterpiece of layers against the ocean. The cliffs always looked most beautiful in the sunlight, but this morning the sea mist cast everything in dim, opaque light.

Somewhere amidst the beautiful rock lay the Hidden Path. The long trek wound upward to the peak's summit, hidden in the sea mist. Though Ophiera had never climbed the cliffs, it didn't take her long to find the concealed trailhead. And after a brief breakfast, they began their climb.

A low mist hung over the coast, coating the rocky shore in cold, sticky brine. The summit remained obscured in the salty clouds as they made their way upward along the Hidden Path. It could barely be considered a path in the same way the marsh road could barely be considered a road. It was simply where the stone had weathered enough to allow someone to pass.

After a good while of precarious climbing, Ophiera made the poor decision to look down. Her stomach twisted as she realized just how far they'd climbed. And how much farther remained. She guessed they were about as high as the Pellucid Falls and yet the destination remained veiled.

"Ophiera," Myronor said, pointing to a dark mass in the ocean below. "I think the ippomares may have followed us."

She squinted toward the dark spot in the ocean and recognized the slithering bodies of the horse serpents. Strange behavior from strange creatures. She still couldn't understand why they followed the shoreline, especially north of all directions. For a moment she feared they fled from something; but what? Not everything was so dire, she reminded herself.

"If they remain there when we return, perhaps I'll greet them," she said before turning back to the rock.

"We'd best hurry this along then," Myronor said.

Though his enthusiasm was admirable, it was also foolish. Ophiera watched his progress carefully throughout the morning. His staff proved useless on this terrain and thus he minimized it to his belt, freeing his hands to climb. He had kept up with her pace, despite his clumsy feet. But every time she heard a rock shuffle, she whipped around in a panic, only to find him smiling up at her. Each time, it grew harder to shake the image of a crumpled heap of blue robes cast alongside a riverbank.

After some time, she decided she couldn't handle the stress of his clumsiness anymore. She spotted a small alcove, protected from the winds and with enough room to sit down.

"Let's rest our legs for a bit," Ophiera suggested.

Myronor didn't argue.

Once settled in their rocky nook, he expanded the minimized packs and extracted two of Berwyn's muffins. But as he unfurled the bindle, only crumbs were left. He must have fallen and crushed them at some point. But as was his nature, he merely smiled sheepishly and pulled from his belt the minimized staff. It looked more like a wand than staff now, but still, he used it to conjure two water skins and two pastries of his own making.

"The staff works even minimized...interesting, huh?" he said, handing her the food and water.

She grunted her acknowledgment. Staff or wand, she didn't care at the moment; she was preoccupied trying to decide on how to best keep Myronor alive.

"Is everything ok?" he asked, looking worried.

"This climb is more treacherous than I expected," she said, watching Myronor drink deeply.

"Worried about me?"

"I'm worried about your corpse in a broken heap again."

He laughed. "Lucky for us, the ekath prevents my death...as long as you don't fall too."

Ophiera glared at him. "Do you wish to test that?"

"I can't tell if you're asking or threatening." He smiled, chewing his pastry. Ophiera snatched the pack away from him. "Ah, so it *was* a threat."

He could joke all he wanted, but she needed to see him safely to the top. It was her duty, after all. She rummaged in her pack with one hand, inhaling her food with the other. Eventually, she found the rope she knew she always kept. The thick cords grazed her fingertips, undamaged by his blundering up the cliff.

She waited in silence, holding the bundle of rope until he finished his meal.

"Stand up," she said with no hint of playfulness in her tone.

"I thought we were resting our legs?" Myronor chuckled.

By the flames, he knew precisely how to draw her ire. Slowly, she unraveled the bundle of weathered rope.

"Stand up and lift your arms."

He cocked an eyebrow, but this time did as she asked.

"Are you going to tie me up and have your way with me? Hardly seems the place, but you'll hear no objections from me."

Despite her flush, she continued her task without meeting his eyes. As she wrapped the length of rope around his waist, she tugged a bit tighter than necessary. He grunted against the binds. She measured a length of slack before tying the same knot around her own waist.

"I never imagined you would add yet another tether between us," he said with a teasing smile.

"At least this one can be cut with a knife whenever I please," she muttered in a dangerous whisper. Myronor sobered slightly, looking somber. "You'll lead from here. If you feel yourself slip, tell me...Don't wait until it's too late." She tugged the rope, and he stumbled forward. The flash of surprise on Myronor's face caused her to smile, and she was forced to remind herself the intent of all this was to keep him upright.

After finishing their rest, they began their trek again. The winds increased steadily as they ascended, howling between the rock faces in disorientating gusts. Although the elements slowed their climb, Myronor's spirit never faltered. Fatigued though she knew he was, he pushed on steadfastly. Ophiera trailed behind, ready at any moment to brace and catch him should he tumble.

She guessed they'd surpassed the height of his tower and the Pellucid Falls stacked atop each other. Though the sea was beneath them and could theoretically break their fall, they were too high now to survive a plummet into the ocean. And as Myronor said, one of them *must* stay alive if they were to rely on the ekath for their lives. But she'd rather not rely on anything but herself to keep them safe.

Now and again, Myronor found enough breath to crack a joke. He often asked her if she was enjoying the view from below, followed by some other inappropriate comment. Each prod disrupted her concentration and her composure. She wasn't sure what had gotten into him.

"I didn't know paladins could blush so much," Myronor said through heavy breaths. "Why do you fluster so easily?"

"I'm not flustered!" Ophiera snapped. "I'm just embarrassed by your idiocy."

The cliffs' summit came into view and yet Myronor abruptly halted in her path. He looked down at her, like a gambler before a critical roll. "Have you ever had a lover before?"

This time, anger triggered the reddening of her face.

All of Tanvik knew the answer to that question. "Prude as a paladin" and "chaste as a cleric" were both popular sayings Myronor must have known. The current situation was precarious enough without his immature banter.

"Climb!" she shouted.

He obeyed, taking a single step before opening his mouth again.

"I suppose I should've asked if you've been in love before?"

Ophiera's hand slipped from the cliff face. She didn't fall, but her heart thundered as if she had plummeted. There were only a few ledges remaining to reach the summit, and she could not afford to have her concentration broken.

"If you can shut your mouth until we reach the top, I'll answer your stupid questions!"

He grinned down at her. "Deal."

To her relief, Myronor didn't utter a single word until they reached the summit. The strain of the climb only hit them once they stopped moving. They both lay splayed out on the flat, cool stone, allowing their shaking limbs a moment's rest. Although Ophiera was ashamed to admit it, the second leg of the climb had nearly exhausted her. And there was yet more to come.

"Time to fess up," Myronor said, his breath steadier now.

His persistence on the matter irritated her beyond reason. And to her surprise, she felt a tickle of the Aether surge beneath her. Strange; she had been so good at ignoring the call of her power these last few days. Yet now, she could no longer ignore the fire churning beneath the stone. Perhaps her anger had drawn the holy flames forth. She placed a steadying hand over her eyes, willing herself to calm.

"Didn't your books give you all the answers? I know the *Book of the Aether* describes *in detail* the answers you seek."

She heard him release a breath without a laugh. "Is the Cloister training truly that strict?"

"Yes," Ophiera said, eyes still covered. "Our Oaths demand devotion. Any sort of...relationship would compete for that commitment."

"Is that fair?"

Perhaps the better question, Ophiera thought, was whether that was *practical.* She removed her hand from her forehead and met

Myronor's eyes. He had perched himself on his elbow, hovering nearby—too close, as usual.

"I find it cruel to force anyone to choose between a lover or their Oath. The Cloister simply removes the burden of that choice."

Ophiera rolled away from his gaze, slowly rising to a stand. She shook the fatigue from her limbs and gazed beyond the cliff's edge. The view of the ocean was breathtaking, a welcome distraction from Myronor's probing questions. As she gazed farther inland, the mist still clung to the rocks and dunes, veiling the coast far past where Iluka lay. But the waters had cleared of clouds and mist, enough to spot a ship on the horizon. Probably one of the fishing vessels from Iluka or Cantheas heading out to the deeper waters of the Lucent Strait.

Myronor joined her, holding the rope that still attached them.

"What if it comes to a choice between me or your Oath?" he asked quietly.

She sensed the deeper question with his query. *What am I to you?* It was a question she wished to avoid answering. He had started as her charge—a burden of duty. But now, between her Oath and the ekath, all her priorities felt jumbled. Her mind, soul, and heart faltered constantly with indecision, with questions and doubt. How could she provide him with an answer she did not have herself?

"You *are* my duty, for now. So there would be no choice to make."

Though she could not see him, she felt his disappointment through the tether. Despite his philosophy of living in the moment, she sensed the fear of their choices ahead. The unknown direction of their fates perturbed his thoughts as often as her own. He simply hid it better.

"According to Kaikora, the tomb lies in the cliff face. We have to drop from the farthest edge facing the sea," Ophiera said.

Myronor moved toward the ledge reaching to the ocean. With one hand, he still held the rope in caution. "Well, this is the farthest point...and there is a small ledge below. Perhaps this is it?"

Ophiera joined him, winding the slack of the rope across her arm. "Maybe...I can lower you down from here to check."

"Do you have the strength left for such a feat?" He grinned with false concern. "I can always just try that spell again to slow my fall."

"Do you have the mana left for such a feat?" she said with a sneer.

"Perhaps," he said with a smug grin.

She knew the only way to combat his teasing was retaliation.

Without a word, she faced him and slipped her fingers between the rope at his waist. She pulled him against herself forcefully and watched as his smile faltered. She had begun to understand why he enjoyed provoking her so much.

Silently, she wound her arms around him, inspecting the rope and ensuring the knot was tight. Myronor remained ignorant of her hands, his eyes never leaving hers.

"What are you doing?" he asked.

Ophiera reached for the back of his neck, pulling him close to her. She grazed her nose against his own, watching his pale eyes grow even wider. She had finally caught him so off guard he was silent.

With one hand on the rope and one at his neck, she brushed her lips against his cheek and whispered. "Hold on tight."

A gentle push sent him toppling over the cliff's edge. As he teetered with a look of shock, she wrapped her arm around the slackened rope, pulling it taught. He cried in alarm before bracing himself against the cliffside.

He stared up at Ophiera and for once, *she* wore the devilish grin.

"That was exceptionally cruel," he said. "And not the part where you shoved me over a cliff!"

Ophiera dropped the rope another few inches, laughing at his yelp of surprise. She blamed exhaustion for her silly behavior, but wasn't this what Myronor asked for?

"Tell me when you see something!" she shouted down to him.

With the rope secured across her arm, she lowered Myronor another few feet, unable to understand his mutterings. For a moment, she worried she had gone too far. Was he even capable of being angry?

"There is an opening in the cliff face, maybe a cave of sorts, but it's too dark to see within."

Ophiera held the rope steady. "Untie yourself when you reach the ledge, and I'll join you shortly."

A moment later, she gathered the freed rope and tied it around a protruding rock nearby. For good measure, she checked the knot at the front of her waist and adjusted it for comfort. With a deep breath, she grasped the rope and lowered herself down the cliff face.

Halfway down her rappel, her arms began to tremble. Between the climb to the summit and lowering Myronor down, she had perhaps overdone it. She could ask him to levitate her down the rest of the way, but that would be akin to admitting defeat. Even if she fell from this height, she'd survive as long as she landed on the small ledge below. She looked down and saw Myronor watching her descent.

Suddenly, a loud crack broke the air, and Ophiera's foot slipped. The rock beneath her boot had broken and fell with a thud to the ledge below. Quickly, she attempted to compensate, but her grip on the rope had slackened too much, and she felt her body fall away from the wall.

Myronor yelled as the air whipped past her ears. But to her surprise, the impact never came. She felt nothing; no hard stone, no pain. She cracked an eyelid to find a blue light surrounding her as she hovered inches above the rocky ledge.

"Thanks," she muttered. Shakily, she got to her feet, rubbing her raw hands.

"Were you not satisfied throwing me off a cliff? You had to throw yourself as well?" His voice trembled despite his smirk.

"The rock broke, so it's not my fault. Plus, I would have survived the fall as long as you stayed alive, remember?"

As she had twisted through the air, the knot of her rope now sat against the small of her back. It proved difficult to undo blindly with numb fingertips.

"Allow me," Myronor said. Before she could protest, he had stuck two fingers between the rope and her waist, tugging her toward him.

She sensed this was only the beginning of her payback.

Pushed against his chest, she felt his long hair tickle her shoulder as he leaned over her to examine the knot. His hands traveled around her waist to the small of her back and she stood still, not breathing for fear of revealing how much this affected her. She stood like this for some time while he fumbled with the knot.

"Just cut it loose," she said into his shirt.

Myronor laughed, rumbling against her cheek. "You tie knots like my father."

As he spoke, the rope fell to the ground, and she tried to step away. But his hands at her waist held her still. He shifted closer, placing his lips near her ear. His breath was maddening—tickling and frustrating as he gripped her tightly. She held no doubt he knew the reaction he had caused; his own retribution for her earlier chaff. Soft lips nipped her earlobe, and she shivered.

"Please don't ever do that again," he whispered.

Myronor let her go and walked away, leaving the rope and her heart completely unraveled at her feet.

~ Thirty ~

REGRET

Ophiera's scars tingled as she approached the mouth of the cave. She thought the sensation of the Aether was due to her frustration. But now, she knew something called to her from within the crack of darkness. It felt similar to the pull of the ekath but different—less desirable and somehow of greater consequence.

Every step toward the cave brought the Aether closer to her awareness. It smoldered beneath her feet, reverberating alongside the burn in her chest.

She wanted to turn back.

"Think this is it?" Myronor asked.

She nodded, unsure if she could speak. Sensing her hesitation, Myronor took the lead and stepped through the opening in the rock face.

As she followed, Ophiera reached behind her shoulder in a failed attempt to grasp a nonexistent hilt. She wasn't sure what she found more disappointing: her lack of a weapon or the depth of her conditioning to reach for it. The pathetic handle of the machete on her hip felt pointless to even hold, and so she didn't.

In the cave, the light dimmed after just a few short steps, enveloping them both in inky darkness. Though Ophiera saw well in dim light, the pitch black was a different story. She was about to curse out loud for forgetting a torch, but then a soft, pale light illuminated the walls of the cave. In Myronor's outstretched hand, a clear crystal pulsated brightly.

"Mallow likes to be helpful on occasion," he said with a smile. The crystal flashed dangerously in response. At least Ophiera knew she wasn't the only target for his teases. "Oh, you know I was kidding. Don't let your pride keep Ophiera in the dark."

Mallow's crystal shone brightly, illuminating the narrow path of swirled sandstone before them. Myronor held out his free hand to Ophiera in expectation, and she took it unquestioningly. Together, they walked. And walked. And walked.

Vibrant layers of sandstone wavered in the light of the crystal, creating an illusion of dancing flames. The Aether still churned beneath her every step, as if drawn to her while simultaneously drawing her toward something else. The sensation felt foreign but familiar, as if she were guided toward a fire by heat alone.

Eventually, the passage expanded, widening until Mallow's light no longer reached the walls. Ophiera craned her neck into the blackness surrounding them. The radius of Mallow's light seemed to grow smaller in the endless dark. Had they been walking on a downward slope the entire time?

A trickle of anxiety brushed down her spine as she gazed into the void.

"What exactly are we meant to look for?" Myronor whispered with a nervous tone.

"I'm not sure...but I can feel the Aether calling in this direction."

The words left her mouth before she fully comprehended the sensation. The Aether called to her.

Myronor's hand remained clamped on hers like iron, fearful but composed. It kept her grounded, or at least distracted from the odd sensations. She wondered if the cave reminded him of the dark place. She still found it difficult to comprehend another realm of existence, let alone one she had visited twice, albeit while unconscious. But his fear, transferred through the ekath, was proof enough for her that the place existed. She was the only reason Myronor ever returned there. And now she led him into darkness again.

Suddenly, the edge of Mallow's light reflected against an object ahead. Ophiera's heart skipped as a white dais of foreign yet familiar stone came into view. Her thoughts flashed to the Sacramentum and the dais that had held the endless pillar of holy flames. But unlike at the Cloister, there was no white fire before her now. Only an ornately carved, ovular stone. The pale rock looked blasphemous against the colorful sandstone floor, unnatural and foreign, and placed, not carved.

At first, Ophiera thought the polished surface reflected Mallow's light. But as she drew nearer, she recognized the glow of a runic seal. The door to the Sacramentum had a similar circle of glowing runes. Someone from the Cloister had been here before.

"What does it mean?" Myronor asked.

She had almost forgotten he was there. The Aether and her memories occupied all her mind's space, and despite his hand still firmly wrapped around her own, she felt far away. As if she were in a dream.

"I don't know," she said. "But there's a line around the rim, like a lid."

Releasing his hand, Ophiera circled around the dais, examining the presumed casket. The runes pulsated, responding to her presence, and her scars suddenly itched. She didn't know what else to do but listen to what the Aether demanded.

"Stand back," she said to Myronor. "Don't intervene. And if I say run, you run. Understand?"

Myronor backed away a few steps, taking Mallow's light with him. She wanted him to leave the cave entirely, but the ekath prevented her from uttering that command. His eyes never left hers, amplifying the tension building inside her. The Aether and the ekath each tugged her soul in different directions.

Ophiera examined the casket in its own light now. The runes glowed brighter the closer she reached toward the seal. And without warning, the Aether's humble churning turned into a storm beneath her feet. She hadn't even called upon the holy flames purposefully; she only thought to break the seal, and yet her scars flared to life. With a shuddering breath, Ophiera watched the symbols emblazoned on her arm resonate with the runes upon the casket. And just as quickly, both arm and seal faded to nothing.

"That was simple enough," Myronor said in the distance.

It had been. But Ophiera felt something stir within the casket—a draw she couldn't explain. Or resist.

"Stay there," she said in a dry, dead voice.

She didn't know why, but she needed to open the casket. She placed both her hands along the top of the pale, smooth stone, and pushed. The weight was considerable, even for her. She slid the stone top open only enough to look inside.

Even in the darkness, she could tell the casket held nothing. No corpse, no armor, no sword. Nothing. Her heart sank, but her disappointment was quickly replaced by rage.

Kaikora.

How could the shaman have been so wrong? The sight was far from infallible, but Kaikora always held a firm line between what was and what could be the truth. There were only two possibilities: Kaikora was wrong for the first time in her life, or she had lied to Ophiera. The possibility of betrayal burned through her chest, harmonizing with the roar of the Aether beneath her feet.

A sudden light pierced the darkness within the casket. Ophiera realized with a jolt this wasn't an empty casket; it was a hole. A fathomless, downward spiral of chromatic stone, illuminated by a pinpoint of light far, far below. She blinked, trying to understand what she saw. And then she felt it surge.

"Run!" she yelled to Myronor.

But it was too late. Like a geyser, the holy flames rushed upward through the hole, emerging from Erum itself with a roar. She stumbled back from the stone dais, instinctively reaching for her poor excuse for a weapon. A vine of white fire broke from the pillar of flame and wrapped itself around her scarred wrist. Her machete melted into nothing as her arm fulminated in holy flames. Like a lasso, the tendril of white dragged her back toward the pillar of holy fire, drawing her arm into it.

She was a terrified girl again, back in the Sacramentum and full of endless agony. As the white flames engulfed her arm, she screamed. Her whole body felt aflame, yet the fire didn't spread beyond her arm and the pillar. Pain alone burned away her senses, including the pull of the ekath.

Why would my own deny me, yet still come here?

The voice spoke over her screams, though it didn't really speak. It was more as if the voice *thought* directly into her mind, surpassing the need for sound or language.

Even if Ophiera wanted to speak, she couldn't through the screams. Instead, she simply thought the only question that came to mind.

Who are you?

The voice laughed, mirthlessly. *My child, you'd succumb before I could fully explain who I am. So why don't we start with you?* The fire licked painfully over her scars. *Why are you here, my Aspect?*

The voice clawed at her mind, using the flames to pry at her thoughts. It needed an answer, whether volunteered or forced. Her body convulsed against the surge of flames, and so her mind began to falter.

I seek...the means...to fulfill my Oath...to acquire...a weapon...armor...for Retribution.

The voice was silent for a moment, but Ophiera could feel its fire blazing through her mind. It riffled through her soul with ease.

But you've only ever rejected my gift.

Overwhelmed, Ophiera struggled to comprehend.

I-I've always obeyed my Oath, Ophiera thought to herself and to the voice. *Despite what I've wished...I've always claimed the anathemas for the Aether...I've enacted endless Retribution across all of Tanvik.*

Laughter filled her mind again. *You've just done what you were told. Endless Retribution, you say? Pathetic. The anathemas you've claimed were nothing but minions—inconsequential compared to what lies in wait. She is ever encroaching on Erum, ruthless in her pursuit of this world...an Aspect as pathetic as you couldn't hope to stop her.*

The world faded away, leaving only pain behind.

I d-don't understand, Ophiera pleaded. *I'm not trying...to stop anyone. I'm...just fulfilling my duty.*

But you're not! The voice snapped, anger now fueling the flames. *You were chosen as my Aspect. The first in centuries, born from the flames. Yet after all this time you know nothing of importance; nothing of Retribution. Duty? I can taste the regret for every soul you've claimed for the Aether. And yet, you yourself proclaimed that regret and Retribution cannot coexist. You are fractured, my Aspect. Broken.*

The voice's words made little sense to Ophiera.

It was true that she always despised her fate. She had questioned almost every life she had ever claimed. She could only think of one soul she had felt *satisfied* in claiming. The Reverend with his yellow robes and sallow face.

The fiery pain subsided as she recalled his throat blistering beneath her hand. The fear in his eyes had sated a deep need within her, flavored by his ashes upon her flaming lips. She wished she could kill him again. And again.

But the vehemence of her thoughts frightened her. As she suppressed the violent memory, the pain returned.

You accepted my gift that day and unleashed it on her thralls. Yet now, even in my grasp, you still deny me! How can you possibly embody my power when you cower before it?

Thrall? Embody? She couldn't think, couldn't respond; there was only pain.

So weak...and such a disappointment. You don't stand a chance against her like this...and we're nearly out of time.

Ophiera couldn't argue. She was weak and pitiful. She couldn't stand a chance against anything at the moment. All she wanted was to end the pain, by any means necessary.

Come then. Return to the Aether and we will try a different soul to bear my burden.

Return to the Aether? Ophiera had often prayed for such an end. Accepting death sounded like the best option to escape the suffering.

Darkness overtook the burn, dragging her down and down.

"Ophiera!"

This voice wasn't in her mind, but frantic in her ear.

She knew that voice.

Hadn't she told him to run?

It didn't matter. Soon she'd never hear his voice again.

"Don't you dare give up, Ophiera!"

She felt a new jolt of pain, not of fire or flame, but sorrow. She'd felt this phantom pain before from her charge. And the thought of Myronor alone drove back the darkness. But her eyes wouldn't open, and her lips wouldn't move. The ekath reverberated his pain, and like a rope beneath the surf, she groped for it through the chaos.

The tether felt different now. Stronger and more tangible, though she couldn't explain how she knew. With the ekath, the darkness receded in full. The pain of the flames returned, but Myronor's despair hurt her far worse than any burn. She felt him straining against something but didn't understand until she heard the grinding of stone nearby. Blue light filtered through her eyelashes.

Interesting...no Aspect of mine has ever been bound to another. The voice laughed, this time with true amusement. *It seems you won't be returning to the Aether after all. You'll have to do then...so find me again when you're ready.*

Suddenly, the fire emanating from the casket extinguished, and Ophiera fell to the ground. She gasped against the residual burning as the flames retreated, leaving her in the dark. Echoing steps approached from behind the casket, but she couldn't move to rise. Mallow's light illuminated Myronor's drawn expression as he knelt before her.

"Are you alright?" he asked shakily. "What the hell was that?"

"Didn't you...hear...the voice?" Ophiera rasped between breaths.

"No," he said. "Something spoke to you?" She groaned in acknowledgment, her mind still swaying. "What did it say?"

Her arms shook as she tried to sit herself up. With her back pressed against the stone casket, she took a few steadying breaths. "It said I was too weak..."

She couldn't continue. None of it made any sense, especially spoken aloud.

"I only heard your screams as you burned...and they only stopped when you started to fade."

Ophiera sensed his emotions through the ekath with painful clarity. The tether transferred more than just hints of his feelings after the ordeal. Like the day Kaikora drowned her, the ekath seemingly grew stronger when challenged by death. The pain Ophiera felt now wasn't her own anymore. Where she'd felt only traces of his emotions before, she now felt the full brunt of his heartache. It left her speechless.

"Are you truly unharmed?" he asked.

"I'm fine," she said, not meeting his gaze.

Using the casket, she pulled herself up to standing. She leaned against the smooth, white surface of the stone, realizing what it truly was.

"I think this is a font," she said. "A source of the holy flames, just like in the Sacramentum. I doubt there was ever any Aspect buried here."

The Aether still called to her from within. But what was the voice she heard if not an Aspect? It spoke as if it knew her, yet...

"Why did Kaikora send us here?" Myronor asked, his voice sharp with frustration.

"I don't know...but it wasn't for armor."

"Did she know you'd face death in this cave?"

Ophiera felt his anger mingle with her own confusion. "Or maybe she knew I wouldn't, as long as you were here too."

Speculation served no one now. The armor wasn't here, so she had no more reason to stay. Ophiera stepped away from the dais, ready to put as much distance between herself and the font as possible. Her legs quaked as she stepped, a poor start to the long trek back outside.

"Put your arm around my neck," Myronor said, coming to her side.

He held most of her weight as they traversed back through the darkness. The path out felt longer than when they entered, but they eventually reached the portal back to the bright sunlight. The mists and clouds that had hindered their way up the cliff had dissipated now, revealing bright, clearing skies.

Ophiera let go of Myronor. She needed to walk on her own two feet if they were to ever make it down the Hidden Path. But she instantly regretted it. She leaned herself against the mouth of the cave briefly before collapsing to the ground.

The holy flames had taken quite a toll on her stamina. Myronor reached to her, offering to pull her back up, but she shook her head in protest.

"I just need a moment to collect myself," she said.

Myronor nodded, understanding as always.

When he sank down beside her, she found his presence eased the fatigue. It reminded her of when they recovered in Iluka after the encampment. Her soul felt soothed. She leaned her head against his shoulder, giving in to the ekath's draw.

"Sure you're alright?" he asked.

"No," she breathed.

Wordlessly, he conjured a skin of water and a small pastry. She knew it would be filled with chokecherries before he passed it to her.

"Thanks," she said, forcing the word past the lump forming in her throat.

She didn't deserve his care after everything that had happened. For three days, she had led him on a wasted journey. They could have reached Cantheas by now, and booked passage on a vessel to Krysas. But she'd wasted so much time and energy searching for what she lost. She had been so desperate for a solution to her own weaknesses, she had believed in Kaikora and even hoped, actually hoped, to regain her armor.

But she had left the cave with nothing—not even the machete.

After nibbling a few bites, she eventually offered Myronor the remainder. Her exhaustion went far beyond what enchanted food could remedy. Fight it as she may, she couldn't even win against her heavy eyelids.

Warm hands maneuvered her until she was lying down, her head in Myronor's lap. He rested his hand on her shoulder, running his thumb in circles against her skin.

Maybe she hadn't left the cave with nothing.

"I would not have survived without you," she said, her eyes closed in fatigue.

"The ekath has its perks, that's for certain."

"It wasn't just the ekath. You closed the font, and stopped the flames from claiming me."

She felt his stiff smile above her. "It seemed the right thing to do."

"Why? I asked you not to intervene. I told you to run."

"Because I'd rather take my chances angering you than risk losing you...even if it's what you wish. Just sleep for now. We can talk when you're rested."

~ Thirty-One ~

BOUND

Ophiera started awake as two hands shook her shoulders. Bleary-eyed, she was still lain on Myronor's lap atop the rainbow cliffs. The sun was all but gone now, disorientating her further. She looked up, trying to focus on Myronor's worried expression.

"Someone is here."

His words were as good as a dousing of cold water. She sat up and whipped her head around. Twilight had settled, providing just enough illumination to discern the layered rock from the horizon. But as far as she could tell, they were alone.

"There's a boat down in the water," Myronor said, gesturing with his chin to the sea.

"Whose?" Ophiera said, her voice ragged. She hadn't realized how much she cried out during the ordeal with the flames. Her throat felt raw, straining against use.

"I'm fairly certain it's the *Mistral.*"

"Berwyn?"

Myronor shrugged. "His ship at least."

She rose to her feet shakily before walking to the cliff's edge. Out at sea, the *Mistral* bobbed in the waves.

She didn't understand why Berwyn would have sailed to the Cliffs of Eidolon. No ships came near these cliffs, and for good reason. Beneath the colorful stone and turbid sea lay a graveyard of unfortunate choices. Every fisher in the Southern Coastlands knew the warnings; it's why she had made them walk here in the first place.

The sails were down on the *Mistral* and by the way it moved, she knew it sat anchored. It had to be Berwyn. He would have known to keep far from the tumultuous waters close to the cliffs. But her relief was short-lived as she studied the vessel.

"Where's the crew?" Ophiera asked.

Myronor shook his head. "I haven't seen anyone yet, but that doesn't mean much. There's barely enough light left to see you beside me."

Instinct turned Ophiera's attention down the coast.

Despite the darkness, the fog had cleared from the dusky horizon. Now her eyes could follow the stark shoreline south toward Iluka.

Her vision swam at the sight.

A dot of flames blighted the dark horizon, illuminating thin tendrils of smoke rising above the sands. She couldn't tell if a battle raged on or if she was viewing the aftermath of a great catastrophe. Either way, Iluka burned.

"No," Myronor said in barely a whisper.

She couldn't speak.

The Aether roared to life beneath her feet, screaming with the agony she somehow kept silent. The rage building inside her burned away her sorrow before she even felt it. Her scars itched, fueled by the holy flames that called to her so loudly she could barely hear Myronor's mournful pleas. If not for his grief grounding her through the ekath, she would have burst into flames then and there.

Tears streaked down his cheeks as he watched the horizon. It was strange to *feel* him falling to pieces through the tether as if his very soul imploded within him. Somehow, his pain gave her the strength to act.

"Berwyn's ship must be here for a reason," she said. "We have to get to Iluka. Do you have enough mana to get us down there?"

He had already cast so much today, conjuring their food and breaking her fall. She wasn't sure how much mana he had left after the ordeal in the cave.

"I can't span," he said, turning his gaze away from Iluka. Slowly, his composure returned. "But I should be able to get us to the ship another way."

Ophiera tried to think of any other option, but what other choice did they have? They needed to get back to Iluka. The climb down would be too long and arduous. And every moment, the Aether's cry grew louder, begging her to unleash it.

"I trust your judgment," she said, meeting his sorrow with determination. "If you say you can get us to the ship, I know you will."

Myronor's eyes softened, still grief-stricken but with something else behind them. He reached for her hand and, again without question, she took it.

"On three, we jump," Myronor said wearily. "Push as far away from the cliff as you can—it will make it easier to guide us."

From this height, the impact with the water would kill them for certain. But she trusted he knew that. As he counted, she felt the Aether burn alongside her anticipation. And then they jumped.

She fell, free from the Aether and its rage for a moment. The wind stung her face and made it difficult to breathe. Her stomach joined her heart in her throat as they plunged toward the dark sea. Yet she wasn't frightened. Without the fury of the Aether, all she felt now was numbness; even when her eyes found Iluka burning on the horizon again.

Myronor held her hand as they plummeted. Halfway down the cliffside, his hands glowed blue and their trajectory shifted slightly, angled toward the *Mistral.* Their fall slowed as he pulled her against him. At first, she thought of their night in the death marsh. His spells were easier to maintain in close proximity. But the ekath revealed that magic wasn't his reason for wrapping himself around her now.

Grief bound them together more than his trembling arms as they fell. She returned his embrace, hoping to shield him against the reality in the distance. Numb as she was, she felt the loss of Iluka in full through him. And it was unbearable.

She knew he wasn't well long before their rough landing on a wooden deck. He leaned against her, heavy and awkward, as something else dragged her down with his weight. Her chest began to ache horribly.

"Sorry—might have underestimated—" he muttered before collapsing to his knees on the deck. The ekath pulled her down beside him, his weakness hers now too. She brushed the hair from his sallow face. He closed his eyes and leaned into her hand, scars pressed against his cheek.

"I'm fine," he said. "Just...manasickness."

A rush of footsteps sounded from below. And a moment later, Berwyn appeared.

"Warden! Thank the sea you and—what's wrong? What happened?"

"Never mind us," Myronor said, raising his eyes to meet his fathers. "What's happened to Iluka?"

Berwyn's eyes widened in grief. "I don't know. I only just saw the flames on the horizon a few moments ago. I went below deck to find a spyglass, and heard the thump of you both."

"Why are you here then?" Ophiera asked. She assumed Berwyn had come for them when the village was attacked. But if he only just saw the flames...there must be another reason.

"Kaikora sent me," Berwyn said, helping Ophiera lift Myronor to his feet. Together, they walked him over to the center mast and sat him down, leaning against the post. "Last night, the sight showed her something or other—you know the shaman, no details—but she asked me to sail to the rainbow cliffs immediately. Her only instructions were for me to go alone. She said that you'd find a way to reach my ship if I simply waited. But..." He turned his sea-glass gaze up the shore, toward the glowing spot on the horizon. "How could the sight not have shown her this? She wouldn't have sent me away if she knew...or...I...I just don't understand."

Ophiera felt sick.

Throughout her retirement, nothing had escaped Kaikora's sight. The shaman had warned Ophiera every time there was a threat to Iluka, whether it was simple thieves or the Marauders' attack. What had changed?

Nothing made sense.

"How fast can we sail back to Iluka?" Ophiera asked.

Berwyn sobered quickly. "I can get us there before dawn; the current is with us and the winds should hold."

If the attack happened recently, then maybe there was enough time to find whoever was responsible. To make them pay. She didn't like having these thoughts without the Aether beneath her and yet, it was all she could think at the moment.

"Let's not waste any more time," she said. "We need to get to Iluka."

Myronor tried to stand, but both Ophiera and Berwyn scolded him back into stillness. Then she and the fisher fell into a dance of muscle memory, readying the ship for departure. She had only sailed with Berwyn a handful of times as Warden, but she knew his ways. Rather, she preferred them.

Once the main canvas had caught the wind, Ophiera began cranking the anchor hoist. She struggled against the weight, still weakened from the encounter in the cave and the drawn ekath. Without the connection to the Aether beneath her feet, she felt even more diminished. Alone.

Despite herself, she managed to haul the anchor on deck with tendrils of ink kelp still attached. Berwyn joined her by the hoist, his eyes glancing warily at his son.

"Warden, I can take it from here. Can I ask...can you take my son below deck to rest? I'm worried about you both."

Of course he was, Ophiera thought. The man was only capable of thinking of others. Berwyn had sailed here on his own, so she knew he'd get back just as well. Myronor looked drained as he slumped against the mainmast. Dark, puffy circles cradled his pale eyes in grief and exhaustion. She'd never seen a more defeated man.

"Come," she said, holding her hand out to Myronor.

He didn't protest but struggled to stand, even with her help. Ophiera could feel it wasn't only manasickness that afflicted him now. With a grunt, she shouldered the majority of his weight, guiding him below the deck of the *Mistral*. She had never spent much time beyond the deck of Berwyn's ship. When she had sailed with him as Warden, she always stayed on deck, no matter the weather or time of day. The Cloister left her wary of confined places and tolerant of the cold.

In the cargo hold, Mallow's crystal shone brightly from beneath Myronor's tunic. He didn't even attempt to pull her out, giving the light a dim, hazy edge beneath the cream material.

Ophiera found a cozy spot near the starboard hull where a newly woven fishing net lay piled high. She knew it hadn't been used by the way it fell, and by the bolt of cord that remained attached. Perhaps weaving the net was how Berwyn occupied his time while waiting for them by the cliffs.

"Lie on this for now," she said, bringing Myronor before the net. It was larger than her bedroll, which remained minimized at Myronor's belt. It would stay there until he recovered enough of his mana to cast.

She helped lower him down onto the net, a maneuver that proved more difficult than she anticipated. He wasn't the only one whose strength had been sapped away, and the rocking of the ship threw off her balance. Just when he had settled on his back, a rough wave caught the ship. She didn't have the strength to fight against it and toppled over, landing on top of Myronor and the net. On hands and knees, she braced herself over him, careful not to land directly on him and injure him. The ship rocked back and forth a few times before settling back into a calmer rhythm.

Berwyn's voice boomed down the hatch. "Gonna be a little rough until we get away from the cliffs! Nothing I can't handle alone, but batten down!"

"Aye!" she called.

If they could make it to Iluka without any more trouble than a few strong waves, they'd be lucky. As another wave jostled the boat, Ophiera realized just how precariously she hung over Myronor. She made to remove herself from him, but cold hands gripped her thighs, sudden but gentle.

"Stay here, please," he said quietly. "I feel as if my life depends on having you as near as possible."

His words hit her heart harder than the next wave. She remembered all too well that desperate feeling the ekath evoked when she'd been near death. Now, the strain she felt through the tether went far beyond manasickness, and she wondered if the ordeal in the cave had affected him as well. Unable to deny the plea in his voice, she leaned back on her knees, resting herself atop him.

Mallow's crystal flashed, a gentle reminder of her presence. Without asking, Ophiera reached beneath his shirt and gently tugged the crystal free. She looped the leather tassel around a protruding floor nail beside them, ensuring the familiar didn't roll away with the waves. Her dim light illuminated the curved, worn hull. Besides themselves and the net, the hull stood empty, a good sign for a swift sail.

Another wave teetered the boat, and Ophiera set her hands on Myronor's chest for stability. The rough sea forced them to move against each other in a way she wasn't ready to acknowledge. Needing a distraction, she stared at the wood-planked floor, studying it with unwarranted scrutiny.

Years of wear could be read across the heavily worn boards. Each gash, scratch, hole, and stain had been made by Berwyn or one of his crew over the many years. She wondered just how many people had left their mark on this ship. And how many of them still lived. Before her eyes, every imperfection in the wood became the epitaph of those who burned in Iluka.

"Please, don't," Myronor said, covering his face with a trembling hand. "Don't think those kinds of thoughts right now."

She knew the ekath shared her emotions more clearly than before, but by his response, it felt as if Myronor read her thoughts directly.

"I nearly can," he said. "At least the stronger ones. Not words, but intentions, and decisions layered within the emotions. Your thoughts dwell on Iluka, as do mine...and I can't bear them both at once."

Myronor shuddered beneath her, his face still obscured by his hand. Though she couldn't see the tears, she felt them through the ekath. The loss of Iluka struck him deeply, leaving him fragile in a way she'd never seen before.

"I'm sorry."

But Ophiera wasn't apologizing for her thoughts. She was apologizing for her failures.

The Justicar of Feyralis had uttered the word first, like a prognostic curse for the entire journey. Ophiera had failed. Over and over again.

She failed as protector of her charge. She failed as a Warden to Iluka. Even the voice in the cave thought her worthless of her Oath. And she'd proven it correct already, by losing her armor and sword to the Brotherhood. She only had the scars on her arm left now; the ones she couldn't hope to live up to after the voice tried to return her to the Aether. Was death really her only option left? Self-destruction in hopes of rebirth? To do what? So much of what the voice asked of her made little sense. And without the Aether burning beneath her, she found a hopeless, hollow pit opening within.

"Stop," Myronor said, his voice breaking. "Now your thoughts hurt me worse than what we sail toward."

She didn't understand how the truth of her misgivings could hurt him worse than knowing Iluka was likely destroyed.

He removed his hand from his face, revealing stark eyes that stared at her intently. The shade of blue reminded her so vividly of his vesper.

"All I have left is on this ship," he said. "And I fear at any moment I will lose it. I can't lose you again, Ophiera." She still didn't understand. Or maybe she didn't want to understand. But Myronor wouldn't let her feign ignorance. "I felt it, you know—the moment you gave up in the cave." He took her scarred hand in his and pulled her farther down to him. Their chests lay pressed against each other, sating the ekath as he spoke. "I felt your relief too—your hope of finding peace within the Aether."

She didn't want to have this discussion. Now, or ever. Her apathetic tendencies toward her own existence were justified. A life of servitude and fire had left her with few other ways to cope. Apathy and avoidance had saved her heart from the burden of her duty and the tribulations of her quiddity.

"You should rest," she said, avoiding his eyes. It was difficult given how close they lay. "We shouldn't look backward when our path forward holds so many unknowns."

Myronor placed his hand on her cheek, guiding her eyes back to his own.

"I am looking forward," he said in a solemn voice. "You say *our* path, but I've sensed the wax and wane of your heart since the very beginning. And I can't blame you for your uncertainty regarding us or the ekath. But, Ophiera, I need you to swear to me that you'll never give up like that again."

Her face grew warm under the intensity of his gaze and touch. "Why?"

He smiled up at her sadly. "Because I love you, Ophiera. And I will continue to love you, no matter if you reciprocate, or sever the ekath, or break your Oath. I don't care. I only care that you are free of all burdens, including me if you still view me as such. But please...do not burden me with a world free of you."

The emotions pouring from the ekath were like a storm against her heart. Adoration and need churned beneath his burning blue eyes, as did unbearable grief—for Iluka, yes, but mostly for her.

He relived that moment in the cave, and she felt his dread of losing her repeat over and over through the ekath. The depth of that fear terrified her just as much as his proclamation of love.

"Even if I wished to die, the ekath prevents my death. So there is nothing for you to fear."

He shook his head. "You, more than anyone, should understand the power of intentions. It's the thought of you finding nothing in this world meaningful enough to live for that hurts me more than anything."

The words struck her, but the scholarly man beneath her was wrong.

It wasn't that she found nothing in this world meaningful; rather she despised the fact she never had a choice in what had meaning. The Cloister dictated her entire existence while her Oath bound her to resentful compliance. But in her retirement, she had found something worth fighting for in Iluka. And years later, something worth sacrificing for in Myronor.

The moment she laid eyes on his pale blue vesper, she knew she couldn't let him leave this world. In the encampment, she had felt the same inexplicable need. She had watched the Reverend beat Myronor within an inch of his life, a sight more painful than anything the Cloister ever put her through. It was enough to awaken the flamed monstrosity within her. That was something meaningful, wasn't it?

"I can't promise what you ask of me," she said in a strained whisper. "But as long as you're my charge, I swear to never give up on you." Regardless of Oath or ekath, that was a promise she could keep. She hoped it was a sufficient.

"It's good enough for now," he said, wiping the tears from her face. She hadn't realized they fell.

Despite their ordeals or maybe because of them, she finally understood her own turbid heart. And Myronor was the only point of clarity. Truth flared to life within her heart, burning with a need she didn't understand. Reminiscent of the holy flames, she felt a draw she could neither explain nor deny. And just as she knew to give herself over to the Aether, she knew to give herself over to this new conviction.

Ophiera drew closer to Myronor, pressing her forehead against his; their noses brushed together as their shallow breaths and tears mingled. Neither blinked as his hand slipped from her cheek back into her hair, weaving his way through the loosened white braid. His body tensed beneath her, paralyzed by the same overwhelming need that drove her to press her lips against his.

The connection was instant. Their tether resonated like a chord struck in perfect harmony, binding them in a concert of moving lips and quickening breaths. She felt everything through him; their despair, their fear, their loss, and yet it all was suddenly replaced by something far more powerful exchanged between them.

She loved him, just as he loved her. She couldn't explain why she now believed him, or her own heart. Regardless of comprehension, these were the simple truths she now accepted.

Embracing their connection, rather than resisting, Ophiera lost herself in him. The rhythms of their lips crashing combined with the rocking ship into a glorious tempo that drew her breath ragged. She had never understood why the people of Tanvik exchanged their affections physically until now. Regardless of the ekath, the kiss conveyed more than words could ever communicate. And she had always preferred actions to words.

Myronor's lips pulled beneath hers into a smile, and she removed herself from him, curious. Moments ago, he had been worn with exhaustion and grief. But now, he smiled up at her like he never had before.

"What?" she asked, breathless and confused.

He chuckled, covering her hands with his own, pressing them against his chest. "This is the second time I've jumped from a great height only to have you atop me, returning me to life."

~ Thirty-Two ~

CATACLYSM

Myronor awoke to the smell of smoke.

The scent evoked a grief that not even Ophiera's touch could stave off. She still lay cradled in his arms in the tangled pile of netting. But her eyes were wide and aware. She'd smelled the smoke before he did.

Together, they had rested throughout the night as Berwyn sailed them to Iluka. The ekath finally felt settled again and his mana at least partially replenished. But he wasn't yet ready to face the reality above deck.

Ophiera was the first to rise. She stretched in silence against the hull, turned away from where he lay. He no longer felt warm affection from her through the ekath. As she turned to him, he saw her amethyst eyes returned to crystal, cold and hard as they fell upon him.

"Are you ready?" she asked.

Like her eyes, her voice was devoid of warmth. Her frost stung him worse than it should.

"Not really," he said. He would never be ready for what they were about to face. "Are you?"

She dropped her gaze. "I'm ready to find who's to blame for the smoke in the air, but beyond that...well, beyond that doesn't matter. I'm going to see if Berwyn needs help docking the ship."

Her boots echoed throughout the hull, leaving Myronor alone in the makeshift bed. He didn't wish to follow in her callous wake. But the dim glow of Mallow's crystal pulsated with words of comfort.

"I know," Myronor mumbled. "I know it's her way of coping...but it doesn't make it hurt less."

He tried to understand Ophiera's dramatic mood shift. Through the ekath, he now sensed a growing void within her. A numbness that overtook all the warmth shared in their kiss last night. The indifference hurt him more than any anger she could have expressed. But he knew that Ophiera, like himself, was doing everything she could to keep her heart together before facing the destruction of Iluka.

Returning Mallow's crystal to his neck, Myronor rose and dragged himself out to the deck. The smell of smoke grew stronger with every step. Against his chest the crystal bounced, giving him enough strength to at least make it to the deck.

Above, Ophiera stood at the bow of the ship against a backdrop of orange flames and dark smoke. It was too early for sunrise, thus Iluka provided the only light. Myronor joined her hesitantly, dreading to see what lay before her. His knees gave way as his eyes fell to the shore.

The dock stood intact but was devoid of any ships. Suspicious lumps lay strewn across the dark pier and Myronor's breath disappeared. They couldn't all be bodies, could they? As his eyes followed the path to the beach, he saw even more corpses and fires marring the sand. Iluka lay before them in utter ruin.

On his knees, Myronor gasped for air that would not come. The same question rolled over and over again in his mind: Why? Why would someone do this? Why Iluka?

He felt the rough skin of Ophiera's hand caress the back of his neck. Her touch somehow brought his breath back to a steady pace.

She held it there until he calmed, but again, he could feel nothing from her. No grief or anger or pain, only a numb purpose.

"I understand if you can't come with me," Ophiera said, her voice still emotionless. "But I'm going to look for Kaikora."

Myronor wiped his face, composing himself. She held out her hand, knowing his answer, and helped drag him to his feet. But she let go of him at once and began tying the ship to the dock.

With a graceful lope, Ophiera disembarked and stood expectantly on the dock. He realized now that Ophiera still had no weapon. Despite this deficit, she led the way toward the beach, expecting him to follow. He remembered the minimized staff on his belt and expanded it to size as they walked. The chances of him needing to fight were slim in the wake of such destruction, but he hoped Ophiera had a plan in case. It wasn't until her boots touched the sand that he understood her intentions.

He felt her sudden fury burn through the ekath, an inferno alongside the surge of Aether. Reconnected with Erum, the holy flames flocked to her again, and even Myronor could feel their wrath.

Ophiera stumbled a moment, finding her bearings against the raw power surging beneath her. He felt it as it nearly overwhelmed her. Yet somehow she resisted the flames overtaking her.

Composed, Ophiera led Myronor through the center of town. The fires lit their way, casting the destruction in an eerie, flickering light. They walked past the collapsed inn, a devastating sight on its own. He remembered when Berwyn was too tired to cook, he'd bring them to the inn for a meal. The innkeeper at the time, Yelena, would always give him extra of the day's sweet pie while keeping his father's stein full to the brim. She never charged Berwyn for any of it. He wondered if...but the thought crushed the air from his lungs again and he turned away from the broken inn.

Many of the stilted buildings remained standing, but no structure was left unscathed. Rows of thatched roofs burned, some in total collapse. Signs of struggles remained imprinted in the sand, yet there were no bodies this far into town. He didn't have the mind to question why; all his effort was dedicated to putting one foot in front of the other now.

As they climbed the hill to the shaman's hut, Myronor barely recognized the place. It was worse inside.

Pale ash and blackened timbers were all that remained of the round roof above. The walls somehow survived, but the shelves surrounding them only held a few clay pots, covered in soot. Everything else had been burned or smashed.

Ophiera stepped over the rubble to the stone fire pit in the center. The coals within were dark, and a crushed kettle lay nearby.

"Kaikora..." Myronor whispered in a voice warbled with grief.

"She's alive," Ophiera said in a dead tone. "Gone, but alive."

He shook his head in disbelief. They hadn't come across anyone alive, and judging by the state of the hut, no one could have survived. There was no sign of a body, but that didn't mean the shaman lived.

Ophiera took a handful of coals from the fire pit and crushed them in her hand. "She hasn't been here for some time; she likely left when Berwyn set sail, long before the attack. Her travel gear is missing too."

He saw the shaman's traveling bag and cloak were gone. Between the destructive clues and Ophiera's darkening thoughts, Myronor reached the same conclusion that drew her ire. It seemed as if the shaman had fled before the attack. As if she *knew* what was coming and yet abandoned Iluka.

"Let's keep moving."

He followed Ophiera back along the central path and past the destroyed inn toward the outskirts of the village.

As they left the village proper, a few charred corpses lay strewn in the sand. Myronor's stomach lurched at the sight. Their last moments had been burned into place. He couldn't tell if they were friend or foe; charred flesh left little to recognize. But he could imagine their screams and pressed a hand over his mouth as he followed Ophiera.

The destruction was far worse in the outskirts compared to the village proper. Myronor wondered where the attack had started and ended, but he stopped himself quickly. He didn't really want to know.

They passed the burning storage house. Small barrels crumbled into charcoal as iridescent pearls poured forth into the sand. Though a fortune lay within, the blushed sea gems remained untouched. The attack on Iluka wasn't driven by greed, only destruction. Somehow, that made it worse.

Myronor held his silence, trying to quell the shock and pain. He didn't want to witness any more of his beloved home destroyed. He just wanted to go back to the *Mistral* and forget any of this ever happened. But Ophiera's cold rage was a respite compared to the mournful anguish he felt, and he latched on to it as they approached her cottage.

Then, it became Myronor's turn to fall to numbness.

The door of her home hung open, lopsided on a single hinge, a prelude to the destruction inside. Her oasis, untouched by the Cloister or Magistrate, now lay in ruin. He remembered how she spoke of Iluka; of her home as the only place she'd chosen. In the flashes of memories he acquired when they bonded, he remembered this place with a sense of peace. As her cold eyes lingered on the smoldering remains of her kitchen, he knew any chance she had of returning to Iluka died within the flames of her home.

"When we recovered here," Myronor began in a shaking voice, "I often imagined what it would be like if we could stay. I liked to dream of what our lives might be...what your life may have been without Oath or duty." Tears broke through as he took a breath. "Not only is Iluka lost, but so is the smallest sliver of hope I had that I could free you from your bonds and return here."

Ophiera turned to him, a softness returning to her hardened eyes. But before she spoke, another voice pierced the night.

"How sweet, confessing yourself like that right in front of her burning home."

Both Ophiera and Myronor whipped their eyes toward the voice. A woman in blackened robes stepped out from behind the ruined cottage. As she drew back her hood, she revealed short, mouse-brown hair that hung straight and flat over her bloodshot eyes. The yellow armband was dirty and worn, but still bright against the dark dawn.

"Marvena!" he spat.

"I must have left quite an impression if you remember my name." She cackled. The sound brought forth a flood of horrific memories in Myronor's mind. "But you can call me the Reverend now."

Ophiera watched her, unblinking. "Reverend of what? I destroyed your faction."

Marvena laughed again. "That's a very arrogant assumption, especially from one of the Cloister. You know it's impossible to destroy an ideology, even in white flames."

"So the Brotherhood is to blame for Iluka?" Ophiera asked, her voice dead.

"And they say paladins are all brawn and no brain." Marvena tapped her temple with two fingers. "Yes, I heralded Iluka's destruction. Happy with your answer?" She bore down on Ophiera, her eyes shimmering with cruelty. "But now, it's my turn to ask a question. How did you survive my arrow? I know my shot was true; I watched your blood spray all over him and heard his pleas and sobs, yet—"

Myronor started forward, staff at the ready, but Ophiera grabbed his wrist and yanked him back behind her. The woman laughed again.

"Why?!" Myronor screamed. He wanted to cast, to do something to this vile woman, but Ophiera's iron grip kept him still.

"Well, I'm curious if she…oh…oh you mean why Iluka? But you skipped the *how*! And you call yourself a scholar? Don't you want to know how the village fell first?"

"All I care about is who," Ophiera seethed through gritted teeth. "I'll make you and every one of your remaining followers pay for this!"

"All of us?" Marvena said with another cold laugh. "You'll be on a murderous rampage for decades then, my dear. Our order has existed for centuries, operated across continents, and infiltrated governments, all under the nose of the Cloister and their precious paladins. Your order might have set us back before—even you have, on this very beach! But we rose again, even stronger, from the ashes. And we will continue, as long as Aud wills it."

Myronor connected her words in a terrifying realization. The Vespula Brotherhood wasn't some new fanatic cult, but a cycling faction of worshippers reborn throughout time. The Grey Marauders were their predecessors, and who knew how many iterations came before them?

He felt Ophiera's heart race and through the hazed ekath sensed where her mind toiled. The voice in the cave had spoken something similar to her, hadn't it? He couldn't pull the words from her thoughts, but the feeling there was...hopelessness.

"What could possibly be worth this much suffering?" Myronor asked.

Marvena's face fell into seriousness. "Suffering is subjective, a point of view, a threshold easily adjusted with experience and resolve. How is what I do any different than what the villagers of Iluka were famous for? I'm simply shucking oysters and collecting the pearls; I just give my harvest to the Void instead of selling it in the market."

"Why Iluka?" Ophiera asked, echoing his previous question.

"Please, I thought that obvious," Marvena said, rolling her eyes. "We were looking for you two; my Mistress wants him back," she said, pointing to Myronor with an upturned palm. "And Aud needs your soul," she finished, gazing at Ophiera. "No one in the village would tell us where you or that monstrous shaman went off to; so the Abyss Mother feasted upon the souls of those who denied her. Looks like you *failed* yet again, Aspect of Retribution."

Myronor felt the words ignite Ophiera's rage. Her fury kept him from collapsing, but only just. He remembered the night in the encampment, watching the Reverend sacrifice souls to the Void. He imagined the terror as they died, and how their vespers crumbled into blackened smoke. The thought of that fate falling to the villagers of Iluka terrified him; not only were they dead, but they were no longer part of the Aether. Sacrificed to the Void.

"Who is your Mistress?" Ophiera asked.

Marvena cackled again. "Clever girl. Just hand him over and he can find out."

Ophiera dragged him farther behind her by the wrist. She trembled with a fury he'd never felt from her before.

"He's mine," Ophiera growled. "Tell me where the Mistress is and she can be the first to burn instead of you."

Despite the vehemence in her voice, Myronor couldn't help but appreciate her possessiveness over him. He was hers. Some of the fear he felt receded, knowing who stood guard over him.

"First?" Marvena asked.

"I told you I'd come for you all. And I won't stop until you've all joined the Aether."

For the first time, Marvena looked fearful. She glared at Ophiera with sunken, cruel eyes. "I know you won't dare set yourself ablaze here, paladin. I remember your pathetic whimpers, unable to control your own powers! You'll destroy all of the Southern Coastlands if you're unleashed here. And as I'm sure you recall, you have no weapon or armor. You're nothing anymore! Nothing but a broken soul of a failed Aspect. And all Aud desires is to be the one to crush that final light from your vesper."

Marvena's arms twirled before her as if in a dance while the air rippled and distorted. Myronor watched, paralyzed in fear. He sensed the darkness before she began the guttural chant, the same one from the encampment. A suffocating air fell upon him, but this time he had nothing left in his heart to resist. Fear wound its way through his chest, strangling his breath and crushing his heart.

He couldn't go back to the dark place.

He couldn't witness this again.

"Get back to the ship!" Ophiera yelled, pushing him away from her.

A loud crack pierced the night. Hysteria opened within him, alongside the rift now cutting through the air. The darkness blighted the beach, at first a small tear no wider than a hand, but it widened with every spiteful word from Marvena. Beyond the Void, something called to him.

"Myronor, go!" Ophiera screamed as her arm ignited in white flames. "Please!"

The pain of her words and the fear in his heart forced his feet to move. Obstructed by sand and debris, Myronor cast his spell to lighten his feet, running on air as fast as he could to the *Mistral*. The sounds behind him turned his stomach, but he kept running without looking back. He wasn't proud of his cowardice, but wasn't about to abandon Ophiera.

When Myronor reached the *Mistral*, he immediately began untying the boat. A few moments into his frantic toil, Berwyn surfaced from below deck.

His pale green eyes were wet and bloodshot, mourning the loss of their home. But grief would have to wait.

"Help me prepare the sails," Myronor said.

"Where's the Warden?" Berwyn questioned, wiping his eyes. "We can't leave without her."

"We're not, but she's in trouble," Myronor said, hoisting the downwind sail. "We need to sail down to the shore by her cottage. Now!"

Berwyn didn't question Myronor's frenetic request. His father gave the boat a few more shoves away from the dock before taking his place at the helm.

Ophiera's screams pierced the night as they sailed.

Myronor didn't require the ekath to know she burned. Up the beach, a white light flashed in harmony with her screams. A beacon of holy flames that guided their way.

His chest ached and his skin began to crawl. The ekath transmitted only a fraction of the pain he knew surged through Ophiera now. And he didn't know how she withstood it.

Berwyn followed course and as they sailed closer, Myronor saw the pale, curved form of an enflamed entity screaming into the night. Against the dark beach, Ophiera's body outlined in flames was both beautiful and terrifying. Her hair burned upward, serving as the pillar they saw from the distance. Before her, the portal dwindled, curling to ash as her flames spread across the beach. A dark shadow fled, hovering above the sand in darkened robes and a pale glow of magic.

Marvena was escaping again.

A few dark tendrils shot toward the burning figure, disintegrating upon contact before the portal closed. The oppressive darkness vanished from his heart, and Myronor felt relief in its absence.

Ophiera hadn't needed his help after all. But though the portal closed, Marvena had fled, and the paladin continued to burn. Her screams tore through the night.

Panicked, Myronor threw a leg over the side of the *Mistral*. He didn't know what he planned; he just needed to get to her. But Berwyn's hands pulled him back by the shoulders, toppling him painfully to the deck.

"Look, you fool!" his father bellowed, pointing toward the shore. "She's forcing the very ground asunder! We have to get farther away before she causes a wave and capsizes us!"

Myronor stayed down on the deck, held there by a pain gripping his chest and squeezing away his breath. The ekath had been drawn taut as Ophiera neared the Aether.

As long as he held her soul anchored to his, she would survive this ordeal. But her piercing screams made him question the price.

The sound of collapse drew Myronor's eyes away from Ophiera and toward Iluka. Fault lines of white flames traversed the town, burning any inanimate object to ash. The ground shook with the rifts and flames, and the sands began to swallow the village whole.

In her agony, Ophiera buried the corpse of Iluka.

As Berwyn predicted, the ocean wasn't immune to the shock waves of the ground, and the boat began to rock harshly. If she didn't stop soon, who knew how far her destruction would spread. He needed to stop her. He needed to disconnect her from Erum.

Myronor used his driftwood staff to stand himself upright. With all the mana he had left, he followed the path of the tether and concentrated his spell. With a glow of blue, he channeled his mana to lift her from the ground. It proved difficult from a distance, and the rocking boat threw his concentration. But the ekath kept him locked on her.

The white flames disappeared abruptly. Darkness fell for only a moment before the sunrise broke the horizon. In the pale dawn, he saw a glint of shine where he knew Ophiera had fallen, alive but barely.

Myronor collapsed on the deck. She drew on him now more than ever, his soul unable to bear the burden of her cataclysm. Despite the rising sun, darkness encroached on him.

~ Thirty-Three ~

CONVICTION

The moment Ophiera saw Marvena, the flames growled beneath her feet. She stalled the fight as long as she could, holding back just long enough to hear what she needed to know. But there was only one way this could end.

She knew the Brotherhood was to blame for Iluka. A thread of understanding connected the nonsense Marvena spouted to the words from the voice in the cave. But she was too distracted by the vacuous rift opening before her to think too hard on it.

Sending Myronor away was her best bet to protect him, but it hurt more than she expected. His fear dragged on the ekath as he ran, like a thread unraveling her control as he went. Every moment, the floodgates holding back her flames faltered.

He would be safest away from her.

Proof came as the dark portal opened in full. Dripping black tendrils shot out toward her charge as he ran for the *Mistral.*

Ophiera summoned a wall of white flames without uttering a single word. The shock of how easily the Aether bent to her will was short-lived as another set of tendrils circumvented her barrier.

With another pulse of will, she burned them too before they could reach Myronor.

"He belongs to my Mistress! He belongs to the Void!" Marvena screamed. Her hands gyrated behind the rift of darkness, coaxing forth the power from beyond.

Endless thralls of blackened vines tried to pass Ophiera, but she managed to catch them with bursts of white flames erupting from the ground. The tendrils cried out in sizzles and steam before vaporizing into nothing.

The ekath nudged her awareness and she knew Myronor had reached the ship. He and Berwyn would be safe there, for now. But her relief drew her attention away from Marvena for a split second too long.

Suddenly, the flames disappeared and the runes on her arm dimmed. A crushing weight pressed against her chest as a blackened tendril wrapped itself around her. With her arms pinned to her sides, it lifted her from the ground. The Aether fell silent in their disconnect.

"This time, I'll make sure to watch you die," Marvena said. Her laugh became a scream as she coaxed the Void forward. The ichor seeped from the binds, burning Ophiera's skin in a pain worse than any flames. It wasn't the pain of death, but a violation of her very existence, as if the ichor drew from her soul. She was being dragged toward the dark portal, away from the Aether and away from Erum.

But she couldn't let that happen.

It wasn't her soul she cared to preserve, but Myronor's, still anchored to hers. And somehow...the darkness *knew* he belonged to her. It sought him as it tore through her, as if she were simply in the way. But she would not yield.

The Brotherhood had taken everything away from her, but they wouldn't have her charge too. She would make Marvena pay, just like the other Reverend. Every last soul who wore a yellow armband would pay for her suffering. They were like every other corrupted soul she'd claimed in the name of Retribution, except this time, she *wanted* to kill them.

Ophiera flared with white fire, igniting from her runic arm and traveling up her body. Disconnected from Erum, she summoned the flames from within. As the tendrils burned in the flash, she fell to the ground and the Aether surged through her once more. And this time, she willingly let the holy fire claim her.

The white flames overtook her the same way they had in the encampment. And though she screamed into the night, it wasn't with pain. She screamed in rage.

"No," Marvena breathed, stumbling backward.

Ophiera drew her gaze away from the pathetic soul and toward the violation before her. She summoned the flames beneath the dark rift. The edges of the portal burned like parchment, shrinking with every moment spent in the white flames. Marvena had already begun to run, but instinct drove Ophiera to take her Retribution on the Void first. She needed Aud to know that she was coming, that she'd never rest until all her followers were burned alive by her scarred hand.

Ah...are you finally ready, my Aspect?

The fiery voice from the cave once again brushed her mind. Now, engulfed in flames, Ophiera felt closer to the voice than ever before—a closeness beyond a physical sensation. She understood its intentions so clearly now. She knew what it needed her to do.

I will burn the Brotherhood from Erum. I won't stop until Aud has nothing left but fear of me. My scars command my Retribution, but my soul demands vengeance. I claim their souls not for duty, but for me. For the Aether; for Iluka; for my ekath.

The voice laughed through the roaring flames around her.

I hope you survive.

Ophiera fell to her knees, dragged down by the flames and voice. The sand vibrated violently around her, grains bouncing themselves into a building cloud. Beneath her, the ground quaked and yet she still burned.

She raised her eyes and saw the fault lines of white fire extending far beyond her. Try as she might to quell the flames, they only seemed to spread farther away. The sand now reached her elbows, slowly consuming her in the burning quake. She heard herself screaming still and knew she couldn't stop. The power pouring from her could destroy the Southern Coastlands and everything beyond. Was utter annihilation the only way to cleanse Aud from Erum?

Through the erupting fire, Ophiera saw the *Mistral* sailing across choppy waters. The tether dragged her heart out to the sea, adding more agony to her screams. But at the thought of Myronor suffering her reaching flames, she imploded, turning them inwards instead. The pain tore apart her very soul, the torture of fire without the relief of ash. She screamed into the dawn as the sand swallowed her, flames and all. The white fire became blue light, and then the darkness took her.

* * *

Ophiera hated the feeling of sand in her armor. And it took her far too long to realize what was wrong with that thought.

Aware of the heaviness set upon her body, she opened her eyes. She recognized the hold of the *Mistral*, open and empty. Her back rested against the hull, but with some barrier in between. She looked down at her body, confused by the sight.

Armor of a swirled-patterned gold covered every inch of her limply laid body. The pale metal looked both silver and gold in the dim light, and she knew it to be adamantrium. She lifted a weighted hand and examined the gleaming gauntlet. Her eyes followed the path of the gilded plate, passed the vambraces and rerebraces on her arms to the heavy pauldrons on her shoulders. Curved upward like flames themselves, the pauldrons connected organically to her breastplate, formfitting without the need for straps or ties. The armor interlocked somehow and hugged her body without gaps or breaks. She feared it was a part of her until she saw her scarred skin through the open-palmed gauntlets.

"Ophiera?"

Myronor's voice called to her from across the hull. She hadn't noticed him, or perhaps he'd just arrived. His pale hair fell lank around his gaunt face. She wondered if he hadn't slept or perhaps still suffered from what...what happened.

The memory of her cataclysm exploded in her mind, reliving every moment as she lost control. She remembered how far the faults of flames had spread, how the ground quaked beneath her, and how she screamed for it all to end.

What had she done?

She opened her mouth to speak, to beg Myronor to tell her what happened. But only a whimper escaped her, followed by metallic, salty warmth flooding her mouth.

"Don't," Myronor said, crossing the hold. He bent before her and wiped the blood trickling down her chin with his sleeve. "Your screams...You'll need time to recover your voice."

He conjured a skin of water with a wince and handed it to her warily. As she drank, her throat burned with the foul taste of blood. Surely her voice couldn't be the only casualty of her eruption. What happened to Iluka?

The only thing that matters is you're alive.

Ophiera jolted, surprised by the familiar tone of his voice, yet Myronor's lips had not moved. His eyes fixed on hers as he smiled sadly.

"The ekath has changed yet again. I can hear your thoughts, clear as day. And I take it you can hear mine."

How? she asked, testing his theory.

Myronor shrugged. "I don't know. It seems the bond changes the more we use it...the closer we become. I don't know how or why, but the more entangled our souls become, the tighter the ekath binds us."

She couldn't process the consequences of his revelation now. There were too many other questions on her mind.

Did I...destroy Iluka?

Myronor's eyes fell from hers. "It was already destroyed...You simply put it to rest."

Her heart sank.

And Marvena?

"Escaped," Myronor said shortly. *I'll kill her with my bare hands next time if I have to.*

Ophiera heard Myronor's afterthoughts and winced. She'd never heard him so violent, so angry. It wasn't right.

How did this happen? she asked, raising her gleaming hand before him. He took her gauntleted hand in his, and the open palm allowed their skin to touch. The ekath purred in satiation though her heart ached.

"I was hoping you'd tell me," he said with a smirk. "We found you like this: gilded and unconscious, buried in the sand. You held *that* in your hand."

Myronor pointed to the far wall where a long, gleaming blade rested against the hull. Like her old claymore, this sword had no sheath. But that was where the similarities ended. The blade was nearly twice the width and seemingly forged from the same swirled adamantrium as her armor. It carried a wider guard and longer hilt to accommodate the broader blade. Massive and beautiful as it stood, she wondered if she could even lift a claymore in her current state. The weakness that plagued her felt irreversible; a tiredness she'd suffer the rest of her life. *Broken.*

"It's only been a day since you collapsed. Give yourself time to recuperate, voice and body," Myronor said gently, brushing a few stray hairs from her brow. "Why don't you lay down? Now that you're awake, I can help remove your armor."

No.

Even her thoughts sounded defensive. After everything that happened, the weight and discomfort of the bulky armor was a welcomed burden.

"Very well," he said. With a glow of blue, he expanded one of the packs strapped to his belt. From within, he pulled a straw-filled pillow and a woolen blanket. "More gifts from Berwyn," he said as he tucked the pillow behind her neck and covered her lap with the blanket.

I'm sorry for everything.

"Just rest now," he said before pressing his lips against her forehead. The warmth of his voice flooded through the ekath, allowing exhaustion to take hold of her once again.

* * *

Rest only gave Ophiera the energy to fret and toil. Below deck with her thoughts, she unpacked the recent events. Like the *Mistral* itself, her heart tossed and churned on choppy waves throughout the storms at sea. For two days, the weather prevented them from sailing. And for two days, she weathered another tempest within.

Ophiera had lied to the voice in the Aether. The more she reflected on what had happened, the more she realized she wasn't ready for this power. She may have gained the gifts of armor and a sword, but she didn't deserve them. The armor fit her as if forged upon her body; and in actuality, they had been. She remembered a burst of energy that threatened to undo her and everything around her. Had that been the armor forming around her? Or had it simply been the next wave of her cataclysm? What would have happened if Myronor's spell hadn't disconnected her from Erum?

One thing was clear: she didn't understand the full potential of her power. All she knew was that beneath the ground lay an endless source of energy that she could unleash with a mere thought. The Aether bent to her will easily, yet constantly threatened to overcome her; a precarious balance. One she couldn't maintain.

Aspect of Retribution or not, whatever she was now, she was a threat to others. To everyone. She feared what those first steps back onto dry land would bring. She feared how quickly the Aether would claim her again, and set her off into another uncontrolled eruption. She feared what else she would destroy. She feared destroying Myronor.

Through the storms, Ophiera reached the same conclusion she had before. Her charge would be safest away from her. Together, her power would consume them both—kill them both. But at least at a distance, the ekath would keep him alive as long as she lived on as anchor. At least until she could severe the tie. Once the ekath was broken, he would truly be free from her fate. Safe from her and what the Aether demanded of her.

Her Oath still demanded she discover Pyra's fate, after escorting Myronor to Krysas. But the voice of the flames had commanded her so clearly, and now she no longer knew how binding her Oath remained. Regardless, she feared the consequences of being wrong. The Magistrate and the Cloister would hold her accountable, even if the Aether didn't. Extinguishment would be her punishment for breaking her Oath, and she had burned long enough.

So, as was her way, she justified the choices she must make with duty and flames. The Brotherhood was subject to her Oath and sanctioned for death by the voice. And Marvena aimed to capture Pyra's son, meaning she was the only clue Ophiera had to the Ambassador's death. All paths led to the Brotherhood, to Aud, and yet the problem lay in Myronor.

By Magistrate and Cloister, she was still sworn to escort him to Krysas. Yet, her own power and the Brotherhood were the real threats to his life now. Wouldn't he be safer separated from her? Wouldn't sending him on his way with his father be the best way to protect him now? Every thought felt more like a loophole than a reason, but it didn't really matter, as long as he was safe. Their fates had always been disparate, no matter what her heart and soul desired. No matter how wrong her choices felt, what she planned was for the best.

Myronor watched her from across the room, his blue eyes dark with worry. He and his father had weathered the storms too, all while mourning the loss of their home. They both suffered a grief too deep for Ophiera to understand. For her, the need for vengeance quelled much of her sorrow.

Since the storms began, she and Myronor had barely spoken to each other. Though they could exchange their thoughts through the ekath now, Ophiera had kept hers purposefully hidden. Like a floodgate, the tether could be manipulated, opened and closed at will. Shut, the connection no longer exchanged her thoughts and emotions with Myronor, and vice versa. The silence was lonely. But it made what she was about to do that much easier.

"How much longer will the storm last?" Myronor asked Berwyn. The old fisher flexed his stiff hands, studying the joints of his knuckles. He then stuck a pinky in his ear and closed his eyes. It was an old tradition in the Southern Coastlands to predict the weather in strange ways. Ophiera still didn't understand how Berwyn did it, but he was rarely wrong. She waited with bated breath.

"Should clear out by morning," he said finally, reaching for the lantern. "I best let you both rest; are you sure you don't want to sleep in the captain's quarters?"

Myronor chuckled and the sound broke Ophiera's heart. "No, no, we're comfortable here. Goodnight, Father."

Berwyn nodded, his bald head shining in the lantern light. "'Night, son. 'Night, Warden."

She bowed her head in farewell to Berwyn, still unable to speak without spilling blood. It suited her just fine. Goodbyes were never her strong suit.

Myronor came to sit beside her. She still refused to take off the armor, making it impossible for her and Myronor to sleep near each other. It was for the best.

While she lay back against the hull, resting in upright position, Myronor laid out his bedroll beside her. She watched him unroll the leathers and furs, flattening them with his bare hands. Some part of her wished to reach for them, to hold them and feel his hands on her again. But she resisted.

It was for the best.

"Are you alright?" Myronor asked, sitting down on the pile of furs.

No, no she wasn't. But she nodded to him and kept the gate of her mind closed. She knew he could sense it, the ekath clamped shut, but he didn't question her lack of communication. His gracious way of always tolerating her idiosyncrasies made her feel even worse.

"If the storm clears, we can head to Cantheas in the morning," Myronor said, studying her face. "Berwyn says there's little chance the *Mistral* could make it to Krysas. But he knows of a good charter in Cantheas, a relative of Yelena's. We could be on a boat to Krysas by this time tomorrow."

Ophiera nodded her understanding. By this time tomorrow, he could be on his way to Krysas.

"You know, as an Ambassador, I'll have access to both the Magistrate and Consortia archives. Plus my mother's personal library. I'm certain I can find out more about the Brotherhood, about their history, and this Aud. We need information before we can go after them anyway. So, between your Oath and my obligations to Krysas, continuing on our journey there would be the best option. Right?"

Ophiera nodded again.

She wasn't lying. She did agree with him. Continuing on the journey was the best option. But she withheld the fact they wouldn't be continuing together.

The Vespula Brotherhood was her duty, not his. Like she always said, fate would not have been so cruel as to bind his soul to one like hers. Once she took her Retribution against Marvena, she would find a way to break the ekath. To free him of her endless duty ahead.

"Might as well rest until morning," he said, laying his head down on the mat. "You sure you actually rest sitting up like that?"

Ophiera smiled and nodded. It was a real smile this time. She'd miss his teasing most amongst everything else.

"Goodnight then," he said, closing his eyes.

Goodbye was more accurate.

EPILOGUE

The ocean looked the same despite all that had changed.

Berwyn held the note in his trembling hand, the latest crashing wave against the hull of his heart. He still recognized the Warden's script.

"Ophiera!"

He closed his eyes. Below deck, Myronor's pained voice penetrated through the thick wooden planks. The sound pierced him like a harpoon, dragging him back to the memory of the day Pyra left.

Love wasn't enough to describe what Berwyn had felt for Pyra. What he still felt for Pyra. She was more important to him than anyone in any world. Long before a child was even a hope born in their hearts, he knew the day would come when Pyra must leave. She had always been honest about her intentions, her past and future duties. Her true purpose in Erum. Some part of him hoped that Myronor's birth would have changed her perspective. But on the day she left, Berwyn was the one screaming her name in desperation from below deck.

"Ophiera! Where are you?"

For years, he mourned her absence, just like Myronor would now. And just when he thought himself settled with his new life as a single father, his son's magic awakened. In a note so akin to the Warden's, Pyra left her instructions for their son. Berwyn delivered Myronor to the mage named Rheta, just as she asked. He discouraged him from returning to Iluka—especially by his own *special* means—just as she asked.

Now Berwyn read similar instructions from the Warden. He was to deliver Myronor to the city of Krysas, unharmed, and discourage him from going after Ophiera. At least Pyra had spoken to Myronor before she left, explaining her reasonings as best she could. But the Warden had left it to him to break the news to his son.

He never thought she'd be so cruel.

Berwyn heard the rapid footsteps of both Myronor and Mallow as they rushed up to the deck. His son's eyes were wide with panic, eyes the same pale blue as his beloved Pyra's.

"Have you seen her?" Myronor asked, searching the deck with those eyes.

When Berwyn didn't answer, he watched his son's eyes fall to shore, where a small wooden boat lay beached. The pain that fell over his son's face was too much for his heart to bear. He couldn't do as the Warden asked. Not again.

Rather than hide the note as she wished him to, Berwyn held out the scrappy piece of parchment to his son. With a scowl, Myronor snatched the note and read it hastily. Berwyn held his breath as he watched his son's face crumple under the truth of her writing.

"She wants *you* to take me to Krysas?"

"Aye," Berwyn confirmed.

Myronor's eyes fell to the letter again. "But she hasn't said where she's going or where we are to find her."

"We'll set sail for Cantheas today. There we can book passage to Krysas on a cargo vessel—Yelena's cousin's or some other."

"No," Myronor said with a bite. "We have to find her first."

Berwyn clenched his fist, trying to find the words. "She doesn't want to be found."

With a growl of frustration, Myronor crushed the letter against his heart. It was as if he tried to smother a great pain. "You don't know that. She—she wouldn't abandon me. I'm her charge! Her ekath!"

Now it was Berwyn's heart that broke, reliving Pyra's departure all over again. No parent should have to hurt their child. But his son wasn't a boy anymore; he was a grown man, an equal, if not a greater man than himself. That was how it was meant to be, wasn't it? A parent's dream should be that their children surpass them, not relive their mistakes.

"The Warden always reminded me of Pyra, at least in spirit," Berwyn said with a sad smile. "They were both strong, powerful beings with the weight of duty bearing down on their shoulders. It's only natural that we get caught in their wake as they leave us behind."

Myronor watched him speak with a broken expression, still clenching a hand to his chest. Berwyn could see the torrent of thoughts rushing behind his son's eyes. Then Myronor threw the letter to the ground and started raising the mainsail.

Berwyn sighed in relief. At least his son had accepted his fate far faster than he had before. He reached a hand out to his son, hoping to provide some comfort. But Myronor turned to him and thrust the rope into Berwyn's hand.

"Ophiera isn't Pyra—and I'm not you," Myronor said with a solemn smile. "I don't care if I drown in the wake of her path, she doesn't just get to make the decision for me. I'm going after her. You're free to help me, but don't you dare try to stop me."

TERMINOLOGY

Aether – The life stream of souls in Erum and source of mana for the disciples of the Cloister

Adamantrium – An indestructible and rare metal thought to be forged from the Aether

Alchemician – A professional potion tinkerer, loosely referring to anyone who mixes

Anurola – An amphibious creature of the Sloughmire

Apfelpom – A fruit with a bite, often used in making suggestive beverages

Auxis – A deep-water fish that inhabits the Lucent Strait

Anathema – A cursed soul; someone who has committed murder and stolen a soul from the Aether

Birzhan – An ancient ritual evoked to bind two souls (ekath) together (ekatma)

Blazecap – A bioluminescent mushroom found in the Severed Wood and often sought by alchemicians

Chaplain – Leader of the Cloister

The Cloister – An institute of religion in Tanvik whose disciples' study, utilize, and worship the Aether

Conjura – A magical affinity possessed by some mages involving the conversion of mana to matter

Crabita – A freshwater crustacean of the Sloughmire

Ekath – Refers to both a bound soul and the bond that forms during the Birzhan

Ekatma – The collective term for the one soul, those bound together after the Birzhan

Extinguishment – Death of the disciple of the Cloister

Echelon – Rank within the Cloister

Familiar – A rare being originating from Nijeka that bonds with mages

Font – A source of the Aether

Gemfruit – A bright, soft stone fruit found in the wild or grown on orchards in Tanvik

Goldencress – A yellow flower that only grows in the Western jungles

Holy Flames – The name for the Aether coined by the Cloister, most often applied when evoking their rites

Ippomare – A horse-like sea serpent of the Lucent Strait and the subject of many fisher's tales

Imbuteria – A magical affinity possess by some mages, involves impregnation of materials with mana

Justicar – Members of the Magistrate and leaders of Tanvik. There are five in total to rule and represent each realm

Kindled – The disciples of the Cloister that have received their Oath from the holy flames

Magistrate - The ruling body of Tanvik, composed of five Justicars

Majflies – Bioluminescent four-winged flies that glow blue in the spring swamps

Manasickness – Ailments suffered when mana is drained, using life instead

Mana – Refers to any source of power utilized by the souls of Erum

Mercy – One of the three Oaths bestowed by the Aether; healing Rites

Metamagi – A classification of magic wielded by mages that include conjura and transmutation magic

Murklouse – A flesh eating, parasitic insect of the Sloughmire

Navarra – A mythical sea monster with dark scales and yellow eyes

Nijeka – An alternate plane of existence where familiars originate

Oath – The literal and figurative doctrine that binds the followers of the Cloister to the Aether and its will

Phratries – The order of the shamans

Paladins – Disciples of the Cloister that are branded with an Oath of Retribution. They wear golden armor and claim anathema for the Aether

Protection – An ancient Oath of rumor among in the Cloister

Retribution – One of the three Oaths bestowed by the Aether; requires the return of anathema to the Aether

Rubyfin – A delicious and common fish that schools off the coasts of Iluka

Sacramentum – A place within the Cloister where the unkindled receive their Oaths

Sacrifice – One of the three Oaths bestowed by the Aether; serves the Cloister and the Aether

Shade – Refers to the color of a vesper

Shadeweed – A flowering plant common to Tanvik, with individual florets that release and float on the wind; named after its similarity to a vesper, spherical and bright

Swardhop – An insect common to the meadows around Feyralis; considered a pest in large numbers

Span/Spanning – An affinity of magic unheard of in Tanvik, where one can traverse between places near instantaneously at risk of traversing through an unknown plane.

Shaman – Village leaders in the Southern Coastlands, utilizing the mana of the sea for their mystics

Troynt – A large boar only found deep within the Severed Woods.

True fire – A term used by the disciples of the Cloister to distinguish between regular flames and those derived from the Aether.

Vesper – Manifestation of a soul after death

Vespula Brotherhood – A faction of anathema that wears yellow armbands in solidarity

Warden – An appointed protector of the village, a tradition of the Southern Coastlands

Winesap – A common bush in Tanvik with waxy leaves and branches that leech a sticky, white substance when broken

ACKNOWLEDGEMENTS

Though my life has dramatically changed throughout the process of creating this story, the support I've received from my loved ones has only grown. I must first thank my real-life Myronor. He's the healer to my tank and the love he's demonstrated to me over the years has been truly magical. With our two familiars, Sputnik and Bear, we get to live in our own fairy tale. I also have to thank my two sisters, Alanna and Leslie. If my partner and I live in a fairy tale, then my sisters and I live in a graphic novel. I genuinely think we three have superpowers that, if organized properly, could change the world. I also have to thank my honorary sibling, Nicole. She is quite possibly the most perfect human I've ever met and lives her life as a main character. Our friendship was forged in the fires of a toxic workplace that should someday become a novel on its own. Special thanks to Jennie, a fantastical friend (literally, I love your elf ears), who was one of the first people I trusted to read this story. It's hard finding friends you can trust to call you on your bullshit while simultaneously stoking your ego, but you have mastered the art. Similarly, I owe Erica and Collin all the thanks in the world for reading this story more than anyone should have and always being a source of positivity. Your encouragement always kept me going.

If you enjoyed The Aether Awakens, please rate, review, and connect with me!

Instagram: @wynnwrites16
Tiktok: @wynnwrites
www.cgwynn.com